Duct Tape Isn't Enough
Survival Skills For The 21st Century

By Dr. Ron Breazeale

What *You* Can Do *Now*
To Spring Back From Hard Times

Bounce Back USA
205 Ocean Avenue
Portland, ME 04103

For information regarding permission, please write to:
Permissions Department
BBUSA,
205 Ocean Avenue,
Portland, ME, 04103.

Publisher's Cataloging-in-Publication

Breazeale, Ron.
Reaching home : a novel about conquering fear / story
by Lee Brazil ; foreword and epilogue by Benjamin
Brazil-Woodford ; written by Ron Breazeale. -- 1st ed.
p. cm.
LCCN 2008941520
ISBN: 978-0-615-23421-2
1. Nuclear power plants--Fiction. 2. Nuclear power
plants--Environmental aspects--Fiction. 3. People with
disabilities--Fiction. 4. Nuclear terrorism--Fiction.
5. Bio-terrorism--Fiction. 6. Southern States--Fiction.
7. Boston (Mass.)--Fiction. 8. Maine--Fiction.   I. Title.
PS3602.R435R43 2006   813'.6
ISBN: 978-0-615-23421-2
Library of Congress Catalog Number: 2008941520

Cover Art and Design by David Jarratt
Book Typography & Composition by: RMS Freelance Writing and Editorial Services
Visible Earth image courtesy of NASA http://visibleearth.nasa.gov/
Printed in U.S.A.
First Edition: 2009

What People Are Saying…

"The talking tradition of storytelling to impart wise and serious truths is successfully employed in this novel and workbook. Dr. Breazeale brings in focus researched and teachable tenets behind the quality of human resiliency. A number of individuals have attempted to bring these learned skills to students and teachers, relief workers, and others but none have been found to do so as well as Dr. Breazeale.

"The application of storytelling is a particularly successful vehicle in teaching these proven skills and shaping problem solving approaches in times of need. Throughout the ages myths, legends, and stories have effectively presented important messages of human nature and trials of life to listeners in a manner that pervades our awareness and fosters growth in not only an entertaining manner but also one that has a subtle but profound impact.

"By employing a novel he had authored, Dr. Breazeale has kept the topic instantly meaningful in our new day and age of the twenty-first century. The foundations of resiliency have been discovered in a wide range of problem solving and trials faced by people. We understand that the application of adaptation to the real issues confronting us is of paramount importance, as well as recognizing and acceptance of our social dependency. We have found that simple socialization markedly improves thinking skills and problem solving in the elderly. We have discovered that steadily persevering in actions that earn us self-respect create a reservoir from which to draw when the going gets tough. We know that finding meaning in our lives builds resolve and provides direction when a storm hits. Dr. Breazeale has created an excellent mode of delivery in teaching these and related concepts to those that can put them into action and best cope and manage that which life presents us. This novel and workbook can be applied in groups or individually, in high school or junior high school classrooms as well as senior centers or adult education programs.

"This is an example of applied psychology based on solid research that can be employed to strengthen not only individuals but groups and cultures of any kind. Providing a new framework in which to help others to meet individual, family, and group needs Dr. Breazeale has stepped into the future of psychology." — RJ Parker, PhD

"Ron Breazeale has used his life experiences to present a format for resilience training. Inoculating people with resilience before disaster strikes is the next logical step to debriefing after the disaster." — Diana L. Prescott, Ph.D. Clinical Psychologist

"Fear and panic are normal reactions to abnormal situations. In our lifetime we have witnessed the apparent escalation of the frequency and magnitude of traumatic events affecting western culture. Through storytelling, Dr. Breazeale is able to capture one individual's journey for establishing a system for self-regulation in the face of adversity. His process is well-organized and uses methodologies, concepts, and systems easily understand by professionals and laypersons alike." — Michael Burd

"Thank you very much for the effort you have put forth on the Maine Resiliency program. There has been a great deal of interest in the project since you first introduced it at our Cumberland County Fire Chiefs meeting. I look forward to the video tools and further implementation of the program throughout the fire, police, and EMS services. It is a worthwhile and important project and I wish you continued success and support for future grant funding opportunities to continue the good work you and your team have started. — B. Michael Thurlow, Fire Chief, Scarborough, ME

"I have been working closely with the Resilience Project and Dr. Ron Breazeale. The program parallels a lot of what we do here in the Portland Police Department to assist employees in developing positive coping mechanisms in their difficult environment. We have a long history of developing peer support programs in conjunction with employee assistance. I have also attended a training program on resilience and found it to be helpful and worthwhile. I believe in this project and the work of Dr. Breazeale. It is paramount for the health of emergency workers in the field. The work completed so far have been successful and has made a difference in people's lives.

"We continues to face many challenges and support programs as this is important for the well-bring of many who not only deal with day-to-day crisis, but for those to manage their lives in many difficult situations." — Joseph K Loughlin, Chief of Police, Portland, ME

"*Duct Tape Isn't Enough* takes a timely look at the pressures we face in today's world. Through his original story and guided exercises, Dr. Ron Breazeale offers workbook users a concrete way to explore resilience and other survival skills needed in the 21st century.

"Dr. Breazeale combines compassion and insight into human nature with practical advice for becoming prepared. The story he tells will give readers many ideas for integrating the skills and attitudes they need to build personal resilience, as well as that of their families and communities." — Glen H. White, Ph.D., Director, Research and Training Center on Independent Living, University of Kansas

"First there was the terrorist attack of 911, then Hurricane Katrina, followed by the economic meltdown and widespread unemployment. And now fears of pandemic flu. We all need to be resilient during these difficult times and *Duct Tape Isn't Enough* is 'spot on' as a manual for surviving tough times. Ron Breazeale has created a tool that teaches resilience skills; he has brilliantly identified that people with disabilities are skilled practitioners of survival. They have the know-how and are eminently qualified to teach these skills to others. It has been a pleasure to be involved in the development and testing of this fine manual." — Dennis Fitzgibbons- Executive Director, Alpha One, South Portland, Maine

"In *Duct Tape Isn't Enough,* Dr. Ron Breazeale has created a remarkably innovative and highly effective method of instilling resiliency. It is timely and much needed in an era when Americans are experiencing increasing personal and economic stress. His unique use of the novel, much of which is autobiographic from his own triumph of resiliency over adversity, is accompanied by a step-by-step method of marshaling one's own resiliency. If you are facing a crisis or know of someone who is, or if in living your daily life you wisely want to increase your survival skills for an adversity that may befall without warning, this book is a must." — Nicholas A. Cummings, Ph.D., Sc.D., distinguished professor, University of Nevada, Reno; president, Cummings Foundation for Behavioral Health; former president, American Psychological Association

"An intriguing perspective on the impact of long-held personal experiences on one's response to life's unexpected challenges…insights of a gifted clinician." — Pat DeLeon, Ph.D, former president, American Psychological Association

"Interesting, fascinating reading...I'm sure it will be a contribution to the field." — Charles Rothstein, Ph.D., former president of the Maine Psychological Association

"Dr. Ron Breazeale and his colleagues bring a variety of perspectives to create a stimulating learning environment for participants to delve into *Survival Skills for the 21st Century,* i.e., resiliency. Their knowledge, techniques, and materials engage the participants effectively. The story telling and sharing are especially valuable. Participants relate to the applicability of the skills learned to the classroom, their personal lives as well as relationships with colleagues in today's ever-demanding world." — Cheryl Lunde, director of training and professional development, Maine Education Association

"*Duct Tape Isn't Enough* opens one's thinking to possibilities and strategies to address adversity and fear. A compelling story carries the reader through obstacles and solutions outlining pathways where personal resilience provided valuable safeguards to threats on health and wellness. The book offers self-help and a model to train others in resilience, a powerful combination for any individual or group."—Richard C. Lumb, Ph.D, criminologist and contributing author, *The Police Journal*

Table of Contents

Special Thanks To Our Co-Trainers

Marilynn Morel
Georgeanne Small
Tony Strodel
Carl Pabst
Marilyn Cramer
Sue Breazeale
Richard Lumb
Lisa Smith
Lou Pelletier
Perry Grant
Brian Harnish
Joseph Loughlin

Introduction

Our nation survived 911. The dead were remembered. Iraq and Afghanistan were attacked and Wall Street in time went back to business as usual. Our government focused its energy on preventing another attack on this country by "fighting them over there" but not, perhaps in part because it might be seen as a sign of capitulation, on preparing the public for dealing with the aftermath of another financial collapse or another terrorist attack on American soil. Part of their effort has been focused on preventing those who might carry out an attack from entering the country, and tracking down and killing the bad guys, the suspected terrorist leaders. These efforts have often relied on new technologies such as unmanned aircraft, high tech surveillance and new screening devices in airports and at border crossings.

Duct Tape Isn't Enough focuses on old and new technology, *human technology*. It is not focused on preventing adverse events from occurring, but on preventing human beings from being devastated by them, on building the skills and the attitudes that are required to survive adversity. Tragedy and adversity are a part of life. We alone cannot control the world economy, but we can exert restraint and insist on effective regulation and oversight of our stock market and our financial institutions. Unfortunately, "greed is good" has been the motto of too many Americans for far too long.

And we certainly cannot control the weather or natural forces, and most likely we will not be able to prevent, forever, another terrorist attack on American soil. Some experts believe that our new president has a 30 – 50% chance of having to deal with some type of nuclear crisis in one of our major cities. It is certain that during his term, President Obama will spend much of his time dealing with the financial mess that we are in and that more will be expected of him than any human being could possibly deliver.

Duct Tape Isn't Enough does not focus on blaming the bad guys for our problems or finding the right good guy to act as our savior. There are no messianic good guys or demonic bad guys in this book. Many of those who survived the tragedies of 911 and Katrina, and who will be able to survive the present financial crisis and the tragedies of the future will call upon the skills and the attitudes of resilience to manage the situations they confront. Optimism, flexibility, teamwork, confidence in ourselves, and the rightness of what we are doing has sustained human societies throughout history. To survive the hard times of the 21st century, we need to go back to the past and practice what we know works. Many of the skills and attitudes that we need are the same ones that our parents and grandparents used to survive the Great Depression, World War II, and Vietnam; the same skills and attitudes that their parents and grandparents used to build our nation. They are the spirit of America. Blinking lights and computer screens, like duct tape, are wonderful inventions, but they're not enough to hold our world together. A GPS unit may help you find your way to the hospital, but it will not help you find your way when you're feeling lost in the ICU waiting room as your husband or wife clings to life.

If we look with clear eyes at the past and our present, we can see what works and what does not. In the past, many would argue that we were better at acting on our values and beliefs, and at being optimistic and confident about ourselves and the future of our country. Indeed, we may have been better at staying connected with family and friends and creating and supporting our communities. But, today it is clear that we know better how to communicate effectively than past generations. (Although some would say that our seeming obsession with the Internet and texting instead of face-to-face communication would suggest otherwise.) We also know better how to manage strong feelings and emotions than in the past. (Despite the fact that politicians can still use fear to manipulate our society.) And we clearly today know better how to care for ourselves physically. (Even when our waistlines and those of our children point to the reality that we are not practicing what we know.)

We need to value and reassert these skills and attitudes from the past and the present, but most importantly, we need to practice them. Research in the social sciences, (human technology), and our own experience tells us that:

DUCT TAPE ISN'T ENOUGH: Survival Skills For The 21st Century

1. Connecting with other is better than isolation
2. Flexibility works better in most situations than rigidity
3. Communicating with others is almost always better than not talking
4. Looking to ourselves to solve our problems rather than to others works best
5. Recognizing and dealing with rather than ignoring our feelings and the feelings of others can help keep us emotionally healthy.
6. Acting on our values works better than acting on our fears
7. Being optimistic is better than being pessimistic
8. Caring for ourselves and for others serves everyone best
9. Laughter is better, at times, than tears
10. Greed and going shopping will not solve our problems

These skills and attitudes are the focus of *Duct Tape Isn't Enough* and *Reaching Home*. They are survival skills for the 21st century, whether the adversity is a national or regional disaster such as a hurricane or a terrorist attack or a personal disaster such as the death of a child or the loss of a spouse.

Duct Tape Isn't Enough is divided into Six Modules. The first defines resilience and reviews the skills and attitudes that build and maintain resilience. In the second Module, I give you an opportunity to "take your inventory" through a series of questions that ask you to examine the skills and attitudes that you've utilized in dealing with adversity in the past. We ask you to focus on what you have learned from the past about yourself and from the role models that you have had, both good and bad.

The third Module focuses on teaching resilience skills and attitudes through storytelling. The module utilizes *Reaching Home* as a tool for learning and teaching these skills. *Reaching Home* is a novel about conquering fear that I wrote and first released in the fall of 2006. It has a love story, is fast paced, and doesn't take itself too seriously. There are no superheroes in this story, just ordinary people living their lives as best they can. They have all the blemishes and the vices of the average person as well as the courage and strength that all human beings possess. There are discussion questions and author's comments to help you look at and better understand how the characters in the novel are making use or not making use of resilience skills and attitudes. You are encouraged, in this section of the workbook, to put down in black and white your own story.

In the fourth Module, you will have the opportunity to develop your own plan for building your resilience. We encourage you to develop a SMART Plan that is Specific, Measurable, Attainable, Realistic and Time specific. To assist you in this process, we provide you, again, with questions to hopefully stimulate thought and to assist you in developing a plan. This module focuses on skill #10, taking care of yourself.

Modules V and VI focuses on Resilience Skill #11, Helping Others. Teaching others the skills and the attitudes that you have learned. This module focuses on how to integrate these skills into the activities that you are presently doing. You are asked to look at the challenges that you will face in doing this and to develop a plan for maintaining your own resilience while assisting others in building theirs. In Module VI we review the resources available to assist you in developing discussion groups, classes or workshops in resilience. This includes descriptions and contact information regarding videos you may want to use in your discussion group or workshop, different formats for presentations, tips on working with various groups, e.g., fire, police, health care, etc., and information on how to obtain copies of PowerPoint slides and videotapes of the modules.

Duct Tape Isn't Enough focuses on human technology and what you can do to survive the challenges facing our society in the 21st century. The program is based to a large extent on our experience with the Maine Resilience Project which began in January of 2007 and has as its goal building on and sustaining the resilience of all Maine citizens. It is right that the program was developed and implemented first in the great state of Maine. The people of Maine, with their calmness and strength, demonstrate on a daily basis so many of the skills and attitudes that are the cornerstone of the program. They are its Maine ingredients.

Ron Breazeale, Ph.D
December 12, 2008
Ice Storm
Limington, Maine

Module I

What Is Resilience?

Resilience is the power to adapt well to adversity. It is the process of coping with and managing tragedy and crisis in your life. It is "bouncing back" from hard times, whether these be national disasters, such the current financial crisis, a hurricane, or a terrorist attack, or personal disasters such as bankruptcy, divorce, or the death of a loved one. Research since 911 suggests that resilience may be much more common than we thought. Although certain forms of temperament may be inherited that may help people to be more resilient in a crisis, and although certain forms of psychiatric or cognitive disorders may interfere with the learning of these skills, most of what makes up resilience is learned and can be taught. This is especially true of one of the key components of resilience: Optimism. Being optimistic does not mean that we look at the world through rose-colored glasses or that we avoid pain or do not experience intense emotions when going through a crisis. Just the opposite. Resilient individuals are aware of their feelings and are able to discharge and manage them as well as deal with and manage others in a crisis. Resilience does not involve avoiding one's feelings; it involves confronting and managing them. Being able to use thinking as a way of managing emotion is a major part of resilience.

Preparing for a national disaster or a terrorist attack by putting together an emergency kit and planning and practicing an evacuation route utilizes many of the skills in resilience such as realistic planning, communication and being willing to look at the big picture, e.g., the possibility of a hurricane, ice storm, terrorism, or the meltdown of Wall Street.

Why Resilience Training?

The experts tell us that there will be another 911-like event sometime in the near future. It is not a matter, they say, of if, but when. A number of countries have accepted this fact, such as the United Kingdom and Australia, and have developed fairly elaborate programs in assessment and training in resilience. They have defined resilience both as resilience of the citizenry of their country as well as the infrastructure. Unfortunately, many of us in the U.S. have slipped back into believing that there will not be another 911.

Whether we believe that there will be another 911-like event, we would all agree that there will be natural disasters and probably no shortage of them, given the climate changes that are occurring. Hurricanes, ice storms, floods, and tornados are likely to be more frequent in the immediate future. And there are, of course, other threats that loom on the horizon such as a pandemic, bird flu, or the California earthquake, the big one.

Perhaps you are saying, *I have never been affected that much by a natural disaster in my life and probably will not be.* This, indeed, may be true for many of us. But life has no shortage of personal disasters. The current financial disaster is global and will touch everyone. Death and taxes come to us all. We are living longer, but because of our longer lives, we are more susceptible to health problems and crises. We know that the skills and attitudes defined through research on resilience can be learned and applied and can assist individuals in adapting to and surviving difficult times. Training in resilience may reduce the frequency and intensity of post-traumatic stress disorders and other health problems that occur after a national or a personal disaster. Such training may allow our society and the individuals and families affected directly to recover more quickly and completely. Just as we know that reinforcing a bridge may make it stronger and less likely to be washed away by a flood, we know that reinforcing an individual's coping skills, their resilience, can make it less likely that they will be overwhelmed, washed away, in the same flood.

We also know that people who cannot deal with their emotions, specifically fear, may become more narrow, exclusive, and rigid in their view of the world and less able to see the bigger picture. This "circle-the-wagons" mentality can increase the level of paranoia in a society and result in the rejection and persecution of those who are different from the mainstream by their religion, race, sexual preference or physical or mental ability. Witness our society's reaction to these groups immediately after 911. Reacting out of emotion rather than thought and rational problem-solving can result in decisions being made through fear that negatively affect the entire society and are later regretted. Defending our society and our culture can be inclusive rather than exclusive involving the seeking of alliances, cooperative problem-solving and consensus building regarding what actions need to be taken.

We should all have an investment in building our own resilience and in supporting the resilience of our family members, friends, and other members of our society, since we are all in this together.

Eleven Skills And Attitudes That Can Increase Resilience

We know that individuals handle adversity in many different ways and that the different approaches and strategies that they have learned have been shaped by the culture, society and family systems that they grew up in and of which they are a part. But some common skills and attitudes emerge.

1. **Being connected to others**. Relationships that can provide support and caring are one of the primary factors in resilience. Having a number of these relationships, both within and outside of the family, that offer love, encouragement and reassurance can build and support resilience, e.g., developing new friendships.
2. **Being flexible**. By definition it is a key component of resilience and one of the primary factors in emotional adjustment and maturity. This requires that an individual be flexible in his thinking and his actions, e.g., trying something new.
3. **Being able to make realistic plans and take action to carry them out**. Being able to see what is rather than what you would like is part of this skill. Being proactive rather than reactive, assertive rather than aggressive or passive are all components of this skill, e.g., taking a Red Cross course in CPR and First Aid.
4. **Being able to communicate well with others and problem-solve both individually and with others**. This includes basic communication, listening and problem-solving skills, e.g., working as a team member within your community.
5. **Being able to manage strong feelings**. This requires being able to take action without being impulsive and responding out of emotion and being able to put emotions to the side when clear thinking and action are required. Being able to use thinking as a way of managing one's emotions is a key component of this skill, e.g., when you're angry or hurt, thinking before acting.
6. **Being self-confident**. Having a positive self-image is critical if a person is to be able to confront and manage fear and anxiety in his/her life, e.g., helping someone else.

7. **Being able to find purpose and meaning**. Being able to make sense out of what is happening and to find meaning in it is critical if one is to be able to manage the feelings that are aroused in a crisis. Spiritual and religious practices are often a component of this factor, e.g., acting on your values.

8. **Being able to see the big picture**. This factor is often closely aligned with #7 and #5. Optimists in general are better able to see the bigger picture than pessimists. They are more likely to see good and bad events occurring in their life being temporary rather than permanent. This, too, will pass. They are also more likely to see events having a specific impact on certain areas of their life rather than having a pervasive impact on their entire life or their future. And last of all, they are less likely to blame themselves or someone else for the hard times. Optimists avoid the blame game, e.g., hold yourself and others accountable without the emotional dose of blame.

9. **Being able to appreciate and use humor appropriately**. Whether humor is "sick" or "dark" often depends on the setting. Laughter may have healing powers, e.g., if you're not feeling well; watch a funny movie.

10. **Being able to take care of yourself, e.g., diet, exercise, financial "health," etc.** First responders and health care professionals are often major offenders in this area. We often assume that the rules do not apply to us but they do, e.g., make a SMART Plan for exercise.

11. **Being able to care for others physically and emotionally.** Occupations and volunteer activities that involve caring for others can often build resilience, e.g., volunteer in a shelter or a food bank.

There are other attitudes and skills that aren't included in this list that can build resilience. What do you think they are?

As you read *Reaching Home*, you will have the opportunity to think about these factors and how they are reflected in the lives of the characters in the story. The Readers Guide will give you an opportunity to look more closely at these factors.

Module II

Learning From The Past

Before you begin reading *Reaching Home*, spend some time learning from your past. Unless we learn from our history, as Winston Churchill once said, "We are doomed to repeat it." This is just as true for us personally as it is for our society. So as you explore the past, ask yourself the following questions and write down the answers.

Seeing things in black and white is different than simply thinking about them or even talking about them. This exercise is for you. No one will see what you've written unless you wish to share it with them. Letting a friend or a family member read and discuss with you what you have written may be helpful. You decide.

1. **What events have I experienced in my life that have been extremely stressful for me?** *A natural disaster like a tornado or hurricane, a personal disaster like the death of a spouse or child, a house fire, divorce, bankruptcy, job loss, illness, disability?*

2. **How have I managed these events?** *How did I deal with my feelings? Did I avoid talking about what was happening? Did I allow myself to discharge the feelings about the event? Did I think about significant others in my life and how they had dealt with similar crisis?*

3. **Did I ask others for help or did I go it alone?** *How did going it alone work for you? If you asked for help, who helped you through these hard times?*

4. **Who have been the role models in my life for dealing with adversity?** *What did I learn from them?*

5. **Have I helped others through bad times?** *Did helping them help me? How?*

6. **How was I, personally, impacted by 911?** *After 911, did my attitude toward others who were different from me by religion or race change? If so, how?*

7. **Have I thrown myself into work or other activities as a way of coping with hard time: was this helpful?** *What was the upside and what was the downside?*

8. **What have I learned about myself and about others from managing difficult situations? How has the global financial crisis effected me?**

9. **During hard times, was I able to use my head?** *Able to think clearly and problem-solve in a crisis? Did my ability to think help me to manage my feelings, specifically the fear and the anger that may come up in a time of crisis?*

10. **How did adverse events in my life change my way of thinking about myself and about the world I live in?** *Am I a stronger person for having gone through a life crisis? How?*

Module III

Why Teach Resilience Through Storytelling?

Storytelling has been around since the first human beings set down around a fire and talked about their lives. These first training sessions on resilience occurred thousands of years ago. From campfires to fireplaces to pot belly stoves to water coolers, we continue to tell stories about resilience. In more recent times, we've written these down in the form of novels and biographies, and even more recently recorded them on tape and film and most recently on the Internet. We will use a novel, *Reaching Home*, as one of our primary tools in teaching the skills and attitudes of resilience. A novel, I would argue, is one of the best ways to teach these attitudes and skills since the average person requires twelve to fourteen hours to read a novel. This time is often spent over weeks or months and is done frequently in the late evening before falling asleep. The activity is usually seen as enjoyable with the reader often identifying with one or more of the characters in the story.

If you are participating in a workshop, you may have the opportunity to hear other stories told by participants and may also review videotape interviews of individuals from a variety of different backgrounds who have demonstrated resilience in their lives. These may include police officers, educators, persons with a disability, fire and rescue personnel and others. Based on our experience with this program, we believe that storytelling is an ideal vehicle for teaching these skills and attitudes far better than lectures, textbooks or brochures.

As part of this process, we would encourage you to consider telling or writing your story. Sharing your story with others may be a way of building your resilience and teaching others these skills and attitudes. Writing a story down may also be a way of building resilience since putting things down in black and white can help people to better understand the situations that they have confronted and the way in which they have dealt with them. If you are participating in a workshop, we would encourage you to consider using the opportunities available to talk about your life and tell your story as well as to listen carefully to the stories of others. Needless to say, you should only write or tell your story if you believe it will be helpful to you.

Research by James Pennybaker, a psychologist, and others have found that writing about difficult things may actually improve our health. In a series of studies, one group of individuals was asked to write down their deepest thoughts and feelings about a traumatic event they had experienced. Another group wrote about ordinary matters such as their plans for the day. Both groups wrote for 15 – 20 minutes a day for three to five consecutive days. The results were surprising. When compared with the people who wrote about ordinary events, the ones who wrote about their traumatic experiences reported fewer symptoms, fewer visits to the doctor, fewer days off from work, improved mood and a more positive outlook. Their immune function was enhanced for at least six weeks after writing.

These studies suggest that words can help us understand and absorb the traumatic event and eventually put it behind us. It can give us a sense of relief and control. Confiding our feelings in others can have a similar benefit.

Introduction To *Reaching Home*

You are about to take a trip into the future. The first stop will be in the year 2042. Your tour guide is a young fisherman who has discovered a manuscript written by his grandfather. With the help of his mother, he has assembled it into the story of his grandfather's life in the year 2013.

Lee, the young fisherman's grandfather, is the main character in this story. He transcends the typical notions of how heroes look and act. He has never made peace with the South he grew up in as a child without a left hand or with the prosthetic hook that he wears or the nuclear industry he blames for his disability. He returns to the Southeast to research material for a book that he is writing. While there an explosion occurs at one of the Department of Energy Plants and Lee is caught up in the ensuing disaster and implicated in what is mistakenly believed to be a terrorist plot. He manages to escape from the detention center.

Much of the story focuses on his journey back to Maine and the unlikely allies he meets along the way. Now on the radar of federal agents tracking a terrorist cell in Boston, Lee is arrested before he can reach home. He is offered a deal: help the federal agents foil the plot and avoid prosecution. To reach home, Lee must confront his fears and question his perceptions of good and evil.

The story is divided into four parts. Book One: Fear, Book Two: Flight, Book Three: Fight, and Book Four: Hope. Each book is followed by a synopsis of the chapters in that book and specific questions regarding the characters and the story. These are followed by my comments.

Your journey ends as it began in the year 2042. The epilogue written by the young fisherman reflects a future that we may not want to create for our children and grandchildren. The future can be different from that of the story if we, as a society, choose to make it so.

I would suggest you read each book or section through and then review the chapters, answering the questions and then review my comments. As you read, observe how the characters in *Reaching Home* either apply or do not apply skills and attitudes of resilience to the situations they confront. In many cases the characters will fail to use these skills or will chose to do things that will make a bad situation worse. The process of reviewing the chapters and answering the questions will take you longer than simply reading through the novel but it should help you begin to integrate the skills and the attitudes of resilience into your life. Enjoy your journey.

Reaching Home

A Novel About Conquering Fear

**Story by
Dr. Lee Brazil
Foreword and Epilogue by:
Benjamin Brazil-Woodford**

Written by Ron Breazeale, Ph.D

For my family and
for all of the people,
both with and without a disability,
I have met on my journey.

Foreword

This book is about my grandfather and our family in the years before the last Great War when the United States of America was still a superpower. It is based on a manuscript written by him, which my mother and I found after his death. I had heard my grandfather tell me these stories many times during my childhood, but I never knew he had written them down. I suppose he was too busy to complete and publish them. Or perhaps he was afraid that, by doing so, he would endanger us.

The focus of his story is terrorism; acts of terrorism perpetrated on our people by our nation's enemies and by the disabling mechanics of our own society.

My grandfather was a quiet man, an ordinary man in most ways, with brilliant blue eyes and a mustache he had grown in graduate school and had never shaved. He had, as the Census Bureau counts such things, a disability. He was born without a left hand. He was small in stature but always stood up for what he believed. He enjoyed laughing and making other people laugh.

For most of his life he had what he called a "love/hate relationship" with his first home, the South. He was a "southern refugee," he'd say. Although he did not find acceptance in the South of his day, before his death he apparently found it here and within himself.

I am not a writer. I fish for a living during the summer, and help build houses and plow snow during the winter. With my mother's help I edited my grandfather's manuscript, filling gaps in the story from our memories. The writing may be rough, but I hope we have done my grandfather's work justice.

My grandfather's story begins when he was sixty-six. He is alone on a road near Pine Grove, in the area where the nuclear bombs that were dropped on Japan in World War II were created, where research on and development of nuclear devices continued until the morning of that first day of Passover, 2013.

Benjamin Brazil-Woodford
Winter Harbor, Maine
March 25, 2042

BOOK ONE: FEAR

CHAPTER 1

For I will pass through the land . . . and when I see the
blood I will pass over you. — Exodus

Tuesday, March 26, 2013
Pine Grove

When Lee awoke the sun was high in the eastern sky. He was lying in a ditch on his stomach in his own vomit. He tried getting up, but felt sick again. Waves of nausea swept over him. Lee heaved again, but there was nothing left in him.

Out of the corner of his eye he could see his car. The engine was still running. He muttered something about thanking Christ he hadn't died of asphyxiation and began to crawl toward the open driver's door.

As Lee struggled to move he realized exhaust fumes were the least of his worries. In his mind he could still see the bright blue flash that had lit up the entire sky, and hear the sounds of an explosion. He could see the flames and the smoke rising over Pine Grove. He looked to the west. Black smoke hung low over the town. The sounds of the previous night, the alarms, the sirens, the cars, the trucks, all had fallen silent. It was spring in the Valley, but there was no sound. Not the song of a bird or the buzz of an insect.

Lee pulled himself into the car and turned the ignition off. And then he heard it; the sounds of a school bus. It stopped, took on passengers, and then started again. As it came towards him, he thought he had truly lost his mind. He blinked as if to clear his eyes. No, his eyes hadn't deceived him. The driver was wearing...a space suit.

The doors of the bus opened and two spacemen got off and headed in his direction. Lee tried to speak, but couldn't. The spacemen said nothing. They pulled him from his car. His legs felt and moved as if made of rubber. They dragged Lee up the steps of the bus and down the aisle to an empty seat. It was then he noticed the insignia: U.S. Department of Homeland Security.

His fellow passengers were draped over seats, or balanced precariously between them. Some were lying on the floor. No one spoke. A low repetitive moan came from the back of the bus.

The door closed. The bus was in motion again, moving on to pluck its next victim from the roadside. He lost consciousness again.

Lee opened his eyes. The bus was hot. The windows were closed. The bus stank. The air conditioning wasn't working or wasn't being used. Sunlight streamed through the bus windows. In a strange way it relaxed him. Lee closed his eyes.

When he opened them again a young woman with long, black hair and olive skin was standing near him. She smiled. He smiled.

Lee was no stranger to nuclear accidents. He was the product of one. He had been born with only one hand. His other "hand," well it wasn't really a hand, was an ugly stump. A wrist. No fingers or thumb. In so many ways, it was a useless appendage. Lee hated it. Hid it in his pocket or under his other arm when he could, before he had the hook that is. Some people said it looked like an elephant's foot. Lee agreed.

His dad worked for the Atomic Energy Commission and they lived behind "the fence" in Pine Grove. In those days even small children and babies needed badges to enter or leave the town. The Cold War was at its height. Accidents happened at the Labs, but all this was secret, classified. After a number of miscarriages, Lee was born. No one knew for certain, but his father apparently had gotten a good dose of something, radiation or mercury. There was no history of birth defects in the family.

The bus rolled to a stop. The jerk of the emergency brake being set startled Lee awake. They were at the hospital; the hospital where Lee had been born. What closure, he thought, to die in the hospital where one was born. People stood outside smoking and waiting, just as they had always done. Lee and his fellow passengers waited, expecting a swarm of white uniforms to descend on the bus. People pointed and talked, but no one came near. Finally, the radio dispatcher snapped at the driver.

"Look, Jim, you're going to have to get these folks cleaned up before we can do anything with them. We got our hands full right now." The hospital staff was overwhelmed with the more seriously injured. The bus and its cargo were ordered to Camp Liberty.

The bus moved slowly, veering around abandoned cars, furniture, and clothing scattered along the way. Some streets were completely blocked. It was forced to back up a number of times. They pulled finally into the parking lot of an old motel. A church had a few years earlier converted the motel into a Christian Academy that, in the last twelve hours, had been transformed into Camp Liberty. Lee and his fellow travelers were to be the first campers.

One by one they were led, carried, or dragged from the bus to the swimming pool of the old motel/academy. Each was stripped of their clothing. No one seemed to care or notice. They were too sick, too busy throwing up to care. They were sprayed with a strong detergent and rinsed with what looked like a garden hose. They were given towels and blankets and bars of Lava soap, the kind mechanics use to clean their hands.

A large man, his face obscured and his voice muffled by his space suit addressed the small, semi-conscious audience. A few stood. Most sat or lay on the concrete.

The man held up one finger of his large, gloved hand. "First, you all got covered with some stuff that came from the lab when it blew up last night. You've got to wash it off." He held up the bar of soap. "Now you got to really scrub yourself."

"Second," he held up two fingers. "The thing you've got to do is drink at least a gallon of water. That will help get the stuff out of your system. I know you don't feel like drinkin' cause you're sick at your stomach, but you got to," he pleaded.

"Third," he held up three fingers. "You've got to take this pill right now." A small pill appeared between the thumb and forefinger of his other hand. "Potassium iodine. To keep the radiation out of your thyroid."

Lee thought he should have been given one of those pills when he was a kid growing up around here, but he wasn't. The drug that could really help Lee and his fellow victims was stockpiled in New York, but there were only a small number of doses. There had been no money in the federal budget to mass-produce it.

"Until you've done these things," said the man in the space suit, "we can't do nothin' else for you."

There was silence. No one had the stomach for food, and most doubted that modern medicine would be their salvation.

One of the spacemen helped Lee up the steps, although his legs were working better now. His room, at the end of a long row of large glass windows, had doors that opened onto a balcony. A room with a view. A small piece of the eastern sky could be seen over the top of the motel's restaurant, now the school's cafeteria.

The room was small and crowded and dark, a standard 1970s motel room. A television hung from the wall. Books and papers were scattered across the floor. Someone's clothing was piled on the bed.

Lee's rescuer, now more a captor, flipped on the overhead light, raked the clothing from the bed, and deposited Lee on top of the bed. He pulled a blanket from the closet and covered Lee.

"Wash good," he said, "and remember to drink as much water as you can hold."

He left. Lee fell asleep.

The sound of voices outside the room roused Lee. Another "camper" was being shown to a room. He rolled out of bed onto the floor and tried to stand, but couldn't. He crawled toward the bathroom, having to stop along the way. His head rested atop one of the books scattered on the floor. *Better Living Through Chemistry*, the book's spine read. Lee would have laughed had he not felt so ill.

When Lee finally reached the bathroom he pulled himself into the shower and tried to stand. He could not. He sat on the shower's floor bleeding, it seemed, from every orifice of his body. Lee just kept on scrubbing. What else could he do? The water turned cold. He continued to scrub. As the water cooled, he tried to drink it. It came back up, but on its return it was filled with blood.

Finally, the water stayed down. He drank more, felt it move through his system. "The plumbing, thank God, is still working," he mumbled to himself as he urinated in the shower. The last time he had done that he had gotten a lecture from his mother. How she knew, he never did understand. His urine was now filled with blood. He sat in it. "In trouble again," he mumbled and lost consciousness.

When he awoke the bathroom was dark. The power was out. He felt sick again. He tried to stand but couldn't. He began to shake. He was burning up and freezing, all at the same time.

He stumbled back to the bed, sat on the edge, covered himself with a blanket, and lay down curled in a fetal position. The fever came in waves. His body ached. Around the edge of the heavy drapes he could see the eastern sky. Still clear and blue, but the light outside was a strange gray hue. Lee picked up his watch from the nightstand. They had let him keep his watch and his hook. It was 5:00 P.M. Where was the sun? He then remembered the black smoke to the west.

Lee's sleep was fitful. His dreams a jumble of images. His father was there, sitting in the chair by the window, just as he had always done when Lee was sick as a child. The young woman with the black hair and olive skin stood by his bed. The bright blue flash came again. It interrupted breakfast with his daughter. It intruded into his lovemaking with his wife. When the morning came and Lee awoke his father and the young woman were gone. And so was the fever.

March 26, 2013
South Boston

The ringing telephone woke Douglas Jennings. He groaned and fumbled for the handset on his nightstand. No one else was disturbed. He was alone and had been for six years, since Margaret left him.

"This is Agent Jennings," his voice sleepy.

He quickly snapped to attention as the caller told him of the accident at Pine Grove. He was being assigned to the investigation. He must pack and be at Logan by 6:00 A.M. "You'll be catching a flight to White's Fork with four other agents from the Boston office."

"What about Project Outbreak?"

"It will have to wait. For God's sake Jennings, this has got priority. This may turn into a friggin' nuclear disaster...a Chernobyl."

"But what about Muqtada? We've got to keep the pressure on."

"Just be on the six o'clock flight," the voice said before hanging up.

Jennings rolled over and looked at his watch. 3:00 A.M. He groaned again and pulled himself out of bed. He flipped on the television and began to throw clothing into an old, battered, leather two-suiter that, like him, had seen too many early morning flights.

The newscaster only repeated what Jennings had just heard. No one knew what was going on down there. An accident or an act of terror? But Jennings knew that the real act of terror was yet to come. A terrorist cell was planning on carrying out what the Cold War Soviets had only schemed and dreamed of, unleashing a disease that could spread not just death, but panic across the U.S. in a matters of days. The Black Death. The plague!

"But Project Outbreak will have to wait," said Jennings to an empty room. "Some accident in Hooterville is the priority."

Jennings showered. He had lost a lot of weight since the surgery. Prostate cancer. He had not gained it back. He needed a new wardrobe, but he refused to take the time to shop for one. Margaret had always helped him with that, but that was before the divorce. Before the cancer.

He started to shave. His face was pale from the winter. Just another sign of my age, he thought, like the thinning hair and the increasing number of wrinkles in his face. *No time to think about that. I am off to Hooterville to find the drunk technician who pushed the wrong button.*

March 26, 2013
Burger Village, South Boston

"Are you sure you don't want to Super Size that, sir?"

"No thank you," said Muqtada. "This is more than enough."

Muqtada stared down at the hamburger and cola, scooped the tray up with one hand and settled at a table near the television.

A crowd had gathered. The coverage from White's Fork was live. Muqtada, who had been lost in his thoughts, began to listen.

"What is being called by officials a major accident at Pine Grove Labs occurred at 9:21 P.M. last night. Evacuation of residents of the town and surrounding area is proceeding. The number of injured or dead is not known at this time. Officials fear that the containment structure of one of the older nuclear reactors at Pine Grove Labs has been seriously weakened."

"An opportunity for someone," Muqtada mumbled under his breath as he ate, and then it came to him. *It is the opportunity we need. Their government will be occupied with this. They will not be watching my brother Ibraham that closely. I can finally talk with him.*

Muqtada, a man in his mid-sixties with thinning hair and a light-gray beard, believed he had spent most of his life in transition. He was an average man in many ways, height and build, but his life had not been average. He fled Iran with his family in the early 1970s when the Shah's regime collapsed. His father reestablished the family in New England, but Muqtada always dreamed of returning home. He dropped out of college and tried to create his own future in business, but failed.

After his father's death he took his inheritance and traveled in the Arab world. It was there that he found a way back home. He would prove himself not as a traitor to his country and his faith, as his father had been seen, but as a true believer in the cause of his countrymen, the Besiege. He had lost a hand and part of an arm in one of his failed efforts to prove himself. He now wore a gloved prosthesis as a means of keeping him from being easily recognized by the authorities, and not because he felt it was of any other use to him.

Muqtada saw the opportunity clearly. *The time is now*, he thought. He and his allies had planned and waited. They were ready. Now, with the help of his brother Ibraham, they could have the device. They could carry out their plan without it, but the device would assure their success now and in the future. With the device this would not be the last attack. Other attacks could be much more easily executed.

It is time to restore honor to our family. Ibraham will have no choice but to help me.

CHAPTER 2

...A country will have authority and influence because
of moral factors, not its military strength,
because it can be humble and not
blatant and arrogant;... — **Jimmy Carter, 1978**

Wednesday, March 27, 2013
White's Fork

It was the second day of Passover. Lee continued to sleep. He slept the sleep of the dead. He did not move. He did not dream. Morning passed into afternoon.

On a normal school day residents of the Academy would have been up early. There would have been a prayer circle after breakfast and then the students would have been off to their first class, Bible study. The Academy believed in getting the day off to the right start. It had been modeled after the teachings of a television evangelist. Unfortunately for the school, shortly after its opening the evangelist was arrested for sodomizing a fourteen-year-old. The resulting media attention, to say the least, had not been helpful to the school already struggling financially from the deep recession and conflicts within the church.

When a church deacon approached the board about offering the school to the U.S. Department of Homeland Security as a decontamination site, "should one ever be needed," the decision was an easy one. The school would receive a monthly fee for storing DHS supplies needed for such work and would be well compensated should the school ever be used. When the headmaster received the call the evening before, the Academy was quickly evacuated. Students packed what they could carry and left along with most of the city's population.

A knock at the door startled Lee awake. He jumped from his bed and looked out the window but could not make out who was at the door. The gray hue remained. The spacemen were gone, replaced by robotic young men and women in Army fatigues wearing surgical masks. They hurried about. People were coming. None seemed to be going.

"Dr. Brazil," the voice said, "Major Henderson wishes to speak to you." He paused. "Get dressed. You will find your medication and clothing in a plastic bag outside the door. I'll be back in thirty minutes."

Lee looked through the plastic bag. A surgical mask. Toothbrush and toothpaste. Deodorant. Thyroid medication. The right dosage. He wondered how they knew. Prison pajamas and sandals. No underwear. Lee wanted underwear, boxer shorts, something that would feel normal.

In the clothing left behind in the room he found an old flannel shirt. It was big, but it would do. He found some boxer shorts, probably not clean, but a little Right Guard and, oh, what the hell. He found some socks. Same story. In the closet was an old pair of tennis shoes. With two pairs of socks, they would work. But no pants? "What? This kid only had one pair of pants and he took them with him?" Well, pajama bottoms it would be.

Lee washed the dried blood from his face and neck. He put on the surgical mask and looked at himself in the mirror. He looked like an escapee from a sanitarium.

Lee switched the television on, but nothing happened. The TV wasn't working. The knock and the voice were back. "Dr. Brazil, Major Henderson is ready to see you now." It hadn't been thirty minutes.

Major Henderson had taken over the headmaster's office. He was a big, overweight man. Big-boned, as they say in the South. He was not muscular. His hair was cut short, military style. He wore camouflage fatigues. He neither stood nor offered a greeting when Lee entered the room. Instead, without looking up, he pointed to the chair directly in front of the desk.

Lee took the seat. He said nothing. He waited. He was still having trouble with his voice. His throat was sore and his voice weak.

Files, books, and papers from the previous occupant's desk had been piled in a corner of the room. The desk had only a few files, a coffee cup, and a stack of two or three manuals. The one on top read, *The Physician's Guide to Managing Nuclear Radiation Exposure.*

When Major Henderson spoke it was with a deep southern accent. "What is it you do, Brazil, and what were you doin' in Pine Grove?"

"Well, I'm a retired psychologist who works part time." Lee stumbled over his words. "I mean you have to these days. Social security is a joke, and Medicare. I guess after we made the drug companies rich, there wasn't much left to pay benefits." The major didn't seem to appreciate his comments about the plight of the nation's retirees. "I also write. Well, I try to write. I've been working on a book." Lee suspected they had found his manuscript, *Ten Years in the Not-So-New South* in the car. A book he had been trying to write—a kind of catharsis—an indictment of greed, racism, and the Religious Right. A step, he thought, towards finally making peace with the South and with himself.

"Yes, we know all about you and your book," he said impatiently. "But, what were you doin' in Pine Grove?"

The SOMOP meeting-*Save Our Mountains and Our People.* He replied with hesitation. "I was at a meeting."

"Yeah," said the major "a meeting of that group of tree huggers that want to close down things."

The government had opened an incinerator for nuclear waste in Pine Grove in 2004. SOMOP had felt for a number of years that the incinerator was creating more health problems for area residents.

The major continued, "Some of those folks have said some pretty crazy things."

Lee said nothing.

"You were supposed to be on a 7:00 A.M. flight back to Maine this morning, the morning after the accident." He stopped. "Maine's pretty close to Canada, isn't it?"

"Yes," said Lee. There was silence.

Major Henderson continued, "You have a very mild case of radiation poisoning."

I'd hate to see severe if this was mild, thought Lee.

"You were over ten miles from the plant when the accident occurred. You will recover completely."

And die of cancer next year, thought Lee.

"We will be keepin' you here until we can make other arrangements."

"Can I call my family?" Lee asked.

"That will not be possible at this time," said the major looking down at a stack of papers on his desk. "You need to rest. We will talk again tomorrow." He did not look up. "When you are ready to eat, the corporal will show you to the cafeteria." And with that Lee was dismissed.

Lee did not like the major. He was sure the feeling was mutual. He felt his old prejudice coming back, what his wife referred to as "internalized oppression." In his last years in the South he had developed an intense dislike for all things southern: football, southern accents, fundamentalism, Republicans, and did I mention football? Maybe because he had grown up in the old South he had had a difficult time adjusting to the "New South." When he had moved with his family "back home," most of what he found new in the South was Sunbelt money. After ten years he and his wife were homesick for New England. That summer they returned to Maine for a vacation and stayed.

When Lee and the corporal returned to his room he found the robotic young people in Army fatigues and masks had installed a padlock on his door. When he protested, the corporal's response was one word, "Orders."

He pushed Lee inside, closed the door. The lock snapped.

Lee was alone. What was the major's interest in SOMOP? What was that business about Maine being close to Canada? Maybe the accident wasn't an accident.

The war on terrorism was still being fought. No one really knew who was winning. People were scared. The government encouraged their fear. If people worried about terrorism, they wouldn't have time to worry about a soon-to-be bankrupt Social Security and Medicare system, or the increasing number of jobless and poor. Bickering over how to fix these things had continued, but no one had done anything. God knows saving the country from the enemies out there, over there, was the first priority. Most people still believed that tanks and bombs could protect their families.

The formal war in Iraq had ended after a few weeks, but the occupation of Iraq and Afghanistan had continued and so had the killing. Both countries had become a breeding ground for terrorists of all stripes.

In the years since 9/11 there had been a couple of suicide bombings in the states. A number of U.S. Embassies had been attacked. The foreign press had reported that the U.S. had assassinated a number of suspected terrorists. The FBI had rounded up a few. Some of them had been tried. Two had been executed. Capital punishment and assassination had become more popular. There was less concern with killing the innocent. What right-minded American politician could object to putting a terrorist to death?

There had been no acts of nuclear terrorism, but there had been many threats. In fact, the main casualty of the war on terror had been the President who had begun the war. During his second term, after hurricane Katrina, his popularity, even among his major supporters, faded. Charges of corruption and cronyism and the congressional investigations that followed drove his numbers even lower. The public seemed to finally realize that his tax cuts were mainly for the rich, that going shopping wasn't the answer, and that his brand of compassionate conservatism was much more conservative than compassionate. His popularity reached a new low and historians began to compare his presidency to that of some of his more incompetent predecessors, such as Buchanan, Harding, and Hoover.

After the meltdown of Wall Street, a new presidential election in 2008 did not prevent the country's slide into recession, one of the deepest since the Great Depression. People were impatient. They wanted more change than the new president or, for that matter, it would seem anyone could deliver.

Hope for something different faded with the incumbent's defeat in 2012. People were looking for a savior, not a president. After the election, the nation sank back into a familiar, although uncomfortable rut. The country circled the wagons again and braced for more. Little had apparently been learned from the past. The politics of fear, once again, replaced the politics of hope.

But, SOMOP a terrorist organization? They had to be kidding. But Lee knew the major wasn't. The major was a very serious man.

Lee banged on the door and yelled. He was hungry. Finally one of his keepers came. Of course he could go to the cafeteria.

Lee sat at a long table. There was no one else in the room. The young woman who had helped him down the stairs to the cafeteria asked, "What do you want to eat?"

Despite being 10:30 at night, Lee said, "Breakfast."

She smiled. "No problem," she replied and disappeared into the kitchen. In five minutes she was back. "Here's some OJ and milk. Would you like some coffee?"

"That would be great." She had a nice smile.

"I hope you like your eggs scrambled and your sausage in links. That's the only way that stuff comes."

Lee had to admit it wasn't half-bad, even if the eggs were dry and the sausage tough. Lee thought this was the best thing that had happened to him since his arrival.

When he was returned to his room the corporal was waiting.

"Get enough to eat?"

"Yes, it was good."

"We're runnin' out of space and we didn't want you to get lonely so we decided to give you a roommate." He opened the door and pointed to a man sitting on an Army cot that had been shoved into the opposite corner of the room.

"This is Howard. Howard meet Dr. Brazil. Since you're a shrink we figured you'd be good for Howard." And with that he closed the door, snapped the lock, and left.

Howard didn't speak or look in Lee's direction. He was busy sorting through a stack of papers, many covered in plastic. They had been arranged in a particular order that had been disturbed. Howard wore large glasses with black, plastic frames. He was balding slightly and needed a haircut and a shave. He was not dressed in Camp Liberty prison pajamas. He apparently hadn't been exposed. He wore gray coveralls and a pair of old work boots. A long chain ran from his belt to a large wallet in the rear pocket of his coveralls. A toothbrush, a tube of toothpaste, and an assortment of pens and pencils were tucked tightly into the coveralls outer breast pocket.

Howard was the first resident of Camp Liberty that Lee had seen close up.

"I don't like that guy," Lee muttered to himself loud enough that Howard could hear. Howard said nothing.

A few seconds passed. "How did you end up here?" Lee asked.

"I wouldn't get on that bus."

"What bus?"

"They sent that bus to the mission." Howard continued his sorting. "But they wouldn't tell us where they were takin' us."

"Well maybe they didn't know exactly," Lee offered.

"They knew. I wouldn't lie to you." Howard looked up from his papers. "They knew. They just want all of us out of there so they can close the shelter and the mission." He stopped. Lee waited. "So I run off. Somebody left the door to the Salvation Army Store open. I slept in there last night." He smiled and nodded. "Everything was going just fine until this afternoon when I walked back to the mission to get my stuff. I didn't see them until they were on me." He nodded. "That young cop. Boy! Could he run fast! So I stopped."

Lee listened and Howard talked.

"I've lived here all my life, Doc. Never left here." He paused.

"Guess I should have, but I ain't going no place but home."

Lee broke in. "But isn't home here?"

Howard ignored Lee's question and continued. "They sent me to that special school cause I run off from home. I got tired of hearin' it. They argued all the time." He shook his head. "You would've run off too, Doc. But I didn't like the school." He shook his head again. "A lot of crazy people in there. I finally got outta there, I got myself a job." He smiled again.

"What kind of work do you do, Howard?"

"Construction." He hesitated. "I used to. I couldn't take the way they talked about me." He paused. "They talked about me, they talked about Jesus," he asserted. "They made fun of both of us. I told my boss about it, but he didn't do nothin', so I did." He nodded. "I hit that guy real hard." He paused. "They fired me. Tried to get me arrested, but the police let me go."

Lee nodded and smiled, and thought about personally smacking the person who was responsible for putting Howard in his room. He had had enough in thirty-five years of clinical practice. He didn't need to sleep with it.

"I needed that job to support my daughter. My wife, she wouldn't work. She wouldn't take care of her, so I did." He closed his eyes. "But the state lady didn't care. They took my baby. Wouldn't let me see her. They gave her to these people." He began to slowly rock back and forth. "They said she'd be better off there, but I knew she wouldn't't." He nodded again. "I tried to get her back." He opened his eyes. "I wouldn't lie to you, Doc. I tried. But the lawyer said it was too late." He stopped rocking and looked at Lee. "I hate those people, Doc. They shouldn't ought to have done that." He nodded and began to rock again.

Efforts by Lee to end or redirect the conversation had little effect.

"I wouldn't lie to you, Doc. I've been on the streets for years now." He began to rock faster. "They wanted me to move into the projects, but I wouldn't." He shook his head again. "They didn't like that. They think we're all crazy." He paused. "I ain't crazy." He looked at Lee again. "There ain't nothin' wrong with my brain, Doc. I got the results of the test to prove it."

He pulled out a copy of a test that he had found on the Internet and showed Lee.

Lee changed the subject, "What do you know about the accident?"

"I know there weren't no accident. That's just them again. Tryin' to scare you." He paused. "Tryin' to make you leave. And once they get us out of here, they won't let us come back. I know 'em, Doc." He nodded again.

"Howard, listen to me." Lee leaned forward "I saw the flash. I heard the explosion." He tried to make eye contact with Howard, but failed. "I've been dog sick for the last three days."

Howard closed his eyes refusing to look at Lee. "Doc, it's all fake. That blue flash. The explosion sound. Your sickness. They just gave you and the rest of them somethin' to make you sick." He stopped. "I know 'em, Doc." He nodded again.

Lee shook his head.

Howard continued on for the next hour. He was a reserve police officer and he showed Lee his card. And so it went on and on. He talked about energy fields and intelligent life on other planets. About a machine that could travel to these worlds.

"I tried to help 'em make one, Doc, but they wouldn't let me so I just made one myself." He stopped. "It works. But they wouldn't even come and see it."

It was after three in the morning before Howard finally talked himself to sleep. The third night of Passover was ending. Lee thought of his wife's Seder dinner. He thought of his friends and of his daughter. They didn't know whether he was alive or dead. When he closed his eyes the blue flash came again. He opened them. He closed them. He repeated the cycle. Sleep finally came.

CHAPTER 3

*Political liberty must be based upon virtue and sustained
by the intelligence of the citizens.*
— J.W.M. Breazeale, *Life As It Is*, 1842

Thursday, March 28, 2013
White's Fork

When morning came Howard was up, sorting through his papers. Lee struggled to open his eyes. "What time is it?"

"Seven o'clock. They'll be here for us soon. You better get up, Doc."

Lee moved slowly. He felt stiff. His body ached. Before he could get in the shower the corporal was at the door. "Breakfast in thirty minutes."

Lee looked in the mirror. He was losing more of his hair. Some of his teeth felt loose. He tried not to disturb them, hoping by some magic they would not fall out.

"Great, bald and toothless living through science," Lee said aloud.

The shower had always been a place to think. The spray hit his face, warmed his back. Maybe when he saw Henderson today he could convince the guy he wasn't "a threat to national security." God! What a crazy situation. The whole thing was out of a bad, B-movie. He had to at least convince the good major to let him call his wife. He turned the shower off.

Howard and Lee had the same meal Lee had had the night before. Lee ate more. As before, there was no one else in the cafeteria. Only Lee, Howard, and their keeper. When they finished Howard was taken back to their room and Lee was escorted to Major Henderson's office.

Major Henderson seemed in a better mood. "Have a seat, Dr. Brazil." Lee sat.

Major Henderson was not alone. Leaning against the wall with his arms folded against his chest was a tall man in a dark suit that clung weakly to his slender frame.

"This is Special Agent Jennings," said Henderson.

The man nodded, but did not speak. Jennings' mind wasn't on the interrogation. He was thinking about Muqtada and wishing he was back in Boston. He had not been back to this part of the Southeast since his father was stationed at Tyson Field in the 1950s. He remembered that he hadn't liked being here then and he didn't like being here now.

"You've been traveling a lot this year, haven't you?" said the major looking at Lee.

Lee nodded.

"Business?"

"Some of the trips have involved my work."

"What business did you have in the Middle East?"

"My wife is Jewish. We have friends in Israel," Lee offered.

"And South America?" The major continued to flip through the pages in a file that Lee could see had his name on it. "My daughter was born in Peru. We visited her birth family."

They found my passport in the rental car, Lee thought. Lee's wife always made him carry his passport. He used to tease her about sleeping with hers. She was the daughter of Holocaust survivors. Passports were important.

"You had dinner with David Smith on Sunday night."

"Yes I did," Lee paused. "Since you guys seem to have spent a lot of time in my rental car, going through my passport and appointment book, I hope you returned the car to the airport. The late charges are murder." Lee smiled, but the major did not. Special Agent Jennings continued to stare. He said nothing.

"Dr. Brazil, you don't seem to understand how serious this situation is," said the major in a grim tone. "What business did you have with Mr. Smith?"

"He's an old friend." Lee was looking for words. "We grew up together. I always see him when I come down here."

"Did he talk about his work?" The major pressed.

David worked at the Labs. "Well . . . some. Why are you asking me this?"

"He's dead, and so are a lot of other people."

"What do you mean, he's dead?" Lee had assumed for some reason that David had not been working the night of the accident. That he was okay.

"Why do you look so surprised, Dr. Brazil? He was killed in the explosion at the Labs on Monday night." He paused and watched Lee's reaction. "Were you planning on meeting him later?"

The next few minutes were a blur for Lee. The major kept asking questions about SOMOP. Lee said little, at least little that made sense. Finally, the major gave up. He ordered the corporal to take Lee back to his room.

The room was empty. Howard wasn't there. Lee sat down. He thought of Dave. In the last ten years they had seen more of each other than in the preceding twenty. Lee and David had been friends since the first day of school. They had double-dated, contemplated the mysteries of the universe, mainly women, together. Talked about the future. But, when high school ended they had steadily drifted apart.

David married his high school sweetheart, Mary. Soon after their marriage David's father died of alcoholism. His mother died a year later. His brother Richard followed in his dad's footsteps. Alcohol and hell-raising weakened his heart. He died peacefully one night in his recliner, only forty-five.

But the hardest thing for Dave was Mary's death. She had died after a car accident. Their two children were grown. Loneliness drove Dave to marry again. The marriage did not last. He missed Mary too much.

Dave had worked for the Labs for twenty years. He wanted to retire, but couldn't. He was still paying Mary's medical bills. She had lived in intensive care for two months after the car accident. The doctors said they had done everything they could and apparently they had.

David was not a happy man. He was bitter, but he was no saboteur. Lee felt rage building inside. Who did Henderson think he was accusing his dead friend? Tears came to Lee's eyes. He had not cried since this whole nightmare began. He cried. He cried for his dead friend. He cried for himself. He cried for the screwed up world of which he felt very much a part.

The door opened. Howard was back. The keeper closed the door, snapped the lock. Howard went directly to his own bed. He said nothing. Lee did not acknowledge his presence.

An hour passed. Howard broke the silence. "They asked me about you. They want to know what we talk about. I didn't tell 'em nothin'. They even gave me a sandwich. I saved half of it for you." Lee didn't respond. "Are you okay, Doc? You don't look so good."

"I had bad news. An old friend of mine is dead." Lee repeated the last sentence again. "An old friend of mine is dead! At least that's what they told me."

"I'm sorry, Doc. I wouldn't lie to you." Howard stood up. "I didn't have nothin' to do with it."

"I know, Howard. I know." Lee was not up for dealing with Howard.

The two sat again in silence. Howard pulled out his papers and started sorting through them. Lee didn't move. Finally, Lee reached for a legal pad and a pen he had found under the bed. Writing helped him to make sense out of things, figure things out.

He needed to write and "need" was the right word. Sometimes he would be all frozen up inside. The words wouldn't come. He would feel like he was falling into a dark hole with no bottom. He would spin and turn and grab at the air. He would struggle with it. Push at it. Set it aside. And finally it would come, like a stream in the Cherokee Mountains after a spring rain, moving fast, overflowing its banks. Gushing out onto the paper. The spillways were open. The pressure was down. The paralysis gone.

Tonight the words came easily. Lee began writing.

The group was organized in the early 1970s by a local man He fought the strip miners. I met him while working in a clinic in the mountains. I visited him at his home. I remember that we talked in the kitchen. The man said it was safer. The picture window of his front room had been blown out by a shotgun blast the night before. By the mining company, he was sure.

Lee wrote on and on, recounting the evolution of the grassroots group.

SOMOP has had some success. Mining has changed for the better. SOMOP has expanded its mission. Most recently, the focus has been on toxic releases from the nuclear waste incinerator.

SOMOP's numbers have grown and their protests have become noisier and more confrontational. For an area like the Valley, civil disobedience has always been an embarrassment. When sit-in demonstrations at the lunch counters started in White's Fork in the late 1950s they lasted only one day. The lunch counters were integrated.

But racism did not disappear from the Valley, it only went underground. As the years passed, White's Fork has become more segregated rather than less as whites moved west leaving the center city and the eastern suburbs to an increasingly invisible black minority. The people with the new money thought of themselves as colorblind. They didn't see themselves as racists. As the 20th century came to a close they just had more important things on their minds: lowering the estate tax and buying the right SUV.

Student activism at the university faded by the mid-1970s. As the Sun Belt grew, new money and people flooded the city. The university had been shut down with a strike after Kent State, and students had been arrested — "The 22" — but that was many years ago. The campus no longer sees protest. Corporate America, through the funding of research, now controls the school as it does most American universities. The university prides itself on its football team and on being "research focused." Teaching is secondary.

But SOMOP somehow survived the 1980s and the 1990s. Its activities had obviously caught the attention of the Department of Homeland Security. The last demonstration had gotten out of hand. Thirty people were arrested and some of the protestors, as the major put it, said some pretty crazy things. One protestor was quoted as saying, "An accident," the major seemed to emphasize this word, "was bound to occur if they did not shut down the incineration program immediately."

Lee had gotten involved in one of the lawsuits against the companies at Pine Grove. Interestingly enough, not because of his hand, since "no scientifically proven link" had been made between his type of birth defect and toxic exposures, but because of having had most of his thyroid removed in his early twenties. Science had been successful in showing a link between releases in the area of Iodine 131 and thyroid cancer.

With the energy crisis of 2010 the nuclear industry had been reborn. It was growing rapidly. The present lawsuit had been going on for twelve years. The companies that were being sued had a battalion of attorneys who were very successful in keeping the case out of court. In the last ten years, the federal government had placed limits on the awards that courts could make in these types of cases. The first large awards, starting in the 1990s had been against physicians. But when the trial lawyers started picking on corporations, something had to be done. A consortium of corporations pressured Congress to enact new laws. Trailer trash, those people with no money, had gotten some very large awards from the courts and the old boys and girls, those people with money, wanted it stopped. They partially succeeded. The new laws were hindering the progress of the present suit.

On the night of the accident, I attended a meeting of the members of the class-action suit. An attorney from Nashville representing the group gave a brief update. The judge who had heard the case originally, and who had thrown the case out of court, because there was "no scientifically acceptable way" of proving a link between their illnesses and releases from the Labs, had died of cancer. The attorney felt that the appeal had a better chance before a new judge. Perhaps. The attorney did not appear optimistic. When the meeting ended we were not encouraged.

The corporal banged on the door. "You boys want lunch?"

Lee looked at Howard. "Yeah, I do, but I don't think Doc's that hungry."

Lee nodded. Howard left with the corporal. Lee returned to his writing.

I left Pine Grove around 9:00 P.M. planning to drive back to my hotel in White's Fork. It was a pleasant spring evening. The day had been warm. As the air cooled, fog began to form. It was Monday. Traffic was light. I drove past the now abandoned guard towers, once the main entrance to Pine Grove. The streetlights of the town disappeared in the rearview mirror. The road became darker. Far up ahead I saw the lights of White's Fork. The fog had slowed the traffic. I decided to follow the two cars in front of me.

I glanced at the car's clock, it was 9:21. That's when it happened. A blue flash of light. The entire sky lit up for a few seconds. It blinded me. Instinctively, I steered the car to the shoulder of the road and stopped. I heard the sound of a car skidding, and a crash, but I still could not see. I heard what sounded like a cry for help. A woman was screaming. I could make out a set of taillights, about one hundred feet in front of my car. I switched the headlights on high beam. The two cars I'd been following had collided.

As I opened the car door I heard the sound of an explosion. Looking in the direction of the sound, I saw an orange glow in the western sky. The screams came again. I ran in their direction.

In the car lights Lee saw a young woman with long, blonde hair trying to open the driver's door of her car. Lee grabbed the door and pulled. It popped open. The woman bounced out of the car. She was crying, "Oh, my God. Oh, my God," over and over again. Lee yelled at her to stop. She did.

"Are you hurt?" he asked. She shook her head no.

Lee turned his attention to the other car. There was no sound or movement. He walked to the driver's side and looked inside. A woman was slumped over the steering wheel. Lee tried to open the door, but it was locked. He yelled and beat on the window, but she did not move. He smashed the rear vent window with his hook and opened the door. She fell back onto the seat. She was bleeding from her nose and mouth. She had a gash on her forehead. The other woman helped Lee slowly recline her seat. They tried not to move the woman.

"What's your name?" Lee asked.

The blonde answered, "Melanie." The woman in the car moaned.

"Melanie, dial 911." He shoved his cell phone into her hands.

The 911 line was jammed with calls. The only response was the sound of the phone ringing.

"Do you have a first-aid kit?" Lee asked.

She did. Lee and Melanie were able to stop the woman's bleeding. She regained consciousness briefly and gave Lee a faint smile. Her breathing was shallow and her pulse rapid. Lee thought she was going into shock. They tried 911 again. No luck.

"Let's leave her in the car. I'm afraid to move her," Lee said.

They covered her with a blanket from his trunk. Working together, Melanie steering from the passenger side and Lee pushing, they got the woman's car off the road. The fog was getting thicker. They tried to push Melanie's car, but the automatic shifter seemed to be stuck in gear. They turned the emergency flashers on and hoped they would be seen. There was no traffic. But they could hear sirens in the distance.

Back at the woman's car, Lee got in the front passenger seat and Melanie sat in the back. She searched the woman's purse for identification. "Her name is Pam," Melanie said.

"You're going to be okay, Pam," Lee tried to soothe her.

He turned on the radio. It still worked, but the only stations on the air seemed to be playing the same announcement over and over again. "Residents of Pine Grove and surrounding areas should remain in their homes. Close all windows and doors and turn off central heating and air conditioning systems. Please wait for additional instructions from the Department of Homeland Security. Remain calm."

Lee and Melanie closed the car windows. They put an old raincoat from the trunk over the broken vent window. On the other side of the road they saw flashing lights in the fog. One, perhaps two, ambulances or fire trucks. They couldn't tell. They passed, moving slowly in the direction of Pine Grove.

Melanie began to recite The *Twenty-third Psalm*. "The Lord is my shepherd I shall not want...." She asked Lee to repeat it with her. He did. Three times they said it.

Lee tried the radio again. He couldn't get anything on the radio's FM band except the same announcement. He switched to AM and heard the call letters WLS, Chicago. He had listened to rock and roll on this station as a teenager. Tonight the station interrupted its regular programming for a news bulletin.

"The Associated Press is reporting that there has been a major accident at a DOE Nuclear Facility in Pine Grove, Tennessee. Details at this time are sketchy, but first reports indicate that one of the containment buildings at PG Labs may have been breached by an explosion and fire. An evacuation of area residents is under way. An emergency response team is on the scene. Again, repeating, The Associated Press is reporting that there has been a major accident at a DOE Nuclear Facility in Pine Grove, Tennessee."

Pam was having difficulty breathing. Lee and Melanie were starting to as well. Both began to feel sick. Lee thought he knew what was happening. They were starting to show the first signs of radiation exposure. The fog was getting thicker. They tried 911 again. No answer.

"We can't stay here. We've got to get to a hospital," Lee told Melanie. "We can't wait for them to find us. It will be too late."

Melanie begged him not to leave. He assured her he would be back with his car.

Lee stepped out of Pam's car and into the fog. He closed the door. He started walking toward the headlights of his car. He could hear the motor running; he had left the engine on. He took a deep breath and almost passed out. The fog now seemed to have something mixed with it. Something that wasn't there a few minutes before. It smelled like electrical wiring when it shorts out. Lee pressed on. He fell, got up, and fell again. He was getting closer. The engine was louder. He was almost there. He could see the outline of the car in the fog. Just a few more feet. He reached for the driver's door handle, but fell again. This time he did not get up, not for a while.

The next few hours were a jumble of coming to, throwing up, passing out again, finally getting to his feet and falling again. The next thing he knew it was morning. The sun was warm on his neck.

I don't know what has happened to Pam and Melanie. I have not seen them since that night. No one seems to know anything.

Lee stopped writing. He was exhausted. Writing about it was like reliving it again. It had to be. That's the way it was when it worked best.

He slipped between the sheets. They were cool. He pulled the covers up to his chin and rolled over on his side. The world out-side for a moment slipped away. He felt safe. But just for a moment. Lee fell into a fitful sleep.

In his sleep Lee went back to the banks of the river where he had grown up. He was sixteen, on a caving expedition with three of his friends. They had been walking for most of the morning. They began to climb the river bluff. Finding good footing on the rocks had become more difficult. The climbing was exhausting, but they could see the opening of the cave.

The trail led to a ledge and a drop-off. Water from the cave ran down the rock face becoming a straight, long drop into the river. The only way across was to jump The distance across wasn't great, perhaps four feet. The problem was that the ledges weren't aligned. The ledge on the far side was about six feet higher. The trick would be to find grips and footing on the rocks on the other side and pull up to the ledge leading into the cave. If you were unable to find secure grips and footing, you would slide off the rock face and fall into the river below.

Bill, who had taken the lead in the climb up the bluff, decided he could make the jump. He said he saw a number of possible grips. He didn't seem concerned. He jumped with little difficulty, found secure grips and footing, and pulled himself onto the top of the ledge on the other side.

It was Lee's turn. Bill shouted instructions. Lee hesitated. He began to realize that this was a two-handed task. He would have to pull himself up using one hand and his legs and feet.

The two friends behind him encouraged him. "You can do it. Go on," they said.

Lee always told himself that with one hand he could do just about anything anyone could do with two hands. He knew there were some things he couldn't do, like a difficult rope climb. But Bill made this look so easy. What would his friends think if he said no? If he gave up so easily?

Lee jumped. He secured a firm grip with his right hand. But his "little hand," as his parents called it, could find no grip. And without a firm grip, a secure hold, Lee could not find his footing. His legs dangled in the air. Lee looked to Bill in desperation. Bill stretched down, trying to reach his friend. But the distance was too great. Lee hung by his one hand. He was starting to slip. He was losing his grip. He was falling.

Lee woke up as he always did. Always before he hit the water or before he drowned. And always wet with sweat, his heart racing.

Lee closed his eyes. He said a prayer for himself and for his world. This time he fell into a deep sleep.

March 28, 2013
Tyson Field, White's Fork
5:30 P.M.

Jennings was on a plane again, flying to D.C. The department had arranged a meeting for the governors of the effected states and the agents heading the investigation. Jennings felt it was a gigantic waste of time, a photo op. But shaking hands with the politicians was important to the department, whose budget had gotten smaller each year.

At least he would have some time to himself. He had taken a seat in the back of the plane by a window. He looked out. The sky to the west remained dark. Black with the smoke from Pine Grove. It was late afternoon. It looked like rain.

Jennings thoughts were not on Pine Grove. They were on Project Outbreak. He remembered the day he had had to sell the project to the top brass at the agency.It was a cold, fall afternoon, but not as cold as the reception he received.

"Look Jennings, we know bubonic plague is a deadly agent. It was a favorite of the Soviets. But it is also a very fragile one. Outside of its host, it dies in a few seconds. Right?"

"Not necessarily," said Jennings.

"How could it be spread?" The chief looked puzzled.

"The Soviets developed a special device, a kind of giant atomizer that would allow it to be spread through air conditioning systems or from a low-flying plane." Jennings loosened his collar. "The device coats the germ with a substance, like sputum, that allows the germ to live on just about any surface for weeks."

"So this giant atomizer coats the germ with spit and then they spray this from a low-flying plane?" He smiled.

"Well, yes." Jennings could feel his face starting to flush.

The other agents were smiling. There was muffled laughter.

"The Soviets came up with a lot of crazy ideas during the Cold War, just like we did." He shook his head and looked around the room at the other agents. "How do we know the terrorists could build such a device? Do they have the plans?"

"Not yet." His pace was quicker. "But I believe they could get the plans or get one of the people who built the device to help them. We know they have the germ."

"Who would help them?" The chief appeared impatient.

"Doctor Ibraham Hussein." Jennings smiled. "He defected to the British from the Soviets in the mid-1980s. Worked in our labs in Germany until the end of the Cold War." Jennings thought he had the answers that should impress the chief.

"Yes, I know. MIT grad. Disenchanted. Moved to the Soviet Union late-Seventies." The chief already knew a lot about Hussein and his family. "His older brother, Muqtada, tried to return to Iran. Did not get a warm reception. He has been involved in a number of actions against the U.S. in Europe." He paused. "At least that is what we suspect. Most of these have failed, thank God. Where is he now?" He looked at Jennings.

"We don't know. No one has seen him in the last few months." Jennings stopped. The chief waited. "I think he is here in the Boston area to get his brother's help in building the device," said Jennings with hesitation.

"Jennings, this all sounds a bit far-fetched, even for you. But I will give you Agent Wright. You have been working with him for the last few months and," looking down at the file laying on the conference table, "Agents Gomez and Clark. They are new. This office is their first assignment since the Academy." He caught Jennings' eyes. "They need an experienced agent like you to work with them. I just hope they don't take all of your ideas at face value." He looked back down at the file. "I want a progress report in six weeks."

Jennings didn't know exactly how to take the last comment, but at least he had been given some additional help. It wouldn't be just him and Wright. His thoughts were interrupted by a familiar voice. He looked toward the front of the plane. A heavyset man in a blue suit was dragging a large carry-on bag, with some difficulty, down the aisle. It was Dick Ketting. He hadn't seen Dick in years.

"Is this seat taken?" asked Ketting.

"It is now," said Jennings. "Have a seat. How are you?" He offered his hand.

"Fine, fine," said Ketting pumping his hand. "And you?"

"I'm okay." Jennings looked away wishing he could avoid what was coming next.

"I heard about your surgery."

"Yeah, I'm okay. It's been a year. They say if it doesn't come back in five I'm home free." *Hopefully, that was enough for him*, thought Jennings. "So what's happening in Denver?"

"Oh, I suppose the same as all over." Ketting said looking for his seatbelt. "The old guys like us are retiring. Private corporations are doing more of our work and a lot of young fellows joining the Agency."

"Yeah, tell me about it." Jennings nodded in agreement. "They gave me these two kids who are great with a computer or a lab coat. They grew up watching CSI, but do they have any street sense?" He shook his head. "No. Never worked the street."

"Yeah I know," said Ketting as he pulled out the in-flight magazine. "Same story in Denver. They don't seem to want to get their hands dirty."

Jennings closed his eyes and leaned back. "Everything is by the book. If it's not in the book, they can't do it. And if they can't do it as a 'team,' they don't do it."

"The Agency doesn't encourage individual initiative any- more," Ketting offered.

"But, God, do they have to write everything down?" asked Jennings as he opened his eyes and leaned forward. "I swear these kids must log in when they go to the bathroom and detail how things turned out!"

They both laughed.

"Well, I'm getting out when I can," Ketting looked at Jennings. "Before they completely do in our retirement."

"Sounds nice, Dick, but the divorce set me back. I suppose I'll be working for Uncle Sam for the unforeseeable future."

The stewardess cut their conversation short. "Sir, you'll have to put that under the seat or stow it in the overhead."

Ketting dragged the carry-on into the aisle and heaved it into the overhead storage compartment, swearing under his breath.

"Please check your seatbelts and replace all tray tables to their full upright and locked position."

March 28, 2013
The "T"
Boston
12:30 A.M.

Muqtada was on the Green Line. He would ride it to the end and then back again. He often did this late at night when he couldn't sleep. On these nights he thought about Fran. He had met her on the Green Line. They were both in their early twenties. He had watched her for weeks before he finally got up the courage to find a seat near her. They exchanged glances and smiles for a few more weeks before Muqtada had the courage to ask her about the book that she was reading.

That was all it took. There was an explosion of conversation between the two. The things they wanted to say, the questions they wanted to ask, their feelings, their fantasies had all been building, one upon another, in the preceding weeks.

Muqtada thought she was beautiful. She had long black hair, a small woman. A little overweight, but she had wonderful eyes and a welcoming smile. She wasn't that sure of herself: a bit shy, like Muqtada. She was Jewish.

He could talk with her about anything. She accepted him. She didn't seem to care about the drug use or the problems he had had with his temper, or the fact that he was Arab. They didn't talk about the Six-Day War or the politics of the Middle East.

But Fran was naive. She thought her family would understand. She finally told them about Muqtada. They didn't understand. Her father contacted Muqtada's father. Muqtada was called home to the farm by his father.

He remembered sitting in the high-back winged chair in his father's study. His father was seated behind the heavy mahogany desk. There was no conversation, just a directive.

"You are not to see this woman again. I have talked with her father and we both agree that this is not in the interest of either family. I believe I do not need to explain why. She has withdrawn from her studies and will be transferring to another school in the Northeast. You will not see her again."

Muqtada returned to the Green Line that afternoon. He returned every day for the next few weeks, and went to the shops and the bookstores they had frequented on Newbury Street and Faneuil Hall. His father was right. He never saw Fran again. But he always looked for her.

CHAPTER 4

Tall white mansions and little shacks, Southern man
when will you pay them back...
— Southern Man, by Neil Young
Crosby, Stills, Nash, and Young

Lee woke to the sound of thunder. He jumped from his bed. Howard stood up. He had been sitting at the desk arranging his papers in their proper order; an activity that he said helped him to calm his nerves.

"Doc, you're worrin' me. You're actin' awful strange," said Howard looking at his papers. "That was just thunder, Doc. It's been tryin' to rain all afternoon."

Lee sat down. "You're sure, Howard?"

"Yeah, Doc, I'm sure. I wouldn't lie to you. It was thunder. You've been asleep for a long time."

Lee looked at his watch. It was 7:23 P.M.

Howard sat on Lee's bed. He whispered, "Doc, we gotta' get out of here."

"Howard, haven't you noticed that these guys are carrying automatic weapons and all the exit doors are chained and padlocked?" He stopped. "I guess to hell with fire regulations," mumbled Lee.

"Yeah. But at night there's only two or three of 'em here. We don't have to go far."

"What do you mean, 'we don't have to go far?'" Lee sounded irritated.

"The machine," whispered Howard. "My machine is near here."

"What machine?" asked Lee absently.

"The machine I told you about."

"Oh, God, Howard." Lee was irritated. "Not that flying saucer business. Don't start that again."

"I'm tellin' you, Doc, I . . ."

There was a knock at the door. It was the corporal. "If you boys want something to eat, let's go. The kitchen is closin' in thirty minutes."

"Okay, okay, we're coming," mumbled Lee. "Let me get my shoes on."

"Make it fast," replied the corporal.

A clap of thunder shook the building. Lee flinched again.

"That was close, must have been close," said Howard.

Lee took his legal pad and pen, and Howard his papers. Howard never went anywhere without his papers.

In the cafeteria the corporal turned them over to another keeper. A packet of spaghetti and meatballs was the special of the evening. The keeper went into the kitchen. Lee and Howard were alone.

"You know, Doc, they closed the interstate to everyone except ambulances and police cars, and trucks. What a bunch of crap," Howard smiled. "They closed the exits, too." He nodded. "They've sure gone to a lot of trouble to scare people. To get 'em so scared they'll leave and not come back."

"Howard, this is for real," Lee protested. "There was an accident at Pine Grove. My friend was killed."

"Sure, sure, Doc. Whatever," said Howard as he scanned the room. "They're just tellin' you that."

"Howard . . ." Lee stopped. The keeper was back with the food. They stopped talking and ate in silence. The thunder continued; then it began to rain.

The night shift was arriving. They saw the two guards pull into the parking lot next to the cafeteria. One was struggling to get the canvas top up on their old Army Reserve jeep. He finally gave up and the two made a run for the building. They were soaked to the skin.

The guard changed. The corporal and the rest of the day shift left. Lee recognized the new keeper. He was a young man. He had waited on Lee at dinner last Sunday, the last time Lee had seen David. Lee assumed he was in the Reserve and had been called up for this duty. Lee smiled, but said nothing.

"Hey, man." The young guard pointed at Lee. "I know you from someplace."

"You work at the Westside Grille, don't you?" Lee asked.

"Yeah." The young man smiled.

"Well, I was there with a friend for dinner on Sunday," said Lee, not sure if he wanted to continue the conversation.

"Oh, yeah. You're the guy with the hook. I remember."

Now he was sure he would be happy with no conversation. Lee hated being referred to as "the guy with the hook." He had heard it hundreds of times. He never got used to it.

"What are you doin' here?" The young man smiled again.

Lee looked uneasy. "I don't know. You tell me."

"Hey. No one tells us nothin'. We're the Reserves, and night shift to boot. All I know is we have orders to keep you here." He put his hand on Lee's shoulder, leaning heavily, trying to find his balance. The young man looked uncomfortable. "I'll be back in a minute, boys. Don't go no place." The guard left quickly.

Lee heard the men's room door in the lobby slam open and close. In a few minutes the young man was back, looking a bit pale and unsure of himself.

Howard stood up. "Why don't you set down here, Officer. You don't look so great."

"I think I will." He sat down. His face and neck were turning red and so were his hands.

In a minute he was up again. "I'll be back in a . . . few minutes." This time he did not appear steady on his feet. They heard the restroom door open and close again.

Lee and Howard could see the lobby from the cafeteria. The young woman with the submachine gun, who would normally be at the lobby desk, was not at her post.

"Doc, this is our chance," Howard whispered.

"Howard, don't do anything crazy," Lee pleaded. "Where are you going?"

Howard stood up slowly. "I'm goin' to check this out." Howard walked quietly to the door. He slipped through the door and disappeared into the lobby. Lee watched and waited. In a few seconds Howard was back. He was smiling. "They're sick as dogs, Doc. Commode-huggin' sick. Both of 'em. I could hear her in the Ladies Room, throwin' up her toenails. Wonder what made 'em sick?"

"I think," Lee hesitated, "the rain."

"Huh? Well, it don't matter. Let's get out of here while we can."

Howard grabbed Lee's arm. Before Lee could think he was in the lobby, sneaking past the restroom doors and out the only door in the lobby not chained and padlocked.

The rain had stopped. Lee and Howard walked quickly across the parking lot, with Howard taking the lead.

"Come on, Doc. Move it."

Their walk turned into a run, across the front yard of the church, across another parking lot, and into the woods.

"Where are we going?" Lee gasped. "Do you know where we're going?"

"Just follow me, Doc."

And Lee did. The sky was clearing. The moon was almost full. It lit the path through the woods. The woods were quiet, unusually quiet for a spring evening. The crickets were silent.

"Relax, Doc. I know this place. I used to live out here when I was a kid. I played in these woods."

The air was warm and heavy, rich with the sweet smell of honeysuckle. As they walked Lee remembered nights like this one. As a child, playing hide-and-seek in the shadows with Dave and his brother. They were better at the game than Lee. But one by one he would find them, no matter how long it would take, he would not give up until they were out. Now they were all "out." Gone. Except Lee.

"I'm not out, yet," Lee mumbled to himself. He had stopped walking and tried to catch his breath.

Howard stopped and walked back to Lee. "Doc, come on."

"Okay, okay, Howard, I'm coming."

They began to walk again. "Hey, Doc. What did you mean about the rain made them sick?"

"Well, I think that's what happened. It happened at Pine Grove in the early 1950s." Catching his breath. "The Air Force was testing photographic equipment on the U-2 Spy Plane. They wanted to know what radioactive gasses looked like from high up where spy planes fly. So they asked the Labs to hold their gas releases until the planes were overhead. They released the gasses all at once." Lee gestured with his hands. "It worked great. The Air Force got the pictures they wanted. The only problem was that what goes up comes down." Lee paused. "It rained that afternoon. A number of people who were out in the rain got sick." He stopped. "We just had the first rain since the accident. Right?" He waited for Howard's response, but there was none. "It's gotta' be full of God-knows-what."

Howard didn't say anything, he just grunted.

"You still think there was no accident don't you, Howard?"

Howard just kept on walking, he didn't respond.

"Howard, where the hell are we going?" asked Lee looking around but seeing nothing familiar.

"Home."

Great. Here we go again, thought Lee. "How are we planning on getting there?"

"The machine. Come with me, Doc."

"Howard, I want to go home. But I told you my home is with my family, in Maine." He stopped walking and faced Howard. "How is your machine going to get me there? I need a car, Howard," he pleaded, "not a flying saucer."

Howard wasn't sure. The home he was talking about was a place his machine had taken him before. It was a place he called Home. The Homelanders were an intelligent and peaceful people. He was sure they could find some way for Lee to get back to his family. They understood the importance of family. They knew they were all from one family, unlike the human race who often forgot this, or denied it. God had set things up right on Home. The Homelanders were reminded each day of their oneness. They all looked alike, at least to Howard.

As Howard continued on about Home, Lee took stock of his situation. He was wandering through the woods with no idea where he was. He had no money and no identification. His only possessions were a pair of prison pajamas, someone else's underwear, and worn out tennis shoes two sizes too big. He was following a delusional psychotic after the two had run away from an internment camp for victims of a nuclear accident. An accident that certain people in authority believed Lee was involved in causing. Lee and his psychotic guide were en route to "Home" by way of a space machine that his guide had invented. Great. This was either a very bad dream or God had one hell of a sense of humor.

When Lee tuned back in, Howard was saying he had decided he would go back to Home and stay this time. He wasn't sure why he had come back anyway, but if he was going to be forced to go someplace else, it would be his choice, not someone else's. And his choice was Home.

Lee said nothing. The two walked on. The moonlight was brighter, the air warmer. The sky was almost completely clear. They were walking along a ridge. Below them, through the trees they could see homes. Neighborhoods. Except for an occasional streetlight, they were dark. Much of White's Fork was dark. They could hear the sound of traffic on the interstate. There was no traffic on the city streets. When they reached a clearing in the woods Lee knew where they were. Cherokee Park was just on the other side of the road.

"Howard, that's the fairgrounds, isn't it?"

"Yeah, that's where we're going."

"It's a little late, Howard. I think the rides are closed."

"Well, one of 'em ain't."

"Okay, Howard." Lee sounded very tired. "This is where the machine is hidden?"

"Yeah, in one of the old drainage tunnels that was closed when they built the interstate." He pointed. "You goin' with me, Doc?" asked Howard.

"Howard, I can't go with you. I want to be with my wife and daughter, my family. I have to get back to them. If I could catch a ride on one of those trucks going north . . ."

Howard said he understood. He knew the importance of family. He didn't have one anymore on this earth, but he understood.

"Well, Doc, if you're goin' to try to catch a ride I know the right place. Trucks can't pull off the exits because they're closed, but there's a place near the park where the shoulder's big enough for 'em to pull over." He started walking and gesturing. "Maybe you could hide and wait until one of 'em pulls over to rest or take a piss and you could climb on board." He paused. "A flatbed is what you're lookin' for." He nodded. "You could crawl up under the tarps and hide in whatever they're carryin'."

They crossed the road and slipped through an opening in the fence that Howard knew was there. They were in the park. The county fair had been held at this park each September for over a hundred years. It was his mother's favorite place. She rode the roller coaster until it was condemned and torn down. She passed her love of the fairground down to her son and every year Lee and Dave saved their money for the fair. Lee loved the carney food, but not the rides. He had taken his daughter to the fair each year until they moved back north. Just like her grandmother, she loved the carnival rides and like her dad, the food.

They had walked along the edge of the small pond in the center of the park. Lee's daughter had always fed more of her funnel cake to the pond's fish than she had eaten. They nicknamed him Moby. Moby Carp. Lee smiled.

The carnival would set up on the other side of the pond. Lee remembered the Last Great Sideshow. *World of Awe*, the sign read. The four-eyed Manchurian. Reptilian, Aquafin. It was a freak show, indeed one of the last. Lee had always felt confused about the show. Should he feel the politically correct anger that these human beings were being exploited, being stared at, and pointed at because their bodies were different, even though their souls weren't? He knew how that felt. Or should he be angry that those who were "politically correct" would eventually close the last freak show down and the freaks would be out of work, unable to make a living for themselves since this was all they had known? Lee could see himself and Howard on the stage, part of the *World of Awe* show. Being looked at, and laughed at. The fantasy stuck in Lee's mind as they crossed to the side of the park that bordered the interstate.

Again, Howard found an opening in the fence. They climbed the bank through the undergrowth, beer bottles and garbage. Lee cut his hand on one of the bottles. *Damn*, Lee thought. *One more thing to deal with*. The two waited in some brush behind the guardrail.

They did not have to wait long. They saw headlights. An eighteen-wheeler heading north pulled over. Behind him was another truck, a flatbed. Its cargo covered with a huge tarp. It pulled in behind. Both trucks pulled ahead of where Lee and Howard were hidden. The drivers got out to relieve themselves, to smoke, and to talk.

"Perfecto, Doc. Come on, I'll help you get aboard." The two moved quietly to the back of the second truck. Howard boosted Lee onto the truck's bed.

"You gonna' be okay, Doc?" Howard looked concerned.

"I guess. Hell, I don't know." Lee had no idea what would be coming next. "How about you, Howard?"

"I wouldn't lie to you, Doc. I can take care of myself," he said with confidence. "I gotta' go, Doc."

"Well, good luck, Howard. Thanks." Lee said, a bit awkwardly.

Howard stepped over the guardrail and into the undergrowth. Lee looked around. *Honest John's Portable Toilets.* A whole flatbed full. Lee decided he would pick out a large, clean one. The new handicapped accessible ones were the largest. Most of the toilets on the truck had apparently just been cleaned. The smell of lemon was a bit overpowering.

He opened the vent window. Through it he had a good view of the fairgrounds. He saw Howard, or who he thought was Howard. Someone walking along the fence inside the park. The figure disappeared into the shadows near an old viaduct that ran under the interstate. The drivers finished their conversation and returned to their rigs. The first truck pulled back onto the interstate. Lee's truck followed. The fairground receded into the darkness as the truck picked up speed.

Just as Lee was getting ready to focus his attention on his new surroundings he saw a strange bright ball of light. Or was it a spotlight? He didn't know. It appeared to rise into the air. It hovered over the park for a few seconds and then moved off slowly to the southeast. It must have been a spotlight of some kind. A spotlight from a police helicopter. That would make the most sense. He was certain, but he wasn't. Lee was a thousand miles from home. He wondered how far Home was for Howard?

CHAPTER 5

Some are driven away by edicts and some by silence.
— Fiddler on the Roof

The lights of the city faded quickly. Only a few sections of White's Fork appeared to still have power. The night was dark, even with the moon. The storm could still be heard in the distance. Lee remembered nights as a child when a storm would get caught in the Valley, too full of rain, too heavy to cross the mountains or the plateau. It would move up and down the Valley like a wild animal trapped in a cage trying to escape. Lightning flashed again.

The mountains glowed in the moonlight, a greenish glow that danced across their peaks and valleys. Science talked about gasses from the mountain's bogs and marshes interacting with the light of a full moon. The Cherokee talked of the spirits of their ancestors returning to play stickball in the moonlight. When Lee had first thought of returning to the area, he had remembered nights like this and the warm rain of a spring storm.

As a child Lee never thought about leaving the Valley. He dreamed of visiting other places. Of seeing the world. But he and Susan, his high school sweetheart, planned on staying. She cut out pictures from magazines. They planned a home with a garden and a pond. After they broke up Lee continued to hope of finding someone with a similar dream. But when he finished his dissertation, Jack, his boss and mentor, told him he would not hire him to work at the Center. He said Lee could do more.

"See how things are done in other places," he said. Lee's family seemed to agree. They were certain that there was something better for him someplace other than the Valley. So Lee sent out résumés and waited. He got involved with a young woman who was finishing her master's degree at the university. She was a local girl. She wanted to leave the Valley. He got a job offer in the Midwest. He could leave but he wasn't ready to leave by himself. He didn't. He knew it was wrong, but they married anyway. With her he took a part of the Valley with him.

They moved, but soon found they could not make a home in the Midwest. Maybe it was the flatness of the land, the tornadoes that came at night, and the extremes of heat and cold. Or maybe they just missed the mountains. Lee found a job in New England. But New England couldn't make their marriage work. She moved west again, this time to Seattle. He stayed. They divorced. Lee made a life for himself in Maine.

But after twenty years of living in Maine, Lee was drawn back to the south. Perhaps it was a similar invisible force that had brought his parents back from California at the end of the war. A force that caused men to work in the car plants in Detroit during the week and drive home to the Cherokee Mountains every weekend. He remembered seeing them get in their cars on Sunday evening to drive all night to arrive at the plant gate on time the next morning. They did this for years. There were no jobs in the mountains. But they would not move. They would not leave their families. Returning to the Valley for Lee was to again be where his father and his father's father had worked and lived out their lives. He had come home.

Lee planned on working with his old friend Dan. They had trained together and kept contact over the years. Soon after arriving Lee found that his old friend was an alcoholic, and that women other than his wife were a major interest. An interest only exceeded by his desire to control the lives of the people who worked with him since his own life was out of control.

Lee could not see most of this until it was too late. Until he was in the middle of it. Until he moved back to the South. Lee and his friend parted company quietly and never spoke again. Lee set up his own practice group. The first few years were hard, but the practice grew.

His desire to return to the Northeast had little to do with the practice and much more to do with what he found to be oppressive in the "New South." The philosophy of the "New South" was certainly not "Live and Let Live." If it wasn't the fundamentalists trying to save your mortal soul, then it was the politics of the Right. The two were often the same. With a daughter with brown skin and a Jewish wife from New York City, it was only a matter of time before Lee said goodbye to the Valley and the mountains and his memories of a time and a place in his life that no longer existed. As Thomas Wolfe, who had grown up on just the other side of the mountains had said, "You can never go home again." Wolfe was right.

In the ten years since he'd been back in New England Lee had still not made peace with the New South. It was something he needed to do. And so he wrote about it. Writing was Lee's way of releasing his anger, and the hurt. These feelings had a lot to do with acceptance, he thought. Acceptance of the way things were. Of himself. Acceptance he had longed for as a child but often had not found outside of his family. Being chosen last for baseball or basketball was hard. He was lousy at sports. No matter how hard he practiced, he was never good at shooting a basketball with one hand.

And dating. Before he met Susan, it had been hard. He remembered the girl who wouldn't dance with him because of his hand. She told him so. Thank God for Susan. They were in love. Lee held on tight, too tight.

The truck was slowing down. Turning off the highway. An exit was open. Lee closed the portable toilet door. He waited. The truck was stopping for fuel. Lee heard the driver get out of the cab. He could hear the conversation between the driver and the attendant. He peered out the vent window. The attendant was asking the driver about Pine Grove and White's Fork and what he had seen.

"Didn't see nothin'." He shoved his hands in his pockets and walked to the other side of the truck. "Got all the exits closed." He shook his head. "This was the first one open I've found."

"Well, the radio says things are getting better." Lee doubted they were. "They got the fire out and they say they're bringin' the reaction under control, whatever that means." The attendant laughed a nervous laugh. "I guess it means the damn thing ain't goin' to blow up."

"They're sayin' it wasn't an accident," the driver said. "It was terrorism." He looked worried. "Those damned camel jockeys are at it again."

"No," the attendant shook his head, "they say it was some group of radicals that's been tryin' to close the plants down. Some group called SUMP," he thought for a second, "or somethin' like that."

"Yeah, those damned environment nuts." The driver agreed. "If they don't like it here they oughta' get their ass back up North." Lee had heard that a lot in White's Fork. "If you leave it to them most of us wouldn't have work." He paused. "I'd be pullin' this damn truck with a bicycle." They both laughed. Lee smiled.

The truck was back on the road. As they crossed the state line three large, lighted crosses suddenly burst into view behind the truck. The center one, Christ's cross, was sixty-five feet high. Lee was used to watching them slowly get larger and larger as he approached the border. This was the effect that the church that had erected them next to the interstate wanted to create. They could be seen from both directions, coming or going. Lee watched them disappear into the early morning fog.

Lee grew up in the church. The values he learned there served him well. His God was kind and full of love. He said he would have become a Methodist minister if not a psychologist. When he returned to the area in the early 1990s he hoped to re-connect with that part of his life. And he did. He worked with a number of local ministers and set up a small clinic in one of the larger churches.

But something began to happen. He found himself increasingly uncomfortable with Christianity. At least the way it was practiced in the New South. The lighted crosses were a symbol of the change. In the early 1970s most local churches found it hard to pay their electric bill or have the roof repaired, much less pay for lighted crosses. The area had been in perpetual recession. Lee's family almost starved during the Depression. But all of that began to change after World War II.

The Tennessee Valley Authority brought relatively inexpensive power into the Valley and control over the spring floods. Pine Grove was good for the area's economy, at least at first. In the late 1970s and early 1980s many new businesses were actively courted and recruited. The lure of cheap labor, low taxes, and very little regulation or oversight brought new people and their money into the area and made some of the local good ol' boys and girls very rich.

The people who came and stayed were looking for the good life: low taxes, affordable homes, the lakes, and the mountains. They weren't interested in the public schools. They could send their children to private academies. They weren't interested in other public services since they didn't use them. As long as the university had a winning football team they were satisfied. At least that's the way it seemed to Lee.

Lee remembered one of the ol' boys from his college days. He had hired the man to install a gas furnace in a small house he owned. Being a graduate student Lee had little money. He had been warned by friends, but Bubba's Quality Plumbing gave the lowest price. After a gas leak almost killed Lee's roommate, Lee hired another plumber. Bubba made no apology. In fact, Bubba never returned his phone calls. Bubba, in Lee's opinion, to quote a popular southern expression, "Couldn't be trusted in a outhouse with a muzzle on." But by the 1990s Bubba had become a respected contractor and a developer. His reputation had changed like his bankroll, the latter having a direct impact on the former. He was now a local saint. All had been forgotten and forgiven. No one seemed to recall how he had made his money.

Money, it seemed in the New South, justified provincialism. Proved it right. A popular bumper sticker said it well, "We don't care how you do it up there." And they meant it. If there was money to be made in reinventing the wheel, it was okay.

People with the money, especially new money, believed that their new wealth was deserved and their money justified their past and present behavior. Indeed, the largest religious denomination in the New South felt that God wanted them to be rich. It was God's will.

The South, until the late 1970s, had been on its knees. Although the last of the federal troops from the Civil War had left in the 1890s, the economic impact of the war was felt for another one hundred years. The repressed anger of all those years came out through a kind of arrogance that had not existed, at least as Lee recalled it, in the South of his youth. Friendliness and southern hospitality were still there, but it seemed more superficial now. Maybe it had always been. Lee wasn't sure. In his last years there, the friendliness had felt more like whitewash, easy to apply, but just as easily washed away.

Perhaps he had become more cynical with the years. More critical. It seemed people were less likely to say what they really felt, to your face at least. People in the area had always been known for their politeness or as his father had put it, "Wouldn't say the S-word if they had a mouthful." Funny how that four-letter word kept coming to mind. Lee had excused this character flaw in the past, but as an adult he began to label it as hypocrisy, saying one thing and doing another. The problem was more not doing than doing. Cross burnings were still happening. Some people said they were outraged. Most said nothing. But little was done and the events were conveniently forgotten, until repeated.

There was other trouble in Paradise. During the last summer in the mountains there had been seventy-five days when the National Park Service had issued ozone advisories. The air was becoming more polluted and so was the groundwater. The State's legislature continued to resist passing an income tax and as a result the State's public schools continued to decay. In national ratings, they passed Mississippi on the way down. More and more faculty, especially those in liberal arts, left the university.

And disability rights. No, privileges would be more correct. Lee remembered his brief tenure on a board of a disability advocacy organization. He remembered his argument with a member of the board, the issue was choosing a new director. Lee, along with a few other board members, had argued for the hiring of a person who had a disability. The man objected. He believed that giving preferences to applicants with a disability would be discrimination. When Lee asked the man when in its history the NAACP had chosen a white person as their director, the man became even more enraged. But the charity model prevailed. The old boys and girls had their way. The new director was a person without a disability. The rationale, which Lee had to agree was a very valid one in White's Fork, was that he would be an excellent fund-raiser. He was well connected. Directors of organizations set up to service the disabled waved the big tin cup and said, "Thank you very much."

But the road system was still in great shape. They added another lane to the interstate that served the western suburbs. There was still money for the right people in road construction. In general, the old boys and girls were happy with things as they were. The football team had a good season, God was in His heaven, and all was right with their world.

So, money flowed into new church construction, not into solving the problems of the community. Of course, as many saw it, the main problem to be solved was the saving of souls, the churching of the un-churched. The bigger and the grander the House of God, the more likely people were to be saved, so the logic ran.

Perhaps they were right. Perhaps they were right about it all. Lee was too tired to think about it anymore.

During the night Lee was sick a number of times. He made good use of the portable toilets that surrounded him.

His dreams took him far away from the truck and his old home and questions of right and wrong. He was walking on a beach with a young woman he had known in his mid-thirties. It was a cold winter afternoon. The sun was bright on the water. The wind was so strong that they could not hear each other when they talked. But they didn't need to talk.

Lee woke to the sound of "The Old Rugged Cross." He had sung the hymn once as a child for the entire church before his voice changed. He still knew the words.

Lee was cold and stiff, but he was hungry so he knew he hadn't died in the night. He slowly got to his feet and looked out the side vent of the toilet. The truck had stopped. They were in the parking lot of a fast-food restaurant, Harvey's. A gospel group was entertaining the breakfast patrons. It was a bright sunny morning. It was Good Friday. The driver was on his way back to the truck with his coffee and take-out bag. *Biscuits and gravy*, Lee thought.

The driver polished off his breakfast quickly. He was back on the road but he did not turn onto the interstate. The road he took ran parallel to the interstate. Soon the truck was pulling off the road again into a parking lot. *The Mine*, the sign said. Lee knew where they were: West Virginia. A tourist attraction. An old coal mine, a deep mine. *Open To The Public.*

A woman emerged from the mine's gift shop and directed the driver to the back of the building. He carefully backed the truck up. He was going to load or unload. Lee wasn't sure what to do.

"Hey, Stella. How you doin'?" The driver smiled a toothy smile. "John said you could use one of 'em until you get your plumbin' fixed."

"Thanks, Bud," she said looking away. "That's real nice of him. Tell him we 'preciate it." She looked at Bud. "Money's hard to find. As soon as we open, should be able to git the bathroom fixed, but don't know." She looked away again. "Things were real slow last year."

"Yeah," he said. "Guess nobody's doin' that good these days." Bud pulled the toilet next to Lee's, to the edge of the truck bed.

"Need help? Can help," said Stella looking concerned. "Don't mind helpin'."

"Nope. When they're empty they're light as a feather." He pulled the toilet off the truck. It struck the ground with a metal *thud*. "Where do you want it?" Before she could answer he added, "Grab that jug of solution." Bud pointed to a bottle setting in one of the toilets.

Bud put the toilet on the dolly and with Stella directing, took it to the other side of the building. Through the vent Lee could see the entrance to the mine. Just outside the entrance water dripped slowly from a faucet. Lee was more thirsty than hungry. He needed to straighten his legs, but most of all he needed a drink of water. He was only ten or fifteen feet away. He could do it and be back on the truck before the driver was back. He cautiously opened the toilet door and on the tips of his toes, without making a sound, he climbed down. He moved quickly over the bed of coal and rock that covered the ground. He slowly opened the valve on the rusty faucet. The water was cold. It tasted good. Just what he needed.

Lee heard the squeaking of the dolly. The driver was coming back. Lee tried to pull himself onto the truck, but couldn't. His hand was too swollen and sore. The mine's entrance was only a few yards away. The truck, he thought, blocked their view of it. They wouldn't see him. He had no choice. He ran into the mine. He was at least out of sight. Bud put the dolly away. He said his goodbyes to Stella and pulled back onto the road. The truck, his ride north, was gone.

What now? Lee looked around. There was a crate full of miner's helmets. Each with a light. A first-aid kit and fire blanket hung from the wall. The coal train, the mantrip, the tourists rode down the four-foot high shaft into the mine was visible in the gray light. Lee sat down on a crate. He needed to figure out what he was going to do, but he best find a safer place than the entrance of the mine to do his thinking. Where would he go if someone came up to fix or check on something?

Oh, what the hell. He grabbed a helmet and a light. He'd always wanted to tour a coal mine. He wrapped the fire blanket around his shoulders, and started down the shaft, walking, crouching next to the train's rails. The cool dark of the mine seemed welcoming.

CHAPTER 6

From the sixth hour until the ninth hour there was
darkness over all the land . . . the earth quaked
and the rocks were split.
— Luke

March 29, 2013
Eblen, West Virginia
Good Friday
The 4th day of Passover

Lee moved slowly down the mineshaft. Crouching, at times crawling. The rock and the gravel cut through his prison pajamas. The ground was wet and cold, the air smelled old and musty. Light from the entrance faded, then disappeared completely. Lee hoped his helmet lamp wouldn't fail. He should have grabbed a second one.

Where was he going? He had no idea. The shaft stretched on as far as he could see. The light seemed to be swallowed up by the darkness. He stopped to rest. He turned the light off, total darkness. He had explored caves as a teenager. They would turn off their lights and with their eyes wide open describe what they saw: a waterfall, a man with a long white beard, an ice cave. Everything, of course, was black and white. Just the way the brain works in total darkness. Lee understood why people went crazy after only a short stay in total darkness.

Lee turned the light back on. To his right, a few feet ahead his lamp illuminated an emergency sign. An airshaft, he figured. He reached it quickly. The rust-colored metal door was partially open. Lee looked inside. He pushed the door open and was surprised to see what looked like a sleeping bag spread on top of some crates. There was a first-aid kit, a couple of blankets. The room was a large metal box, big enough for seven or eight men to stand or sit. A large air vent was on the wall opposite the door. Two ten-gallon cans labeled *Water* sat on the floor. The room seemed warmer than the shaft. Lee closed the door.

Lee decided he had found what he needed, at least for the next few hours. Drinking out of the ten-gallon can wasn't easy, but he managed using his helmet as a cup. He opened the first-aid kit and found some disinfectant for his hand. It burned and smelled like peroxide. He wrapped his hand as best he could with one of the bandages. Using his teeth and his hook he was able to tighten the bandage.

Lee was cold and wet. He crawled into the sleeping bag. He had slept very little on the truck. He tried to stay awake, but couldn't.

In his sleep Lee saw the mantrip car moving down the shaft toward him. It stopped. He climbed aboard. It began to move again, slowly picking up speed as it descended the shaft. It moved faster. Up ahead Lee could see light. Suddenly the car was moving along a track outside the mine. There were trees and mountains in the distance.

The car was coming into a station. *Bourbonville.* The small town Lee had grown up in. The town near Pine Grove where his parents had moved when Lee was still a baby. A banner hung from the wall of the station: *Welcome Home.*

The car stopped. Lee stepped onto the platform. *It's the same,* he thought. A block over from the train station is Broadway. He walked there quickly. On the corner is the Rexall, where he would have five-cent cherry cokes with his friends. Lee looked through the window. Two teenage boys were at the fountain. They looked a lot like Dave and Bill.

Up a few blocks is his grandparents' home. Lee walked down Broadway to the jewelry store where his mother worked. He looked in. She was busy with a young couple. She didn't notice him. She was a pretty woman with blue eyes and shoulder length brown hair that was getting grayer each year. Lee watched. She smiled as she showed the young couple wedding bands. Lee thought she was probably telling them the story about how she could not afford a wedding band for Lee's dad when they got married. She was patient with the young couple. "Take your time," she was saying. Patient, like she had always been with Lee. He would come back.

He headed up Hill Street to his old high school, first walking, then running. He could see the school. A young girl sat on the steps. She must be waiting for the late bus. She had olive skin and long black hair. It had to be Susan. This was their time in the afternoon, waiting for the bus. She saw him. She smiled and stood up. He called her name. He ran even harder now, but the sun was in his eyes. It was so bright. So bright he could barely see her. In a flash she was gone. The school was gone. A new building sat on the hill: Bourbonville Assisted Living.

Lee sat up and opened his eyes. The room was dark except for the weak light coming from his helmet lamp. He had fallen asleep with the lamp on.

Lee scrambled to his feet, looked at his watch: 3:15. It was time to go. Maybe he could find another way north. His heart raced. His head pounded. He started crawling up the shaft to the entrance.

As he reached the top of the shaft a rumble of thunder shook the ground around him. The rain came hard. The lightning flashed. It was afternoon, but the sky was dark. Except in the southwest, where on the horizon the sky glowed a strange bluish orange. A sky Lee had not seen before.

Lee waited for the rain to stop and night to come. He looked for his watch. It was gone. The band must have broken on his way up the shaft. His only possession other than his wedding ring and his hook. It wasn't an expensive watch, but his daughter gave it to him one Christmas many years ago. He had to find it. Lee grabbed another lamp and started down the shaft.

Lee carefully retraced his steps back to the metal room. He found his watch lying on the ground. He breathed a sigh of relief. The band was broken. *Like me,* he thought. His heart started racing again. A panic attack.

"No way," he said out loud. "Get a grip. Breathe slowly, deeply. Distract, re-focus." Instructions he had given to his patients a few hundred times over the years.

He thought of his daughter, of pillow fights when she was five, of dinners in a little Italian restaurant they loved. She always ordered the same thing, spaghetti with butter and parmesan. And chocolate milk. The waiters knew them, they knew to expect them on Wednesday nights. She was grown now, twenty-four, finishing a graduate degree in oceanography.

Lee thought of his dream. The school now gone, converted to a nursing facility. Lee had lost track of Susan, married now, he was sure with children and grandchildren. His mom, resting next to his dad in the family cemetery. The town, the train station had been boarded up for years, most of the downtown burned in the mid-1990s. A community college now occupied the space where the jewelry store and the hotel had stood. The rest of the businesses had been killed many years before by the superstores that had sprung up around the exit from the interstate.

In the years he had lived in White's Fork after his return, he had visited Bourbonville only a few times. His family was gone. His purpose on most visits was to attend to their graves. His grandfather had cared for the family graves until he was too ill to do so. Lee wanted to make sure that the graves, especially his grandfather's, were cared for. On this trip he had visited the cemetery a day before the accident.

Lee had arrived late, having been distracted by other things in White's Fork. He had tried in vain to locate a couple of old friends. Diana had moved. And Robert? Well, Robert was dead. A heart attack, they said.

It was a cool evening. Nearing sunset. The wind came up and blew the dead grass from the last mowing across the graves. Lee's family plot was near the crest of a hill. It faced east and was shared by Lee's parents, his mother's parents, and her sister's first husband, George. When the plot was purchased money was tight both for living and especially for dying. By sharing the cost the families could afford the large, pink marble stone. *Brazil, Henshaw, and Stevens.* Lee had always thought it sounded more like a law firm than a family grave.

As the light faded, Lee removed the poinsettias and holly that his mother had always insisted be put on the graves in late November. Lee replaced them with spring flowers, red and yellow tulips. He liked the spring ones best. More life and energy.

Lee finished arranging the last vase of flowers, the one between his grandfather and grandmother's graves. He sat down next to his father's grave. Further up the hill his grandmother's sisters and brothers were buried. At the bottom of the hill lay his father's parents and his father's older sister, who had died as a young child. His father had never known her.

And then there were the graves of George and Emmit. To be so close in death, yet so far apart, so different, in life. Lee had always puzzled over that. The two men had been neighbors. They had grown up together. They had been born in the same year and they had died in the same year. George it seemed to Lee had treated life as a precious book to be read slowly and carefully. Emmit had treated life as a dirty joke to be told carelessly and quickly and taken lightly. Perhaps this had to do with the scarlet fever that spread through the Valley that summer when they were nine. George took the fever, Emmit did not. The fever damaged George's heart. George had fought to live. He wanted to live.

He married Lee's mother's younger sister, Rose, his high school sweetheart. They both knew George would die young. But they went on. They lived their lives. George drove a truck like his father and grandfather until he could no longer do it safely, because of his heart. They had a child, Glennell. She was just a baby when George died. Lee was twelve years old. He answered the phone that afternoon. Rose's voice was soft and calm. She asked to speak to Lee's mom. Lee knew what the news was before his mother's voice cracked and the tears welled up in her eyes.

Emmit Smith was a handsome man like George. And smart. Things came easy for Emmit. He loved women and fast cars and to drink and raise hell. He seldom worked and when he did, it was just long enough to make his car payment and pay his bar bill. His only health problem was a hangover. Lee's grandmother said he "wasn't worth killin'."

Sheriff Cates was the one who came to tell the family. It was a Sunday evening. The Pentecostal Church down the street was holding its evening service. The sound of *Hallelujah* and *Amens* filled the warm night air. Lee remembered the sheriff's car parked in front of Mrs. Smith's house. Emmit had been out with one of his ladies, drinking, driving too fast. They had rolled over in the white Firebird convertible he loved so much on the highway just a few miles south of town. To comfort the family the sheriff had said that Emmit and his lady friend had died instantly.

"Didn't suffer," he said.

Lee lay back on the ground. It was warmer than the air. Lee stared up at the sky. To the east the evening star, Venus, was rising. Overhead the first real stars of the evening were starting to appear. Lee remembered his grandfather, Papaw. He was always willing and able to wake at any hour of the night, with Lee, to watch a planet rise or the moon eclipsed by the shadow of the earth or a shower of cosmic rock and ice, balls of fire that would streak silently across the sky. He had always loved Lee. But college and work had taken Lee away. He had not been there when his grandfather could no longer care for Mamaw. They had moved to a retirement home and then, after his grandfather's stroke, to a nursing home. If Lee had stayed in the Valley he could have helped. He wondered if he had really understood. It was a long time ago. He had wanted Lee to leave the Valley.

Lee looked up at the sky again. He lay there for quite a while. Images of his family came in and out of his mind. They were there, around him again. Talking, laughing, crying. Around him again.

His breathing was slowing down. He was starting to relax when he heard someone coming down the shaft.

"Alright, know ya're in there, so come out here. Not goin' to hurt ya." It was a woman's voice. Stella's voice.

"Okay, guess we'll just have to come in there after ya. Ya know this is private property."

The woman pushed the door open and scanned the room with her light. It only took a few seconds for the light to find Lee's eyes.

"Well, now ya look pretty harmless, don't ya? Guess won't need old Betsy after all." She was carrying a pump-action shotgun under her left arm. "Why ya hidin' down here?"

Lee shielded his eyes and said nothing.

"Ya not much of a talker, are ya? Guess we'll just have to call Sheriff Jenkins."

"No, don't do that," Lee pleaded. "I'll go. Just let me go."

"Ya ain't goin' no place, Mister," she said as she propped the shotgun up against the wall of the tunnel. "Saw ya run in here this mornin'. Been wonderin' all day when ya were gonna' come out and why ya was hidin' in those toilets." She set her light down.

"Now ya ain't the first to do that. Bud caught a guy hidin' in one of 'em toilets a month ago." She paused. "Gave him quite a lickin'. Good thing he didn't catch ya." She shook her head.

"Now, since ya ain't goin' no place, thought we might have ourselves a talk over a meal." She reached back into the tunnel and produced a basket. "It's not much, just some beans and cornbread, but it's hot and I'm assumin' ya ain't gonna' be too choosy."

Surprised again, Lee nodded and smiled. He ate and talked. He talked about Pine Grove.

"My dad worked there all his life. I think the arthritis that finally killed him had a lot to do with the place."

He talked about the lawsuit, "I doubt anything will come out of it. Much of what happened there is still classified...secret, I mean."

About the accident, "I lost one of my best friends in that accident or whatever it was. I grew up with the guy. They think he's a terrorist, that we all had something to do with this."

About his family and trying to get home, "I haven't been able to talk to them. I assume the government has." He sighed. "That is, if they still think I'm Public Enemy Number One." He stopped. "The whole damn thing is ridiculous."

Stella listened for a long time. "Well, figured ya might be mixed up in that mess down there. There's been a lot more trouble today." Lee waited. "This afternoon some damn fool drove his airplane into that thing. The one that blew up on Monday and got the whole thing goin' again." She paused and looked down at the lump of coal she had been rolling around in her hand. "This time they say it's real bad. They're movin' everybody out one hundred miles of the place. There's a big fire and they say they ain't sure when they can put it out." She looked at Lee. "A lot of people 'round here are real scared."

There was a long silence.

"It's comin'."

"What?" asked Lee looking puzzled.

"End of time."

Lee had thought the end of time was coming during the Cuban Missile Crisis. He could still remember digging a small fallout shelter in their basement in the little house he had grown up in Bourbonville. He was sixteen. He wasn't sure it would have done any good. A hole in the ground, bags of red clay on top of some old boards, but it was all he could think of to do that afternoon. He could still remember Stevenson, the U.S. Ambassador, speaking to the United Nations as the word came. The Russian ships had turned back. The world wasn't going to end, at least not that day.

Stella didn't remember.

"Didn't pay much mind to what went on outside of there. Didn't have a TV."

Lee tried to change the subject. "I suppose you miss your family?"

"No," said Stella, shaking her head and looking down at the lump of coal. "Don't miss none of it. Came here to get out from under it after Thomas died."

"Thomas?" asked Lee.

"Yeah, my boy. Got himself killed in a car wreck." Stella began to clean up. She put the dishes in the basket and began wrapping up the leftover cornbread.

"Got me this job the first day here. Reckon God was lookin' out for me." She smiled. "The job don't pay much, but they let me use the room behind the gift shop." She put the cornbread away.

"Big enough for me. All I need."

Stella took care of the mine in the off season, which lately had been most of the year. People didn't seem to be interested anymore in deep mining.

"Like to come down here. Need to be to myself sometimes." She paused. "Think better. People get on my nerves awful bad these days." The sleeping bag was hers.

Stella sometimes could feel the devil's presence. "Felt him strong today, but ain't scared of him." She was ready to die, she said. "Don't care. Don't matter no more."

She knew something bad was going to happen today. She felt it in her bones. She knew things. She had known something bad was going to happen to someone in her family before her son died. She just didn't know it would be him.

Stella said the mess at Pine Grove had gotten the weather all screwed up. The weatherman said a tornado might be coming. She said she felt safer in the mine, especially on nights like tonight.

Lee agreed. He remembered those nights from his childhood and his time in the Midwest. The storms when they passed overhead sounded like a freight train plowing through the night.

Stella's dad had been a miner. He died young of black lung. Stella was just a baby. Her mother had remarried within the year; the man was an alcoholic. He wouldn't work, didn't like Stella, but left her alone. For that she was thankful. It could have been worse. He liked her sister. He used her up.

Stella married the first man who told her he loved her. "Did it just to get away from home, I guess. Shouldn't have, but I did. He wasn't worth killin', just like my step dad. Drunk all the time. Never worked a lick the whole time we were together."

Lee said nothing, but she could see the question in his eyes.

"Stayed 'cause of my boys," she sighed. "Johnny got into drugs. Never came back. Don't know where he is." She looked away. "But now Thomas was gonna be somebody. Was smart as a whip. Good in school, liked it." Her voice rose as she talked about Thomas. "Loved music. Could play it. Not just country, but that 'classical' stuff."

"Why the Lord took 'im don't know. Girl he was goin' with was drivin.'" She stopped and looked at Lee. "Shouldn't hold it against her, but do." Stella sighed and turned away. "But know he's saved. Gave his life to Jesus when he was twelve. That's all that matters."

"Do you talk to your friends about Thomas?"

"People here been good. But can't talk to 'em. Guess don't care no more. Gettin' too close don't pay. More trouble than it's worth."

Stella talked like a woman who hadn't been listened to in a long time. Lee was safe to talk to. He was a stranger. His home was a thousand miles away.

"Well, Mister, don't know what to do with ya, but will pray on it and know by mornin'. Ain't goin' back up there tonight with those twisters out there."

She told Lee he could have the sleeping bag if he liked. She didn't sleep much anymore. She was going to listen to her tapes of Sunday sermons by a local minister. One of the people who liked Stella would bring them to her. They knew she had to work Sundays, so they understood.

Stella dug an old cassette recorder out of one of the crates. She took the recorder and a blanket and sat down with her back against the metal door. Lee tried to make himself comfortable on the sleeping bag on the crates. Stella turned off the lantern. Lee drifted off to sleep that night in total darkness with the muffled sound of a Baptist minister preaching about the fate of the unsaved and the fires of hell.

Boston

In his dreams Muqtada is back in the intensive care waiting room at Massachusetts General. He is alone. The waiting area is crowded and hot. It is July and New England is experiencing a rare heat wave. Muqtada finds a seat in the corner of the room. He was called to the hospital earlier in the day by his father's housekeeper. His father has been taken to the hospital by ambulance after he collapsed in the barn. Muqtada had warned him about overdoing it, especially in the heat. His father is still recovering from his second heart attack, but he does not listen. He seldom has listened to Muqtada.

Muqtada has not been at this hospital in years, but he remembers it well. It has changed little. The police had brought him here after a drug overdose in his early college years. He was never charged with anything. His father, with his connections, saw to that. He remembered being alone then too. His father came only one time to the hospital. He said little. He was angry. Ashamed. Ashamed of his oldest son whom he felt had brought more dishonor to the family.

The conflict with his father had started much earlier. When they were still in Iran. Muqtada had gotten in trouble there early on because of his temper. But his mother had kept all of this from his father. She died there. Before they had to leave. Nothing had been right since her death. Since they had to leave. Muqtada could still see her in his mind's eye. In the late afternoon light. A beautiful woman with long black hair, small, with a kindness that shown through her eyes. Sitting in her garden. Waiting for him. Ready to listen. But his mother was many years dead. Buried in Iran.

"Will the family of Mr. Hussein, please come to the desk?"

Muqtada looks around, then quickly remembers he is the family. His younger brother, Ibraham, has not been heard from in a year. He is somewhere in the Soviet Union. There is no way to contact him. Muqtada approaches the ward clerk's desk.

"You wish to speak to me?" he asks.

"You're a member of Mr. Hussein's immediate family?"

Muqtada hesitates. "Yes, I am his son."

"Are there others here too?" she asks looking past Muqtada and scanning the room.

"No, I am the only one here," Muqtada replies, trying to intercept her gaze.

She nods. "Please come with me. Dr. Alexander wishes to speak with you."

Muqtada is led down a long corridor filled with equipment and hospital staff who are moving in and out of rooms and corridors. He is taken to a small room. A young man is paging through a chart, occasionally stopping to make a note or sign his name.

"Dr. Alexander, this is Mr. Hussein's son."

The young man stands and extends his hand. Muqtada takes it and the two strangers shake.

"Please sit down," says the doctor as he removes the files from the chair next to his. "Your father has had another heart attack. His third. I'm sure that's no surprise to you. It is not unusual for one to follow another so quickly."

"Yes, I am not surprised. I warned him about the heat, but still he only laughed."

"I'm sure you did," says the young doctor staring at the file in his hand. "Unfortunately, this time his heart has sustained considerable damage."

"You are saying he will die?"

The young doctor continues to stare at the file. "The prognosis is not good. You see in these types of cases..."

Muqtada finishes his sentence. "He will die?"

The young doctor finally looks up from the chart. "I'm afraid that is very likely." The doctor looks uneasy. "He was asking for you."

"He was?" Muqtada sounds surprised and pleased.

"Yes. He said he must see you and talk with you. He understands his condition. He talked about you."

Muqtada's face begins to brighten. "He is very proud of his son, Ibraham."

"But I am Muqtada." The darkness returns. Muqtada repeats himself a second and third time. "But I am Muqtada."

CHAPTER 7

Real liberty is the will to grant another the freedom
to do or be what you yourself wouldn't care to do or be.
— Richard Ford

Saturday, March 30, 2013
Eblen, West Virginia
The 5th day of Passover

"Wake up," Stella shook him. For a moment Lee was confused, he thought he was back at Camp Liberty and the voice was Howard's.

"Prayed on it last night. God told me to help ya. First thing we're goin' to do is clean ya up. And then goin' to wash those clothes and find somethin' warmer for ya. Come on."

Lee rubbed the sleep from his eyes and followed Stella up the mineshaft. The rain had stopped. The sky was overcast and gray. The wind cut through Lee's clothing as he crossed the yard to Stella's apartment. It had turned colder in the night.

Stella opened the door and showed Lee to the bathroom. "My plumbin' still works. It's the toilet in the shop that's screwed up. Some kid broke it last fall." She opened a small closet next to the bathroom door. "Here's a washcloth and towel." She handed them to Lee and smiled. "Ya can use one of my old razors if ya want to risk it."

In the morning light Lee finally was able to get a good look at his host. She was a small woman with sandy-brown hair pulled back into a ponytail, mid-forties. Her face showed her age. She wore no make-up or jewelry.

Her apartment was small, but clean. One large room, part of it a small kitchen. The walls needed painting. Pictures of her family in simple wood and metal frames covered the wall next to her bed. An old couch and chair, and a floor lamp and television were at the other end of the room. A small table with two chairs separated the kitchen from the sitting area. The bathroom was next to the kitchen.

"Give me those clothes out here and we'll wash 'em. Here's a spread ya can cover up with." She laid a faded bedspread on top of the towel and washcloth. "Goin' to make breakfast. How ya like your eggs?"

"Any way you want to fix them, Stella." Lee paused a moment.

"Can I use your phone? I've got to call my family."

"Phone's on the table." She pointed. "Ya can try it. But it ain't worked since yesterday afternoon when everything down there blew up." She paused. "Television says the phones are out in the whole state."

Lee found the phone and dialed the number for his wife's cell phone. It didn't go through. He tried again. Just a strange sounding busy signal. He put the phone down. On the table was yesterday's newspaper. The headlines were about the accident at Pine Grove. There was a large photograph of the governors from the region surrounded by federal officials trying to reassure the public that the situation would soon be under control. The second explosion hadn't happened when the paper was printed. Lee thought he recognized the man in the last row. A tall man. The way he was standing reminded him of Major Henderson's spooky friend, Special Agent Jennings. "Nah," muttered Lee to himself. "If he's that important, he's got better things to do than play second fiddle to Henderson and worry about me."

He pulled off his clothes, slipped them outside the door and climbed into the shower. The water was hot. His skin tingled. It burned. But it felt good. His skin was alive. He was still alive.

So what now? A mountain woman, a good soul. Her God has told her to help you. You can't stay here for long. You don't need to get anyone else involved in this mess. So what are you going to do? He repeated all of this in his mind a number of times.

The hot water was running out and so were Lee's ideas. Lee got out of the shower. He needed a shave and tried to give himself one. Stella was right, using her razor was risky. He nicked himself three times.

The smell of country ham and sausage cooking drew his attention back to the kitchen. He checked to make sure all his important parts were covered by the spread and opened the door.

"Ya clean up pretty good," said Stella looking Lee over. "Have a seat. Poured ya some coffee."

He took a seat at the table. "Thank you!" he said feeling a bit embarrassed sitting at the table of a woman he barely knew wearing only a bedspread. "You don't need to go to all this trouble for me."

"No trouble, like to cook, but don't git much chance to cook for anybody. So don't cook much." She smiled.

"Well, it's great." He had always loved the smell of breakfast.

"Made the eggs over easy. Ya like country ham? Said you were a Southern boy."

"Yeah, I guess I was, or am, at least when it comes to food."

Stella served up a southern feast: eggs, country ham, grits with a lot of butter, country sausage, and buttermilk biscuits. Lee hadn't had biscuits like these in years. He didn't think they knew how to make biscuits in the North. That's not to say that New England popovers weren't something to kill for. Lee stuffed himself. He hadn't eaten like this in weeks.

Lee and Stella made small talk over breakfast. Lee mainly ate.

"Gonna be a real cold spring. Summer's gonna come late," said Stella. "Happens when ya git a winter like we had."

Lee nodded.

"Mother Nature a tell ya if ya just listen. See that catbird over there?" She pointed. "Shoulda been back two weeks ago. Just showed up day before yesterday. Look at that tree over there." She pointed again. "Buds on it should be bigger."

Lee nodded in agreement and grunted. He knew very little about the signs.

"Well, decided I'm goin' to give ya the old truck, one they let me have when they bought the new one for the place."

"I can't take your truck."

"Don't get in a lather. Haven't used it in months." She paused. "Sure the battery's dead. Thing might not run. It's an old F-150."

Lee helped Stella clean up. She washed, he dried. She asked him about the North and what he liked about it. He said the people. Their "Live and Let Live" attitude, at least in Maine. And the ocean.

Stella could relate to that. "Too many people want to stick their nose in your business. Don't take to that." She paused and looked at Lee. "People got the right to live their life the way they wanna." She didn't like hypocrites either. "Lot of people don't do what they say they're gonna do. Some of 'em are two-faced." She shook her head and sighed. "Say one thing on Sunday, do somethin' else on Monday." She had heard that in church.

When Lee talked about New England, she thought it sounded "real pretty. Like to see that ocean. Never have seen one."

Lee's clothes were done. "Here's somethin' else for ya," said Stella. "Overalls. Warm. When they took over the mine found two in the store-room." She pulled a second piece of clothing from the small closet. Here's a coat some woman left last summer. Don't guess she'll be comin' back for it." She held the overalls up to Lee to size them. "Think the overalls are a fit. The jacket?" She shook her head and smiled. It was black and across the front and back in pink was written "I Love West Virginia" with a large pink heart in the center on the back.

"Good souvenir." Stella chuckled. "Beggars can't be choosers. That's what they say."

The overalls were a good fit. The jacket was too big, but it was warm and Stella was right—a fitting souvenir.

"Well, ya look better than ya did, and that's sayin' somethin,'" Stella said when Lee reappeared. "Okay, let's see if we can git the truck goin'."

The sky was still overcast, the wind colder than before. Stella said it looked like snow. The old truck was in a shed on the other side of the main building. Stella brought the new truck around. A black F-150, a 2010 model. Lee hopped in. Stella drove to the shed.

As he entered the shed Stella flipped on the lights. The truck was old. A 1996 F-150 with a lot of rust. Lee didn't hold much hope it would run. Stella reached in the bed of the new F-150 and pulled out a can of gas.

"Let's pour some in her. Give her a little taste." She stopped. "Ya' know this old one's still got a carburetor in her? Bet ya haven't seen one of these in a long time."

Lee hadn't.

"Grab this cable, and we'll jump her off. Bet she'll start."

"Well, it is almost Easter, so maybe she'll rise from the dead," Lee joked. He did that when he was nervous. Stella smiled, but it was clear she didn't appreciate his humor.

It took a couple of tries before the truck started. "Well, let's let her run a while and see how she does. Don't know how far she'll git ya'."

"Stella, let me write out an I.O.U. or something."

"No need. She gits ya there just sell her. Send the money. We can use it." She put the hood of the truck down. "Now, don't know how far New England is, but figure this should help ya git part way." She shoved an envelope with ninety-six dollars into Lee's hand.

"Stella, thank you. I'll pay you back," he promised. "Write down your address." She did.

"Write me, let me know what happened to ya." Her voice was softer. "Don't know what's goin' to happen to any of us."

He kept thanking Stella until she told him she had had enough of it and that he should get on the road.

Lee headed for the interstate entrance north. Life was, as William Goldman had said many years ago, "Just one long string of temporaries."

As soon as Lee got on the interstate he turned on the radio. The news was not good. The fire continued to burn at Pine Grove. A team of volunteers had been organized to go in and put it out. Although they would have protective gear better than that used at Chernobyl when the Russian reactor blew up, they would probably suffer a similar fate. Most of those folks were dead from radiation exposure within a few months after the accident. Not a pleasant thought.

From the reports it sounded like thousands of people in the surrounding area had already gotten a good dose of toxins from the fire and radiation. A few hundred had died. The government wasn't releasing the exact numbers. Hospitals as far west as California and as far north as Boston were treating the victims of the explosion. The last explosion was clearly the work of a terrorist group that had claimed responsibility for the attack and seemed to also be claiming responsibility for the "accident." There was less talk about radical environmentalists and SOMOP.

Lee wasn't sure what all of this meant for him. He didn't feel moved to stop at the next police station and turn himself in. If he were going to do that it would be in Maine. He knew the police there. He had provided training to a number of departments in the area. Richard, a criminologist and friend with ties to a number of police agencies, both state and federal, would know what to do. He might call Richard, explain the situation. Joe, Lee's attorney, would help him decide.

Well, I need to get there, he thought. I can be there by late tonight. He had driven the route many times—nine, maybe ten hours of driving. Well, maybe closer to eleven or twelve, since the truck's top speed was about fifty. If he just spent the money on gas he might make it. Stella had put three quarts of oil on the floorboard on the passenger side, saying she was sure the truck would use the oil and maybe more. It would be close, but if he got to Boston he could call Jean.

He hadn't thought of Jean in a while. He used to think of her everyday. He hadn't seen her in years. She had written him a few weeks before he left Maine to say that she would be in the States for a few months, visiting her sister in Memphis. She had lost her husband, Ian, in a skiing accident in January. Jean said she wanted to see him, to visit, to catch up, to talk about old times. To talk. Lee hadn't written, called, or e-mailed. He wasn't sure how he felt about seeing Jean. It had been a long time.

Lee had been in love with Jean most of his life. In their twenties they had planned on marriage and children, yet for many different reasons it didn't happen. They had kept in contact, but after her marriage to Ian they had drifted further apart. Seeing each other became painful.

Well, maybe he could call someone else? Maybe Molly, his old business associate. She lived in Boston. She would help him out. Hell, all he would need would be a little gas money. He could tell her he lost his wallet and that his car had broken down. Well, he would think of something. No need to see Jean, not like this. She would help, but . . ..

It was starting to snow, light dry flakes. It was getting colder. The truck's heater wasn't that great. *But better than a Volkswagen,* Lee thought.

The snow was getting heavier. It covered the road. The plows were out. Lee thought of Maine winters, the snowplows on the interstate running three abreast, clipping along at forty miles an hour, cutting into a Nor'easter as it blew south. The snowplow drivers working sixteen-hour shifts with little relief, for days at a time when the weather was bad.

Lee remembered one of his first patients, a plowman who had broken his neck when his truck's plow hit an exposed manhole. God, he was an angry fellow, and with every good reason to be, this young man with a wife and young children. Lee's role had been only to complete a psychological evaluation and make recommendations for treatment. He wondered what had happened to the man and his family? He had never heard.

Lee suddenly felt sick. He had eaten too much. He felt the urge to throw up. But the food stayed down. A few miles later the truck's engine started to make a weird noise. It shouldn't need oil. He had put a quart in a few miles back. Now the engine was hissing. The oil light was on again. He pulled over.

Lee opened the hood. He checked the oil again. It did need more. He put a quart in. It still needed oil. He put in the third quart. The light went off. He pulled back on the road this time with some difficulty. The snow was building up.

It only took a few more miles and the oil light was on again. He pulled over. What now? He put on the emergency flashers and waited. They worked for a couple of minutes and then went dead. If the police stopped he had no license or identification. Maybe someone else would take pity on him.

CHAPTER 8

Perseverance and spirit have done wonders in all ages.
— George Washington

March 30, 2013
I-81 Pennsylvania

Two trucks passed by, then a car. Two cars, then another truck. A half-hour went by. Lee was getting cold. He decided he would get out and try to flag someone down. Just as he was stepping out of the truck an old, green wrecker pulled up behind him. He waited for the person driving the wrecker to get out. Lee walked around to the front of the truck and looked down at the engine for the whateverth time, but the person in the wrecker wasn't getting out.

"What the . . . ?" Lee muttered to himself. He walked over to the driver.

The wrecker window rolled down, "You, you, you need help?" the driver stuttered.

"Yeah. Will you see if you can figure out what's wrong? It must be an oil leak."

The driver got out and, avoiding Lee's eyes, walked around to the front of Lee's truck. Lee eyed the driver. *Is this a man or a woman?* he wondered.

After some poking at the engine and again, without looking at Lee, the driver said, "I, I think the main seal is buh-buh-blown."

"That doesn't sound good. Can you fix it?"

"I ca-ca-can't, but Vi-Vi-Vinnie can. I-I-I'll have to tow you."

"Sure," said Lee. What other choice did he have?

"We'd better do it now before the r-r-roads get wuh-wuh- worse."

The driver pulled the wrecker around, backed into position, and attached the cable and chains. Lee looked on.

"I have AAA, but I've lost my wallet. It's a long story." The driver said nothing. Lee got in the wrecker on the passenger side. "How much to tow it?"

"Fi-fi-fifty."

Lee decided he would wait until they got to the garage before mentioning that he only had ninety-six dollars.

"Nice jacket," the driver smiled.

"You like it?"

"Yeah. Are you fr-fr-from West Virginia?"

"No, but a friend gave it to me as a souvenir." Lee decided he would introduce himself. "I'm Lee."

"I-I-I'm Bird."

Well, that didn't help very much, Lee thought. He looked more closely as they drove. He finally decided that he was a she. It was her voice. It sounded more female than male. Her hair cut short. Dressed in brown work coveralls and a heavy blue parka. She seemed younger than her years. It was her shy, almost childlike manner.

Bird took the next exit and within minutes they were at the garage. "Why don't you ge-ge-get out and g-g-go in the office, I'll buh-buh-back her in."

The office was cluttered and small. A kerosene heater burned in one corner. Stuffed into the rest of the space was a beat-up wooden desk, covered with work orders and invoices. Cartons of oil were stacked neatly in another corner. A beautiful blonde woman in a bikini looked out from an A.J.'s Auto Parts calendar. Vinnie didn't seem to be around. Lee sat down on an old green couch and looked around. He noticed the coffeepot on a small table behind the cartons of oil. He sniffed the pot. Left from the morning. He wasn't that desperate.

Bird entered and motioned to Lee to come into the garage.

It was more crowded than the office. Car and truck parts covered the floor and hung from the walls.

Bird wanted to show Lee something in the engine. Bird hung over the front passenger-side fender with a drop light in one hand and a screwdriver in the other. "S-s-see?" she pointed. "I-I-I told you it was the seal."

"Okay, but can you guys fix it?"

"Do-Don't know. Vi-Vi-Vinnie will know."

"Well, where's Vinnie?" Lee didn't think this was the best place to be snowbound.

"Ba-Ba-Bambi's."

"Can you call him there?" Lee was tired of waiting.

"H-h-he wouldn't like that." Lee didn't care whether Vinnie would like it or not. He wanted to be back on the road.

"When will he be back?"

Bird shook her head and shrugged.

As Lee walked back into the office, thinking he might be desperate enough to try the coffee, he saw the sign, a bright pink neon sign, *Bambi's Exotic Café and All Nude Review.*

Lee turned around. "He's at Bambi's? Across the street? The people over there know him, right?"

Bird nodded.

"They could point him out?"

Bird nodded again.

"Well, maybe I should just go over there and find him." Lee was feeling more anxious and impatient.

"Uh, I-I-I don't think he'd like that. He's buh-buh-busy."

"Well, maybe I could go over there and have a sandwich and maybe I would run into him." *Why am I waiting on her to give me permission?* Lee thought.

"I guess that..." said Bird as Lee opened the office door and stepped into the snow. The wind had picked up and it seemed to be snowing harder. The tennis shoes were soaked. His feet were numb.

What would he do if he found Vinnie? He barely had enough money for gas much less for engine repair. Maybe he could sell the truck for parts. Use the money for a ride to Boston or New York. There were a lot of trucks in the parking lot. Maybe he could find a ride with one of them. A hundred dollars should convince someone to take him along.

Some food and drink, why not? He wasn't going to get to New England on ninety-six dollars and the way it was snowing he wasn't going to get there tonight.

Bambi's was a two-story brick building. It looked like it might have been used for another purpose in the recent past. The Review and the café were on the first floor and what looked like two or three apartments on the second. The parking lot was filled with cars, transfer trucks, and flatbeds. The snow appeared to be driving more people from the interstate. And it was Saturday night.

The door to the café opened into a foyer. An elderly black woman in a wheelchair sat behind a small table. Lee hesitated.

"Come on in, young man. What will it be? A little entertainment or some food first?"

"I think the food."

"Okay, well follow me." The black woman led Lee into a large, dimly lit room with eight tables, each with three or four chairs. Two tables were occupied, an older man sat alone at one of the tables, and two younger men at the other. The younger men were talking about the fire and evacuation at Pine Grove.

"The land lines are all out. So are the cell towers. Can't talk to nobody unless you got one of them satellite phones."

"Can I have a table near the television?" asked Lee.

"Sure, but it won't do you no good." She smiled. "Cable's been out since this morning. Weather, I guess. Usually is." She paused. "Could be 'cause of that stuff that's goin' on in Tennessee." She waited for Lee's reaction. He gave none. "Don't know." She pointed with one hand while she rolled the chair with the other.

"Here's one," she said. She led him to a table near the giant television in the corner of the room. "You know we got better things to look at here than television."

Lee smiled.

"Hey, Lynn, can you bring this young man a menu?" Lynn appeared from a door behind the bar with a menu and not much else. She was dressed in a pair of pink panties and black knee boots with spike heels. "Lynn will take care of you."

I'm sure she will, Lee thought.

The elderly black woman began rolling her chair back to the foyer.

"What can I get you, sweetie? A beer? Redhook IPA is on special."

Lee smiled. "Great. I love Hooks."

"Yeah, sure," she said and headed back to the bar. She didn't get it.

Lee opened the menu. The Mouse's Ear Steak Burger with fries was the day's special.

"So what will it be?" Lynn had returned with Lee's beer. "You can't beat our meat." She stared off into space.

"I'm sure I can't. I'll have the special, medium-well."

"Okay," she popped the gum she was chewing. "Be out in a few minutes."

Lynn was a tall woman with pale skin and long red hair—the kind that comes from a bottle—late twenties. Large breasts that were just beginning to sag. Heavy, red lipstick. Her empty brown eyes and the look on her face, a forced sort of smile, reminded Lee of the expression, "Lights on, but nobody home." The young woman inside had left years before.

Lee could hear music coming from the room next door. The first show of the evening was starting. The black woman in the chair was showing two men to a table. They looked to Lee like they might be truck drivers. She joked with them about their accent. "Southern boys a long way from home," she said.

"Hell no, Millie. You know my home's the road," turning to his partner. "Now Bob here, he's the guy that gets homesick. Misses that sweet little wife." He paused and smiled. "Worries about what she's doin' on these cold nights when he's not there!"

"Well maybe she ought to be worryin' about what he's doin'," she said, looking at Bob. "Bet that sweet woman don't know you're at Bambi's!"

"Are you kiddin', Millie? She'd kill me!" They all laughed.

Lynn reappeared. "Here's your burger. Would you like some ketchup?" Lee nodded.

She returned with his ketchup. "Do you get cold?" Lee asked a bit sheepishly.

"Everybody asks me that and I always tell them I grew up in northern Michigan and like the cold. Besides it makes my..." She hesitated. "The guys like that. I usually get bigger tips." She paused. "Another beer?"

"Not right now, Lynn." He felt his face flush. Why the hell was he embarrassed? She was the one with no clothes on. "Do you know Vinnie from across the street?" he asked.

"You mean that little snake that runs the garage? Yeah, I know him. Do I know him." She suddenly appeared interested in the conversation.

"Have you seen him? I need to talk to him."

"Yeah, he was in earlier. I think he left with Sue. It's her night off, so she's probably with the jerk." She paused. "I warned her. Is he in trouble?"

"I don't know," said Lee. "Can I ask you something else?"

"Shoot," she snapped.

"Do you know any truckers that might be heading for Boston or New York? I need to find a ride."

"I don't know these guys like Millie does. I've only worked here a few months, but Millie's been here for years." She looked around the room. "For you, sweetie, I'll ask her." She smiled a vacant smile.

Lee tried the fries first and then the burger. They were okay, nothing to write home about. Of course, people didn't come here for the food.

Millie showed four men to a table. They looked like college students, and seemed uneasy and out of place. Instead of returning to the foyer, Millie rolled over to Lee's table. "Lynn says you're lookin' for a ride."

"Uh, yeah I am."

"Where you goin'?"

Lee hesitated. "Maine."

"You in some kind of trouble?"

Lee tried to lie. "No. My car, uh, I mean my truck broke down." It didn't work.

"Yeah, you in some kind of trouble. You goin' to tell me what kind of trouble so I can decide what I'm goin' do?"

Lee hesitated again. "I was at Pine Grove the night the accident happened." He waited for her reaction. She waited for Lee. "I was getting ready to go home. I got sick. I lost my car, wallet, everything else."

"Why didn't those rescue folks help you?"

"They did, but . . ." All of her questions were making Lee very nervous.

"But? You're not tellin' me the whole story."

"It's a long story."

"I got all night."

Lee tried to lie again, but Millie stopped him. "Look, I'm not goin' to waste my time on a white boy that's lyin' to me and not even very good at it. Why don't you just tell the truth?" She paused. "You tell me your story, and I'll tell you mine."

Over another beer Lee told her his story. The flash of blue light, Melanie and Pam, Howard, SOMOP, Honest John's Potties, the mine, Stella, the truck, and Bird.

"Well, I wouldn't trust Vinnie."

"That's what Lynn said."

"For different reasons. She says she was in love with that rooster fightin' cracker and she thought he was in love with her." She looked at Lee and shook her head. "Ain't that pathetic? She wouldn't listen to me, or the other girls." Lee looked distracted and tired. "Well," said Millie, "if you can't pay, you won't get your truck back from that redneck."

"I just need a ride, Millie. To hell with the truck." Lee felt desperate and on the edge of panic. "Do you know anyone heading for Boston?"

"Maybe." There was a long pause. "Yeah, Jim and Ben. They run out of Boston. They're watchin' the show. Table sixteen."

"Can we talk to them?" Lee started to get up.

"Now just sit back down. They ain't going no place tonight, not in this weather," she scolded. "Just wait until they've had a chance to see the show."

Until they're half-drunk, Lee thought. He took a deep breath and sat down.

Millie was thinking about something else. "Now Bird, she's a strange one. I think she's scared to death of Vinnie. Just showed up here one day. Don't know where she sleeps." Millie rubbed her chin. "That girl is a piece of work. Somethin' bad happened to her a long time ago."

Lee nodded, but he had little attention for speculation regarding Bird.

"So what's your story, Millie?" Lee started to accept that he would have to go at Millie's pace.

"Well, I don't usually have to tell mine." She chuckled. "People get so wound up in their own they forget about mine."

"Like you said, Millie, we've got all night."

"Well, as you would say it's a long story." And it was. "Grew up not far from here. Dirt poor. There were eight of us. Farmers. I guess you could call us that." She looked for Lee's reaction. "Sure you want to hear this?"

"I got the rest of the night," said Lee and he smiled.

"When I was ten we moved to Chicago. Daddy had a job in a plant. The war was on and us Blacks were being hired. We did pretty good until the war was over. Then the white boys came back and wanted their jobs. My daddy's job was one they got.

"I was the oldest girl. Could never do nothin' right, not in my ma's eyes. Trouble in school." She laughed a nervous laugh. "Slow, they said. Couldn't read. Took me forever. Ma gave up. She thought I was a lost cause." Millie shook her head. "I ran off at fourteen. On the streets. Guess I learned quick I could make more money turnin' tricks than flippin' burgers. And I was damned good at it. Opened my own place. Treated the girls right." Millie looked pleased with herself. "Made money. Lots of it. Sent some of it home." Millie stopped.

"And?" said Lee.

"Ma sent it back. I tried to visit 'em. Well, I tried once." She looked at Lee. "They wouldn't even open the door. Wouldn't even open the damn door."

"That must've hurt a lot."

Millie looked away but continued. Lee smiled and nodded. Millie's tone became softer. "I drank and started dealin' out of the house." She looked at Lee. "Just the soft stuff. But money was in the hard stuff. I started usin'." She looked away. "Don't know why. Got in deeper. Cops were tryin' to close me down, but I was too screwed up to care. So wha' did I do?"

"You left Chicago."

"Yeah. One Sunday afternoon I went for a drive. Ended up not far from here. My car broke down. Good ol' Vinnie gave me a tow. Didn't have no money. Didn't care. Didn't want to go back to Chicago. Vinnie took me to the shelter. They sent me to rehab at County. God, what a place." She slapped the table with her hand. "Crazy people." She laughed. "I mean real crazy. Got outta there in a hurry!" She smiled. "So I was sittin' on a bench in front of the County Hospital when a white woman sat down next to me. She was old. Dressed to kill." She paused. "She was cryin', said her sister had died. Said she didn't want to go home. Said she had never lived by herself." She paused again. "We talked. Hit it off." She nodded. "To make the story short, finally found a mother, even though she was a white one." She stopped. "I took care of her for years, until she died." Her eyes filled with tears. "Karen was a sweet thing, she was." She nodded. "It would've been fine if I hadn't had that car wreck. I was doin' good. Had an apartment. Karen had left me money, so I only had to work part time." She paused. "But didn't have any insurance. A crazy kid, on drugs, ran into me. On drugs." She shook her head and laughed.

"God was teachin' me a lesson. Serves me right! I had done too much for Him to let me off easy." She nodded again. "The car was totaled. Was in the hospital for months. Couldn't work. In a wheelchair."

"So what happened?" asked Lee.

"Gave it back over to the Lord. Lou, the guy I work for here, owns Bambi's. He just up and gave me this job." She looked at Lee. "I like workin' here. I take good care of the girls. Try to keep the drugs out. It's hard." She paused. "But life is."

Lee nodded. "You can certainly say that."

The snow was still coming down. It was getting close to midnight.

CHAPTER 9

Bambi's
Exit 283, I-81
Pennsylvania

As midnight approached the café was getting busier and the noise from the Revue louder. Millie said it was time. Time to find Lee a ride north. Lee followed her as she rolled into the hall where the second show of the night was just ending. The room was packed. Filled with smoke. Millie moved through the crowd, stopping to talk to the men that she knew. She appeared to know most of them. They liked her. They saw that chairs were moved to help her pass.

Millie stopped at a table near the stage where two men were sitting. Lee joined her.

"Boys, meet Doc. He's tryin' to get back to Maine."

One of the men stood up. "Jim Hawkins," he said. He grabbed Lee's hand and squeezed it hard.

Millie continued. "He needs a ride. I told him you might give him one. He's been in West Virginia for the last few days. Got friends there."

Jim smiled. He was a large man, long brown hair pulled back into a ponytail and a beard streaked with gray. Late fifties. "West Virginia? What part?" asked Jim.

"Near Eblen," said Lee.

"That's just down the road from where I was born. Sit down, Doc. Take a load off. This is Benedetto McGill. He's from Boston." Ben nodded. "His dad was a Mick and his mother a Wop," Jim laughed. "Hey, Barb, get my buddy, Doc, here a beer. A Hook?"

Lee nodded. "Sure, isn't it obvious?" Jim got it and for a moment looked unsure of himself. Lee laughed. Jim nodded.

"Ya got good taste, Doc."

Jim continued to talk. Ben appeared to listen and occasionally shook his head in agreement. Ben was younger than Jim by quite a few years, clean-shaven, well groomed. Like Jim he wore gray insulated coveralls with the Peterbilt logo on the breast pocket.

"So, Doc, are ya down on your luck?" asked Jim

Millie interrupted. "It's a long story. He'll tell you later. He needs a ride. Vinnie's got his truck."

"Yeah, somebody's gonna kill that little bastard. Pardon my French, Millie. If you break down here, that little snake will take your ride and your last nickel."

"Yeah, that's right," Lee agreed.

"Sure we can help him. Can't we, Ben?" Ben nodded again.

Millie smiled. "Well, I gotta get back to the front. The mid-night show will be startin' in a minute."

Lee's eyes followed Millie as she rolled back through the crowd. The cigarette smoke was thicker and the guys were getting louder and more obnoxious. A drunk at one of the back tables yelled, "Come on, girls. Show us what you got. Take it all off!"

"Yeah, we want what we friggin' paid for," another patron hooted.

Lee thought of little boys on the playground doing things to impress each other. He remembered his friend, Bobby, from high school and the song *Little Egypt*. Bobby would play that song every morning on the jukebox in the diner across from the high school. "Little Egypt came a-struttin' wearin' nothin' but a button and a bow." Lee couldn't remember the rest of the words. For a month Bobby played the song and just like these boys, he did it Lee thought, to impress the other kids. Playing it made him feel bigger and more important than he felt most of the time.

The show was starting. A recording of a drum roll crackled over the loudspeaker. The M.C., somewhere offstage, announced Miss M's entrance. She was a tall blonde woman with long, thin legs. She circled the stage. Prancing, not dancing. The crowd yelled for her to "Take it off!"

She slipped her pink sequined bottom off one leg at a time and then she fell to her knees. Putting her arms behind her back she stretched her long, thin legs out in front of her and opened them slowly. The pink G-string began to vibrate. The boys went wild.

"What do ya think about that, Doc?" said Jim. "Damndest thing I ever saw! What I wouldn't give . . ."

Lee looked uncomfortable, but nodded approval.

After a few more minutes of pelvic gyrations the music ended. Miss M picked up her top and bottom and left the stage. The men continued to hoot and clap.

The second exotic dancer was a young, petite woman with short brown hair, olive skin and a firm, muscular body. She made her entrance by sliding down a pole that was part of what looked like an old jungle gym set. The M.C. introduced her as J.J.-- Jane of the Jungle, and a recording of African drumming reinforced the theme. As J.J. swung from the pole and monkey bars she stripped. Lee thought her parents must have spent considerable money on gymnastic lessons. He remembered the cost of the lessons he had paid for his daughter. But J.J.'s talent was wasted on the crowd who spent most of her act talking about Miss M.

Triple T was the final act of the midnight show. She made her entrance twirling a baton and was dressed in a silver majorette uniform. She was an older woman, early thirties Lee guessed with long, bleached blonde hair. Slightly overweight. She looked sad, Lee thought. Her breasts were far too large for the uniform, but the guys certainly didn't mind. To the sound of a marching band she took her uniform off while she continued to twirl and march around the stage in her silver majorette boots and matching G-string.

"Twirling Terry," the M. C. announced, would now perform the Triple T. This consisted of attaching small drain plungers, the kind used on kitchen sinks, to each breast and while twirling her baton with one hand, she placed three brightly colored plastic rings on the handle of each plunger and began to twirl them.

"The Triple T," the M. C. said. A difficult, and Lee assumed, somewhat painful feat. The boys loved it, but not as much as they loved Miss M, who came back to close the show and received a standing ovation from the boys.

Lee had never found places like Bambi's very exotic. Embarrassing, humiliating, were words that better described the experience. But he had to admit that on that cold winter night Miss M's performance did raise his temperature. Lee took this as a good sign, a sign that he might not die from radiation poisoning, at least not any time soon.

Lee had always worried about his health, worried that what had caused the birth defect and the thyroid tumor, radiation or mercury or whatever, had caused other defects in his body that were just waiting for the right moment to show themselves.

He dreaded his yearly physical. The first year he was back in New England it happened, or at least he thought it had. His physician called him after a routine chest x-ray. There was something abnormal about it. He ordered a CAT Scan. The results raised more concerns. Lee was told to cancel a trip he had planned back to the South.

"We need to get started on this now," his physician said. Trying to be reassuring he told Lee, "You'll survive this. I'm sure of it."

Lee wasn't so sure. In fact, he was certain that this was it. Lung cancer. Lee started planning for being away from his practice, maybe even closing his practice. Maybe dying. He wrote a letter for his daughter. A letter for her if he died. He talked to his wife, Liz. Her father had died of lung cancer. She was scared, but she was there like she always had been in a crisis.

He saw the pulmonologist. A young man. He wasn't sure what it was either. But he was sure that a biopsy to find out would require open chest surgery. Whatever it is was in a place that the radiologist could not reach with a needle. There was the possibility that it was just scar tissue. Not very likely.

Lee called his physician in White's Fork. Phillip located some old chest x-rays he had made a few years before and FedExed them to the pulmonologist who planned to review them at a case conference the next morning.

That night Lee woke in the early hours of the morning. The first word that came to his mind was faith. "Have faith," a voice inside seemed to say. "It's about faith." Sure, he thought, that was okay for other people. But for Lee it was hard. He tried. A calm settled over him and he fell back to sleep.

The calm, however, was gone when the new day arrived. Lee left for his office expecting a call from the pulmonologist that would give him direction on making arrangements for chest surgery. The call came mid-morning. "Good news," said the pulmonologist. It appeared, indeed, to be scar tissue. Nothing needed to be done. A follow-up appointment in six months. "Sorry for the scare," he said.

Since then Lee had worried less about his health and had found more time for his family. But now, God knows what this would do. What this would stir up.

Lee needed a break from the smoke and the show. His body still wasn't used to food, especially bad food. And beer…that was another story. He needed to find a john. He thought about all the time he had spent in the one on the back of the flatbed. He laughed.

Bambi's Men's Room was jammed and filthy, but it served the purpose. Instead of going back to the main hall, Lee saw an exit door and decided he would get some fresh air. The snow had stopped. The sky was starting to clear. The air was cold, but clean. Lee took a slow deep breath. He closed his eyes. He could see his wife and himself walking in the woods near their cabin. It was winter. The river was frozen.

Lee's fantasy was interrupted by the sound of someone clearing his or her throat. Lee opened his eyes. It was a woman. Her small body was tucked inside a large heavy overcoat.

"Pretty night," she said.

"Oh, a beautiful night," Lee replied.

"Haven't seen you before." She sounded nervous, but interested.

"No, I'm just passing through," said Lee, trying to think of what he would say next.

"I know you're going to ask me why I do this job."

Lee looked more closely at the woman. "You're J.J. aren't you? I didn't recognize you with your clothes on." He wasn't sure how she would take his effort at humor.

"J.J.'s my stage name. My real name is Beverly."

"And my real name is Lee." His efforts at humor failed. J.J. didn't respond. There was an uncomfortable silence. Lee tried to revive the conversation. "You must have been really good in gymnastics."

"You never know what's going to come in handy later in life." She sounded more confident.

"I would certainly agree with that," he said. "So what is a nice girl like you doing in a place like this?"

"Saving for college."

Lee smiled and rolled his eyes.

"No, really. I'm not going to medical school, but I'm going to do something with my life."

"Good. Good for you," said Lee, looking and sounding more sincere.

"Your accent," she said. "You sound like you're from the South. I'm a southern refugee myself. Alabama."

"Tennessee," Lee replied. "Why did you leave the South?" Lee asked, sounding like he really wanted to hear the answer.

"Oh, I'm not really sure. I just couldn't be who I wanted to be. Everybody thought I should get married when I got out of high school." She paused. Lee waited. "I wasn't ready for that. My friends said I was too pushy. Southern boys," she looked at Lee, "no offense, don't like that. I should follow their lead they said. God forbid I should say what I thought." She paused again. "To hell with that, I said. So I left. And you?"

"Oh, same reasons."

She closed her eyes and smiled. "You're making fun of me."

"No, I'm not. Our daughter was thirteen when we left. My wife and I, we both were worried about some of the same things. You remind me some of my . . ." Lee didn't get to finish his sentence.

She glanced at her watch. "I've gotta be getting back. The next show, you know."

"Well, good luck with college," Lee said, almost apologetic. She was gone.

Thinking about the way women were treated in the South still stirred anger in Lee. He muttered under his breath, "I guess not much has changed. Assertiveness training for southern women is still an oxymoron."

He decided to go in. His feet were numb again. He could use some distraction and maybe another beer. After all, he wasn't driving. He headed back to Jim and Ben's table. As he crossed the floor he heard someone mumble, "Hey, the wuss from West Virginia with the pink heart jacket is back."

Lee kept on walking. He wasn't in the mood to deal with Bubba and his brothers.

"Hey, Capt'n Hook, where'd you get that coat?" a voice said.

Lee continued to walk. He didn't need any more trouble.

"Hey, Pop, I'm talkin' to you," the voice said.

Lee could feel the anger rise inside his chest. His heart was pounding, his fist clenched. He stopped, turned and faced the voice. It was a young man, early twenties, sitting at a table with two other young men.

"So did they let you and some of the other gimps out of the nursin' home for the weekend?" The young men laughed.

Lee said nothing. The young man stood up. He was about a foot taller than Lee and considerably heavier.

"So, what ya got to say, Pop?"

Lee took a deep breath. He wasn't really sure what he was doing. "I say would you like to play Connect the Dots?"

The young man looked unsure of himself. "Yeah, sure old man. I'll play."

"Good," said Lee. "The way Connect the Dots is played is I go first and try to use my hook to connect your asshole with your belly button."

Those watching who had suddenly fallen silent began to laugh. Lee noticed that Jim was standing behind the young man and his two companions. "Well, Doc," said Jim, "Are we goin' to play or not?"

The young man looked confused. He turned around and swung at Lee, but Lee ducked. On his way back up Lee landed a solid, left, literal hook to the young man's crotch. The young man collapsed to his knees. His two companions started to come to his aid but Jim's large hands closed around the back of their necks and slammed their heads into the table. Once, and then a second time, for good measure.

While the young man lay moaning on the floor holding his not-so-brass balls, Jim helped his two companions to their feet and guided them to the exit door. He kicked the door open and while counting shoved "one potato and two potato" out the door into the snow.

"And now, last but not least," Jim said as he walked back to the young man. He picked him up by his belt and using it like a luggage strap, dragged him to the door. After a couple of wind up swings he tossed him into the snow bank with his friends and closed the door. He noticed Millie had come back into the hall to see what was happening.

"Just takin' out the garbage, Millie. No problem," he said, pleased with himself.

Recorded music again crackled over the loud speaker. The M. C. was introducing the first act of the last show of the night. Bang Bang Lou Lou rode onto the stage on a wooden stick pony wearing two six-guns, a ten-gallon hat, cowboy boots, and nothing else.

Jim slapped Lee on the back. "Well, David, I think we better get the hell out of here before Goliath and his two brothers come back. Let's collect Ben and head for the truck. I want to be on the road early." Jim motioned for Ben to join them, but Ben didn't move.

"Dammit," Jim said as they walked to the table. "He's drunk on his ass again. I told him not to have that last one."

Jim helped Ben to his feet. "Come on, buddy, we've got to go."

Ben muttered, sounding very drunk, "I'm sorry, Jim. I know I promised ya."

"Yeah, yeah. I know."

"But that Barb, she's somethin' else isn't she, Jim? Isn't she?"

"Yeah, she's somethin' else, Ben. You just had to keep buying drinks from her, didn't ya? Why didn't you just buy a couple of lap dances from one of the girls? At least they wouldn't make you stinkin' drunk."

Jim turned to Lee, "It's that damn Mick blood."

Lee grimaced. "I don't know, Jim. Maybe . . . here, let me help you." Lee took Ben's left arm and helped Jim guide him toward the main entrance of Bambi's.

Millie was at the small table in the foyer as they left.
"Now, you all come back," looking at Lee, "as they say down South."

"I don't know when that will be, Millie," said Lee.

"Well, Ben and I will see you the next time we're through."

Jim gave Millie a warm smile. "Take care of yourself," he said.

Jim opened the large metal door of Bambi's and the three men stepped out into the night air. A foot of snow had fallen. A plow was clearing the entrance to the interstate.

"Keep your eyes open for that little bastard," said Jim as he looked around the parking lot. "You never know what a redneck like that will try." Ben groaned as the three struggled against the wind. "Most of 'em just go home and lick their wounds," said Jim, "but sometimes they come back with Uncle Billy Bob's shotgun and half their family."

"Why do you say he's a redneck, Jim?" Lee asked.

"Didn't you notice the ten-pound belt buckle and the sideburns?" Jim said.

"Well, yeah, but . . ." Lee decided he shouldn't take it any further. "I'm sure you know your rednecks."

"Yeah, I do! We're in my world, Doc, not yours," said Jim sounding a little irritated.

"Well, if he looks like a redneck what do I look like?"

Jim laughed. "You don't wanna know."

The three men walked through the snow in silence until they were standing in front of a fire engine red Peterbilt 379. A monster of a truck with a massive polished aluminum grill and bumper and double polished aluminum stacks.

"Isn't she a beauty, Doc? Ben and I bought her new two years ago. She's a fine rig." He opened the door to the sleeper and turned to Lee. He didn't wait for his response.
"Let's get Ben in," said Jim.

He climbed in and with Lee's assistance he pulled Ben into the sleeper and hauled him onto the top bunk. "Now, Ben, here's a paper bag," Jim said. "If you get sick, throw up in it. I don't want to have to clean up a damn mess like last time."

Ben grunted.

"Here's a pillow and a couple of blankets, Doc. You can make a bed on the cab seats. One thing this truck doesn't have is a John so if you feel the urge, use the parking lot."

"Well, that's fine with me. I've spent enough time in Johns lately."

Jim didn't appear to hear Lee. He was still busy tucking Ben in. He turned to Lee, "I'd give him a plastic garbage bag but the last time I did he passed out with his head in it and almost suffocated his damn fool self." He paused. "I'm goin' to turn in. I'll have to do most of the driving tomorrow. Ben won't be worth a crap." Jim crawled into the lower bunk.

Lee propped himself up on the passenger seat and stretched his legs out using the driver's seat for his feet and ankles. It wasn't that comfortable, but it was better than the sleeping bag and crates he had slept on the night before. Lee closed his eyes. It had been one hell of a long day.

CHAPTER 10

Now on the first day of the week
very early in the morning . . . — Luke

March 31, 2013
Easter Sunday

That night the dream came again. Lee went back to the banks of the river where he had grown up. He was sixteen again. And again, on a caving expedition with three of his friends. They climbed the river bluff to the opening of the cave. The ledge was there as always in his dreams. Water from the cave ran down the rock face, becoming a straight, long drop to the river. The only way across was to jump. The problem, as it always was, was that the ledge on the far side was about six feet higher than the ledge they were standing on. Without the right grips and footing one would slide off the rock face and fall into the river below.

Bill slowly surveyed the ledge for possible grips. He turned to Lee, "I think I can do it," he said. He positioned himself like a cat getting ready to strike its prey. Lee waited. Without a word Bill flung himself against the opposing ledge. His feet and hands quickly found secure grips and footing. With only a low groan, he pulled himself onto the top of the ledge on the other side."All right, way to go," shouted Bobby, who stood behind Lee. Lee and Fred said nothing. Fred looked scared.

It was Lee's turn. Lee hesitated. From the other side Bill shouted. "I did it. You can too."

"Yeah," said Bobby. "You can do it."

But Lee began to realize that this was a two-handed task. Bill had made it look so easy. What would Lee's friends think if he said no? If he gave up so easily?

Lee looked down. The Tennessee River was two hundred feet below. The fall alone could kill him. Lee looked across at Bill and back at his friends. He positioned himself for the jump. But then he shook his head "no." He turned to Bobby, "Go ahead, I can't."

Lee didn't jump that day. He gave up. He was sure he would have died if he had not given up, if he had denied his fear. Bobby turned to Fred and shrugged his shoulders. They both looked at Bill. Bill looked a bit confused at first, but then decided to rejoin the other three. He jumped back across. They began to walk. Lee followed them down the bluff. Little was said. They seemed to understand.

Lee awoke. He felt cold, but his heart wasn't beating rapidly. He was breathing normally. Lee had analyzed this dream many times before. As a psychologist it was much easier to look at others than at yourself. Lee knew the dream was about facing fear. About trying to find a balance. Lee had had to make that choice many times in his life. Between being cautious and giving up when it was wise to do so and white knuckling it and pushing through when it was best to continue. This was often confusing for Lee. He talked to one of his friends, another psychologist, about the dream.

"I know the dream's answer is to listen to yourself rather than to others. Trust your own perceptions." That day changed the way Lee looked at fear. "I guess I had forgotten that fear is to be respected, not ignored."

His friend Terry agreed. "It sounds like fear saved your life."

Although Lee had had the dream many times, it now seemed to make even more sense to him. His present world was a world filled with fear. Fear of being arrested, of jail, of dying, of never being home again. Maybe some of it had been the beer. He had drank too much. But most of it had to do with what Jim had said. Jim was right. Lee was in Jim's world, not in his own. In Lee's world, Lee was in control most of the time. At least he thought he was. In this world he had little control. It was difficult to listen to yourself and to make choices based on your perceptions of an unfamiliar world. A world in which you are a stranger.

Lee looked out the truck cab's window. The sun would be rising soon. To the east the sky was starting to brighten. It was Easter morning. Lee thought of his family, of his parents. Of an Easter sunrise service when he was seven. Of a rabbit he had been given by his parents that had gotten away from him at the service. Of he and his father on their hands and knees chasing the poor creature through the crowd of worshipers, through the sea of legs.

Lee closed his eyes. He wanted to stay with thoughts of his family. Lee's parents had grown up in Bourbonville. They'd lived a few houses apart. His father quit high school to help support his family. Lee's grandfather never recovered from his wife's death. She had died of cancer in her thirties and he was bitter. He quit his law practice, saying that you could not be both an honest man and an attorney. He became a union organizer, a difficult job in the South of the 1930s. He traveled a lot. Began to drink. Rumor was he drank too much. He lost his money and the family was broke.

Lee's dad, Frank, was the oldest, and so he had to work. When Frank finished high school, it was the middle of the Great Depression. "I was lucky," he said. "I found a job in a laundry and I found your mother. You know son, we didn't have any money, but we got married anyway. Ray, my boss, gave me a fifty-cent a week raise." He said proudly. "That was a big deal, to get a raise during the Great Depression."

Lee's mom, Mary, was also the oldest child. Her father was a good man, a laborer. He was a hard worker, but the family was poor. Her mother was a "nervous" person. She usually spoke her mind. In the last years of her life, she lost it to Alzheimer's.

When the war came, Frank joined the Army. "I was thirty-two and out of shape, too old for basic training some people said. But I showed 'em." He was trained as a medic and rode the trains that carried the wounded home, depositing them at hospitals across the country. "Our company moved from camps in Louisiana to Texas and finally to California. At Camp Sananita I even got to sleep in Seabiscuit's stall," he laughed.

Lee remembered his laughter. "Your mom moved with me. God love her." He always teared up when he told Lee about the ring. Lee remembered his tears. "You know when we got married your mom didn't have any money, not even enough to buy my wedding band. Well, when we were in San Francisco she worked and saved her money." The tears started to come. "One Saturday night she said, 'Why don't we take a walk on the bridge.' The Golden Gate Bridge. Our apartment wasn't very far from it. When we got to the middle of the bridge she gave me the ring. Put it on my finger. I said I'd never take it off." And he never did.

Lee's parents loved California. But when the war ended the Valley drew them back home. Frank took a job in Pine Grove with the Atomic Energy Commission as a clerk. He worked in the vault where they kept classified material. He did not like his job. It made him crazy. Depressed. Paranoid. At least that's what Lee thought. He remembered the time when his father was convinced he was being watched, that they suspected him of giving some of their secrets away. Lee remembered him at the kitchen window with the lights off, watching a car parked across the street from their house. Watching the person he thought was watching him. Maybe they were. Lee never found out. Nothing came of it.

Lee's dad continued to work at Pine Grove for thirty years. In the last years he was quite ill with rheumatoid arthritis. His doctor told him to retire, but he would not. He continued to climb the ladders and lift the crates. He was going to see his only son through college. And he did.

After the war Lee's mom had to take care of her younger sister. Her mother had a nervous breakdown near the end of the war. They said some of it had to do with the death notification that she had received—that her only son had been killed in a plane crash, a B-17, in which he was the tail gunner. But they were wrong. He was not killed. She was notified of the mistake a few weeks later. He was the only survivor of the crash, but the damage to her was done.

The first rays of the morning sun flooded into the truck's cab. The snow covered Pennsylvania mountains were ablaze with the yellows and gold of the early morning. The world was quiet and appeared at peace. Lee felt at peace. A fragile state that ended with Jim's knock on the sleeper door. Lee had not noticed that Jim's bunk was empty.

"Hey, guys, open up. I got breakfast." Ben was still asleep. He didn't move. Lee opened the sleeper door. Jim climbed in.

"I got some doughnuts and coffee," Jim said. "They're both fresh. Home-made doughnuts. That's about the only thing they make in the morning that's worth eatin'," Jim continued, "I saw Bird. I told her I know someone who is interested in buyin' your truck. Vinnie'll meet us at eight o'clock."

"Who's interested in the truck?" asked Lee.

"Vinnie is," replied Jim. "He just doesn't know it yet."

"What do you mean?" Lee asked, confused.

"Well, Vinnie owes me a favor. A couple of months ago I ran into one of Vinnie's ex's. She works at a truck stop on 81. She's been lookin' for the little snake for a while. He owes her money, alimony I guess." He paused. "Now, normally I wouldn't get involved. I figure it's none of my business helpin' a woman track down her ex, but in Vinnie's case I could make an exception." He looked at Lee and grinned. "So, I think after I have my little talk with Vinnie he'll be wantin' to buy your truck real bad."

After a breakfast of glazed doughnuts and coffee the two men walked through the snow to the garage. Bird was in the office. Vinnie hadn't arrived yet.

"Bird, are you sure Vinnie is coming?" asked Lee.

Jim answered for her. "He'll be here. He never misses an opportunity to make a buck."

Bird, looking at Jim said, "Y-y-you're the gentleman who wants to buy the truck?"

Jim smiled "Let's just say I want to make Vinnie an offer he'll have a hard time refusing."

"G-g-good," said Bird.

Bird turned to Lee, "You s-s-sure you don't want to trade me that c-c-coat for this p-p-parka?"

"I might," said Lee, sounding distracted.

Vinnie pulled up in front of the garage. "I'll take care of this," said Jim. "Just give me a minute." Jim walked out to meet Vinnie.

"Will your parka fit me?" asked Lee, turning his attention back to Bird.

"T-t-try it on." Bird took off the blue parka and helped Lee off with his jacket. Lee pulled the parka on.

"I-i-it fits you b-b-better than the j-j-jacket," said Bird excitedly.

"You're right, Bird. It's a deal."

"G-g-great," said Bird as she slipped the jacket on.

Jim and Vinnie entered the office from the garage bay."Well, I hope you ladies got the fashion show finished. Vinnie has an offer to make, Doc," Jim said.

"Yeah," said Vinnie. "I'll give you four hundred dollars for the truck minus fifty dollars for the tow."

"Wait a minute, Vinnie," Jim's voice had an edge.

"Oh yeah. I've already deducted the tow from the offer, that's right, uh yeah….Four hundred dollars cash."

"Sounds like a good deal to me, Doc," said Jim smiling. "The seal is blown and she'll need some other work."

"Four hundred dollars cash sounds okay to me. I can't give you the title. I don't have it with me." Lee didn't have it, period.

"No need," said Vinnie. "I'm goin' to cut her up for parts anyway."

Lee took the money, wished Bird and the jacket well, and walked with Jim back to his truck.

"So, you're square with that little fool?" asked Jim.

"Yeah. Thanks for saying whatever you said to Vinnie."

"Well, Doc, it was a pleasure. I have been waitin' to get that little bastard for years." Vinnie had always reminded Jim of his father. The kind of man he thought his father had been. Jim didn't know whether his father was alive or dead. He had never met his father. All he knew was that his dad had left his mother pregnant and with nothing.

When they got back to the truck, Ben was awake. "So, how's your head, buddy?" asked Jim.

"Not so good," said Ben, sounding in pain.

"Yeah, I bet. Well, I'll take the first shift. Log me in. We're outta' here."

They pulled onto the interstate. Jim turned on the radio. "I guess we should find out if the rest of the world is still around or if the ragheads have blown it up."

The news was better. The team of volunteers was having some success in bringing the fire at Pine Grove Labs under control. The National Code Red Alert remained in effect, but no incidents had been reported. The Canadian border crossings had been closed and would remain closed, at least for the next few days. Roadblocks had been set up in a number of New England states. Exactly who they were looking for was not clear. In the Pine Grove Labs "accident" and subsequent bombing, the small private plane that crashed into the Labs had been loaded with explosives. Names and descriptions of suspects either did not exist or were being withheld.

"So, Doc, have you got kids?" asked Jim.

"Yeah, a daughter. She's in her twenties."

"Do you see her?" asked Jim as they pulled onto the interstate.

"Yes, quite a bit."

"Do you worry about her?" He grinned.

"Sure I do, I'm her father. That's my job."

"Well, I've got a daughter. Somewhere," said Jim with hesitation. "Haven't seen her in a while. She's in her thirties. Married to some guy I've never met. She has a daughter. I've got a picture, but never seen her either." Jim adjusted one of his mirrors. "After the divorce I tried to see her but her mother was mad as hell at me. And drivin' like I do..." Jim shrugged his shoulders. "But I still worry about her. Especially as screwed up as this world is. What about your daughter, Doc?"

"My wife and I adopted her when she was three months old. She's from Peru." Lee waited for Jim's reaction.

Jim stared at the road, but asked a lot of questions. "How did you ever end up with a kid from Peru?"

"We weren't really planning on adopting. Liz had had a few miscarriages." Lee's voice became softer. "The doctor said keep trying. We decided to try for another year and then adopt. We put our name with one of the adoption agencies in town."

"So how long did it take?"

"Well, we weren't even done with the application when they called us on a Friday. My wife was out of town. They told me they had a picture of this little girl who had just been born in Lima. I talked with Liz over the weekend and we decided we would go." Lee paused. "But, when I called them back on Monday they said they were sorry, but they had made a mistake and that she was going to be adopted by another family."

Jim shook his head. "Boy, that must have been a real bummer." Jim down shifted and the truck slowed.

"The crazy thing about it is they called us two months later and said the family that was planning on adopting couldn't, and she was available again. Two weeks later we were in Peru and she was in our arms." They both smiled.

"Well, great. So you guys flew back and you had a baby."

"It wasn't quite that easy." Lee paused. "The late eighties were a crazy time in Peru. You remember the Shining Path?" Lee was sure he probably didn't.

"Not really." Jim stared out at the passing traffic.

"They were a group of communist rebels. On the day we arrived they assassinated the Minister of Defense near our hotel. Things were really nuts. The police questioned me that night, since I had just arrived in the country."

"You, Doc?"

"Yeah. They kept asking me how I lost my hand. Had I lost it in an accident with explosives?" Jim grinned. "Things got worse. Two days later they blew up the Marine barracks of the U.S. Embassy guards. The power and the phone services in the area we were staying in were knocked out. There was fighting outside the hotel." He paused. "I can still remember laying on the floor with our baby, Dru, between us." He remembered it very well. "Liz and I had argued about how dangerous Peru would be. I had talked with a pilot a few weeks before we left. He had worked in Peru and warned that the rebels were planning an offensive in January. Liz said I was exaggerating."

"Women," said Jim.

"As we lay on the floor, I reminded her," said Lee, "that it was January eleventh, and I had told her so. We both laughed."

"So, how long did it take to finally get back?"

"Well, we finally returned from the land of Panama shirts and submachine guns two months later. I realized I had been under a lot of stress when I got misty in customs looking at a picture of the first President Bush." They laughed.

"When we told Liz's mother about the bombs and the gunfire, she just said that's the way we have babies in this family. She talked about hiding under a table in her apartment in Shanghai while the allies bombed the city. She was pregnant with Liz."

"Why the hell was she in Shanghai?" asked Jim, looking a bit puzzled.

"They were Jews. She had fled to Shanghai from Vienna with her mother to escape the Nazis." Jim looked at Lee. "Shanghai was one of the few open ports that would accept Jews in the 1930s. But her father stayed in Austria. He thought things would get better." Lee shook his head. "He was wrong. He died in a concentration camp." Lee paused. "Liz's mom met Liz's dad, in Shanghai. He was a German Jew, a physician. He had left Europe at the urging of his parents."

Lee cleared his throat. "His parents stayed behind in Germany like Liz's grandfather and died in a concentration camp with the rest of the family." Lee's tone was matter of fact. He had told the story so many times, but inside he felt the sadness he always felt. Jim's tone wasn't matter of fact.

"Those dirty little Nazi bastards. I get mad as hell just thinking about those SOBs." Jim was turning red again.

"Well even in Shanghai, if you were a Jew, life was not easy." Lee sighed. "After the attack on Pearl Harbor, the Japanese took control of Shanghai. They put all of the Jews in a certain section of the city they converted into a ghetto. My wife was born in that ghetto near the end of the war. You remember the Germans had formed an alliance with the Japanese."

Jim shook his head "yes" and mumbled "those little slant-eyed bastards."

"They were advising the Japanese. They had definite plans for the Jews, the Final Solution, extermination."

Jim grimaced, "I didn't know that."

"Fortunately for Liz and her family, Shanghai was liberated before their plans could be carried out. Liz's birth certificate was destroyed in a fire caused by the allied bombing of the city. She still has a pearl necklace that was given to her mother by one of the Nazi officers' wives a few days before the woman and her husband fled Shanghai and the allies occupied the city. Liz's mother had worked for the woman as a seamstress." Lee paused. "You know in a strange way I think the two were friends. They had both grown up in Vienna. They had a lot of the same memories. Knew a lot of the same places, and even some of the same people."

Lee relaxed as he told these stories. "I have a lot of respect for Liz's family. I also respect the impact of all of this on Liz's view of the world."

Jim nodded, "Yeah, I suppose it has."

"You know, Jim, I think she's a lot like you."

Jim laughed. "What the hell are you talking about?" Jim avoided Lee's eyes.

"Well, she carries around a lot of fear, and she needs to control situations or at least think she is in control of them."

"Oh hell, Doc, don't start that psychology stuff again."

Lee laughed. "Okay, Jim, I'll shut up."

"Is Liz's mom still alive?" Jim shifted again. The traffic was thinning. The truck picking up speed.

"No. She died quite a few years ago. Right before her death I spent some time with her. I drove her back home to Connecticut. She talked about her last months in Vienna. We talked for a long time." Lee stopped to clear his throat and regain his composure. "You know, it was sixty years later, but she could still hear the sound of the German officers' boots on the stairs outside her family's apartment, as they came in search of her older brother." There was silence. There was nothing else to say.

Lee was forced back to the present by the shudder of the truck as Jim downshifted. The traffic was moving slower. Perhaps there was a roadblock up ahead? Perhaps they were searching for Lee? Perhaps they would find him? But why did he have to flee? This wasn't Germany in the 1930s. This was America, Land of the Free and Home of the Brave. People had rights here, or did they anymore? After what had happened at Pine Grove, would they? Would he? Lee felt a surge of panic run through his body. His breathing became shallow. His heart was beginning to race.

Jim switched the CB on. The chatter on the radio was about an accident, a bad one just up ahead. An SUV pulling a trailer had flipped and rolled down an embankment. Multiple injuries. People trapped in the wreckage. Emergency medical services were en route.

"Okay Ben," Jim commanded. "Get your ass out of that bunk. You're going to get to use that EMT certificate again." Jim flipped the emergency flashers on and pulled over. "Grab that emergency kit under your seat, Doc. Let's go."

CHAPTER 11

A crowd had gathered at the top of the embankment. Jim pushed his way through. Ben and Lee followed close behind. The car, an old SUV, and trailer had rolled over a number of times on the way down the embankment and had partially disintegrated in the process. A set of kitchen chairs, a table with two broken legs, a smashed lampshade, a shoe, children's clothing, a girl's bicycle, a thermos, playing cards, all scattered along the way.

The three men plunged down the hill. It was steep. All three lost their balance a number of times. Through a combination of running, sliding, and walking they reached the bottom. Four other would-be rescuers had already made the descent. Three were trying to open the door of the SUV, which lay on its roof. The fourth stood quietly next to a figure lying on the ground. Ben decided he could be of most assistance to the victims pinned in the wreckage. He started pulling things from the emergency kit that Lee was holding.

Additional help from the highway was arriving. With the assistance of a crow bar the door was opened. Two children, a boy and a girl, eight or nine years of age with dark brown hair and almond eyes, Vietnamese, Lee thought, were pulled from the SUV. The boy's right arm was badly cut. Ben placed a bandage on it and Lee applied pressure. The young girl appeared more frightened than physically hurt.

Lee noticed Jim's absence and asked one of the others to take his position with the boy. Sirens could be heard in the distance. Emergency medical services were arriving.

Lee found Jim standing over the figure on the ground, a young Vietnamese woman, the mother, Lee assumed, of the two children. Standing next to Jim was a young man, also Vietnamese. Her husband, Lee thought. She did not move. Lee bent down. She was not breathing. Lee tried to find a pulse in her neck, but couldn't. He started to re-position her head on the ground, but Jim objected. It was then that Lee noticed that her neck was broken and the side of her face and head she was resting on no longer existed. She was dead.

The young man did not move. He said nothing. He continued to stare blankly at the ground. He seemed unable to hear his children's cries. The family dog limped from the SUV to the side of his mistress and then back to the children.

The EMTs arrived and took over the care of the children. A small circle of rescuers formed around the man and his wife. A young state trooper joined the circle. Jim took the young Vietnamese man's hand in his. Lee followed Jim's direction and took the hand of a young woman. A middle-aged black woman standing next to Lee took hold of Lee's hook. The joining of hands continued until the circle was complete.

Jim noticed the silver cross that hung around the woman's neck. He suggested that the group might say a prayer for the woman and her family. The young trooper began to recite *The Lord's Prayer*. "Our Father, who art in heaven . . ."

There was little left for the three men to do. They climbed the hill slowly. Nothing was said. They pulled themselves into the truck, Ben into the driver's seat, Jim into his bunk, and Lee into the passenger seat. The young highway patrolman waved the truck back onto the road. They headed north again. It was early afternoon.

An hour passed without a word between the three men. "You think he's asleep, Doc?" Ben asked. Lee glanced back at the bunk.

"Well, he's got his eyes closed," said Lee.

"You know he's really 'wound,'" said Ben referring to Jim.

"What do you mean? He's asleep, isn't he?"

"Yeah, that's what I mean. When he gets too much of something he just turns it off. He may stay in that bunk for the next three days."

"Well, he just watched someone die," said Lee.

"It's not just that," said Ben. "It's because that somebody was Vietnamese. He's still fighting that damned war. In his first week in Nam he killed a Vietnamese woman. I bet she looked a lot like that one. Blew her head off. She was the lead driver in an NV convoy." Ben paused for a moment and glanced back at Jim. "He was a sniper. Went to school for it. And was damn good at it. He's never gotten away from it. Stuff like this will stir him up for weeks. Sometimes he won't talk at all."

"God, my head is killin' me," said Ben. "Get these damn sick headaches when I drink. I think I got one comin' on." A few minutes passed. "Jim," shouted Ben, "can you take over? I think I'm goin' to throw up."

Ben pulled the truck over. Set the brake. Turned the flashers on. Jumped out of the cab and began to vomit.

Jim didn't respond. *We can't stay on the shoulder for long. The police will stop. They will ask questions,* thought Lee.

"Jim," pleaded Lee, "help Ben out. He's really sick. Jim!" Lee yelled this time. "Come on, Jim! For God's sake, we need your help."

Jim rolled over. He climbed out of the bunk and into the driver's seat. He didn't say a word. Ben scrambled back into the truck through the sleeper door. Before Ben could close it Jim was pulling back onto the highway. Ben sat down on the bunk holding his head.

Another hour passed. Lee tried to reach his friend, Molly, in Boston with Jim's cell phone, but just weird busy signals was all he heard. Ben was asleep.

"So what's with you, Jim. What's your story?" asked Lee. "I told you mine."

"I don't know, Doc. Small town boy goes halfway around the world to kill Commies for Christ. How would that be?"

"That's what you did?"

"Hell, yes. That's what I did. I was a damn Marine. I blew the crap out of those little yellow bastards. But did it do anybody any good? No." Jim's face was starting to turn red. "But I made it back. At least part of me did," he sighed. "I almost didn't. One day me and three guys in my recon squad were waiting for our ride. The VC knew we were there. We didn't have a snowball's chance in hell." He stopped but then pressed on. "They left us for dead. Three of us were. When the chopper got there they hauled my ass back to Saigon. I spent the next six months being cut on and learnin' to walk. They let me out. Gave me thirty percent for my legs.

"I remember when we flew back to the States. They unloaded us in a hangar away from the terminal." His voice became louder. "No friggin' brass bands for us. The best they could do was to sneak us back so we didn't have to face those damn hippies with their peace and love B-S. I got a job that summer drivin' and I've been movin' ever since." He was finished. His face was beet-red.

"So, is that a good story, Doc?"

"What do you think, Jim?" asked Lee. There was silence. "I've got a question. What is it with all the names? Wop? Raghead? Redneck?"

"It helps me keep things straight. Know who's who—the good guys and the bad guys. In Nam you never knew."

"You sure some of it isn't because you're still just a little pissed off with the entire world?"

"Well now, Doc, you could have a point. Usin' those names does help some days to take the edge off. So does getting really drunk or beaten the hell out of some little fool who's askin' for it."

"I'm sure you have a lot of reasons to be angry."

"Whether I do or don't or should or shouldn't, some days I am one angry son-of-a-bitch. Especially on days like today. When somethin' happens to bring all that crap back up." He looked at Lee. "So let's just leave it there."

Jim had said a lot more than he wanted to. Lee decided not to push it. Jim's knuckles were white from the death grip he had on the truck's steering wheel.

The young woman's death had made Lee think of his wife. Endings somehow always seemed to make Lee think of beginnings. Of when they had met. She was a young woman then. Full of energy. A woman with a mission. She was ready to have a child and so was Lee. But Lee had just ended a relationship with another Jewish woman, Rita. The difference in religion was just part of it. They had talked of marriage too, but it was Annie Hall in reverse. What had attracted and in the end repelled Lee from Rita, were the same things he saw in Liz.

Lee and Liz tried living together. They talked a lot about marriage and children. But one weekend when she was away, Lee moved out. He became involved with another woman, but he kept in touch with Liz. Months passed. He couldn't commit to the new relationship. He kept thinking about Liz. Finally one night he showed up at her house. They talked. She wanted a commitment. He got down on his knees and proposed. She accepted.

The next few weeks were crazy. He seemed more ambivalent than ever. The wedding was on, then it was off. She told her parents and friends it was on and then she had to tell them it was off. She had had it with Lee. He knew it. Finally after a sleepless night he went to her house. It was early morning. The neighborhood was just waking up. He beat on her door. When she asked from her second floor window who it was he shouted for her and her neighbors to hear, "It's your future husband." She opened the door.

They were married by a Justice of the Peace a few weeks later at an old inn on one of the islands. Before the wedding she told Lee he would have to call her friends and family and explain to them that the wedding was back on. He did.

But his confused feelings about the relationship had stayed with him. The debate in his head had gone on for the twenty-five years they had been together. It never ended. They were different. She was Jewish. He was Christian. They had different attitudes about money. He had grown up working class and she had grown up upper middle class with a mother who was a fashion designer and a father who was a physician. Her parents had divorced. His parents had stayed together until death separated them. He had grown up in a small southern town. She had grown up in New York City. These differences often sparked conflict that fueled the ambivalence.

But they were also so much the same. They might fight to the death over small things, but their core values were the same. They loved their daughter. She was first in their lives. On that they always agreed. There was energy and passion in the relationship. More than Lee had ever found in any other relationship. And trust. Their relationship had weathered many a storm. They were both risk takers. Fighters. They loved each other deeply. *A mature love,* he thought. He had told himself when he was angry with her that he would leave her some day. But he had never taken the first step.

Their daughter was gone now, grown up. Living on her own. Since she had left their arguing had increased. Lee was tired. Tired of the conflict. They argued about his trip south. She asked him to reschedule it. He refused. She wanted him home for Passover. He assured her he would be.

Lately the ambivalence seemed to come in waves. It was stronger than before. The tide was high. Thoughts of leaving came more often and troubled him more.

It had started to rain. They were an hour out of Boston. He decided to try Molly again. The cell phone worked. She answered.

"Sure," she said. "What are friends for?" He could stay over. She had business in Portsmouth tomorrow afternoon. She could drive him to Portland in the morning, if that's what he wanted.

He wasn't sure. He could call his family and Joe, his attorney from Molly's tonight. Joe would know what to do. Maybe Lee was just being paranoid. They probably weren't concerned about finding him. With all the confusion they had probably forgotten about him. An old man and a homeless person running off into the night. Who cares? Major Henderson and the boys certainly had bigger things to worry about now. If he turned himself in they would probably laugh at him. Lee drifted off to sleep. He was tired.

When he woke up, the truck had stopped. Traffic was at a standstill. "We're almost at Somerville, Doc" said Jim. "But we got a problem. They're searchin' everything that takes the exit. The guys on the radio say they're lookin' for some guy who looks a lot like you. He's got a hook." He smiled. "Now, Doc, I'm sure they're not lookin' for you, but I'm sure you don't want to have to do any explainin', do you? So I thought you might want to slide over that guardrail." He pointed. "We're close to Broadway. You can catch a cab." He paused. "You said your friend lives a few blocks from the exit."

Lee couldn't get his thoughts together. "Yeah, yeah, Jim. You're right. I don't want to slow you guys down."

"Sure, Doc. Let us know when you get home." Jim smiled again.

"Okay, sure." Lee hesitated.

"Doc, I think you better go while you can."

Lee nodded. He opened the door. Stepped onto the tarmac. The rain was getting heavier. He slid over the guardrail and down the embankment. A cab, to his amazement, was stopped at the light. He hailed it. It pulled over. He was on his way to Molly's.

CHAPTER 12

We have met the enemy...and he is us.
— Pogo

"Where to?" asked the driver.

"Can you drop me on the corner of Moran and Broadway?" asked Lee.

"Sure, bud. It's your nickel."

Moran was the street that ran behind Molly's brownstone. He would walk two blocks down Moran and then a block over to Molly's. Maybe he was being too cautious. But if the police were looking for a guy with a hook, well. How would they know about Molly? God, this whole thing was pushing him over the edge. *Clinically paranoid,* he thought. *Molly will think I have completely lost my mind.*

"We're here," said the driver when Lee didn't move after they stopped.

"Yeah, okay, thanks," said Lee sounding distracted. Lee handed the driver the fare with a good tip.

The cab pulled away and Lee began the two-block walk down Moran. The rain continued. A cold rain. Lee's pace quickened. He wanted to get to Molly's. She would have some dry clothes and something to eat. Lee was hungry. Really hungry. But it felt good to be really hungry. His appetite was coming back.

Molly had been a good friend for years. She was a great lady. A nurse, turned healthcare consultant, turned author of children's books. A woman who acted on her values. She was often referred to as the conscience of any organization of which she was a part. God knows managed healthcare of the late 1990s needed a conscience.

For the last fifteen years she had focused her energy on writing and publishing children's books. It was a hard market but she loved it.

Lee turned up the side street that ran past Molly's brownstone. He could see her condo. The lights were on. She was waiting for him. He began to run.

Sunday, March 31, 2013
Agency Offices, Boston
3:15 P.M.

Jennings looked out at the rain. It was a miserable afternoon. His small office was in an old building that the Feds had converted to the anti-terrorism unit of the Bureau. He shared it with his partner, Agent Wright, a much younger man with more education, but less street experience. The one thing Jennings always said he had was experience, and probably too much of it.

The anti-terrorism unit had been located in this relic of a building from the 1950s, not in the new federal building. For a purpose, they said. So they could be close to the people they were working with. Most of the facility had been converted into a detention center. The conversion wasn't difficult. The building was relatively new as structures in Boston go. Built as a small private psychiatric hospital. When managed care had arrived in the 1980s, the facility had struggled on for a few years, but finally closed in the late 1990s. It stood empty for a number of years, until the Feds saw an opportunity with minor renovations, such as adding more security doors, fencing, and cameras to make it into a detention center. What went on there was a mystery to the surrounding community. The Bureau liked it that way, since they didn't want the center to be that visible.

There were a few senior agents who worked in the facility, like Jennings, but most of the bright and the best were downtown at the new Federal Building. A large conference room off of Jennings' office filled with dividers created cubicles for the agents and staff. Most of the agents were young and were just pleased to be working with the Bureau. They didn't seem to mind the beat-up, gray, metal desks and the old office chairs that had been left by the hospital.

Agent Wright entered the office, but Jennings continued to watch the rain. It was getting heavier. Wright sat at his desk and immediately started going through his e-mail.

"Jim, remind me again why we arrested Angus Smith, the scientist-turned-would-be novelist? I don't think he has a clue about what's goin' on. Which genius ordered this one?"

"I think it came from the top, Doug."

"Well, I think they are wasting our time. They want an arrest, that's all. As far as Pine Grove goes, they should be concentrating on those two with the plane that did the job on the containment building and give us the manpower we need to prevent a second disaster. You can bet Muqtada knows what's happening and will seize the opportunity." His voice was getting louder as he spoke.

Wright continued with his e-mail and didn't respond.

"Doug, remember that guy you saw in White's Fork? The psychologist? Brazil? He left the decontamination center. Took off without anyone's permission."

"Naughty boy," said Jennings sounding bored.

"In all of the confusion down there they lost track of him. Clark put taps on the phones of the names we got out of his appointment book."

"He didn't have anything better to do?" asked Jennings, appearing irritated.

Wright ignored his response and continued. "An hour ago Brazil called a friend in Boston, a Molly Cohen. He made arrangements for her to drive him to Portland tomorrow."

"Yeah, yeah, so pick him up if you want to, but give me a motive for him doing anything as crazy as sabotage." Jennings shook his head. "Give me a history. I think he's as clueless as his friend Smith."

"Maybe so Doug, but what is most interesting is that he is close friends, very close friends, with our Dr. Kudrick, Hussein's friend. Her name wasn't in his appointment book, but I recognized his name from her background check."

"Yes, interesting," said Jennings rubbing an old scar on his left hand.

"Well I think it might be even more interesting if he spent the night at Dr. Kudrick's rather than at his friend Molly's condo."

"So how do you want to arrange that?" Jennings sounded engaged for the first time.

"He needs to know that we are expecting him at his friend Molly's. Dr. Kudrick may be the only friend he has in Boston who isn't in his appointment book. Remember he knows we have his appointment book. I think he will go there. We have her place wired, so maybe she will talk with her old friend and confidant, Dr. Brazil, about Dr. Hussein."

"Why not." Jennings' interest faded. "If we pick him up now, we will just have another lost soul in detention." Jennings stared out at the rain.

Boston

Lee saw them. Two black Crown Victoria's. He had worked enough as a consultant with law enforcement to know an unmarked police car. One of the cars was parked across the street from Molly's. The other on the side street.

Lee stopped. He stepped off the sidewalk into the shadows. He watched. He waited. He thought of his dad. Watching the people who had been sent to watch him. He listened. He took a few more steps forward. He could hear, at least he thought he could hear, a police radio.

Maybe he was mistaken. Maybe if he walked back up to the corner and waited a few minutes they would leave. Maybe they were there for someone else.

So he did. There was a Mom and Pop convenience store on the corner. He decided to go in. He desperately wanted to get out of the rain. He'd get a cup of coffee and a sandwich and wait. An Italian sub would taste really good.

He opened the door. A young man was behind the deli counter. He ordered a small tuna Italian and a large cup of coffee. He looked around the store. Maybe a bag of chips. *No, let's not overdo it,* he thought. He noticed his reflection in the window. He looked like a drowned rat. A very old and thin drowned rat. He had lost weight. He had needed to lose weight. One of the unsung benefits of radiation poisoning.

The sandwich and coffee were ready. The clerk rang them up. "Anything else?" asked the clerk.

Lee looked around. "A *Globe,*" he said. He put the newspaper under his arm.

There were a couple of tables in the store. He sat down, opened the sandwich and took a bite. It did taste good. The coffee was hot. A few sips of it took some of the chill off, but he was still shivering.

He opened the newspaper. Most of the front page news was about Pine Grove. The fire was out. An estimate of fatalities was still difficult to make. Hundreds of people were still missing. In the past day forty-six of the survivors had died from their injuries.

Lee looked at the banner headline at the bottom of the page.

Search continues for Pine Grove saboteurs. Retired nuclear scientist arrested. Lee read the article. *Dr. Angus Smith was arrested at his home in Winterport, Maine on Saturday evening.*

Lee read it again. My God, why would they arrest Angus? Lee read on. The article didn't say. There was a picture of Angus being led away in handcuffs, looking confused, scared. Behind him was a face Lee recognized. Special Agent Jennings. "This guy certainly gets around," Lee muttered to himself.

He fumbled with the paper to find the article's conclusion on page twelve. He ignored the sandwich and coffee. He was no longer hungry. There on page twelve, next to the article's conclusion, he saw his own name under the header. *Maine psychologist sought for questioning.* It was only a few lines. It said no one had heard from Lee since the first explosion at Pine Grove.

"A lie," Lee muttered. A description of him followed emphasizing his hook, of course, and a request that anyone knowing his whereabouts should call the following number.

Now Lee understood. It was Angus' manuscript that they had found in his briefcase. Angus was a friend of Lee's. He was part of a writer's group Lee participated in. He liked Lee and valued his opinion. Lee didn't think he was that good of a writer. Very technical, too technical. *Dry,* Lee thought.

They both shared an interest in Pine Grove for different reasons. Angus thought it was a disaster waiting to happen. Aging nuclear facilities, tons of nuclear garbage. A terrorist's dream. Lee thought the disaster had already happened: residents with thyroid cancer, ALS, and birth defects.

Angus had brought his manuscript over the night before Lee left for Pine Grove. Lee had thumbed through the hard copy, but hadn't read it. But the title, *Blueprint for Disaster,* and the storyline, "Terrorists take control of the Pine Grove Labs and blow up one of the old reactors," was enough. He had forgotten he had even brought the manuscript with him. He must have thrown the disk in his briefcase. Henderson and Jennings must have found it.

Poor Angus. He had worked in the Middle East before he retired. He married an Iraqi woman, Shorey. And he was very critical of the Nuclear Regulatory Commission. A perfect suspect. And so was Lee. Poor Lee.

Lee noticed that the young clerk was looking at him. He was on the phone. What if he had recognized him? How many people in Boston have a hook for a left hand?

Lee got to his feet, ditched the rest of the sandwich and coffee in the trash. He tucked the newspaper under his arm, shoved the hook into his pocket and left the store.

Molly's was out. If they had his briefcase, they had his address book too, so everyone else he knew in Boston was out. Except Jean. Her number and address weren't in the book. What else could he do? Surely they would find him if he stayed on the street. A hotel? His money would run out in a couple of days. He had to get off the street. He hailed a cab. Again, luckily the cab stopped.

"One Wadsworth Place."

"Downtown?" asked the driver.

"Yes." Lee knew the address well. Jean lived in the same building in the early 1980s. In those days he was either in Boston on the weekend or she was in Portland, but they were together. The best of times. They were in love. The worst of times. She would have to return to Europe at the end of the year when her post doctorate was over.

As they crossed the Charles River he could see Jean's building in the distance. He remembered how his heart would race as he got closer to the exit. He would park his car in the underground garage and grab his bag. Michael, the doorman knew him. He would buzz him in. Up the elevator to the fourth floor. Down the hall. She would be waiting. A late dinner, a bottle of wine, soft music, and a woman he had been in love with for most of his life. What more could a man ask?

The cab pulled in front of Wadsworth Place, one of the more exclusive apartment buildings in Boston.

"You sure you want out here?" the driver asked staring at Lee.

"Yes, of course." Lee looked like a cartoon character soaking wet in miner's coveralls and worn out tennis shoes.

"Okay, just checkin'."

Lee paid the driver, tipping him well. It was an expensive ride from Somerville. Lee shoved his hook in his pocket.

Michael was not at the door. Lee was sure Michael had retired many years before. The new doorman watched his approach with apparent concern.

"Hey, Mack. I told you guys no panhandlin'. Now get lost before I call the cops," said the doorman.

"Now, now wait a minute. I'm here to see a friend of mine. Jean Kudrick, apartment 410."

"Dr. Kudrick is out for the evening. She apparently wasn't expecting you."

"No, no she wasn't."

"Why don't you come back tomorrow? I'll be glad to give her your card," he smiled.

Wiseass. "I'm afraid I don't have any cards with me. It's a long story."

"I'm sure it is," said the doorman.

"I'm Dr. ...Brown. An old friend of hers. I really must see her tonight." Lee sounded desperate.

"I'll tell her you came by, but you need to leave now." The doorman reached for the phone to call the police, Lee assumed.

"But you don't understand, I. . ."

"Look, you better understand that..."

"It's all right, Roger," said a familiar voice from behind Lee.

"Right, Dr. Kudrick. Right. I was just getting ready to take down Dr. Brown's name and number for you."

Jean put her arm around Lee's waist and ushered him to the door as Roger buzzed them through.

"Well, Dr. Brown, what brings you to Boston?" asked Jean. Lee just stared at her and smiled.

"It's a long story," he said as they stepped into the elevator. Lee looked penetratingly at Jean. He hadn't seen her in over ten years.

"What? What are you looking at?" she asked.

"At you. Your hair, it's brown again." Jean had colored her hair blonde for many years.

"I could always do wonders with a bottle of chemicals. All those years of lab work." Jean had run a research lab in Europe. She was a psychopharmacologist, with her specialty, behavioral toxicology, the study of the impact of toxins on the behavior of animals and human beings. She had worked for the German government for most of her career. When the Cold War ended, the lab she worked for lost much of its funding, most of which came from the United States government. Some of the things they were working on, better left unsaid, just wouldn't be needed if the Soviet's were out of business.

"I mean ...you look beautiful tonight."

Jean was a petite woman with green eyes and a fair complexion. Since she had retired her body had become more athletic. She had time to ski and bike with Ian. She was now in better shape than Lee. The worry lines and wrinkles of her early fifties were gone. "Thanks to modern medicine," she said.

She opened the door to the apartment. "I think this will remind you of my old place," she said. And it did. "Four-fourteen is just around the corner." Lee remembered the old apartment well. It was a small studio with a balcony that overlooked the courtyard. They often left the balcony door open at night. He could still see the drapes blowing in the wind. Four-fourteen had been sparsely furnished. Much of the furniture rented. A small bed, but big enough for two small people. Her new apartment was larger, with a bedroom. It had been furnished with care. Original art, not rental store prints, hung from the walls. Jean did have good taste. Solid, dark colors. Not busy. *European,* Lee thought. But what did he know? He hadn't been to Europe in years.

"Let me see if I can find you some dry clothes. You and Ian were. . . ." She looked away. "I think some of his clothes will fit you." She began opening drawers and closets and within a few minutes she assembled an outfit for Lee. A blue button down dress shirt, a dark blue sweater, khaki pants, and black socks.

"I don't know about the shoes. Here. Try these loafers on. He always loved them."

"Oh, that's okay, these are fine." Lee felt he no longer deserved her kindness.

"No. You look like you ran away from the Salvation Army thrift store."

"No, that was Howard," said Lee trying...he wasn't sure what he was trying to do.

"What?" Jean sounded confused.

That was stupid, he thought. "Never mind."

"Ian liked you. He didn't understand you or the relationship that you and I had."

"I was sorry... to hear of his death." Lee hesitated again. "He was a good man. He was good for you. Better than I would have been."

"I suppose so. I guess we will never know, will we?" she said staring at Lee. Lee had no response.

"Here, change. We'll see how you look in my dead husband's clothes." As she turned to leave the room Lee did something he had wanted to do since he saw her. He put his arms around her. At first she resisted. Then she began to cry. They both cried. For Ian. For things that never were, or would never be again.

In a minute it was over. Jean pulled away. "Take a shower and, please, shave. There's a razor in the medicine cabinet. I'll see what's in the fridge. I assume you're hungry." She left the room without waiting for a response.

Lee found Ian's razor. He hadn't shaved or showered for a couple of days. He climbed in the shower. The warm water seemed to wash away the past week. The pain. The fear. The cold.

He was in Boston with Jean. Something he thought would never happen again. The trouble he was in seemed unimportant now. He was with Jean. He felt . . . yes, he felt...happy. He was up to his ass in alligators, but he felt happy. He felt at home. He always felt at home with Jean.

He finished his shower and dressed. The shoes were a little big, but two pairs of socks would work again. With his weight loss the pants were a good fit. He looked for cologne or after-shave. At first he couldn't find any. But when he looked under the sink he found an old bottle of Pierre Cardin in the back corner. He thought for a few seconds that it might have been his. *Couldn't be,* he thought. Lee inspected the bottle more closely. On the bottom was a faded water-spotted "Jordan Marsh" tag, an old New England department store that no longer existed. Closed twenty years ago. The cologne was his. He smiled. Jean hung onto it for all these years.

When Lee reappeared, Jean had prepared a table and put on an old Bocelli CD, *Cieli Di Toscana.* Lee remembered it well.

"I'm afraid you'll have to settle for gouda. It's good. And the bread is fresh. I picked it up this morning. You remember the bakery around the corner? And what else?" Looking in the refrigerator. "Hmm, I have some fruit salad from last night."

"Great," said Lee.

She handed the wine and the opener to Lee. "It's a Mondovi. A chardonnay. It will do I guess." She suddenly looked sad. "Ian used to ....Well, it will have to do. There's nothing else in the house."

"It's fine, Jean." Lee was looking for the right words. "I mean it's great. It reminds me of old times. A loaf of bread, a bottle of wine and..." Lee stopped. He wanted to say "my love," but didn't. He felt he no longer had the right to say such things. It had been years and marriages ago. He tried to put the thought of being with her again out of his mind.

"I really like your apartment. How long are you going to be in the States?" asked Lee, suddenly starting to feel uncomfortable with the whole situation.

"I'm not sure. I just wanted, well I guess I needed to come back, to visit my sister and spend some time with friends."

Jean was the younger of two girls. Her father had been a house painter. They had lived in a small house, a lot like the house Lee had grown up in, in a working-class mill town. Jean had worked in high school. She was a bright woman who had been admitted to one of the best schools in the Northeast. College life, however, was not easy for a Catholic girl living at home working her way through an Ivy League college with Jewish kids from upper-middle-class and wealthy families. But academically she did well and was off to graduate school.

"And I wanted to see you. I'm glad you came. I mean I'm glad you're here."

Lee had met Jean during his first year in graduate school when they were working as volunteers at a student crisis center. There seemed to be an immediate connection between them. A way of knowing the other. In the weeks that followed they found themselves telling each other things they had never shared with another living soul. And then it got scary. Jean began to back away. She started seeing someone else. Lee stepped back.

Jean finished her degree. She decided to take a job in St. Louis. They would keep in touch. Lee visited Jean a number of times. The first night was always wonderful. The connection was back. They would talk for hours. But by the time Lee got in his car to drive back to the university the line was dead. Time would pass. Letters would be sent. Phone calls received. Another visit. And then nothing. But neither could let go.

When it came time for Lee's internship, his major professor arranged his acceptance at Menninger. But Lee chose Fort Andrews Hospital in St. Louis. He had worked there for a summer and liked the program and the people. To be honest, Jean was a major reason. But being that close again ended as it had at the university. By the end of his internship the distance was back. Lee returned to the university to complete his dissertation and Jean began to explore teaching opportunities in Europe. By the end of the next year Lee would be married and on his way to a job in the Midwest, and Jean would be in Europe.

"So, Dr. Brown," said Jean, "what's with the costume and the charade? I hope you parked your car in the garage. We're supposed to get some snow tonight and there's a parking ban."

"I don't have my car with me."

"You came down on the train?"

"No, I came up by truck."

"Up? From where?" Jean looked perplexed.

"Pine Grove."

"Oh, God! You were there?" Her puzzled expression turned to one of fear.

Lee handed her the paper. "I know you are always impressed when you see my name in print," trying weakly to make a joke.

Jean read through the article once, and then a second time. "So, what is going on?"

"Well, as a friend of mine said last night, it's a very long story."

"It usually is with you," said Jean and she smiled.

"I went down to work on the book. The one I've been trying to write."

"Yes, I remember you talking about that book a few years ago."

"And to meet with the attorneys working on the suit against the companies at Pine Grove." Lee paused. "I was on my way back to the hotel. There was a flash of light that lit up everything." He could still see it. "It blinded me and the drivers of the two cars in front of me. They smashed into each other. I stopped to help."

"You would," said Jean.

"And that's one of the things you love about me, Kudrick. One of the drivers, a young woman, was hurt pretty bad. The fog closed in. I tried to go for help. The next thing I knew I was being carried to a school bus full of people, survivors, by two guys in hazmat suits. I don't know what happened to the two women." Lee paused. "We were taken to a decontamination center, Camp Liberty, and questioned." Lee stopped, but then continued. "I assume they found my manuscript and Angus' in my rental car."

"You're physicist friend who writes those disaster novels?" she asked.

"Yes. And this one just happened to be about Pine Grove."

"Oh, no," said Jean. The worried expression returned.

"And poor David. You remember Dave?" Jean nodded. "He worked at Pine Grove. They told me he was killed in the accident. Since I had just seen David the night before I assume Major Henderson, the headmaster at Camp Liberty and his sidekick, Special Agent Jennings, decided that David and I and Angus must have planned the whole thing. I suppose my taking off with Howard didn't help."

"Who's Howard?" asked Jean.

"A homeless fella who was being detained at the camp with me. We managed to sneak out of the camp and I hitched a ride north on a truck carrying portable toilets," Lee smiled.

"Good choice, Brazil," said Jean laughing.

"Hey, I had to take what came along. Anyway, I'm here. I'll skip my night in the coal mine and the bar fight at the strip joint."

"Your what?" again sounding more puzzled than worried.

"Never mind. It's not important right now. I got here thanks to a number of people who helped me when I really needed it. You know, I didn't start putting all of this together until a couple of hours ago when I saw the article in the *Globe*. I haven't been able to contact anyone in Maine or anywhere else for that matter."

"So no one knows where you are? Or if you're alive or dead for that matter?" Jean stood up.

"Oh, I think they know I'm in the Boston area. That's why they were waiting for me at Molly's tonight. You remember Molly?"

Jean nodded. "But how did they know you were going to be at Molly's?"

"I assume they've been listening in on her calls. They have my computer and my address book. I called her earlier tonight."

"So, what do we do?" Jean was starting to pace.

"I don't know. I can't stay here long. If they keep digging they will eventually find that you are in Boston. That I might be here. And they will come knocking on your door."

"Where can you go?" She continued her pacing. She said it helped her to think. But it had always made Lee nervous.

"I don't know. But I'm not sure I can keep talking or thinking about this anymore tonight." Lee caught Jean's eyes. "Just talk to me, Jean. About something. Anything. Something that has absolutely nothing to do with them or with Pine Grove."

Jean knew what Lee was asking her to do. He loved to hear her talk. She told great stories. She went on and on. It relaxed them both. She talked to relax. Lee listened to relax.

"I miss Bridget," she said. She had gotten the large black lab a year before she and Ian had married. "Cas and Sam are keeping her. They said they would fly her over with them when they come to the States next month."

"How are they?" asked Lee. They were friends Lee had heard Jean talk about for thirty years, but had never met. "They are doing great. The kids are in college now. Fine young men. Handsome."

Lee tried to make conversation. "You've had Bridget for quite a few years now."

Jean nodded, sadly. "She is getting to be an old girl. She loved Ian. Misses him. Still looks for him to come home some evening." She paused. "It's been hard without Ian." Lee's comment was more a statement than a question.

"Well, yes, of course it has. He was here one day and then...I'm not sure you ever get over that. All three of them. You knew his two friends, Bruno and George, died in the same accident?"

"No, I didn't know. What happened?"

"That was what was so crazy about the whole thing. It happened near our village." She paused. "I know you thought he was some kind of nut when it came to skiing, but he wasn't. All three of them were experienced skiers. They were careful. It was a warm day but the ski patrol had checked the slope they were on that morning." She paused again. "It should not of happened." She shook her head. "Melita, Bruno's wife, and I had thought we might go with them, but we decided we would go to the village to pick up a few things for dinner that evening." She looked away and rubbed her eyes. "Those who saw it said the mountain just opened up and swallowed them."

Lee took Jean's hand. Jean pulled away and changed the subject.

"Did you notice my masterpiece? Here let me show you. I took a drawing class last summer." Jean pointed to a sketch of a young girl. "What do you think?"

"I...I like it," said Lee.

"I really felt out of place at first. Most of the other students had taken classes before. I think one woman said she had worked as a commercial artist. What she was doing there, I don't know."

"Who's the young girl?"

"Oh, that's me."

"Oh yes. I see," said Lee.

"No, you don't. Anyway, it was my first effort. I will certainly improve," said Jean feigning confidence.

"I have no doubt you will, Dr. Kudrick."

"And while we're on the subject of what you like and dislike, did you notice these?" Jean pointed to her feet.

"Well, no."

"I love these. They're comfortable."

"Oh, your shoes."

"Yes, Lee, my shoes. I found them in a little shop on Newbury Street."

Lee was lost. All they were to him was a pair of burgundy shoes with heels. Lee hated shopping for shoes with Jean, with anyone. Over the years Jean had dragged him in and out of at least a hundred shoe stores.

"Well, what do you think?"

"I like them. In fact, the thing I like about them most is that I wasn't with you when you bought them!"

"Oh, you! You never change."

They laughed. They drank the bottle of wine and ate the cheese and talked. They talked about old times. Outside the rain had turned to snow. They remembered walking in the Commons with an umbrella on a snowy afternoon in late March. They were in the center of the city, but no one was around. The city was quiet. Only the two of them. At least that's the way it had seemed. The way they had felt. The way they remembered it thirty years later. The winter was ending. Their winter was ending.

They had drunk too much. Lee knew that if he did not lie down he would soon be on the floor. Jean helped him to the bedroom. She took Ian's loafers off. Helped him undress. She changed into a gown and lay down next to him. He put his arms around her again. Lee could see the balcony door. It was open. The wind blew the drapes just as it had so many years before.

Agency Offices, Boston
7:00 A.M.

Jennings watched the sun rise over the bay. A view of the harbor was one of the few things that his office afforded. He had spent the night in the office again. The colors of red and orange reminded him of sunsets on the North Sea that Margaret and he had watched that summer in the Netherlands. He could not remember the name of the village they had taken a room in. He just remembered the sunsets and Margaret. She was happy then. Jennings was happy then. They talked of going back, but never did. Now he supposed they never would.

Jennings was an Air Force brat, an only child. His parents and he had moved every few years. He swore he would settle down and stay in one place. True to his word, he had married a woman who had never lived anyplace but Boston. Margaret had made a home for them here. Jennings felt like she had taken it all with her when she moved out and back with her family. The office had become his home. He felt he had nothing left but the job.

Jennings heard noise in the outer office. He was surprised to see Wright. He usually wasn't in this early.

"So how are our little lovebirds this morning?" asked Jennings.

"Well we're not sure. I just talked to Clark. The wire went down about 4:00 A.M."

"What the hell do you mean 'it went down', Jim?" Jennings voice grew louder. "What is going on with the equipment in this agency? Did someone forget to change the friggin' batteries?"

"I don't know, Doug. We think they're still there."

"We aren't sure?" Jennings was on his feet.

"Since we had electronic surveillance in place, they pulled Gomez and Clark off last night to work on data analysis from Pine Grove."

"So we don't even know if they are still in Massachusetts? We need to get in there."

Wright began to scroll through Jean's file. "She's got a recently deceased husband who applied for a visa just before his death. We could send someone in from INS. They could plant a new listening device."

"Jim, some days you make me proud." Jennings returned to his chair by the window to watch the morning sun rise higher over the bay.

CHAPTER 13

Love is the sweet surprise.
— *Peacekeeper*, by Lindsey Buckingham, Fleetwood Mac

April 1, 2013
Apt. 410, Wadsworth Place, Boston
The 7th Day of Passover

Lee woke a number of times that night. Near morning he woke to the sound of footsteps. He sat up. It was not Jean. She lay next to him sleeping quietly. Lee waited. A small figure appeared at the door. A child. A little girl with long hair. She quietly crossed from the door to the bed. Without a word she crawled into the space between Lee and Jean and found her way to the top of the bedcovers. She slipped between the covers and put her small arms around Jean. Lee lay back down and put his arms around the young girl and Jean. Katie, he thought, must have had a bad dream. She always gets in bed with us after a bad dream. Lee snuggled up to Katie and drifted back to sleep.

When he woke again it was to the sound of Jean preparing breakfast. She wasn't a quiet cook. The sun had been up for hours. It was mid-morning.

Lee rubbed his eyes remembering the dream. Katie. The baby Lee and Jean had dreamed of having. The child they had tried to create. A child that would have brought Jean home to the States. That would have radically changed both their lives. Commitment would have been easy. There would have been no confusion. No uncertainty. It would have been clear to both of them. Many good things and people had filled their lives in the years since. People and things that would not have been. But for a moment, he felt the sadness again. He missed Katie. He missed what could have been.

Lee slipped into the robe that he found on a chair by the bed. He washed his face and combed his hair. He looked in the mirror. *For having gone through hell the last week, still not a bad looking guy at sixty-six,* Lee thought.

The bedroom door was partially open. Lee stood for a long time watching Jean. He had missed her. She was a strong lady. A professional he respected, but still a woman. Although she had trained in the South, she didn't fit the definition of a Southern professional woman. God forbid. Lee wouldn't describe these women as assertive. Aggressive seemed a better descriptor but often in a very passive manner.

Many Southern professional women, Lee felt, did not like men. Men were definitely not seen as potential allies. But Lee could understand the attitude. Women in the South, especially professional women were often not well treated by men. He theorized that since they had grown up with tutus, and Scarlett O'Hara, they were themselves often confused about how they wanted men to treat them. Most southern men, unfortunately, didn't have a clue about how to deal with this confusion. Each side had learned to expect put downs and betrayal from the other. Unfortunately, these women had to fight for every inch of ground they gained. Often they were just as aggressive with their female colleagues. Feminism in the New South was a dirty word. Other professional women were often seen as a threat, not an ally. The old eat the young and vice versa.

It was good to be out of the South. In the North there were certainly problems and tensions between the sexes, but at least people seemed more open about it. The issues could be talked about rather than denied or made light of. For Lee there had always seemed to be less confusion and more willingness to do what worked for both sexes, rather than what tradition or what the fundamentalists thought the Bible said.

Lee walked into the kitchen. Jean smiled, "You're up. Hope I didn't wake you."

"No, no," said Lee.

"Did you sleep well?"

"I always sleep well with, uh, when I'm really tired." Jean smiled again. "Did you get the paper?"

"Yes. And you're in it again. Page one, not twelve this time. It's on the table." Jean filled a mug with coffee and brought it to the table where Lee stood studying the front page of the paper.

"Well, at least they spelled my name right. Looks like I am no longer just 'wanted for questioning.' Now I am a 'suspect' in the attack on the Labs. It looks like they are building a case, aren't they." He turned to the next page. "They even mention my involvement in the anti-war movement back in the Seventies. And here's something about the class action suit and my involvement with Angus and his wife." He paused remembering them. "She's a sweet lady. I bet she's scared to death."

"I'm sure your wife and Dru are terrified too. Is there someone who knows them, but is not a friend or a colleague of yours, who you could relay a message through?"

"Yes, I'm sure." Lee thought a moment. "There is a woman I worked with years ago. She was a patient in our rehab program. She met my daughter when Dru was at the office," Lee remembered. "Dru was fascinated by Violet. Violet has no speech. She communicates in Morse Code via computer. The two became friends." Lee paused and rubbed his hook. "I doubt they would suspect her of being able to communicate with my family. Or anyone else, for that matter." Lee smiled. "Lack of awareness regarding disability may come in handy for once.

"It's perfect. She knows Elvish and so does my daughter."

Jean looked puzzled. "What is Elvish?"

"You remember, it's the language of the Elves of Middle Earth. *Lord of the Rings.* Violet and Dru both loved the book and the movies and began e-mailing each other in Elvish. I can contact Violet and ask her to contact Dru." He stopped. "I think I still remember her e-mail address."

"But I guess the question is what are you going to say? What are you going to do, Lee?" Jean was on her feet. Lee hoped she wouldn't start pacing.

"Hell, I don't know, Jean. I didn't realize I was such a dangerous character until I read the paper."

"Do you want to go back to Maine right now? It looks like our government is getting ready to conduct another witch hunt and you have the pointed nose."

"I haven't thought of any other options. I have an attorney there and some friends who have connections with the Feds at the Attorney General's office. I'm on speaking terms with Senator Snowe and Senator Collins. I guess that's worth something." Lee shrugged. "I hope it is."

"Some friends and I have been thinking of disappearing for a few months. They have a yacht. We've been thinking about sailing around Cape Horn and into the South Pacific. I've always wanted to do that. I could use a long vacation." Jean's speech slowed as she walked to the window that looked out on the bay. "Maybe you could come along? They're Dutch. They could give a damn about what the U.S. suspects you of, and they have some good friends in the Port Authority here and in the Netherlands," Jean offered.

"Just leave?"

"Yes. Just leave. It's better than being held in detention while your attorney tries to convince them you're innocent. That process could take a long time. Come back in a few months. When the present hysteria has subsided." Jean sounded hopeful. "Have your attorney negotiate your 'surrender.'"

"But I couldn't leave Liz and Dru to deal with this mess alone." Lee turned the coffee mug in his hand as he spoke. A habit that drove Jean crazy.

 "Lee, how do you think you're going to get to Maine? The paper says they're searching every vehicle crossing into Portsmouth." She paused. "I'm sure the Amtrak Doweaster and Logan are no different."

Lee thought a moment. "Griff. You remember Griff? He has a son who is a physician in San Francisco. His wife died a few years ago, you remember? We spent some time with his family in Ogunquit many years ago."

"Yes. I remember. He's an advocate for AIDS research. So?" Jean sounded irritated.

"Well, when I saw him in Portland a few weeks ago he was planning on bringing his lobster yacht down to Boston to participate in some sort of fund-raiser. It was this week. He usually stays at the Parker House." Lee continued to turn the mug in his hand. Jean looked away. "He would help me, and I doubt anyone in the Coast Guard or Port Authority would question Griff. They all know him and his boat."

"Well, I still think my idea is a better one. For a number of reasons. The main being it would give you and me a chance we may never have again and..."

"And what happens after a few months?" Lee interrupted. "I go back to the States to surrender? They track me down? It ends. It always ends. We say goodbye at the airport or the train station, or now a police station." Lee's voice was rising, his face beginning to flush. He turned away from Jean. "God, I don't know that I could do that again. For years I blamed myself. I didn't have the guts or the good sense to follow through. I don't know. I..."

The intercom buzzer interrupted their conversation.

"Yes?" Jean inquired.

"Dr. Kudrick, there is a Mr. Elliot Smith here from, he says the Immigration and Naturalization Service. He wishes to see you. Shall I send him up?" Jean hesitated. They needed time to cover Lee's tracks.

"Yes, George. But wait five minutes before you send him up. I'm not dressed."

"Quickly, Lee, put away the second place setting. Grab your coffee." Lee put away his place setting while mumbling something about it being a quick breakfast. He grabbed the coffee, spilling half of it on the floor.

"It's okay," said Jean. "I'll get it. Are all of your clothes in the bedroom?" She mopped up the coffee with a dishtowel and threw it under the counter.

"I think so," said Lee, as Jean raced across the floor. "What about the bathroom? Are your towel and razor put away?"

"I'll take care of it," said Lee.

While Lee was in the bathroom Jean threw on a pair of slacks and a pullover sweater.

"Are you decent?" Lee called out from the bathroom.

"I'm okay. You can wait in the bedroom while I get rid of this guy. At least I hope I can get rid of him." Jean didn't sound very sure she could.

As he headed for the bedroom Lee stumbled over a kitchen stool, knocking it over.

"I've got it!" Jean caught it before it hit the floor. She rolled her eyes and smiled.

There was a knock at the door. Lee disappeared into the bedroom as Jean prepared to open the door. All Lee could hear through the bedroom door were muffled voices. Mr. Smith could be a federal agent indeed, one that works for the FBI, not the INS.

Lee waited. He thought of his family. He missed them. They must be so confused about what was happening. Lee certainly was. He thought of Jean and a cruise around Cape Horn. And the story of the fish who loved the bird and the bird who loved the fish, but where would they make a home together? He understood their dilemma.

Lee could no longer hear voices. He heard footsteps approaching the door. He took a deep breath. The door opened. It was Jean. Alone.

"Is he gone?"

"Yes," but she was shaking her head. "You look worried. What did he say? What did he want?" asked Lee.

"I'm not sure. He said he was here to discuss Ian's application for a visa. When I told him what had happened to Ian he apologized. He said he was sorry that he had not called." Jean shrugged. "But something didn't feel right. He kept looking around the apartment and he asked me a number of questions. How long I had been in the States? When I was planning on leaving? And how I was planning on returning to Europe?" Jean paused. "Why would he assume I might not be flying back to Europe?"

"What did he look like? Tall, thin, mid-fifties?"

"Well, not that tall. But thin. His suit seemed to just hang on him."

"I don't know, my love, but I think we may have just had a visit from Special Agent Jennings." Lee shook his head. Sadness clouded his eyes. "I think we may have to go with my plan. Our South Seas cruise may have to wait...wait for another life, I suppose."

The two looked at each other. Jean put her hand out and Lee took it. For a moment they were back in time. They held each other so tightly as if by doing so they could make the moment last. And they could. At least they could in their memory.

Lee broke the silence. "If we can find Griff, I can go back to The Cove with him. I can e-mail Violet from the hotel and she can contact my daughter and they can meet me there. A friend of Joe's has a lodge on Loon Lake near Baxter State Park. I could stay there while Joe tries to sort things out for me. I don't know. That's the best I can do. I think we had best act before Mr. Smith or Agent Jennings or whoever the hell he is returns with his friends."

"I'll call the Parker House," Jean said.

"No. Don't do that. They may be listening in. We'll just go to the Parker House."

"Well, you can't go looking like that. You'll need a disguise."

Jean quickly dug a pair of sunglasses, a tam with matching sport coat and handkerchief, and a raincoat out of the closet. "You can put the raincoat over your left arm to cover the hook. And we can't leave together. I'll leave first. Take a cab to the Westin. Take the elevator to the mezzanine. If they're following me I will lose them in the crowd. That place is always a mad house. And I'll take a cab back here. Trust me, I saw this in a movie. You leave after I leave. Go out through the garage and wait for me in the bakery on the corner. I'll have the cab stop and we'll pick you up."

"Well, it sounds good, I guess, especially if they're watching you. Maybe they've searched my office in Maine and found your letter and are just waiting for me to show up here. If they talk to your friendly doorman, Roger, they will know I'm here. I think we need to go now."

"I agree." said Jean. "Here's an umbrella as a finishing touch."

"God, you did work around those cloak and dagger guys too long!" Lee was only half kidding. Security at her old job had been tight, very tight. Jean became close friends with some of the other scientists working on projects at the Institute, projects they weren't allowed to discuss with anyone. Rumor was that some of these projects were funded by the CIA and involved research with bio-warfare agents such as drug-resistant strains of plague and other nasty things that apparently the Soviets were also working on developing. Jean said she never knew for sure, but whatever they had been doing stopped when the Cold War ended.

Jean had continued her friendship with one of these men, Ibraham Hussein. Lee had met Ibraham and liked him. He was a quiet and retiring soul, and Lee had a hard time believing he would be involved in the development of anything that would harm another person, much less be involved in the development of such bio-weapons.

Parking Garage
Wadsworth Place

Jennings pushed the elevator button for Level 1. No one else was in the elevator. As it moved past the other floors Jennings' heart began to race again. He was covered with sweat. His thoughts were moving even faster. What had he believed he would accomplish with this visit? He went there with the intention of planting a listening device, but couldn't. She never took her eyes off of him.

"Screw up. Screw up," he mumbled to himself. The door opened on level 1. A cold blast of air sent a chill through Jennings' entire body. He looked around. Where the hell was Wright parked? He couldn't remember. He wandered up one row of cars and then down another. He heard a voice calling his name. It was Wright. Jennings opened the car door slowly and slipped into the passenger seat.

"What happened, Doug? Did you plant the bug?"

"No," he said slowly, "I wasn't able to."

"I talked to the doorman," Wright said with some energy. "The guy who lives in the condo next door goes to work in the middle of the afternoon. I'll run the bug through when he leaves. Are you okay, Doug? You look pale. You're not having those chest pains again are you?"

"I'm okay," Jennings insisted.

"Gomez and Clark are back," said Wright trying to sound reassuring. "I'll send them over to Hussein's building to keep tabs on him. That's what you want me to do? Right?"

"Jim, you do what you think is best." Jennings' tone was dark.

"What?" He paused. "Are you sure you're okay?" Wright was clearly confused by Jennings' behavior.

"Are you my damn mother? I told you," Jennings continued to insist, "I'm okay."

"Sure, Doug. Fine." Wright wasn't sure what to do next. "I guess we should get back to the office. Command has called a meeting for noon and they expect you to be there."

"All right, get me back so I can get the damn meeting over with."

"Don't worry, Doug, I'll keep an eye on Dr. Kudrick and Dr. Brazil." Wright looked at Jennings asking for direction. "But our main concern is keeping up with Dr. Hussein. Right?"

Jennings didn't respond. He stared out of the car at the bay.

Jean left first. Lee dressed quickly and waited another ten minutes. He took the elevator to the basement. He slowly opened the door to the garage. No one was around. It was mid-afternoon on a Monday. He remembered the garage. He went out the exit door on the north side, followed the sidewalk to the street and walked at a normal pace to the bakery. He ordered a small cup of coffee and took a seat by the window and waited. Five, ten, fifteen minutes passed. He finished the coffee. Where was Jean?

Finally a cab pulled up at the curb. Lee sprang to his feet and in doing so knocked a chair over. The clerk looked at him. Lee picked the chair up, but in the process the overcoat slid off his arm exposing the hook. He picked the coat up quickly and left. He jumped in the cab next to Jean.

"The Parker House," she said. The cabbie nodded. Lee looked back at One Wadsworth Place and smiled at Jean.

"You have always amazed me, my dear."

"Sure," she smiled. "I bet you say that to all the girls."

The "T"
South Boston

"Next station, Roxbury Crossing."

Muqtada got to his feet. He had been going through it all again in his head. He had rehearsed the stops. He had timed it.

The subway doors opened. Muqtada mixed with the crowd of late afternoon riders. He blended in. It wasn't difficult. He found his way up the subway stairs. Some of the lights were out. There was garbage on the steps. Muqtada reached Bassin's building, a three-story, run-down brownstone. He had lived with Bassin for the past few weeks in a small apartment on the third floor.

He let himself in. Bassin was still at work. Muqtada waited for him. Once Bassin arrived they would make their evening prayers and then prepare their meal. They would talk. They would make certain all was ready. They had planned it both ways: If Ibraham honored his family, or if he does not.

The apartment was quiet. Muqtada dozed while he waited. He rarely slept at night. He heard Bassin's footsteps on the stairs. Muqtada met him at the door, filled with questions.

"Bassin, my friend, how has your day been? Have you arranged it?"

"Yes, yes. Do not worry. I have made the arrangements."

Bassin sounded confident. "Amon has use of his company's delivery truck. I will dress like him in one of the company uniforms. We have obtained a key to your brother's apartment." Bassin filled a saucepan with water for tea. "The storage pod was delivered to his building yesterday. We will be at his apartment before he returns. He will come with us." He struck a match and lit the old gas stove. "If he resists, we will sedate him. Do not worry, we will not harm him."

"You must be very careful. They watch his every move. If you are discovered, you will jeopardize our plan. You must not fail," he insisted.

"Yes, I understand." Bassin stopped and looked into Muqtada's eyes. "We will not fail. Tomorrow night you will see your brother. I promise it."

CHAPTER 14

Boston

The promised Nor'easter had blown out to sea and spared Boston. Yet the traffic was still slow. Although, it was mid-afternoon on a Monday, it always seemed on any day of the week and at any time of the day Boston could have a traffic jam.

The traffic started moving, and soon the hotel came into view. The cab dropped them at the main entrance. Lee paid the driver and followed Jean into the hotel lobby.

The Parker House was a beautiful old hotel with a cozy lobby and small rooms. The ambiance lent warmth to this cold April afternoon. Lee loved the oak and gilt. It reminded him of the old Mayflower Hotel in Cleveland that Jean and he had stayed years before.

Jean picked up the house phone. "Griff Martin's room, please." After several rings the operator came back on.

"Mr. Martin isn't answering. Do you wish to leave a message? I'll connect you to his voice mail."

"Please. . . Griff, this is Jean Kudrick. I'm in the hotel restaurant with an old friend of yours. I hope you will join us for . . . for tea." She hung up.

"For tea?" said Lee.

Jean looked around the lobby. "What else do you do at three o'clock on a Monday afternoon at the Parker House?"

"Well, my dear, let's have a spot of tea and a piece of Boston cream pie. The Parker House, after all, did introduce Boston cream pie to the world. And maybe a sandwich?"

"I knew you were hungry," said Jean. She knew Lee's appetite increased when he was anxious.

"Well, we did have a very quick and a very light breakfast, thanks to Mr. Smith."

The restaurant was empty except for two couples having tea and scones. Only one waiter appeared to be on duty. He showed Jean and Lee to a small table in the corner of the main room, apparently sensing that they wanted some privacy. He handed each a menu and left.

"Well, let's hope Griff returns to his room in the next hour or checks his voice mail," said Lee as he turned the water glass in his hand. Jean looked at the menu.

"I wish there was another option. But I think you're right. Going with me and my friends wouldn't be safe." Jean surveyed the dining room.

"In a number of ways," Lee tried making light of it all. "Liz would kill me. That woman takes 'til death do you part very seriously." Lee regretted the words before they were out of his mouth.

Jean didn't laugh. *Stupid, stupid, I say some of the stupidest things,* Lee said to himself. He tried to continue. "It is good to be with you again. It is always so easy when we are together. Until I make it difficult. Why can't it . . ."

Jean interrupted Lee. "Oh, for God's sake, don't."

"I was just going to say that the distance we felt in Nashville seems gone."

The waiter was back. Lee ordered a club sandwich and coffee. Jean ordered tea and scones. Lee had never cared for scones. He thought they belonged on the ice at a hockey game and not on a dining table.

After the waiter left with their order they sat quietly, each waiting for the other to speak first. Neither had pleasant memories of their meeting in Nashville. Jean and Ian had just gotten married the year before. They had lived together for years, but this was marriage. This was different. It meant something very special to Jean. She had retired and was spending most of her time traveling or skiing. Enjoying the things that she had never had time for when she was working eighteen hours a day in the lab. And Lee and Liz were busy being the parents of a young girl. Lee was still cranking out the long days and burning out badly in the process.

In Nashville there was a distance between them that they had never felt. So far apart that they could not bridge it. They had always kept alive the fantasy that someday they would be together again. But that had faded in Nashville. Over the next few years they talked only occasionally, exchanged Christmas cards. They did not talk of seeing each other again. It would be too confusing. Too painful. Over the last few years the cards and phone calls had almost stopped entirely. That is until Lee received Jean's letter. He hadn't replied. He didn't know what to say. If he could have stayed with Molly he might never have replied. No, that was not true.

It was back now, the fantasy. It was just a fantasy. It wasn't going to happen this time. Maybe never. But it was back.

"Retirement changes a person doesn't it, Jean? I remember being jealous when you retired." Lee paused. "But it's...it's great. Now I have the time to do things, like writing, that I never had enough time for when I was working." Lee waited for Jean's response but she stared at her water glass. "It also helps you get a better handle on just what is important in your life. In your sixties you can begin to see the end. You know it's out there. Some days you think its standing next to you, other days you're sure it's miles away, years away." Jean looked up.

"What are you trying to say, Lee?" asked Jean.

"I'm trying to say that maybe . . ."

"Maybe what?"

"That someday. . . well."

"Lee, we're in our mid-sixties." Her tone was one of irritation.

"Are you planning on living to be one hundred?"

"I certainly hope so." He couldn't think of a better response.

"As you pointed out to me last night we had our chance. We had our time. Will you leave the States and live with me in Europe?" She didn't wait for a response. "I doubt it. Will I come back to the States to live? My home, my friends are in Europe. My life is there." She looked directly at Lee. "I would not want to start over again. Even for you." She looked away.

"There was a time, a number of times when I would have done that. But not now. And you? Your family, your life is here in the States. You're hell-bent upon going home to Maine." She rolled her eyes and shook her head. "Even if they arrest you the moment you walk through the door."

Lee smiled. "The fantasy is back for you too, isn't it?"

"Well...yes. I guess." She hesitated. "But it is a foolish fantasy," she insisted.

"Maybe so, but . . ."

The waiter returned with their order. Jean offered Lee a scone, which he, of course, refused. They laughed. Lee offered Jean part of his sandwich, which she accepted. They talked very little over the meal. There was very little, it seemed, left to say.

It was well after 4:00 in the afternoon. They were just finishing their coffee and tea when a large man with a bushy white beard speckled with gray entered the main dining room. It was Griff. He recognized Lee immediately and moved quickly across the room to their table. He looked around a number of times to see if he was being watched. Nervously he said in a whisper, "Lee, what the hell are you doing here?"

"Sit down, Griff, and I'll explain."

Griff didn't move. "Shouldn't we go to my room so we can..." Griff looked around the room again.

"Okay. Sure," said Lee.

"Why don't I go first? Give me five minutes and then come up. It's room 312." Griff exited the dining room as quickly as he had entered it.

"Are you sure you can trust him?" Jean's voice had an anxious edge to it. "He seems awfully nervous. You don't think he will call the police, do you?" asked Jean.

Lee shook it off. "No. We'll just talk with him. If he doesn't want to get involved I'll...," he truly wasn't certain what he would do, "I'll think of something else."

In five minutes they were knocking on Griff's door. He quickly opened the door and waved them in while glancing up and down the hallway. Griff double-locked the door. Lee thought he would be a good role model for "acting suspiciously."

"Griff, calm down. If you don't feel comfortable with me being here, I will leave. It's okay. I understand."

"No, Lee, you just startled me. I assumed you were miles from Boston."

"Well, I would certainly like to be. That's what I came to talk with you about. When are you heading back to Maine?"

Griff was slow to answer. "Early tomorrow morning."

Lee's response was quick. "Can I go with you?"

Griff hesitated. "I'm only going to The Cove." He paused again. "Lee, there is no truth in these news reports is there?" He avoided Lee's eyes. "You wouldn't do anything that crazy, would you?"

Lee put his hand on Griff's shoulder and forced him to look at him. "You've known me for thirty-five years. I have done some crazy things, but I'm not a mass murderer."

"Okay, okay. I'm sorry. I shouldn't have even asked." Griff took a seat on the couch. "I know you're no terrorist. It's just that...I don't know. It's just a crazy world."

With that out of the way, Griff went straight to the details. "I plan to be in The Cove by late afternoon." Griff leaned forward and looked at Lee. "I anticipate rough seas. The storm that came down the coast was a big one. Portland got a foot-and-a-half of snow out of it."

"That's fine with me. I'll have someone meet me there." Lee explained about the Lodge on Loon Lake and Joe, his attorney, and how he thought he could get word to Dru and Liz of his planned arrival. They could call Joe. He could meet Lee in The Cove. That way Liz and Dru could stay out of it. Surely a U.S. citizen still had the right to meet with his attorney.

April 1, 2013
Agency Offices, Boston
6:15 P.M.

"So where the hell are they?" asked Jennings. "You guys managed to lose all three of them, Brazil, Kudrick, and Hussein?" He glared at Jim. "How did this happen, Jim?"

"I lost her at the Westin. When I doubled back to her apartment they were both gone."

Jennings was having a hard time concentrating. His heart was pounding. He couldn't think. Maybe he shouldn't have stopped taking the medication that Dr. Rodriguez gave him. Rodriguez had said it would help him with the depression and the anxiety and maybe the anger. Jennings was losing it.

"Hold on, Jim, just give me a second. I've got to think this out." But the only thought that was going through Jennings' brain was that these little Ivy League bastards weren't going to drive him out; weren't going to cost him his job. He had been worrying about this for a while. There were rumors. Jennings took a deep breath and closed his eyes. He thought about the North Sea and the sunset, and Margaret and he calmed down.

"Okay Jim, let's discuss this logically. Let's review our approach to the problem." Jennings went to the door of the office and yelled "Gomez! Clark! Get in here!" Jennings walked to the other side of the office and looked out at the bay and waited.

"Okay, what do the two of you have to say?" demanded Jennings.

"We followed procedure," said Gomez. "We covered the main exits in his building."

"Dr. Hussein must have gone out another exit. You followed procedure, but you don't know where your man is." Jennings voice was getting louder.

"We do have a lead to follow on Brazil and Kudrick," said Clark. His tone was optimistic. "The clerk at the bakery near her apartment saw them leave in a Yellow Cab. He didn't get the number."

"That means you're going to spend tonight interviewing Yellow Cabs until you find their driver," said Jennings. "Understand?"

"Yes sir," said Gomez.

"We'll get on it right now," said Clark.

"Then do it," snapped Jennings. "Do I have to do everything around here myself?"

Jennings could see the whole thing falling apart. He needed this one. They weren't going to screw it up for him.

"Where are Muqtada and Dr. Hussein?" asked Jennings glaring at Jim again. "When they get through with the Yellow Cabs Jim, have them check out that farm in southern Maine that the family bought when they came to the States. I know they sold it years ago, but Hussein has visited the couple who bought it."

"I'll get them on it in the morning. Why don't you get some rest, Doug. I'm going to grab a sandwich. Can I get you something?"

"No, no. I'll get something later."

Jennings sat at his desk and stared at the day's activity report. A lot of traffic on the Net. But where it led, Jennings didn't have a clue. There were times he missed Ron, his old partner. Ron would have had a clue.

Jennings opened the middle drawer of his desk and after a bit of fumbling, he found it. Ron had always carried it for luck. But on the day he was killed he had forgotten to take it—a GPS unit disguised as a fountain pen. Ron loved gadgets. Jennings remembered the sequence of twists and turns, the combination that turned it on and deployed the miniature tracking screen and control panel. It still worked. But Jennings didn't need the pen to tell him where he was. He knew. No place.

Parker House

Lee e-mailed Violet. "Yes," she responded, "I still know Elvish." Lee explained little and Violet had few questions. "Yes, I will contact your daughter and explain to her when she is to meet you and your friend," Violet typed. "I am glad to help." She still trusted Lee. He had helped her deal with the loss of her speech after the car accident. This, Lee thought, is a little healthy role reversal.

When Lee returned to the living room Griff was still talking about his work and the recent fund-raiser. "That's most of what I do these days," he was saying to Jean. "I still do a little bit of preaching when they ask me, but most of my time I spend sending letters and e-mails to the damn bureaucrats." Griff shook his head in disgust. "You know those guys won't even spend the money that has already been earmarked for research on AIDS?"

Lee's attention wasn't with Griff, which Griff soon realized. "We should get some sleep. You look like you need it, Lee. We will need to be up by 3:30 A.M. and at the wharf by 5:00. I want to get underway by 5:30." Griff stood up and took a few steps toward the bedroom. "I got the boat prepped this afternoon. Everything's on board except us. I'll have to give a little thought to where I put you." Griff paused. "Maybe the forward storage compartment. We could get boarded as we leave the harbor. The patrols have been a little bit more unpredictable lately. You can understand why."

"Great. I have enough of a problem with getting seasick and you're going to put me in a storage compartment," said Lee, half-joking and half-serious.

"Don't worry I'll give you a barf bag." Griff stroked his beard. "Yeah, I think that's the place to put you. It could be easily missed by a routine inspection." Griff nodded. "Yeah, that's where we'll put you."

"Now here's the rest of the plan. I'll leave in a separate cab. You two can follow me thirty minutes later. Jean, you drop Lee off at the dock, but I wouldn't go back to the apartment anytime soon."

"We've talked about that," said Jean. I'll have the cab drop me at Benny's. You remember Benny's on Northern Avenue in South Boston? I'll have breakfast, spend a couple of hours there before going back to the apartment. Hopefully by then the two of you will be out of the harbor and heading north." Jean was beginning to have second thoughts about going back to her apartment. Maybe she would go someplace else for a few days.

For what little sleep they might get Griff offered them the couch. Neither felt like sleeping or, for that matter, talking. They snuggled up against each other and drifted in and out of sleep.

For Lee the dream came again. Lee was on the edge of the ledge. Jean was on the other side. Lee was ready to jump, but Jean begged him to wait. Not to jump. There was time. They could find another way across. Another way to be together. He shouldn't risk it. There was time.

"Lee, Jean...it's time," Griff whispered.

"Oh, God! Is it that time already?" Lee rubbed his eyes.

"Come on guys. We've got miles to go before we sleep," said Jean. She was on her feet.

"I think I've heard that before. You always were disgustingly cheerful in the morning," said Lee.

"Well, some things never change," said Jean as she headed off to the bathroom.

"Yeah," said Lee, "like you beating me to the bathroom!"

Griff was dressed and ready to leave. "Here's the address." He handed Lee a slip of paper. "It's in the Marine Industrial Park. I have an old friend who lets me keep my boat there. Tell the driver it's off Black Falcon Avenue. He'll find it." Griff stepped toward the door. "Give me thirty minutes before you leave and don't be late."

"I made some coffee, help yourself. Oh, and when I check out I'll tell the desk clerk that the two of you are friends of mine who came over late last night, drank too much, and fell asleep on my couch. I'll give him fifty dollars. I know him. It'll be fine." And with that Griff was out the door.

Neither Jean nor Lee had to dress since they had slept in their clothes. They made some effort to straighten out the wrinkles, but with little success. Jean fixed her hair and freshened her makeup. Lee smiled.

"Hey, don't laugh. It's important," said Jean moving the brush through her hair.

"You look fine. How about me?" asked Lee opening his arms and bowing slightly.

"Other than looking like you slept in your clothes, you look great."

Two weak cups of coffee later they cautiously opened the room door. The hall was empty. After all, it was four in the morning. They walked quietly to the elevator.

As they passed the front desk the clerk winked and bid them goodnight. Outside the wind was up and it was cold. *Really great weather for sailing. God help us,* Lee thought.

There was one lonely cab near the hotel entrance. The driver was taking a nap. Lee tapped on the window. The cabbie woke with a start and unlocked the passenger door. He appeared to be Indian or Pakistani.

"Where to?" he said.

"Boston Marine Industrial Park. Forty-six Dolphin Way. It's off of Black Falcon Avenue," said Lee.

"In South Boston?"

"Yes," said Lee a little concerned that the driver might not know where it was.

The city was dark and quiet. The lights of the harbor came into view as they crossed Ft. Point Channel. Lee thought he could hear the muffled sound of an old Tony Bennett and k.d. lang song, "If We Never Meet Again," coming from the driver's CD player.

"You're a Tony Bennett fan?" Lee asked the driver.

"Yes sir, *Wonderful World,*" said the driver, referring to the name of the CD. Lee wasn't too sure that was true. "Love never dies," sang Tony. "Forever I will love you if we never meet again."

Lee knew that would be true. He felt tears welling up in his eyes. He reached for Jean's hand. She took it.

South Boston was still sleeping, but the Marine Park was another matter. At this time of morning it was alive with activity. Trucks were being loaded and unloaded. Workers were arriving and leaving. Finding Dolphin Way in the dark and confusion of early morning was not easy. After backing up a couple of times and turning around at least three times, the driver stopped to ask directions.

"Finally," whispered Jean.

"Don't say it," said Lee.

Another five minutes and they were at the address on the paper. Lee saw Griff's boat, *The John Wesley II,* bobbing at the dock. The cabin and running lights were on. *The John Wesley I* had met an untimely end a few years before. Lee turned to Jean. Here they were once again at a place so familiar. Saying good-bye again.

"Well," Lee said, extending his hand. Jean did not take it. She reached for him and held him for a moment. "I love you." He whispered. "I always have and . . ." She smiled and nodded. She said nothing. Lee stepped out of the taxi. He handed the driver his last fifty-dollars.

"Take her to Benny's on Northern Avenue and make sure she gets in safely." Lee didn't trust South Boston in the daytime much less at five in the morning.

"Thank you, sir," said the driver with a perfect British accent.

The cab pulled away. Lee watched its taillights disappear in the early morning fog.

CHAPTER 15

...It's enough to be moving on home, build it behind your eyes,
carry it in your heart....Enough to be on your way.
— James Taylor

Tuesday, April 2nd, 2013
Boston Harbor
The Last Day of Passover

Lee approached Griff's boat cautiously. The cabin and running lights were on, but Griff was nowhere in sight. Lee could hear the radio. Griff must be checking the weather. Lee climbed down the ladder to the boat and carefully slipped onto the boat's deck. Griff must have heard him because he was immediately topside.

"I see you found us. Now let's get you below before you're seen."

Lee nodded and walked quickly across the deck into the wheelhouse and down the stairs to the forward cabin.

"Here, try this on for size." Griff pointed to a large storage bin tucked neatly behind the port wall of the forward cabin. "Go ahead, I'll boost you up."

The cut on Lee's hand was better, but he still needed help from Griff to climb in. "You should be able to breathe okay in there."

"I hope so," said Lee with concern.

"You'll have to find something to hang onto. I don't want you rolling around in there making noise if we're boarded."

Griff gave Lee an old belt and together they made a hangstrap.

"Now, we just need a subway car to attach this to," said Lee. Griff smiled.

"You'll need to stay in there until we're out of the harbor. Security is so tight around Logan these days. The Harbor Patrol may insist on coming aboard."

"Okay. Just tell me when we're clear and give me a barf bag. The way this water feels I may need it before we're out of the harbor."

Griff replaced the false wall. It was pitch dark inside. *Great for really making someone seasick, Lee thought.*

Griff started the engines. His lobster yacht, a forty-five footer built at the Brothers' Yard in Downeast, Maine, was powered by two Olds 88 engines. Using old Buick and Olds engines in lobster boats was still common practice. They were cheaper to install than diesel and with gas at seven-plus dollars they could be found at a good price.

Griff slowly backed out from the wharf. He gave a couple of loud blasts on his horn, slipped the boat into stop, revved the engines again and yelled down to Lee. "Full speed ahead and damn the torpedoes."

They were heading for the main channel. A northwesterly wind came around the corner of the wheelhouse sending spray from the bow wave onto the gunnel. The harbor was choppy.

Below deck Lee held onto the strap and imagined how the open ocean must be if this was the harbor. Lee loved the ocean but not on days like today. He was not a strong swimmer. He had learned to swim late in life. He had almost drowned as a child and carried that fear with him over the years. But hell, what good was swimming in the North Atlantic? Without a survival suit he would last fifteen, maybe twenty minutes in the water before he lost consciousness. In another fifteen minutes he'd be dead. Most of the lobstermen, especially the older ones, didn't know how to swim.

"Don't need to," they would say. "If you go down the most merciful thing that could happen to ya would be for your hip waders to fill with water and take you straight to the bottom."

"Harbor Patrol off starboard side," shouted Griff. "And they're heading our way. But don't worry the water is too rough for them to board us." Lee could hear their boat drawing closer. "I think they're just going to give us an escort out of the harbor." Lee waited. "Yeah. That's Larry Cutts," yelled Griff. "He's waving. We're okay."

As they left the protection of the harbor the water became rougher. Lee rolled around in the bin in the dark and was getting more seasick by the minute. "Hang on. I'll be down when I can," yelled Griff.

But the swells were larger now. The boat rolled back and forth, up and down, and so did Lee. He had never liked carnival rides and this was much worse. A half-hour passed, then an hour. The storm seemed to be blowing stronger. Griff was continuing to yell down, what Lee hoped were words of encouragement and reassurance. But they were drowned out by the howl of the wind.

Lee's heart was pounding so hard he thought it might explode. He thought of his mother. They say everyone thinks of their mother just before they die. But thinking of her calmed Lee. She had been a strong woman. She broke her hip in her eighties and fought to walk again. She struggled with blindness in her nineties.
She never gave up and neither would Lee.

At some point the boat lunged forward and Lee became fully airborne. He flew headfirst into the bow end of the compartment wall. There was a flash of blue light and Lee lost consciousness. When he opened his eyes he was lying in his own vomit. It was still dark, but Howard was there. He could see his face very clearly.

"Come on," Howard said. "Let's go, Doc." He was inside the flying machine. It was a large silver ball. The top was transparent. He could see Howard leaning over the controls. Studying them. "Let's go," he said again.

Lee shook his head and closed his eyes. When he opened his eyes Howard was gone. It was completely dark again. Lee could hear the drip and trickle of water. He could smell the musty smell of the mine. The sound of running water was becoming louder. He must get out. The shaft must be filling with water. In the dark he could see the outline of the metal door to the escape shaft. He pushed. He pulled. It would not open. He began to beat on it with his fists. Suddenly it sprang open. Light flooded into the shaft. Someone had opened the door.

"Stella?" he said. He could not see his rescuer. He was being helped out of the shaft. He was going to be okay. Everything was going to be okay. He closed his eyes.

Agency Offices, Boston
10:00 A.M.

Jennings was staring blankly at the computer screen when Jim entered the office. "Good news, Doug," said Jim, sounding upbeat. "We know where Brazil is." He waited for Jennings' response, but didn't get one. "He's on a lobster boat heading north. He's with an old friend of his, Griff Martin. Exactly where they're going, we don't know." He waited again, but there was no response. "The weather will make it hard for us to intercept them before they land. But we're tracking them on radar. We've got a chopper in the area."

"Good. Okay, Jim," said Jennings showing little enthusiasm for Jim's news. "But do we know where Kudrick or Hussein is?"

"Kudrick hasn't returned to her apartment and Hussein, no idea. Gomez and Clark are on their way to Maine. They will check out the farm and then assist the local agents in taking Brazil into custody."

"Anything on Muqtada?" Jennings sounded depressed.

"No," said Jim apologetically.

North Atlantic
Maine Coast

When Lee woke, he was lying in a bunk in the main cabin. Griff was talking to him. "I'm sorry but I couldn't leave the wheel. The sea as rough as she was. How's your head? You've got one hell of a goose egg there."

Lee felt the left side of his head. "You're right about that. How long was I out?"

"I don't know. I came down about half an hour ago. You were beating on the wall, talking crazy when I got you out. Mumbling something about a mine and water coming in. We took a little water on this morning but . . ."

"It's a long story, Griff. When we have the time I'll tell you about it," said Lee.

"You alright now? I've got to get back up top."

Lee nodded and the motion made his head throb. "What time is it?" Lee's watch had stopped running.

"It's about 2:00 P.M. We're just passing the Isle of Shoals starboard side. If you come topside, keep your head down. I don't know if we're being watched. A helicopter flew over a few minutes ago. That's unusual this time of year." Griff stroked his beard. "It wasn't a Coast Guard chopper."

Lee tried to get up. The ocean was calmer, but Lee felt dizzy. His head felt all fuzzy. As if it were stuffed with cotton. Sunlight streamed into the cabin from the wheelhouse. The wind had died down. The only sound was the churning of the engines and the crackling of the radio.

Lee decided to lie down. He thought of his wife and daughter. *The John Wesley II* should make The Cove by late afternoon. Would they be there? Would Joe? Would the other they, the Homeland Security folks, be there? Agent Jennings?

Lee fell into a deep sleep. He did not dream. When he woke again it was late afternoon. He was able to stand up without losing his balance. His head still hurt but he was not dizzy. He climbed the stairs to the wheelhouse. The rocky coast of Maine stretched out in both directions as far as he could see. To the starboard side was the open ocean. It was easy to understand why smugglers loved the Maine coast. Hundreds of miles of rugged shoreline with countless coves. Guns for Revolutionary War soldiers, rumrunners in the 1920s and 1930s and, more recently, drug dealers. And now him.

Lee thought about his friend Griff, so willing to help. Griff loved the ocean. His younger son loved it even more. Todd had his own boat and fished until he was so sick he could not haul the traps. He died of AIDS five years ago. The AIDS epidemic had grown worse since his death. In the last ten years seventy million people were dead worldwide. More, as Griff liked to point out, than all the people who had died in WWI and WWII combined. The U.S. unfortunately, had still not gotten the message. Funding for research and prevention was only a fraction of what was needed. The richest country in the world was still spending its money on bombers and tanks, believing the military could protect the country.

Griff had grown up in Texas. He trained for the ministry as a young man. After eight years he left the church and moved his young family to Maine. Griff supported them through working as a grant writer for local human service organizations. They rented a small, hardscrabble farm—a poor man's farm—and home- schooled their children. The two oldest left Maine for college. They were good students and found jobs in other places. They did not return to Maine. Todd, their youngest, stayed to work the farm and fish.

Soon after Todd became ill Griff's wife died suddenly. Griff seemed to recover from Beth's death, but Todd's illness shook him to the core. While Todd was still alive Griff decided to return to the ministry. He took a position as a pastor with a small church near their home and spent the rest of his time caring for Todd and being an AIDS activist. "I need to do both," he said. In a strange way he seemed more content with his life now than in all the years that Lee had known him.

"We'll be at The Cove soon," said Griff. "I'm going to slow her down a bit so we'll enter The Cove after dark.

There aren't too many year-rounders and those who work in the village will be home by then having their supper." Griff paused. "Flo's will have a few regulars, but that should be it for a Tuesday night."

As afternoon turned to evening the sky, which had begun to clear, was again filled with clouds. The wind picked up and a gray, cold, fog rolled across the water from the shore and settled over the boat. As they approached the shore the last light of day was fading. Passover was ending. Griff slowed the engine to an idle and threw it out of gear. They passed under the footbridge and slipped silently into The Cove. The summer cottages and shops were dark. The summer people would not arrive for another two months. A couple of lonely streetlights lit the fog. The only building that appeared alive with light was Flo's.

Flo's stood on a hill behind The Cove. A white clapboard building with large windows. To the east, the Atlantic and to the west, the salt marshes.

"The best view in town," Flo would say. Her specialty was her fish chowder and fried clams. She and her clam shack, as she liked to call it, had been here for as long as Lee could remember. She refused to sell to the out-of-staters who made her regular offers.

Flo was now surrounded by "preppie" shops, as she called them, and "la-de-da" restaurants that catered to the summer people. The summer crowd was welcome at Flo's. But most of her business was local. Peeling paint and worn vinyl booths did not appeal to the summer people who now owned most of The Cove.

As they approached the pier Lee saw the outline of a man. He stood near the gangway that led to the float where Griff would drop Lee before tying the boat for the night.

Griff pulled in close to the float and Lee scrambled over the side. He fell. The man came down the gangway.

"Are you okay?" It was Joe, his attorney and friend. He recognized the voice.

"Well, you tell me," Lee replied.

Joe said nothing until he reached Lee's side. He was Lee's age, but looked a bit younger. When he started losing his hair a few years back he shaved his head. He was in better shape than Lee. He prided himself on eating well and on regular exercise.

"We have a problem," Joe said.

"Are Liz and Dru okay?" Lee's heart was starting to beat faster.

"They're fine. The problem is the Feds know you're here."

"How?" asked Lee and he took a slow deep breath.

"Some kid in a bakery recognized you. The hook. Saw you leave in a Yellow Cab. The Feds must have interviewed half the Yellow Cab driver's in Boston before they found the one that drove you to the Parker House and then they figured out Griff was the person you were meeting there." Joe put his hand on Lee's shoulder. "A few more hours and well, maybe you could have made it to the lodge."

"So, where are they?" asked Lee.

"Chief Dutremble is here. He's on the radio arguing about jurisdiction. But I'm sure the Feds are on the phone right now with the governor's office. We'll lose this one. The Feds always win on jurisdiction. Being a good Southern boy you should know that."

"But why aren't they here?" Lee was feeling impatient with Joe's answers.

"I don't think they've been able to get through. There's an accident that's blocking the only road into The Cove. When Dru heard they knew you were coming she e-mailed Violet. I don't know what she did, but we were the last car to get through before Kim and Steve had one of their trademark 'accidents.'"

"Are they okay?" Lee had to concentrate on his breathing. Slow and deep.

"Oh, it was just one of their 'fender benders.' They managed to block both lanes and the shoulders with their vans. And, of course, they had to drop their lifts and come out in their chairs to inspect for possible damage. I would say it would be an hour or so before the boys from Boston get them to move. Vic has the only wrecker for miles around and I bet he's having supper right now."

Kim and Steve were two old friends of Lee's who were known for their activism around disability issues. They were early members of ADAPT—American Disabled for Attendant Programs Today—a very long name for a very active and some would say radical, organization for persons with a disability. They were experts in the art of tying up traffic and frustrating federal officials.

"So, I would say you have an hour or so to spend with your family before - - "

"Liz and Dru are here?"

"Yeah. They're waiting for you at Flo's. The booth in back. An Agent Jennings . . ." Lee was climbing the steps to Flo's before Joe could finish his sentence.

April 2, 2013
Agency Offices, Boston
6:05 P.M.

"What do you mean the local chief has Brazil in protective custody?" shrieked Jennings. "I talked to Brazil's attorney earlier this afternoon. We had a deal. What are those local yahoos doing up there?" He glared at Wright. "Where the hell are Gomez and Clark?" Jennings was pacing.

"They are tied up with an accident on the road leading into The Cove." He paused. "Apparently two handicapped vans hit each other and are blocking the road."

"Well, tell them to push them off of the road. I want us to do one damn thing right today." Jennings' face was turning red.

"Sir, I don't think they are likely to do that. It's against policy." Wright waited.

"Get me the head of the State Police up there. They damn well know this is our call and not theirs."

"I have already talked to him. He is on the phone right now with the governor's office and Chief Dutremble."

"And the farm?"

"They've checked it. No one has seen or heard from Hussein."

"Great, that's just great, Jim. Time is running out. Something has to break our way soon. Ideas?"

Wright shook his head and met Jennings' cold stare with his eyes. "Doug, we're doing everything we can."

April 2, 2013
The Cove
6:15 P.M.

"Evenin', Doc," said Flo as Lee slipped through the door. "They're in the back." Flo was a very large woman who was always behind the bar. She had jet-black dyed hair, Lee assumed, since Flo had to be in her seventies. She had a large nose and usually wore a loose-fitting dress, often quite colorful, that more resembled a bathrobe.

Two regulars were sitting at the bar. They did not acknowledge Lee. As Lee turned the corner to the main dining room, Dru bounced into his arms. Dru was a petite young woman with short brown hair, large brown eyes, and olive skin. Simply beautiful.

"How are you, Dad?" she said.

"Oh honey, I'm okay." Lee changed the focus of the conversation. "How's your mom? How are you?"

"Well, Mom's taking it pretty hard. She's really worried about you this time."

"Honey, your mom's always worried about me. I'm okay. Joe will take care of this."

"I'm afraid he won't be able to," said Liz who was now standing behind Dru.

"Hey, I told you I would be home before Passover was over," Lee said, wrapping his arm around his wife.

Liz smiled. "It ended at sundown, but you were close."

"Hey, the story of my life. Close, but no cigar." Lee smiled.

Liz's hair was cut short. Almost completely gray. She was a beautiful woman who had retained her shape as the years had passed and threatened to take it from her. She was crying. Her eyes were red and her nose was running. Lee gave her Ian's handkerchief, the one that Jean had given him.

"Honey, this is still America. Land of the Free. It's not Nazi Germany. We're not in WWII. Come on now, I'm hungry and I want to hear about other things." Turning to his daughter, "Tell me about school and this new love of your life, Mr. Woodford."

Dru looked confused, but complied. "I...I don't know. He's different from a lot of the guys I've dated. He's got a direction for his life."

Lee smiled. "Good. What direction...is he planning --"

"-- his direction?" Liz interrupted. "Is this what we need to talk about now? What did Joe tell you to tell the FBI?"

Lee turned to her. "Liz, I'm going to tell them the truth. I've got nothing to hide."

"I don't know that that's the wisest thing to do, Lee. You ran away from that camp, didn't you? That's what Joe told me."

"I walked away. And since when is telling the truth a bad idea?" he snapped. He felt like yelling. He wasn't sure why. He took a deep breath. "Let's just stop. We will have time to talk about this later. Let's just enjoy the fact that we're together." Lee put his hand to his face trying to hide the tears that were welling up in his eyes. "I'm sorry, I just don't understand..." He couldn't finish the sentence.

Flo arrived with three bowls of chowder and Shipyard Ales. "On the house," she said. God love Flo.

Lee listened to his family, trying hard to concentrate on them and nothing else. He ate the chowder and drank the ale. He had a good view of the road from their table. Around 7:00 he saw a string of blue lights coming across the marsh. They would be at Flo's in a few minutes. They would push past Chief Dutremble and Joe. But it was going to be okay. Lee was with his family and his friends. He was close to Home.

SECTION I: FEAR

Chapter Summaries, Discussion Questions and Author's Comments

Foreword - Chapter 15*

Foreword

Benjamin, the grandson of the main character, Lee, introduces the story and describes his grandfather. He tells you that the focus of this story is terrorism: "Acts of terrorism perpetrated on our people by our nation's enemies and by the disabling mechanisms of our own society." He explains that his grandfather had a disability and that one of the struggles for his grandfather was acceptance.

Discussion Questions

1. What do you believe some of the "disabling mechanisms" of our society are?

2. Based on the little that you have been told about the main character, Benjamin's grandfather, Lee, why do you think acceptance might be an issue for him?

Author's Comments

Fear can be one of the most disabling mechanisms that can operate within a society. Lee's disability has much to do with his concerns about acceptance.

*Refer to pages 4 and 5 for a list of the Eleven Skills And Attitudes That Build Resilience.

CHAPTER 1

It is the beginning of Passover in the year 2013. Dr. Lee Brazil returns to the South to work on a book about the New, or as he sees it, the Not-So-New South. Lee has never made peace with the South he grew up in as a disabled child, or with the nuclear industry he blames for his disability.

As Lee is leaving Pine Grove, an "accident" occurs at one of the nuclear plants. He is caught up in the ensuing disaster and implicated in what the authorities believe is a terrorist plot. He is taken to a decontamination center. He is suffering from radiation poisoning.

In Boston, Special Agent Jennings of the FBI awakes to the news that he is being reassigned to the investigation at Pine Grove. He has been pursuing a terrorist cell led by an Iranian, Muqtada Hussein, who he believes is planning a bio-terror attack in the U.S. He resists the reassignment, but complies with his orders.

Muqtada, also in Boston, sees the opportunity that now exists. With the government focused on the disaster at the Pine Grove Labs, he has an opportunity to pursue his plan. If he can only obtain the cooperation of his brother, Ibraham, he will be able to create a device that will quickly spread the virus. His brother, he believes, will have no choice. He must honor his family.

Discussion Questions

1. What are the primary stressors that each character is confronting?

Author's Comments

For Lee, the main stressors are physical ones. He is frightened and confused, but his body is trying to deal with a toxic exposure. Jennings is recovering from prostate cancer and a divorce. The main stressor is being pulled away from his work on Project Outbreak. Since Margaret left, his work is what he has built his life around. Muqtada is without a home and recovering from the loss of a hand and part of his arm. For Muqtada, time is the main stressor. "The time is now." Muqtada has spent too much of his life waiting for an opportunity to redeem his and his family's honor.

*Refer to pages 4 and 5 for a list of the Eleven Skills And Attitudes That Build Resilience.

CHAPTER 2

Lee is interrogated by Major Henderson regarding Pine Grove. Agent Jennings passively participates in the interrogation. Lee is placed in a room with a homeless, schizophrenic man, Howard, who is at the decontamination center because he refused to be evacuated with the others. He tells Lee of having been abused by his family, of having his children taken from him by the Department of Human Services. He believes that he has created a machine that can travel to other worlds and is angry that the government has no interest in his invention.

Discussion Questions

1. In what ways does Howard demonstrate resilience?

2. How do you think Howard's psychiatric illness, which becomes evident as he tells his story, has prevented or helped him adapt to adversity?

3. In what manner does Lee begin to demonstrate his ability to "bounce back?"

4. What are the differences between the politics of hope and the politics of fear?

Author's Comments

Howard's support network is very limited and apparently always has been. He has had few positive role models in his life and little support from others. Due to his illness, his thinking process is disordered and severely impairs his ability to adapt to change. He has, however, been able to survive on the streets for a long period of time and, as it will become clear as the story unfolds, he is much more resilient than he first appears. As you will see, Howard has plans for the future and takes action. He also communicates and attempts to solve problems. He tries to find meaning in what is happening and to make sense out of his world.

Lee demonstrates his ability to problem solve, to communicate and to adapt to adverse situations, e.g., when he puts together an outfit for himself from the clothing left in the room. He does, however, let his feelings about the south color his relationship with Major Henderson.

The politics of fear should be familiar to all of us, having lived through the post 911 years. Leaders of a society may resort to using the politics of fear as a way of manipulating and controlling its members. In general, the politics of fear focuses on exclusion and the questioning of difference. You're either for us or against us. In contrast, the politics of hope focuses on inclusion and the assumption that difference and diversity will benefit a society and should be welcomed rather than always questioned. It is not immediately assumed that if someone disagrees with you or wants to debate an issue that they are against you.

CHAPTER 3

Lee learns from Major Henderson that his high school friend, Dave, who works at the Labs, was killed in the explosion. Lee also learns that a manuscript by a friend of his, Angus, which is a fictional story about a disaster at Pine Grove, was found among Lee's possessions. The government now believes Lee is involved in a conspiracy and that the accident was an act of terror by him and his two friends.

Agent Jennings leaves Pine Grove to return to Boston. He recalls his efforts to convince his superiors that a bio-terror attack is likely. He meets another older agent and complains about the new agents he is working with. They are good with computers and lab coats but have no street smarts.

Muqtada cannot sleep. He rides the T's Green Line late at night recalling the young Jewish woman he fell in love with in his youth, and how the relationship was destroyed by their fathers.

Discussion Questions

1. What resilience skills do you see Lee practicing in Chapter 3?

2. Even though Keating is "an old friend," how comfortable is Jennings in talking about himself? Why?

3. It appears that Muqtada has never been able to get over the loss of Fran. Why not?

4. How does Lee deal with the death of his old friend Dave?

Author's Comments

Lee demonstrates a number of different skills. He manages to use thinking and, specifically, writing as a way of making sense of what has happened to him. He is actively engaged in planning and thinking about the future, and he discharges some of the emotion that has built up by allowing himself to cry, something most men are taught not to do at a very early age. And he prays "for himself and for his world." But the intense fear that has been stirred by the events that Lee is caught up in is reflected in a dream that will appear a number of times in the story.

Jennings has shut himself off from others, has difficulty communicating with Keating and is fearful to share very much about himself with anyone.

Muqtada has never resolved the loss of Fran and has never been able to replace her or create other relationships in his life that can meet the needs that the relationship with Fran met. His "connections" to others that he can trust and seek support from are very few.

Lee allows himself to grieve rather than trying to avoid or deny his feelings.

CHAPTER 4

After being exposed to the first rain after the explosion, the guards at the decontamination center become ill with radiation poisoning. With the help of Howard, Lee manages to escape. Howard leads him to an old amusement park that Lee use to visit as a child. He tells Lee that his invention, the machine to travel to other worlds, is near the park. Lee tells Howard that he must try to get back to his family in Maine. Howard helps Lee stow away in the cargo of a flatbed truck carrying portable toilets.

Discussion Questions

1. Lee leaves the detention center with Howard. Is this an impulsive act? What would you have done?

2. As Howard and Lee cross Cherokee Park (page 35), Lee remembers the "World of Awe," the freak show, and is disturbed by the memory. Why?

Author's Comments

Leaving the detention facility with Howard was an impulsive act. Lee had not planned it or thought it out. He was acting on emotion and the desire to escape, being very human, but not thinking through the consequence of his action, which he finally does on page 34, when he "took stock of his situation."

Lee is both attracted and repulsed by the freak show and confused by how he should react. Lee's own fears and uncertainties about how he is viewed by others, his self-image and lack of self-confidence, are stirred by his memories of the "freak" show. He is sure some people view him in the same way, as a freak.

CHAPTER 5

Lee tries to sleep, but recalls his reasons for leaving White's Fork, the racism and greed, and for returning: his family, his youth in the Cherokee mountains. When the truck stops to deliver a portable toilet to an old coal mine-turned-tourist-attraction, Lee, hungry and thirsty, gets off the truck. But he cannot get back aboard without assistance and ends up having to take refuge in the mine.

Discussion Questions

1. What is your interpretation of the quote from *Fiddler on the Roof* that begins the chapter?

2. In this chapter, we learn much about Lee and his past. What are some of the ways in which he has demonstrated resilience in his life?

3. At the end of the chapter, Lee decides to "grab a helmet and a light" and "tour the coal mine." Is this an impulsive act?

Author's Comments

Lee talks again in this chapter about having used writing as a way of releasing "his anger and hurt." He also shows some insight into his relationships with other people and admits some of the mistakes that he has made in the past, such as in his relationship with Susan, "They were in love. Lee held on tight, too tight" (page 38). The importance of the church and religious beliefs and values throughout his life is also discussed.

Lee thought about his decision about going deeper into the mine, realizing that he could not stay at the entrance to the mine where he would very easily be discovered. He made some effort to reframe with humor what he was doing by saying that he "had always wanted to tour a coal mine."

CHAPTER 6

In the mine Lee finds an escape shaft where there are blankets and water. He falls asleep and in his mind travels back to his hometown. He remembers his family, particularly his grandfather. Soon he is discovered by Stella who runs the tourist attraction at the mine. She tells him that there has been a second attack on Pine Grove Labs and she is frightened. The two spend the night in the mine. Muqtada dreams of his family and recalls the deaths of his father and mother, his father's rejection of him and his father's love for his younger brother, Ibraham.

Discussion Questions

1. When Lee thinks he has lost the watch that his daughter gave him, he comes close to having an anxiety attack. Why is this watch so important to him?

2. Lee remembers his visit to the cemetery and thinks of George (page 44). In what ways did George practice resilience in his life?

3. You learn about Stella and her life in this chapter. In what ways has she shown the ability to adapt to adversity?

4. What does Muqtada's dream tell us about the issues in his life?

Author's Comments

For Lee the watch represents his connection to a very important person in his life, his daughter. Losing it at this point in his life threatens his sense of security since it is one of the few things that he has left that is a concrete connection to his family.

George demonstrated a number of the principles of resilience in his life. He showed flexibility in adapting to his heart disease. He continued to make plans and take action on them and move toward his goals. He did not allow the fear of early death to control his life.

Stella, like Howard, is a survivor. She has had a very difficult life. One of her main sources of support is her connection to her God and her religious beliefs. She demonstrates the ability to communicate, and control her emotions. Her emotional control is perhaps too tight, with her suppressing and not dealing with much of what she feels and choosing to withdraw and isolate herself from others. Her thinking is much more pessimistic than optimistic with her assumptions about her life falling more into the pervasive, permanent and personal blame categories. She has never resolved many of her feelings around the death of her son.

Muqtada's dream reflects again the unresolved issues in his life, e.g., the rejection by his father, the lack of support from family and/or friends, and the failure to create a "home" for himself.

CHAPTER 7

In the morning, Stella tells Lee that God has told her to help him. She explains to him that she has been grieving the loss of her son and that is why she left her family in Tennessee and took the job at the mine. She helps Lee get an old truck running. Lee agrees to pay for the truck when he gets home. Lee heads north again, but the truck breaks down in the mountains of Western Pennsylvania as a snowstorm begins.

Discussion Questions

1. In what ways does Stella show flexibility and demonstrate problem solving?

2. Is Lee thinking clearly about the trouble that he is in (review bottom half of page 49)? Why not?

3. Is Lee an optimist or a pessimist? Explain your answer.

4. Why do you think American society tends to be more reactive than proactive?

5. Are hope and optimism the same thing?

Author's Comments

Throughout the chapter, Stella demonstrates the ability to be flexible in her behavior and thinking. At the beginning of the chapter, she decides that she will help Lee, since this is God's will. She thinks about how she can help him, coming up with a truck, clothing and money that she is willing to give this stranger. She is acting in ways that are consistent with her beliefs and values.

Lee clearly is trying to convince himself, to deny, that he is in trouble and that Major Henderson and Agent Jennings have more important things to do than pursue him. Denial can relieve stress temporarily.

Lee, like most of us is a combination of optimism and pessimism. When negative feelings are upon us initially, it is hard to remember that most things, both good and bad, are temporary rather than permanent. We easily forget that most events have a specific rather than a pervasive impact on our lives and that blaming ourselves or others tends not to make the situation better.

Many people in our society have denied that bad things are going to happen to them. Saving and managing debt has not been a priority. Taking care physically and emotionally is seen as a nice thing to do, especially for the other guy.

Preparing for a disaster, such as an act of terrorism or a financial crisis, may be seen by some politicians as capitulation, as giving in, accepting that we may not be able to prevent them. We need to change our thinking. Denial and minimization do not work well for a society, especially one that is in a leadership role internationally.

The two, optimism and hope, seem very similar to me. With both, bad things don't last forever. They usually do not have a pervasive effect on our lives and blaming ourselves or others is not a necessary step to accountability for either.

CHAPTER 8

A woman in an old tow truck stops to help Lee. She tows the truck to the garage where she works. The mechanic isn't available but is at Bambi's, a bar and strip joint next door. Lee goes there to find the mechanic and meets Millie, an elderly black woman in a wheelchair who runs the place. She takes an interest in Lee. He tells her his predicament and she agrees to help him find a ride north.

Discussion Questions

1. In what form is Lee's resilience demonstrated in this chapter?

2. In this chapter, Millie tells her story. How does she exhibit resilience in her life? How has she dealt with her disability?

Author's Comments

In this chapter, Lee continues to be active and assertive, going to Bambi's in search of Vinnie, engaging Millie and obtaining her help.

Millie has demonstrated assertiveness and risk-taking throughout her life (page 57). When she was unable to get her needs met through her family, she developed her own support network outside of her family. Like Stella, her faith, perhaps different from Stella's in many ways, and her connection to God gives meaning to her life and has helped her to understand and deal with her disability.

CHAPTER 9

Millie introduces Lee to Jim, a Vietnam veteran, and his partner, Ben, a younger man. They agree to give Lee a ride north. Together they watch the show. A number of younger men taunt Lee because of his hook and the way he is dressed. Lee becomes involved in a confrontation with one of the young men and, with the assistance of Jim, wins the bar fight.

Discussion Questions

1. How did the possible diagnosis of lung cancer change Lee's life? How would such a diagnosis change your life?

2. How did Beverly, the exotic dancer, practice resilience in her life?

3. How should Lee have dealt with the young man who heckled him in the bar? What would you have done?

Author's Comments

As Lee points out on page 60, since the cancer scare, he had "worried less about his health and had found more time for his family." But the exposure to radiation and toxins at Pine Grove reawakened these fears.

Beverly demonstrates resilience by being able to leave her hometown and develop plans for herself and her life. As she puts it, "I'm going to do something with my life." She also, as she indicates on page 61, is someone who speaks her mind. She is assertive, perhaps aggressive at times.

In the confrontation with the young man in the bar, Lee clearly felt that he was cornered and he had no other choice than to take the situation on. He felt the damage to his ego and his self-image might be more severe than any physical damage he might receive in the fight. And after all, he finally had the opportunity to use his connect-the-dots line.

CHAPTER 10

Lee spends the rest of the night with Jim and Ben in the cab of their truck. He dreams of his family and remembers his parents and their life during the Depression. He specifically remembers his father and the efforts he made, even though he was ill, to help Lee through college. Jim arranges for Vinnie to buy Lee's truck and Bird and Lee trade coats.

It is Easter morning. The three men pull the truck back onto the interstate and head north. Lee and Jim talk about their families, and Lee talks about the adoption of his daughter from war-torn Peru and about the ordeal of his wife and her mother as Jews in Shanghai during World War II.

Discussion Questions

1. Can fear have a positive effect? Has fear ever had a positive effect on your life?

2. Lee talks about his father. How did his father's life illustrate some of the skills in resilience?

3. How did Lee and Liz exhibit resilience in their adoption of Dru?

Author's Comments

Fear should not be ignored. It should, however, be confronted and managed. For Lee, the conflict that will become clearer as the story progresses, is between being "cautious and giving up when it is wise to do so and white-knuckling it and pushing through when it was best to continue." It is about trying to find a balance. As Lee points out in the story, reflected in the dream (page 64), if he had jumped, he would have died. Fear saved his life.

Lee's father demonstrates resilience in dealing with his rheumatoid arthritis by continuing to move forward with his goals and plans and not giving up. He is able to put into perspective what he is doing and to see the bigger picture. He is acting in a way that is consistent with his image of himself and uses the support of his family and friends to reach his goal (page 65). "He was going to see his only son through college. And he did."

Lee and Liz set a clear goal of adopting a child and were willing to manage their fear and uncertainty about doing this in a foreign country. They were good problem solvers, they were persistent and confident in their ability to carry off the adoption, they supported each other and when things got really difficult, they were able to make use of humor.

CHAPTER 11

The three men encounter an accident on the interstate. They stop to provide assistance. It is a Vietnamese family. The mother has been killed and two of the children injured. The event brings back flashbacks and memories to Jim of the Vietnam War. Lee thinks about Liz, his wife. He remembers the uncertainty and the ambivalence of their marriage. The journey continues and Lee plans to be in the Boston area by nightfall. He decides to call his friend, Molly, who lives in Boston, and ask her if she will help him get to Maine. The call is intercepted by Agent Jennings who decides to take an interest in Lee, since they have discovered Lee is friendly with Muqtada's brother, Ibraham. Agent Jennings and his partner decide that they will use Lee to try to find Muqtada. They try to force Lee to contact his old love, Jean, by placing police units near Molly's condo giving Lee few options other than Jean.

Discussion Questions

1. Explain Jim's strong reaction to the death of the Vietnamese woman.

2. Explain Lee's ambivalence around his relationship with Liz.

Author's Comments

The accident and the death of the young Vietnamese woman re-stimulates Jim's feelings about his time in Vietnam and his role there as a sniper. His behavior is typical of individuals suffering from post-traumatic stress disorder and is especially common in soldiers who have fought in unpopular and confusing wars like Vietnam and Iraq.

Lee's heart tells him to commit to Liz. He is in love with her. His head tells him that this is a bad idea because they are so different (page 72). The scale is finally tipped in the direction of commitment when Lee understands in his head that their core values are the same. But their conflicts, often minor, continue to stir Lee's ambivalence.

CHAPTER 12

Lee cannot reach Molly because her condo is being watched by the police. He learns by reading the paper that his friend, Angus, has been arrested. He realizes that the federal agents have his appointment book and computer and will be watching all of his other friends in Boston. But Jean's name is the only one not in the appointment book. He decides to go to Jean.

They spend the evening together talking about old times. They were lovers from their college days and had planned to marry. They have not seen each other in years. Jean recently returned to the States after the death of her husband. She had attempted to contact Lee, but he had not responded.

The apartment is wired and the feds listen in. The bugging device, however, goes dead in the early morning hours. Jennings and his agents scramble to reestablish the listening device.

Discussion Questions

1. In this chapter Lee comes out of "denial." He realizes the trouble he is in. Why do you think it took so long for him to see this?

2. In this chapter Lee and Jean demonstrate a number of the different skills and attitudes of resilience. What are they?

Author's Comments

A positive self-image is undoubtedly a good thing in helping people to deal with hard times. Sometimes, however, it may get in the way of being able to see reality. It may create a blind spot. The idea that he could be considered a terrorist or a saboteur is totally foreign to Lee. Or being accused by the doorman of being a panhandler (page 77). These images are counter to the way in which Lee sees himself. His refusal to see himself as others do leads to his confrontation with the doorman, which almost gets him arrested.

Even though Lee showed rigidity in how he sees himself, he does demonstrate flexibility by being able to modify his plans and change his behavior when he finally realizes that he must.

Jean and Lee reconnect in this chapter and are able to talk about and express some of the feelings that they have had about their relationship, especially those they have felt in the past few years. They do not allow old feelings of anger and hurt to prevent them from supporting each other through the difficult times they are experiencing in the present. "She talked to relax. Lee listened to relax" (page 81).

CHAPTER 13

That night Lee dreams of Katie, the child that Jean and Lee had tried to have many years before. In the morning their breakfast is interrupted by the doorman, who says an INS agent wishes to speak to Jean. Lee hides in the bedroom and waits. The INS agent is actually Jennings. He is supposedly there to talk with Jean about a visa that her husband had requested. Jennings finally leaves after being unable to replant a "bug" (listening device) in the apartment. Lee and Jean realize that the INS agent is most likely Agent Jennings. Lee decides to contact his friend, Griff, who he knows is staying at the Parker House. Griff has a lobster yacht and is planning on returning to Maine the next day. The two manage to elude the federal agents and to reach the Parker House. Jennings realizes that his agents have lost track of both Ibraham and Jean and Lee. Muqtada with his friend, Bassin, plan a forced meeting with Ibraham.

Discussion Questions

1. In this chapter, what resilience skills are practiced by Lee and Jean?

2. Jennings has a panic attack in the garage on his way back to meet his partner, Wright. Why?

3. How are Muqtada and Jennings alike?

Author's Comments

Three of the primary resilience skills that they demonstrate are the abilities to communicate, plan and, specifically for Jean, the ability to observe carefully and "read" another person's behavior.

Jennings has a panic attack because he feels he has blown it. He has behaved impulsively without thinking through carefully what he is doing and the other options that he might have pursued. His self-confidence has taken another hit. Jennings is not able to keep things in perspective, to slow down and to think carefully and clearly before acting.

Muqtada, like Jennings, is obsessed with his mission and unable to sleep well or eat. Neither Jennings nor Muqtada have focuses in their lives other than their "work" and neither is taking physical or emotional care of themselves (page 88).

CHAPTER 14

Jean and Lee meet Griff at the Parker House. They convince Griff to take Lee to Maine the next morning. Jean and Lee say their good-byes and Lee boards Griff's boat for the trip north.

Discussion Questions

1. How has "retirement" changed the way Lee thinks about his life and relationships?

2. In this chapter, Jennings violates many of the basic principles of resilience. What are they?

Author's Comments

Lee has been spending a good deal of time reviewing his life and trying to understand many of his feelings about the past and his relationship with Jean. He is trying to put their relationship in perspective. As Lee puts it, on page 90, "In your sixties, you can begin to see the end. You know it's out there. Some days you think it is standing next to you, other days you're sure it's miles away, years away."

Jennings is "burning out." He has difficulty controlling his anger and thinking clearly. His pessimistic view of his life and the future is coloring his behavior and his relationship with his fellow agents. His young partner, Jim, is much more the optimist (page 92).

CHAPTER 15

Griff hides Lee in a storage compartment on the boat. The sea is rough and Lee is tossed about. At one point, his head is smashed against the wall of the compartment and he is knocked unconscious. He recovers consciousness but suffers from a concussion. They reach the Cove and rendezvous with Lee's attorney, Joe. Lee is reunited with his wife and daughter. The feds know that he is in the Cove. The local police chief, a friend of Lee's, takes Lee into protective custody and argues with the federal agents about releasing him to their custody.

Jennings' agents check a farm in southern Maine where Muqtada, Ibraham and their father lived. They do not find Muqtada.

Discussion Questions

1. Lee describes some of the things that happen to a person when they have an anxiety attack or a panic attack. What are they?

2. In this chapter, Griff tells his story. In what ways has he practiced resilience in his life?

3. Lee has missed his family. Why does he quickly become angry with his wife when they are reunited?

Author's Comments

With a panic or anxiety attack, breathing usually becomes shallow, your heart may pound, your thinking is not clear, and you may become convinced that you are going to die.

Griff has shown resilience in his life in a number of ways. Two of the major stressors for him have been the sudden death of his wife and the slow decline of his son from AIDS. Griff has dealt with these changes in his life by returning to his work in the ministry and caring for his son, Todd, before his death. He has also thrown himself actively into the support of AIDS research and into his boat, the *John Wesley II*.

Note on page 100 that Lee, when he is reunited with his family, experiences a rush of emotions. "He felt like yelling, becoming angry with his wife. He was able to get control over his feelings and to concentrate on them (his family) and nothing else...Lee was with his family and his friends. He was close to home." He is overwhelmed by the emotions that he has had to control and suppress over the past week. He feels safe and allows this flood of emotion to come out. This is confusing to his family.

BOOK TWO: FLIGHT

CHAPTER 16

A discriminating irreverence is the creator and protector of human liberty.
— Mark Twain

Tuesday, April 2, 2013
The Cove
7:10 P.M.

As Lee watched the blue lights come closer he decided that he had best say his goodbyes. Even though things hadn't worked as planned he wanted to thank Chief Dutremble. As he started to rise, Joe came bounding around the corner from the bar followed closely by Dutremble's Deputy Chief Jules Lavigne.

"What's going on?" asked Lee.

"Get your coat on, Lee. Let's go," Joe said as he buttoned his overcoat.

Liz looked worried again. She had relaxed some, but she was quickly on her feet.

"Hold on. Wait a minute," ordered Lee. "Do we have to meet them at the door? You know I'm in no hurry."

"Get your coat," Joe said again, cutting Lee short. "You can go too, Liz. Dru, you will have to ride up with me. We will meet your mom and dad at the hospital."

"What hospital?" asked Lee.

"The Medical Center. Life Star is on the way. It'll pick you up on the ridge. Only place it can land in The Cove."

"Why?" said Lee, looking even more perplexed by the flurry of activity.

"You got a nasty blow on the head, right?" explained Joe.

"Yeah, but a little ice and a few aspirin..."

"They're on their way back from Boston. Dutremble asked them to give you a lift to the hospital." He looked at Lee. "It's one way of keeping you in his custody for another hour or two." Joe scanned the room. "Jules will ride with you. Liz can come, but we got to move it."

They started toward the door. Liz and Dru followed close behind.

"Take care, Doc. My Jeremy will show you the way," said Flo as she ushered them through the storage room behind the bar and out a back door into the snow.

Jeremy was waiting. "The trail to the ridge is up this way," he said and started up the hill. He led the way with the deputy chief following close behind. At fifteen, Jeremy was a big boy for his age. Flo's daughter, his mother, was dead. Killed in a car accident when Jeremy was a baby. Flo raised him more as a son.

Jules was a small man, middle-aged. French to the bone. Light skin, looking very pale after a Maine winter. Joe and Lee followed with Liz and Dru bringing up the rear. The party trudged through the snow sometimes up to their knees. The moon lit the way. The trail had been beaten down by children who climbed the ridge with their sleds and snowboards. The north slope was steep, but smooth. The top was flat.

As they made their way, Jeremy and Jules talked about Life Star's last visit to The Cove. Last summer, a tourist from New York didn't listen to the locals. They warned him that the ocean, at high tide, tossed the rocks on the south slope and that one could easily get a leg or arm pinned or crushed crawling around on them.

"Learned his lesson, didn't he? He was lucky we got him out before high tide. His leg was beat up bad, but I don't think he lost it," said Jules.

"I helped get him out," Jeremy said proudly. "He was wicked scared."

"Goin' into shock I suppose," said Jules, "Lost some blood and it was getting pretty late and pretty cold."

As Lee reached the top of the ridge he could see the blue lights. The FBI was in The Cove. They were looking for Flo's. To the southwest Lee could see the lights of Life Star moving quickly up the coast toward The Cove. "Well, I suppose this will really piss off the boys from Boston. I'm sure Dutremble will be happy with that," said Lee, referring to the conflict that had raged for years between the Feds and the local departments.

"I suppose," said Joe. "You're still in his custody. He can do what he thinks is best, even if those guys don't like it."

The helicopter switched on its landing lights and descended slowly, its blades whipping the light dry snow from the afternoon into a cloud that enveloped the small party waiting on the ridge.

"Don't worry, Doc," said Jeremy, kicking the snow from his boots. "Unless they find the trail to here they'll be wading in snow up to their armpits."

The side door of the helicopter opened and a figure dressed in a blue thermal jumpsuit and helmet waved them over. Jules led the way.

"Okay, Doc. This is Charlie. Climb in. He'll check you out and get you settled in. C'mon, Liz. You too," said Jules.

Lee looked at Dru. "I'll see you soon, honey." He gave her a quick hug. "Take care of her, Joe." Dru rolled her eyes and muttered "Dad" under her breath.

"Don't worry," said Joe. "We will see you in Portland in a couple of hours. Don't say anything without me, understand? Name, rank, and serial number. That's all."

Lee climbed into the chopper. Charlie told him to lie down on the stretcher, closed the helicopter's side door, and directed Liz and Jules to the jump seats on the far wall. He strapped Lee to the stretcher and helped Liz get her belt on.

"So let me see your head," said Charlie as he touched Lee's forehead. Lee flinched.

The pilot yelled, "All clear." Charlie responded by looking out the cabin windows and echoing, "All clear." The helicopter began to lift off as he started to take Lee's vital signs.

"Well, your pressure's up a little," said Charlie.

"Just a little?" Lee laughed.

"Everything else is okay."

He then conducted a mini neurological exam asking Lee to track his finger with his eyes, touch his nose with his eyes closed, repeat digits forward and backwards, and give the day, date, and year. Jules and Liz looked on and said nothing. Lee passed. Charlie asked Lee if he had lost consciousness.

"Yes." Lee was sure of that.

"How many times?"

Lee guessed. "Twice."

"For how long?"

Lee didn't know.

The helicopter moved northwest along the coast. The lights of Kennebunk and The Port appeared and then disappeared. In the distance the lights of Scarborough and South Portland could be seen. It was a clear night on the coast. Headlight, Ram Island Light, and Spring Point Light could all be seen as they approached the city. The air was rough. To the west the sky was dark.

"Another storm is comin' in tonight. It will probably shut us down until daylight," the pilot said yelling over the roar of the engine.

They circled the Medical Center and then descended slowly, gently touching down on the landing pad. Their arrival stirred the dry snow from one of the afternoon squalls that had moved through the area.

"We're goin' let her run for a few minutes, Charlie," yelled the pilot. "Dry 'er off before we shut her down, if we shut her down. I'll see you inside."

Charlie opened the cabin door, stepped out, and helped Liz and Jules. He turned to Lee. "Can you walk with some help or do we need to use the stretcher?"

"Hell, I climbed the ridge at The Cove without help. I think I can walk the next hundred feet on my own."

"Good, let's go," said Charlie.

He took Lee's arm, but Lee shook it off. "I'm okay." Lee had a hard time accepting help even when he badly needed it.

"Good," Charlie said again.

Lee had worked with the Medical Center many years before. Some of his patients had made notorious visits to the emergency room. One of his favorites had not liked the way he had been treated and had sent an envelope full of nondescript white powder to the ER during the anthrax scare. Since they considered him mentally ill, the Medical Center didn't pursue prosecution.

Lee still knew some of the staff. Maybe his friend, Kathy, would be on duty. As he crossed what used to be a parking lot, he remembered the demonstration. Lee and his colleagues had expressed concern for many years about how patients with emotional problems were dealt with in the emergency room. These patients, like the one with the white powder, were always seen last and were either rapidly released or shipped off to the state hospital with few other options being considered or created.

And God help them if they were homeless and had a problem with alcohol or drugs. In those days they sometimes ended up dead in an alley in downtown Portland from an overdose or the weather. But Lee's protest and that of others in the medical community were ignored. Little change occurred until the patients themselves organized a protest, a noisy one outside the emergency room, just in time for the evening news. By 7:00 P.M. the president of the hospital was in the parking lot shaking hands and promising that changes would be made. And things did change for the better.

As they entered the emergency room a young blonde nurse that Lee didn't know met Charlie, took his report, and showed Lee and Liz to an examining room. She said Jules could post himself outside in the hall. She quickly took Lee's vitals and left the room.

Turning to Liz, "How you doin', hon?" asked Lee.

Liz shook her head. "I don't know. Okay, I guess. I'm glad you're back home, but I just wish there was something more I could do."

"Well, see if you can find Kathy. At least you can let her know we're here. I don't know what she can do, but..."

"All right. I might as well." She started toward the door. "You'll probably be here a while."

"Most likely. Some things never change," said Lee.

Liz opened the examining room door cautiously and stepped into the hall. Lee looked around the room. His legs dangled from the examining table. He climbed down and began his examination of the examining room. Like a kid, he loved to look in all the drawers and play with all of the gizmos and gadgets. He hadn't gotten far in his investigation when the door opened and a young physician entered the room. Lee wondered if the kid was shaving yet.

"I'm Dr. Williams," he said and shuffled a few pages in Lee's chart. "Let me look at your head."

He poked around Lee's head and face, tested his pupils with his light, and asked some of the same questions that Charlie had asked. The answers were the same, and the outcome the same. He said he wanted to do an MRI just to be on the safe side.

"Looks like you've got a slight concussion. If nothing shows up on the MRI, there's nothing to worry about. Are you allergic to aspirin?" Dr. Williams asked.

"No," said Lee.

"Well, aspirin should control the pain. Use ice packs as long as you can tolerate. That should take down the swelling. The bruising will probably get worse tonight. But it should be gone in a few days. Do you have any questions?"

"So, take two aspirin and call you in the morning," Lee wisecracked.

"Yes, but only call me if you really need to."

"Thank you, Dr. Williams. If you see my wife out there, send her back in."

"Will do. I'll send a nurse in and she will prep you for the MRI. We're really busy tonight so it could be a while. I'll see you later."

Lee nodded. Dr. Williams, looking pleased that he had wrapped this one up in five minutes, took his leave. Lee waited. He could hear Liz coming down the hall. She had a distinct walk. Deliberate, hard and fast. The way she approached many things in life.

The door opened. "I found Kathy," she said. "Betsy is back in town for a visit. She was just up here. We missed her. Things are really jammed up out there. They're bringing in a number of people from an accident on Forest Avenue near the university. Kathy said she would try to get back when she can."

"Where's Jules?" asked Lee.

"I think he went up front to help security deal with the drunk college student who hit the family in the other car. It's getting really wild out there."

"Jules isn't by the door?"

"No, no he isn't."

"Well," Lee sighed and made one circle of the examining room. Liz followed him with her eyes.

"Lee, what are you thinking? What are you going to do?"

"I don't know, but I think we should take a little walk while we consider all the options." Lee circled the examining room a second time.

"Do you know what you're doing?"

"No, but I am not sure anyone else does either."

Lee cracked the door. He could hear shouting and crying coming from the ER waiting area. "Come on, Liz," Lee whispered. He took Liz's hand and they started down the hall.

"As I recall," Lee whispered, "the exit at the end of the hall leads to the staff parking garage. And I know for a fact some people leave their car doors unlocked and their keys over the sun-visor."

"Lee, have you completely lost your mind?" shaking her head and looking disgusted. "That blow on the head must have done more than just give you a headache."

"I will plead insanity, my dear. You'll vouch for that." Lee stopped walking. "Look, Liz, at this point what do I have to lose?"

Liz didn't have a good answer for that, so they continued toward the exit.

CHAPTER 17

Tuesday, April 2, 2013
Medical Center
Portland, Maine
9:35 P.M.

When they reached the exit door, Lee glanced down both hallways. Although crowded with gurneys and equipment, they were free of people. "The coast is clear," he whispered. "Come on."

Lee opened the exit door and they hurried down the dimly lit stairway to the ground floor. As they approached the exit to the garage the door suddenly opened. It was Betsy. Barely five feet in height, Betsy was a determined-looking woman. Attractive. Her brown hair, only now beginning to show traces of gray and white.

"Dr. Brazil, are you...lookin' for a ride?"

"That all depends on where you're going."

"Kathy called me and said you guys could probably use a little help. How are you, Liz?" She hugged Liz.

Lee broke in. "If we're going to talk and hug, I think we should find a more private place."

"How about my bus?" said Betsy. "It's just around the corner."

"Sure, great," said Lee, looking up the stairs toward the door to the emergency room.

"Man, I'm glad to be outta' here," said Betsy as they walked toward the bus. "Nursing's not what it used to be. You worry too much about avoiding lawsuits and not enough about taking care of people."

Betsy had retired from the Medical Center and from nursing after thirty years. She was going back to school to be a minister. She had been admitted for the fall term to a seminary in Boston. "I've been wanting to do this all my life. It's time I finally did."

She was a Southern girl complete with a rich daddy. She came north with her first husband, a pilot with the Air Force. They divorced. He left. She stayed. Lee and Betsy had become friends when he worked at the Medical Center, a friendship that had lasted thirty years. The last time Lee saw Betsy was at her retirement party in February. A week later she drove south to visit her family. She loved to drive. She was going to see parts of this country she had never seen.

When they reached the van, Betsy unlocked the side door. Her van, more correctly her bus, was an old, VW from the 1970s that she had rebuilt and repainted at least three times. The bus had antique vanity plates: BETS.

"Watch your head," she said as she pulled herself through the side door.

Liz climbed in next. Lee looked around again and then followed. The bus was crowded with boxes of clothing and books and papers. Lee and Liz cautiously set down on the small bed next to a makeshift kitchen. Betsy stood for a few seconds and then found a seat on the "mini couch" in the rear of the bus.

"Cozy, isn't it?" Betsy said. Liz nodded. "How do like the privacy glass I put in?" asked Betsy as she pointed to the side windows. "We can see out. They can't see in."

"If you ever decide to sell it, I'm sure a drug dealer would be interested," Lee mused.

Betsy smiled. "Still got your sense of humor, even in this mess." She paused. "I've been reading about you in the paper."

"I'm sure you have," said Lee feeling more and more anxious with every passing second. "Look, Bets, can you loan us your bus?"

"My bus?" Betsy grimaced. "Lee, you and Liz wouldn't even get past the ticket taker at the parking gate. Both of your pictures are on the front page of *The Press Herald.* Here take a look." Betsy flashed the paper in front of Lee.

Area Psychologist Sought in Pine Grove Investigation, the headline read.

"I wonder where they got that picture?" Lee mumbled. "Well, it doesn't matter. What matters is we've got to get to a lodge near Baxter."

"Well, you just happen to be in luck. I'm headin' up to Jackman tonight to visit an old friend."

"Great," said Lee feeling suddenly hopeful.

"Betsy, you could get in serious trouble doing this," said Liz.

"Not if he didn't do anything wrong. And I know Lee very well. This is all a bunch of crap dreamed up by those paranoid souls in Washington. And it pisses me off." With that, Betsy got up, slipped into the driver's seat and turned on the engine.

"Lay down on the bed, Lee. Cover him up, Liz. Head to toe. Now Liz, you sit on the bed until we're out of the garage. Here, put this cap on." The cap said *Braves.* "You're an old girlfriend of mine from Atlanta, if anyone asks. Think southern."

They pulled up to the parking gate.

"Hi, Bets," said the security guard. "How do you like not workin'?"

"It's great, Terry."

"Well, I would sure like to try it," she said as she collected the parking fee. "All set. Drive carefully."

They pulled on to Congress Street. It was almost nine. The streets were empty. Soon they were on I-295 heading north.

Lee pulled the cover off and sat up. Liz had moved to the passenger seat and was talking to Betsy. Lee felt a little dizzy and disoriented. Maybe he should have stayed in the hospital. But no time to second-guess now. He decided not to mention the dizziness to Liz. He would sit on the bed until his head cleared. It must be the motion and darkness. It reminded him of the storage compartment on Griff's boat. He began to feel sick. He changed his mind about not talking about how he was feeling.

"Betsy, I'm starting to feel a little...ohh! You wouldn't happen to have a bag or can or something?"

"Lee. I'll look," said Liz. "Don't move around. Lay down. Maybe it will pass."

He did, but it didn't pass. Luckily, Liz found a plastic garbage bag in time. Lee felt relieved and lay down on the bed again.

"Let me tuck you in," said Liz.

"There's a little bit of ice in the trays in the freezer. Make a pack for his head," Betsy said.

"Try to get some sleep. It's a long way to Jackman," said Liz.

"Three hours," added Betsy.

Liz lay down next to Lee. The warmth of her body, the sound of her breathing, and Lee was asleep.

In his dream it was spring. Still a bit cold, even for a sunny May afternoon. The Portland Sea Dogs are playing the New Haven Ravens. Hadlock Field is packed. A sell-out. Dru is scoring the game with Lee. The bottom of the ninth. The score tied 3-3. The Dogs are up. Millar at bat. One player, Honeycutt, on second. The count, 2-2. The pitch. A fastball. Millar nails it hard into right field. It's going. It's gone. A home run. The crowd goes wild. Lee hugs Dru.

"The roar of the greasepaint and the smell of the crowd," he mumbled.

"Lee, what are you talking about?" asked Liz. "You must have been dreaming."

"Oh, God, my head. Where are we?" Lee sat up and rubbed his eyes.

"I don't know. I think we're close to Waterville," Liz said, looking out.

"Yeah," answered Betsy. "We'll be on 201 in a few minutes."

"What time is it?" asked Lee.

"I'm not sure. Are you feeling better?" Liz asked.

"Sleep may not have been the best idea," he said rubbing his neck.

"Hang on back there. I see blue lights comin' up behind us."

Betsy slowed the bus and moved to the shoulder of the road. Lee felt his heart starting to race. He held his breath.

"No, they're goin' around," said Betsy

"Thank God," said Lee exhaling.

They pulled off the exit and started north on 201, a small two-lane highway that ended at the Canadian border. The wind was picking up and large fluffy flakes of snow started to fall. There were only a few cars on 201.

They drove through Skowhegan, passing the giant wooden Indian created by the well-known sculptor, Bernard Langlais, and dedicated to *The Maine Indians .The first people, and* Lee thought, *the last, to use these lands in peaceful ways.* The streets of the town were empty. The two restaurants that were open for dinner had been closed for hours. The only signs of life were a few cars and pickups at The American Legion Hall and the Irving station.

It was approaching midnight when they saw the lights of Skowhegan fade into the snow behind them. The night was dark. It was starting to snow harder. The roads were still clear. The crews weren't out yet.

"How does your dad feel about you going to seminary?" asked Lee.

"He won't talk about it. He's still upset about me getting divorced a second time." The speed limit had dropped. She slowed the bus. "He doesn't have a clue about why I'm going. He thinks I should get married again. He just doesn't understand that maybe I wasn't meant to be married."

They drove on through the sleeping villages of Solon, Bingham, and Caratunk, following the Indian River. At the top of a hill, outside of the Forks, they saw blue and yellow lights.

"Roadblock," said Betsy.

A car ahead of them had been stopped and was being searched. Two state troopers looking more like snowmen than police officers were fumbling through the trunk and back seat of the car.

"Okay, guys. It's show time," said Betsy.

"Get under those blankets on the bed, Lee." She slowed the bus to a crawl. "Lay down on top of him Liz and cover both of you up." Betsy looked around. "Where's that bag of puke? Get it." Liz grabbed it out of the garbage can. "You're very sick, Liz. You got a bad case of the flu and you've just thrown up."

Lee groaned and crawled under the bed covers.

"Okay, Betsy. I think I'm ready," said Liz.

"Well, ready or not."

Betsy pulled the bus up and rolled down the window.

"How you boys doin' tonight? Isn't it a little too cold for standin' out in the road?" said Betsy.

"Yes, Miss. It is. But may I ask what brings you out on a night like this?"

"You may," said Betsy. "I'm on my way to Jackman. Takin' a friend of mine back home. She stayed with me in Portland for the holidays. Unfortunately, she has come down with a bad case of the flu."

As if on cue, Liz began to make gagging sounds. Betsy looked over her shoulder. "Are you okay, honey?" Turning back to the officer, "She's been throwin' up all night. Just can't keep anything down."

"May I see your license and your passenger?"

"Well, now, here's my license." Betsy stepped out of the bus as the officer looked at the license. Betsy slid open the side door.

"And here's Lynn. The doctor said she was pretty contagious so I would be careful."

Liz began to cry hysterically with intermittent gagging.

"Now, Lynn, the officer is just doin' his job." Turning to the officer, "She always gets so emotional when she's sick."

The smell of vomit drifted out the side door of the bus as Liz waved the now open bag in the air. The officer stepped back.

"Okay. Here's your license, Miss." Turning to Liz, "Sorry to have bothered you. I hope you get to feelin' better soon."

Betsy closed the side door and climbed back in. "Well, I hope you gentlemen find what you're lookin' for before the weather gets any worse."

"Unfortunately, I'm afraid we're going to be out here for the rest of the night. Drive safely. The road between here and Jackman hasn't been plowed yet."

"Thank you, officer," said Betsy. She rolled the window up and pulled back onto the highway. "You can come out now," said Betsy. "You were great, Liz."

"It wasn't hard," said Liz. "But you were better. You sure can turn that southern girl charm on when you need it."

"Liz, honey, would you get off of me?" said Lee. "I thought I was going to smother to death while you two were entertaining the state police. But you were something else. She does cry when she gets sick. How did you know that?"

"It's a woman thing," said Betsy.

They drove on. "Well, he was right about the roads not being plowed," said Betsy.

The drive into Jackman took an hour. In Jackman the sign on the only hotel that appeared open for business read: *Guns, Wedding Gowns, and Cold Beer. If you don't stop, smile on the way by.* They smiled.

The side road from Jackman to the inn took even longer. At one point Liz and Lee had to get out and push the bus back onto the highway.

"The Gray Panthers' road crew," Lee joked.

"If this is any indication of what retirement's going to be like I'm ready to go back to work at the hospital!" Betsy added.

It was getting close to 3:00 A.M. when they pulled into the small parking lot next to the inn. The building was dark except for a light in the front hall.

"I hope you are real good friends with this fellow," said Lee. "It's a little late for company."

"Oh, I am," said Betsy. "He knew I would be late. He just doesn't know I'm bringing you guys with me." She paused. "But he'll be okay with it. It's off-season." She stopped and looked at her two friends. "We will probably be his only guests."

The front door to the lodge was open. Liz and Lee followed Betsy. Embers from an evening fire glowed in the huge fireplace in the main hall. Lee remembered the place. Under the mantle there was a large carved wooden sign.

"Flying Fish Lodge," said Lee in a whisper.

"What?" said Liz. "Did you say something?"

"Nothing important," Lee answered.

CHAPTER 18

Wednesday, April 3rd, 2013
Jackman, Maine
3:05 A.M.

"Welcome, my lady," the note said. "Room 205 as you requested. Breakfast at 7:00 — Ray, Your Innkeeper."

"Wonderful," said Betsy starting up the stairs. "The room is a suite. I'll take the couch. You guys can have the bedroom. We'll sort things out in the morning."

Lee and Liz lay down on the large featherbed and that was the last thing Lee remembered until Betsy shook him awake soon after sunrise. "Lee, you got to get up. I talked to Ray. He says the police are searching all the hotels and inns on or near 201."

"Slow down, Betsy. Let me get my eyes open." Turning to Liz, "Wake up honey, we got more trouble."

"Oh, Lee. Go away. Just let me sleep a few more minutes."

"Here this should help." Betsy shoved a cup of coffee in his hand.

Lee sat up, took a sip. "The Golden Road isn't far from here, is it? Maybe we could borrow or buy that old Jeep in the parking lot. I saw it when we drove in last night."

"I don't think that thing has run in years. I don't know why Ray keeps it around. Even if we could find you transportation Golden and Ragmuff are barely passable this time of year. And Loon Lake Road...." Betsy stopped and looked out the window.

"Are you okay, Bets?" asked Lee.

"Yeah. Ray could do it."

"Do what?" asked Lee.

He's a pilot. That's why he bought the place. Don't worry Lee, I'm sure he will." And with that she was on her feet and out the door.

"Oh God, here we go again," Lee muttered as he walked slowly around the room. Looking out the window he could see the small runway, the lone windsock, and a single engine Cessna equipped with winter skis parked under a dilapidated hangar. Each gust of wind seemed to move a different section of the hangar roof. Lee hoped the plane was in better shape than the hangar.

Lee knew the lodge well. It had been built in the 1920s as a hunting retreat for a wealthy family. Sometime in the 1950s it was sold to a couple who renamed it Flying Fish and opened it to the public. Lee wasn't sure who had installed the runway. The lodge itself was a beautiful piece of craftsmanship. All log structure, built from great white pines and red spruce, taken from sections of the Maine woods that had never been cut before. The lodge had a slate roof and a system for collecting the rainwater used for drinking and bathing in the early twentieth century. There was a glacial ice cave near the lodge with an entrance from the lodge's basement. In the early part of the twenty-first century, global warming made the ice unstable and the cave's entrance was sealed.

Lee and Joanne stayed at the lodge a number of times. She was a young social worker whom Lee became involved with in the late 1970s after his divorce. Jean was in Europe. They hadn't spoken for some time. He didn't contact Jean after the divorce. He wanted to wait. Wanted to try something else. Someone else. Joanne was quiet. Lee liked that at first. Joanne let Lee live his life. He was busy building his practice. They had dinner together, mostly eating out since neither liked to cook. And Joanne was leaving social work. She was working on opening her own business. She, too, was busy. So weekends away from it all were fun, and the lodge was away from it all. But after a couple of years Lee knew that the relationship wasn't going where either wanted it to go. Marriage. Commitment. He couldn't. But still, he thought of Joanne often and remembered those peaceful times when the biggest decision of the day was where they would dine.

But this time he certainly had not found peace at the lodge. Lee could hear Betsy on the stairs. She burst into the room out of breath.

"He wants to talk to you. Go on now. I'll get Liz up. She said she hadn't slept much since this whole thing started. Poor baby. Go on now, before he changes his mind."

"What is his name and what are you doing with him? I mean, well, you know what I mean," said Lee.

"His name is Ray Noyes and we've been...friends...for a long time," Betsy said, appearing a bit embarrassed. Lee knew they had been much more than friends. Embarrassment in the old days had been a rare occurrence for Betsy. But time and age change a lot of things, Lee thought.

"And this guy knows how to fly that plane out there?"

"Of course," Betsy said, sounding very self-assured.

"What, what do you mean, 'of course'?"

Look, Lee, he flew in Nam and then as a commercial pilot for Delta before he retired."

"Okay, I'll go. I'm sorry, Bets. I appreciate your help. I'm just..."

"It's okay, just go."

Lee started down the stairs with his coffee cup. He could hear music coming from what he thought was the kitchen. He recognized the music, an old CD by a jazz musician who had served in Vietnam. Willie Bang. The name was easy to remember and the music hard to forget. "Vietnam: The Aftermath."

Lee crossed the Great Hall. It was dark except for a small fire dwarfed by the huge opening of the fireplace. The adjoining dining rooms were dark, the heavy drapes pulled tight to keep winter out. Lee peered through the porthole window of the kitchen door. A large man with a mop of white hair and a rosy complexion was leaning over the stove. His attire, a heavy blue denim apron and camouflage fatigues made Lee chuckle. Without looking around he said, "Well, come in. Would you like a refill on the coffee? Help yourself." He pointed to a coffee maker on the side counter.

Ray turned around to face Lee. "Popovers...eggs on steroids, I love 'em. But I can never get them to rise as high as they should," he said, looking through the oven door. "We'll see how this batch does. And while we're waiting to find out, Betsy said you and your wife want me to fly you to the Lodge on Loon Lake?"

"Yes, I guess." Lee still wasn't sure this was a good idea.

"Do you want to go or not?" Ray pressed.

"Yes, we do." Nothing like being decisive, Lee thought.

"When?"

"As soon as we could...."

"Yes, I would think that would be a good idea," said Ray. "Given my call from the state police, I know you're in some kind of trouble. I don't know what kind and I don't want to know." He bent over to check the popovers. "I moved up here after I retired to get away from trouble. I don't have any TVs in the lodge. I don't get the paper. I've got a radio that I haven't listened to in two weeks." He pulled off an oven mitt and laid it on the counter. "The only news I get is from my guests, and I haven't had one in a month. So if you want to go to that lodge and stay with crazy Robert for the rest of the winter, that's your business." He made eye contact with Lee. "You know he's the only one up there this time of year? You got anything to take with you?"

"Well, not really," said Lee, thinking that maybe he should take a lot of things; a gun, a bottle of anti-psychotic medications.

130

"Good. The less weight the better. Your wife's not a big woman, is she? The ice is getting a little thin this time of year. It's been a wicked warm winter. You know we will have to land on the ice?"

"No, she's not a big woman." Lee was sure this was not the smartest thing he had ever signed on for.

"It will cost you four hundred dollars. I'll give you my best price because of Betsy."

"That's fine," Lee said hesitantly.

"Well, tell your wife we got popovers coming. I got to check the weather again. There may be a clipper comin' through this afternoon. And I got to get Alvin ready." Lee looked a little puzzled. "My plane. Alvin. After Alvin York, the war hero from WW I who believed war was morally wrong. From Kentucky, I think."

"No, Tennessee," said Lee.

"Right, Tennessee," said Ray, realizing that he and his house guest might have more in common than he thought.

"We should be ready to go in a couple of hours. Say 11:00? That'll give me plenty of time to miss the snow and get back here before dark."

Lee headed back upstairs, "Alvin," he said under his breath "All I need is another crazy vet. Jesus!"

When he reached the room, Betsy was sitting on the couch thumbing through a copy of *Southern Living*. "What do you think about this?" She shoved the magazine in front of Lee.

"What?" said Lee, still thinking about Ray and Alvin.

"Those are great colors, aren't they?" Referring to a set of patio furniture with large, deep green cushions.

"Goes with the woods, Bets. But don't you think it's a little bit early for patio furniture?"

"Not for long. Summer is coming. It's been a warm winter up here."

"So I hear. Where's Liz?"

"In the shower. I explained the situation. She is a trooper. She says she'll go, if that's what you decide. You talked to Ray?"

"Yes. He says Alvin and him will be ready by eleven."

"A cute name for a plane, don't you think?"

"I guess," said Lee, still trying to sort out his feelings about Ray.

"I've flown with him. He's a good pilot. He flew people up to that lodge during the summer."

"But not during the winter?" asked Lee.

"I don't know."

"Do you know anything about Robert, the caretaker at the lodge?" asked Lee, remembering Ray's comments. "Not really. People say he's a bit strange."

"Well if we stay here, it sounds like I will be talking with the state police before the sun goes down." Lee was sure of that.

"Then let's get ready." Betsy sprang off the couch.

"I don't think you can go. The less weight on the ice, the better."

"All right. I can at least make up a bag for you and Liz from the lost and found department here at the lodge. Liz is about my size."

Lee nodded. Betsy was out the door and halfway down the stairs before he could form another sentence.

Lee took a shower. He couldn't think. His head felt numb. His mind was blank. He dressed. He thought some about Jean as he put Ian's clothing on. "God, where do the years ago?"

Liz was ready. Looking a bit nervous. Asking a lot of questions about Ray. How long had he flown as a bush pilot? Did he drink?

"Jezum, Liz. I didn't give him a flight exam. Betsy says he's a good pilot." Liz was quiet. "I know what you're thinking. Bets can be a bit of a space cadet."

"Well, she does take unnecessary risks sometimes."

"Don't we all? You have any better ideas?"

Liz was silent again. The silence was broken by the sound of Alvin's engine starting up. It roared once and then sputtered and died. After a few seconds it roared again and settled into a gentle purr.

At a quarter of eleven they went downstairs. They had already had a light breakfast, popovers, juice, and some fruit. Betsy met them in the Great Hall with a small bag she had put together. Some clothing and cosmetics for Liz and a few pieces of clothing from the lost and found that she thought might fit Lee. At exactly eleven Ray came through the patio doors that led out to the landing strip.

"Ready?" he asked.

"As ready as we're ever going to be," said Lee.

The two would-be aviators followed Ray and Betsy out the door, across the patio and down the shoveled walk to Alvin who sat quietly running at the end of the runway.

Lee didn't know much about small planes. He had the same level of interest in riding in one as he had in carnival rides. None.

"Liz, why don't you sit in the back. Help her get settled, Bets," said Ray.

Betsy handed Liz the bag. "And here's a thermos of coffee. It helps Ray stay awake while he's flying." Lee grimaced. "I'm just kidding," said Betsy, laughing.

"Thank you, Betsy. You've been so good to us." Tears filled Liz's eyes. "I hope we see you again soon."

"You will, you will." Betsy turned and hugged Lee. "Now you take care."

"Here, Doc. Go around to the other side. You can sit up front and be my navigator."

Lee climbed in, closed his door and put his seat belt on very tight. *Navigator?* Lee thought. He had trouble with road maps. Ray closed his door.

"Okay, are we all settled in?"

Lee and Liz nodded nervously. Betsy stepped back from the plane and waved as Ray revved the engine. The plane started moving forward. The propeller blade stirred the snow as the plane picked up speed. The snow muffled the sound of the engine and made the takeoff so gentle that Lee was surprised when he looked down and the ground was a few feet below them.

The plane easily cleared the trees at the end of the runway as Ray banked the plane to the left and headed east toward Seboomook Lake. He explained that they would fly east to Canada Falls Lake and then to Seboomook. They would cross the lake to its eastern shore before turning north.

The sun was high in the crystal blue sky. A gentle tailwind pushed them forward and helped them quickly gain altitude. Below were miles and miles of white, broken only occasionally by jagged outcroppings of rock and bluff. Lee had never seen the northern Maine woods from the air in winter. Neither had Liz.

Ray was not much for talk, at least not at first. But he soon realized that the constant stream of questions, mainly from Liz, was her way of feeling more in control and less anxious. He had seen this before. So he answered her questions about where he was from, and how he had got into flying, and how he ended up with the lodge.

"I'm a Maineiac, born in Saco. My dad was a superintendent in the mills just like his dad before him. He worked there until they closed them down." He banked the plane to the left. "He never took that well. He never liked retirement. Only lived a year or so after the mills closed."

"But I wanted out of Maine. I guess I wanted to see the world." He slowed the plane. "I joined the Air Force the day after I graduated from UMO. They taught me how to fly C140s. Sent me to Nam. I almost got my ass shot off a few times over there," he chuckled, "but I came through without a scratch. But career military wasn't for me." He frowned. "Too many damn rules. Too much B-S." Liz smiled. "When they let me go I took a job with Delta. Started out as a navigator and worked my way up. Loved it.

"I bought the lodge while I was still flying. The couple that made the place go, the Levesques, retired and sold it to a couple of good ol' boys who loved to fish and hunt, but didn't know jack about running a place like the lodge." He shook his head and smiled. "They went bankrupt and I bought it for the taxes. My friends in Boston thought I was crazy."

As they turned north, Mount Russell and Little Russell Mountain came into sight. "It took me a while. I flew up when I had time off. Got some help from some of the people who worked for the Levesques."

"Great," said Liz.

"We put it back together. Opened again in 1993. Business has been good. Can't complain. I like it better in the off-season when it's just me. I like to cook and if I need any help I can call Margaret who works for me during the summer."

"That's Bean Pot Pond to our left. We'll head up to Bear Pond and, depending on the wind, I will line him up for Loon Lake."

"Good," said Lee. One of the few things he said during the flight.

"We've got a crosswind coming in from the north. So we may have to make a couple of passes."

As the lake came into view, Ray mumbled something about "those damned springs."

"What?" said Lee. Liz leaned forward to hear Ray's response.

"We've got to keep away from that side of the lake," pointing to what he said were bogs and marshes.

"There are springs there. The ice will be very thin."

Lee and Liz looked worried again.

"Hey, if we break through the ice when we're landing, the plane will nose over immediately and what's left of us will do cartwheels across the lake. It will all be over very fast," said Ray.

"Somehow that's not very reassuring," said Lee.

Ray laughed. "I love ice. I got my own private ice cave at the lodge. Look, I've done this before. We will be okay as long as the wind stays down and doesn't push us over there."

Ray lined Alvin up and started to descend rapidly. The roar of the wind increased as Ray lowered the plane's flaps. Liz took Lee's hand. Lee closed his eyes. A minute, then two, passed.

"You can open them now, Doc. We're on the ice. You okay, Liz?"

"I'm fine," was the reply.

CHAPTER 19

April 3, 2013
The Lodge
Loon Lake, Maine

Ray taxied the plane down the ice toward the lodge. At first all that could be seen of the lodge was the smoke from its double chimneys. The white, two-story structure was buried in snow and ice, a large frosty mound sitting on the edge of the lake. As they moved closer they could see that sections of the roof had been shoveled off. A path was carved in the snow from the lodge to the wooden dock that extended into the lake. The dock was piled with snow. "Supply plane hasn't been here since early March, Ray explained. "Bob Johnson was the last person up here. He flies up twice a winter to deliver supplies and mail to Robert. He won't be back again this winter."

The plane bumped along over broken ice from earlier freezes and thaws as it continued slowly toward the lodge. "The next people you see will be the fishermen who will start coming in when the ice is out in early May. In fact," switching to his Maine accent, "it will get right busy up here." He laughed.

There were faint creaks and groans from the ice as Ray slowly moved the plane closer to the north shore of the lake. "People say they met here in the 1960s. You'll meet them if you stay. Nice people. They'll be up in early May to open for the season. It's not a place I would want to stay in May, or in June for that matter. The black flies are so thick 'cause of the marshes you need a canoe paddle to drive them off."

Ray pulled the plane to a stop. "This is about as close as I can get you. You're goin' to have to unload without my help. I don't trust the ice."

Lee opened the door of the plane and crawled out. Liz handed him their one bag and followed. As they put on the snowshoes Ray had loaned them, Ray said, "Now be careful. Spread out on the ice and walk to the ladder on the dock. See it?" Lee nodded. "The ice will be thin near the ladder." Ray shouted over the noise of the engine and the wind. "Keep your distance from the dock until you get close to the ladder. I'll stay until you're on the dock. Robert will let you in. Just keep banging until he hears you."

Lee nodded again, "Thanks, Ray," he shouted.

"Tell Robert I will pick up the snowshoes the next time I'm up."

Lee slammed the door of the plane shut, having to fight a gust of wind that threatened to blow it open again. Lee and Liz did as they were told. Lee took the lead. The ice seemed firm at first, but as they neared the shore each step with the borrowed snowshoes was met with louder creaking and cracking sounds. Lee was within a few feet of the dock when he slipped his boots out of the snowshoes and threw the snowshoes on the dock. His feet sank into the snow. He leaned forward and lunged at the ladder catching it with his right hand just as his hook slipped off an icy rung. He started to fall backwards. He had a flash from the dream. He was falling, for a second he could see the green water of the River far below, but he caught the rung. He pulled himself up the ladder onto the dock.

Liz followed. She had less trouble on the ladder. The two gathered up the shoes and bag as Ray revved Alvin's engine and turned the plane into the wind.

When they reached the stairs of the lodge they could see and hear signs of life. The entranceway and steps had been more recently shoveled and there was the low hum of an electric generator and the sound of a radio. Lee banged on the door. No response. He banged again. Still no response.

"Well, open it," said Liz. He did.

The entryway was cold and dark. They could see light and hear music coming from what appeared to be a basement door. They crossed the entryway to the top of the basement stairs and waited. Liz pushed past Lee. She heard the sound of paper being shuffled, furniture creaking, and footsteps.

"Robert," she said a number of times, each time louder.

The sound of her voice, a woman's voice, startled Robert. "Who's up there?" There was fear in his voice.

"Joe's friends," Liz said. "Liz and Lee."

"Who? Who's up there?" he asked again.

"Liz and Lee," she said again.

Robert appeared at the bottom of the dimly lit stairs.

"I didn't think you folks were comin'. I thought they had . . . " and he stopped.

"Well, we weren't sure we were either," said Liz, "but we're here." She tried to sound positive.

Robert looked confused and rubbed his eyes. He was a large man in desperate need of a haircut and a shave. His shirt was partially unbuttoned and stuffed inside his pants, which hung low on his waist.

"Uh, any friend," Robert finally said nervously, "of Joseph's is a friend of mine." He started slowly up the basement steps taking one step at a time pulling himself up with his right leg and right arm. His left arm swung lazily at his side with his left hand cupped and turned inward. Robert reached the top of the basement stairs and moved past both Liz and Lee without looking directly at either or speaking.

"I got the bridal suite ready for you a couple of days ago," he said pointing up the stairs to the second floor.

Robert started up the dark stairs with Lee and Liz following. A few steps up he turned around.

"Wait. Let me get a lamp," he said as he pushed past them. He disappeared into another room and quickly returned carrying a lamp tucked against his chest with his left arm and hand.

"Can I help you?" Liz asked.

Robert ignored her and slowly began to climb the stairs. They followed. The bridal suite was at the top of the stairs. Robert opened the door, placed the lamp on a large oak bureau, and moved around the room lighting two more lamps. The sun had disappeared behind Mount Russell into a bank of heavy gray clouds. It was only mid-afternoon, but the shadows were long and the sunlight rapidly fading. The room was cold. Robert apologized as he opened the damper on the small wood stove and lit the paper and kindling he had placed in the stove days before.

"She'll warm up fast," he said, "once she gets goin'. Now you folks are on your own for food. I mean...you wouldn't like my cookin'," sounding apologetic, "but I'll be glad to show you how the cookin' stove works. I keep a fire in her all the time so all you got to do is add more wood if you want her hotter or just pull the damper if you want her cooler. But for God's sake, don't put her out."

Robert looked the two over carefully, wondering if they understood his situation. "The pantry, she's full of food. I'm afraid I've already ate most of the fresh stuff Bob brought," sounding apologetic again, "but there's a lot of good canned stuff, some frozen fish and steak in the freezer."

"You need a freezer up here?" Lee said, trying to make a joke.

Robert didn't laugh and Liz rolled her eyes as Robert opened the door to leave.

"I turn the 'lectric on for couple of hours at noon so if you have somethin' to charge or run, do it then." He paused and then with a loud voice, "I'm runnin' low on gas so I can't run the generator no more."

"Okay, thank you very much, Robert. It's a beautiful room."

She wasn't ready for him to leave. "Will we see you later tonight?" asked Liz.

"No," said Robert. "I, I got work to do." He hurried out of the room. Indeed, the room was beautiful. A large four-poster featherbed. Everything oak, with some bird's-eye maple, like the wash basin stand. There was a full bath. Lee tried both hot and cold and found them working.

"I guess the hot water must run off of the main furnace. I wonder if it's all wood heat?"

Liz didn't respond. She was admiring one of the quilts on the four-poster. "Look at the hand stitching. When did people have the time to do this kind of work? When?"

Lee had walked over to the window and was watching the shadows of the mountains spread across the lake. He thought about Jean for just a moment and wondered where she was and if she had been arrested. And Dru...was she okay? *Oh lighten up,* he thought. *She's twenty-four-years old, for God's sake.*

"I'm really hungry," said Liz. "Let's see what's in the kitchen."

"Well, it's good to see that you've still got your appetite," said Lee. "I'll go with you, but my stomach is still screwed up." He shrugged. "I'm hungry. Then I'm not."

They took one of the lamps and made their way down the stairs and across the giant dining area. The floors of the lodge were stained pine. The ceilings low. The dining room furniture consisted of long oak tables and benches with a large wood stove at one end of the room. At the other end of the room they found a door with a sign that read "Kitchen."

It was a huge room with a large wood-fired cooking stove that served to heat water for dishwashing and to heat the kitchen and large pantry.

Liz found a couple of cans of stew in the pantry and some bread. A bit stale, but edible. Dinner was ready.

They ate mostly in silence with Liz commenting once about the amount of salt in the canned stew. "Too much...way too much. Why do they do that?" she asked. Lee didn't respond. He had stopped responding to that question years ago.

They washed their dishes and returned to the room. It was only 7:00 P.M., but they were ready for sleep. They opened the bag Betsy had packed. Lee found a flannel nightshirt and slipped it on.

"Look at this gown, Lee."

"Honey, you'll look beautiful in it," said Lee. "How do I look in this old night shirt Betsy sent along?" Lee twirled like a model.

"Well, I'm not sure it's you," she said. "You know I doubt that this gown is very warm."

"So why don't you take this flannel shirt? Bets packed two for me."

In a few more minutes they settled into their bed under two quilts and three blankets.

"God, this cover is heavy," Liz both observed and complained.

"Better than being cold. Did you notice that the bathroom has some sort of forced hot water system that keeps it warm?" Lee asked.

"Don't bother me with technical details at this hour," said Liz as she fluffed her pillow..

"But, it's only 7:30." Lee was serious. It was early for him.

"Well it feels like 1:30 in the morning," she insisted, "and I'm a hundred years old." She turned out the lamp.

Lee laughed. "I know, but most days you don't look it." Lee put his arm around Liz.

"I don't know where we're going or what the hell is going to happen, but it's good to be sharing a bed with you again, Miss L."

The room was dark except for faint flickers of light from the wood stove. "At times I wasn't sure it would ever happen again," he said.

"Me too," and she started to cry. Lee kissed her on the forehead. They held each other as they drifted into sleep. That night they slept a deep and sound sleep. The first for both of them in what seemed like a very long time.

April 3, 2013
Black Falcon Ave.
South Boston
10:45 P.M.

In the morning it had snowed. In the afternoon it had rained. Tonight it was cold again. The wind was off the ocean. Muqtada had been walking for an hour. It was late. There was no public transportation to where he was going. At least not at this hour. He reached in his pocket again and pulled out the scrap of paper that he had written the address on. He was on Black Falcon Avenue, looking for a side street and a warehouse. Amon and Bassin would be there with his brother. At least he hoped Ibraham would be there.

The street was dark. Muqtada had difficulty making out the street signs. In Boston, street signs were not a priority. "The biggest little town in the world." That's what his brother had always called Boston.

"Ten Edgewater." He repeated the address a number of times. He was taking a risk walking this late in this area. He might be stopped by the police, but he needed to see his brother. He had to see his brother.

He reached another corner and looked for the street sign. It was lying on the ground. Probably knocked down by one of the snowplows this past winter. Edgewater, it read.

The address was a short walk from the corner. It was an old warehouse. There was no activity at this time of night, at least not in this section of the industrial marina. Muqtada found the door. He could make out a light through a window. He looked around to see if anyone was watching. He had been told to knock four times and he did. The door opened and it was Bassin.

"Come," he said.

Muqtada followed Bassin through a maze of crates and storage compartments. Bassin guided them with a flashlight. In the last room Muqtada saw a faint light. He turned the corner and saw his brother standing with Amon in what looked like a sea of darkness. The faint light came from an old propane lantern.

Muqtada approached. His brother did not move. Muqtada greeted him. "Ibraham, my brother. Did my friends treat you well?"

"They forced me to come," said Ibraham sounding angry. "I told you years ago I do not agree with the things you have done, or are planning to do."

Images of other confrontations with his brother flashed through his head. Anger, like a dark red cloud, rose inside of Muqtada. He felt the muscles of his arms and hands tighten into fists. He thought of their mother and the cloud began to dissipate. For a few seconds his vision had blurred, but now he could see his brother clearly again, standing in front of him. He would not strike his brother. He had promised their mother before her death. He would reason with him.

"My brother you have been corrupted by this country. You dishonor our family. How can you support their government?"

Ibraham's voice rose. It echoed through the empty building. "You know I do not support the policies of the U.S. government, but I do not believe that violence will change them. Violence only creates more violence." He paused. "My friends are here. My home is here. I will not be a party to destroying them."

"Your home is not here. It is in the land you and I grew up in."

"No, brother, my home is where I made it. Not what I was given at birth." He looked at Muqtada. "I am sorry you have not been able to create such a place for yourself."

Muqtada shook his head. "I had it taken from me, as did you, by these people you call your friends."

Muqtada could feel the anger rising in his chest. His younger brother had always been better with words. Ibraham had always been better at most things. He had always succeeded, at least that is the way Muqtada and their father had seen it.

Ibraham looked away. Muqtada did not. "I don't see," said Ibraham, "that we have anything more to talk about. I wish you good fortune brother, but I will not help you. I will not build the device you seek. And the plans for its creation, as of yesterday, are no longer in my possession."

Muqtada spoke in a weaker and almost pleasing tone. "My brother, I wish to spare your life, but I know you are a stubborn man. As a child I could never force you to do anything that you did not wish to do. Neither could our father."

Ibraham smiled. "Yes, that is true. I will not help you, but I will not help them. I believe you will have to make a choice. Is our family's honor, as you see it, more important than my life?"

CHAPTER 20

God has not given us a spirit of fear, but of power
and of love, and of a sound mind. — 2 Timothy

Thursday, April 4, 2013
The Lodge
Loon Lake, Maine

Snow and a sharp wind rattled the windowpanes and whistled around their frames. The clipper Ray had predicted had come and blown up into a raging winter storm. Neither Lee nor Liz had any desire to get out of their warm bed to cross the icy floor and rebuild the fire. They cuddled closer.

By noon the snow stopped and the sky was starting to clear, but the wind was even stronger. Lee felt better than he had in days. He had slept well. And being back with Liz felt familiar. It felt safe. He decided that he would brave the cold. The bathroom was, relatively speaking, warm. But it was not warm enough for a shower. He would have to revive the stove. The fire was easily restored with the additional kindling and wood Robert had laid in.

In the blaze of the fire and the early afternoon light Lee could see the room more clearly. It was large and L-shaped with a bank of windows at the bottom of the ell. Two love seats, a rocker, and an easy chair faced the lake. They must have thought that newly-weds expected a lot of company on their wedding night. There was a small writing desk in the bottom left corner of the room with a chair that looked more decorative than functional. Paintings of wildlife in crude wooden frames covered the walls. A snowy owl looked down on the bridal bed. A couple of 1940s vintage electric lamps set one on the desk, another on the bureau. The floor was rugged wooden planks. Wearing boots except when in bed was a good idea. The walls were logs that had been stripped of their bark and whitewashed just like the outside of the lodge. *Strange*, Lee thought. It gave the lodge a ghostly appearance in the snow. He wondered how it looked with the green of summer.

"Get up, honey. The room is getting warmer." It was a bit of an exaggeration. Liz didn't move.

"I'm going down to see what I can find or make or kill for breakfast."

"Great," said Liz. "Please, honey, will you bring me a very large cup of coffee with cream and lots of sugar?"

Lee started down the stairs. A cold breeze met him. He could hear Robert. From the sound of thuds and clunks, he guessed that Robert was bringing in wood. As he approached the kitchen, the sound grew louder. Through the open door, Lee could see Robert on all fours shoving wood into the cook stove. He mumbled under his breath. Lee was able to make out an occasional "damn" and "jeezum crow."

"Hello, Robert. How's the fire?"

Robert looked vaguely in Lee's direction and grunted. Lee waited as Robert continued his work closing the stove door and getting to his feet with some difficulty. He turned away from Lee toward the door that led into a large room stacked to the ceiling with cords of wood. Lee followed.

"How much wood do you burn in a winter?" asked Lee looking around the room. "Quite a bit, I imagine. The whole place is heated with wood?"

"We got two wood furnaces and an oil back up. Forced hot water. I keep 'em runnin'," muttered Robert as he pulled pieces of wood off the top of one of the stacks.

"How long have you been doing this?" asked Lee.

"A long time. I got work to do," said Robert as he headed for the basement stairs dragging a pallet of wood behind him.

Lee wandered back into the kitchen and found a coffeepot in the sink. He filled it and after a brief search for the coffee, put it on the stove and waited. He located the powdered milk and some corn flakes and made his breakfast. There was even some O.J. in the refrigerator.

Lee stood by the stove warming his feet and legs while he finished his meal. He thought of Pine Grove and White's Fork and wondered who had gotten out before the second explosion. He thought of his old patients and the staff at the Cerebral Palsy Center. Of his partner, Jim, who had taken over running the practice when Lee had left. Lee had been so focused on himself and his family that it was easy to forget the people who must be having a much more difficult time than he.

He found a large cup and poured the coffee, adding the sugar and cream the way Liz loved it. He returned to the room and found her reading. A mystery, he assumed, from the pile of old books stacked under the nightstand. He handed her the coffee.

"I talked to Robert, if you can call it a conversation. He's a real piece of work." A shudder ran through Lee's body. "I wonder what he does when the summer people come?"

"I suppose he hides in the basement," said Liz. "But what are we going to do about the summer people?" She pressed. "In a few weeks the ice will be out and the fishermen will be here." She paused. "We could hike across the border into Canada." Her expression was brighter. Her speech quicker. "We're only a few miles, maybe twenty or twenty five from the border. My family would help us. Sam could help," she was sure of it. "Given the level of tension these days between Canada and the U.S., the Mounties are not going to spend that much time and effort looking for you."

"Liz, we're in the middle of the great north woods. Twenty-five miles is one helluva long way. The temperature even in May can drop well below freezing at night."

"I'm sure Robert knows someone who could get us across," she insisted. "He's lived up here all his life. Here, look at the map I found." She pulled out a dog-eared map a tourist had left in their room. "There's a bunch of small villages just on the other side of the border and the Canadian Railway runs along the border. I'm sure there's a way to get us across."

"Okay, Liz, let me think about this." Lee was feeling irritated, as he often did, with her persistence.

"And I'm sure Joe's trying to find a way to contact us. Robert's got a satellite phone. Joe talked to him a few days ago." Lee wished she would stop. "You know I could call Sam," Liz said.

"No, I bet they're monitoring the calls of your Canadian relatives." *Maybe that would slow her down,* he thought.

"I could call him at the hospital. We could probably catch him in the doctors' lounge. Since he retired, he spends a lot of his time there. I doubt they're monitoring those calls."

"Yeah," Lee brightened. "You could, couldn't you." *Maybe this idea isn't such a bad one,* thought Lee. *Maybe she's right.* "But Robert? You think he can help us? He's such a scared rabbit." Lee shuddered again. "All he wants to do is run back to his hole."

"I'll convince him," said Liz. "Just let me turn on the old charm."

"He's not the sharpest tool in the shed."

"Hey, you're usually the voice of optimism. 'Give him a chance. He can do it.' He appears to me to be more capable than some of the wet puppies you've brought home." *God knows that was true,* she thought. "Why are you so down on him?"

"I don't know. The guy just bothers me." Lee really didn't know. "He seems so scared, so scared of living. You can feel it when you're around him."

"You've worked with a lot of scared people. But he really gets to you, doesn't he?"

It was true. Maybe because fear and anxiety, especially these days, was the most frequent problem people brought to Lee's office. "I…I guess I am just tired of the chase. I feel like a fox, hoping the hounds have lost my scent, yet knowing they haven't."

"Well, my foxy one," she said as she pulled back the bed covers, "why don't you slip into this bed with me and let's do a little intense snuggling while we quietly contemplate the price of tea in China and look for the next foxhole."

Lee pulled himself back and focused his attention on Liz.

"I don't have anything else on my schedule," he responded.

"Gee, thanks." She smiled.

Lee knelt down next to the bed and touched Liz's face with a gentleness she had not felt from him in a long time.

"I don't think you've been on your knees with me since you proposed."

"Thanks," said Lee.

Liz looked surprised. "For what?" asked Liz since she wasn't sure what he meant.

"For just being here. You've always been, especially when things have . . . .Well, you know." He kissed her. For a moment they both felt like making love. But the thought quickly passed. They were tired and cold, and they both knew that not everything had changed. There was still a distance and a tension between them, especially around sex. All of the craziness of the past week hadn't changed that.

The afternoon slipped into evening as the two passed in and out of sleep. It was nearly 7:00 P.M. when Liz woke him.

"I know, you're hungry, right?" said Lee.

Liz was a person who had to have something to eat every few hours, otherwise she started to, in her words, "get cranky."

"How did you know?"

"You learn a few things after twenty-six years of marriage."

Lee lit a lamp for the bath and another for the bedroom. While Liz dressed, Lee sat in the rocker facing the lake and watched the evening star rising in the east. He thought of his grandfather. He remembered his visit to the cemetery. It felt like years ago, but it had only been a week and a half. Before all of this. He closed his eyes. Maybe he would open them and they would be at their cabin on the river. It would be Saturday night and they would be preparing dinner while they listened to *Prairie Home Companion* on Maine Public Radio.

But it didn't work. His efforts at changing reality were interrupted by Liz's voice.

"Let's go. I'm very hungry," she said.

Lee followed her down the dark stairs. In the lamplight they cast long shadows on the walls and ceiling of the lodge. The kitchen was dark, but warm. The lodge was quiet. Robert, Lee thought, must be downstairs asleep. He was making no noise.

Spam, pork and beans, and potato chips was the evening meal. They ate by the stove.

"I wonder why Robert is so devoted to Joe? How does he know him?" Lee asked.

"Joe explained some of that. Apparently Robert came to Portland to celebrate his twenty-first birthday years ago. He got a room in one of the small hotels. It was all he could afford." Liz paused and took a sip of Lee's coffee. "He took the money that he had left and went in one of the first bars he saw and ordered a drink."

"And the plot thickens."

"He apparently had quite a few drinks and decided he would buy himself some marijuana. Unfortunately, the person he decided to buy it from was an undercover cop."

"Nothing like having good luck on your birthday," said Lee shaking his head and smiling.

"Needless to say, he did not spend the night in his hotel room, but in the county jail." Liz paused. "He was arraigned the next day. Joe was a young attorney in those days and assigned the case by the judge. He plea bargained, got Robert on probation and got him transferred back to the county." Liz sighed. "Robert returned the next day and hasn't been out of this area since.

"But don't worry. Come tomorrow morning, Robert and I are going to have a long talk over breakfast. I'm going to put together one of the best meals Robert has ever had."

Liz stood up. "Which means I had better put the frozen egg substitute out tonight so it can thaw," said Liz as she opened the refrigerator. "I wonder what kind of spices they have around here? Spam tastes good, they say, if you season it right." She placed the egg substitute on the counter by the sink.

"So what is Robert going to tell you?"

"Who he knows up here, and who can get us across the border. Maybe he could do it himself?" she said as she fumbled through a second drawer.

"Oh, no. I've already done that once before this week. I've had enough of being led through the woods by folks who don't have their cap on very tight."

"You mean that guy from the shelter?" said Liz, pulling out a jar of red pepper.

"Howard," said Lee.

"Where do you think he is now?"

"I don't know," said Lee as he imagined the ball of light that had hovered over the park that last night in Tennessee. "I hope he made it...home."

"Where is home for Howard?"

Lee shook his head. "God only knows," he said and started to clear the table.

As Lee washed the very few dishes and utensils their evening meal had required, Liz searched the kitchen for items she would need the next morning. She found a drawer of spices and a ton of Spam.

"Ah, potatoes," she said. "They keep all winter if they don't freeze. Okay, I think I'm ready. Why don't you sleep late?" She sounded confident of her plan. Lee always loved her optimism. "You can have brunch after Robert and I have our talk."

"Fine with me. If you get him to say ten words you'll be doing better than me."

The couple returned to their room. Lee filled the stove and banked the fire for the night. Liz read while Lee thumbed through an old copy of *National Geographic*. The wind rattled the windows. The stars and rising moon blinked in and out as the clouds raced across the sky. Lee felt warm and safe and, for the first time in what seemed an eternity, hopeful. Maybe even optimistic.

April 4, 2013
Southern Maine
11:36 P.M.

Muqtada waited for the doctor. He had chosen the wing chair with a high back and the leather trim in front of the doctor's desk. It was late. Muqtada was tired. He had not slept in two days.

He knew the room well. The high, tin ceiling, the long narrow windows, the small painted Italian fireplace that the doctor never used. *A fire would be good,* Muqtada thought. The leather felt cold against his skin.

Muqtada knew the decision had to be made tonight. The others were waiting for him. Watching him. Not sure of him. He tried to put away the memory of past failures, of missteps. *It will be different this time.*

The doctor entered the room. Muqtada stood out of respect. This was the man who had been there after his father's death, who had rekindled his interest in his religion and his culture, who had taught him the prayers and traveled with him on his first pilgrimage. He was also the man who had helped him make his first connection with the movement.

"Sit, my son," said the doctor.

Muqtada complied as he always did. He had known this man most of his life. He both admired and feared him.

"You wish to speak with me tonight? The hour is late."

"Doctor, I know we should act now, but we are not ready."

Muqtada looked away, trying to avoid the doctor's eyes, but this did not work.

"Muqtada look at me." Muqtada again complied. "We cannot wait. The timing could not be better."

"But without the device, I believe we may fail," Muqtada objected.

"You will not fail again, Muqtada. You cannot fail again. Allah will be with you."

"Doctor, I do not wish to be disrespectful of you or your work, but your method of delivery of the virus is primitive. The device would have insured our success." Muqtada thought of his brother.

"Yes, that is true. But you must remember that our goal is not to spread the virus, but to spread the fear of the virus, to create a panic. That is what will bring down our enemy."

The doctor waited. For a moment Muqtada hesitated. Then as if someone was speaking for him he said, "We will act now." He sounded decisive, although he did not feel decisive. But he had made his decision. He knew he must now carry it through.

CHAPTER 21

When God creates disability he seeks perfection
not in the disability but in the reaction to it.
— *The Power of Intention* by Dr. Wayne Dyer

Friday, April 5, 2013
The Lodge
Loon Lake, Maine

Lee woke to someone crying. It sounded to Lee like a man's voice. Sobbing. Liz was asleep next to him. *It must be Robert,* he thought. Lee rolled over hoping the crying would stop. It didn't.

Lee sat up. He pulled the cover back and crossed in bare feet the icy floor to the room's door. He listened. The crying continued. He opened the door. The light from the moon partially illuminated the stairs. He could see that the door to the basement was open. The yellow flicker of an oil lamp mixed with the moonlight. The sound was coming from below.

Lee felt his way down the stairs to the basement door. He listened. A force, an energy of some kind, seemed to be pulling him, pushing him. He descended the basement steps. In front of him set an oil lamp on a small wooden table. He could feel heat to his right. The wood furnaces. In the dark he could see only their outline. The small windows in the furnace doors looked like two large red eyes staring into the dark.

The crying came again. It was to his left. It was coming from what Lee assumed was Robert's room. The door was ajar. A strange blue light streamed from the room. Lee felt the energy again. He tried to turn, to mount the stairs to leave. But he couldn't. Instead, he walked toward the light and pushed the door open.

The room was long and narrow. To his right was a small bed and chest of drawers. To the left an old wooden bookcase. The walls were covered with photographs. There were empty frames on one wall. The room seemed familiar. Like the room he had grown up in as a child. The blue light was coming from the far end of the room. At first he thought he heard the crying. But the crying had stopped.

"Is anyone there?" asked Lee. There was no answer.

Lee took a few more steps forward and stopped. A photograph in one of the frames caught his eye. It was his father in his Army uniform. He looked again. There was another photo, one of his mother as a young girl with her parents in their porch swing on Fifth Avenue in Bourbonville. They were smiling. He imagined that his grandfather was singing. He always did. He looked at the next photograph. It was his Aunt Rose at a party a few months before her death. God could she dance! She had taught Lee and David to dance, to twist, to do the locomotion, to slow dance. But these pictures, where had they come from?

Why?" asked Lee out loud.

He heard a sound and turned to his right. There was another wall of photographs. Lee looked more closely. There was Lee on a white water rafting trip with his friend David, having a great time, smiling for the camera. But he had never taken the trip. He had made up excuses. Fear had stopped him.

The next photograph was of Lee repelling off a cliff with Liz, something he had promised her he would do. She was working the ropes. But he wasn't afraid. He was even laughing. But he had never repelled off the cliff with Liz. He had refused. Again he had made up excuses. Fear was the reason.

Lee looked again. There was a photograph of Lee in a tuxedo and Jean in a wedding dress together. He looked confident and pleased with himself. Certain of his decision. But that wedding had never happened. It had been planned, but "postponed."

The photographs all had one thing in common, they had never happened because of his old friend, fear. They had never happened because Lee had been too unsure of himself. Too afraid.

Lee felt his old friend nearby. Lee's heart started to race. His legs felt weak. His hands were trembling.

He thought he heard someone say something.

"Is someone there?" Lee called out.

And again there was silence. Lee tried to slow his breathing, but couldn't. The blue light was brighter now. It burned his eyes. He couldn't see. And then the room went dark.

Lee turned and grabbed at the dark. He spun around again. There was a light. Someone was at the end of the room, sitting in a large winged chair with a book, a large book, reading by the light that came from a small blue lamp. Lee took a few steps forward.

"Hello," he said.

His voice echoed in what now seemed to be an empty room. The person in the chair did not respond. Lee could see that he was holding a scrapbook. Lee couldn't see the person's face. It was blocked by the chair. Lee suddenly felt irritated and angry. He took a few more steps forward.

"Excuse me," he said. "Who are you?" No response. He was being ignored. His anger was building. It pushed down his fear. He clenched his fist and walked toward the figure in the chair. He could see that it was a man wearing a black tuxedo. Lee stepped around the lamp to get a better look at the man.

"Who?" and he stopped. The person in the chair looked up. His hair, what was left of it, was white and neatly trimmed, as was his mustache. The face was familiar. Lee looked at the man's hands. His left one was small. A hand like Lee's, but wrinkled with age. There was no hook. No need to cover it. No mask for the hand. No need to keep it from view.

Lee looked back at the man's face. It was Lee's face. Lee stepped back. The old man smiled. Lee smiled. Nothing was said. Lee turned to leave. The old man turned back to his book.

As Lee walked toward the door his fear seemed to drop away. His breathing slowed. His heart no longer raced. Wet with sweat, he felt cold, but good. He found the door he had entered. He could see the lamp at the bottom of the basement steps. The red eyes of the furnaces glowed. He could feel their warmth.

"Doc," a voice said from the dark. It sounded familiar.

"Howard." Lee was sure it was Howard.

"It's time to go home, Doc." Lee peered into the dark.

"I know, Howard. I am home," he said as he continued to walk toward the stairs.

"You will be soon," the voice said.

Lee stopped. He turned scanning the dark basement. "Where are you, Howard?" He waited. He scanned the room again. "Howard," he called. But there was no reply.

Lee took the steps two at a time. He felt a surge of the energy again. The light from the oil lamp faded as he neared the top of the stairs. The moonlight was gone. The landing was dark. He let go of the stair rail, and stepped out into the dark. But there was nothing there. He was falling. And he wasn't afraid.

He looked down. The water was there, the river. Lee turned his body so that he was now falling headfirst. He extended his arms and placed his hands together as the woman who had taught him swimming had told him to do. He tucked his head in just before he hit the water. He plunged through the water.

With a few strokes he rose to the surface. The water was warm. He swam with less fear than he had ever felt. He flipped on his back and floated. The bright sunlight was warm on his face. He closed his eyes.

When he opened them he was lying in the four-poster alone. Liz was gone. Lee remembered she was downstairs fixing breakfast and talking to Robert. It had been only a dream. But something was different with Lee. He felt lighter. Stronger. At peace with himself in a way he had never felt.

Lee could decide to not wear the mask, his hook that he had been hiding his hand with, just as he had done when he had shoved the hand in his pocket as a kid.

But more than that, he could stop hiding with lies and excuses, his fear of failing, of not being able to do and be with one hand what others could do and be with two. He could finally accept and let go of this old fear. Take the risk. Conquer it.

Liz found Robert in the basement putting wood in one of the furnaces. "Morning, Robert. I cooked a big breakfast. More than Lee and I can eat." Robert continued stoking the furnace. She pressed on. "Lee is still in bed. Please, have breakfast with me. I would really enjoy your company."

Robert followed her up the stairs. She had a place set for him at the table. He nodded his appreciation.

"Have you always lived in the county, Robert?" Robert nodded yes. "Your family is here?"

"I don't have no family. They're all dead or livin' someplace else."

"Your mother?"

Robert closed his eyes and leaned back from the table. "I don't know where she is and I don't care. She never cared about me. Not me or my nana." He paused. "Nana tried to raise me. No one would help her cause of my fits. They wanted me put away."

"Is Nana still alive?"

"No," he said, appearing irritated. "She died when I was a kid. The state took me and put me in a home."

"I guess it was hard, Robert, with no family." Her smile was sympathetic.

He looked up from his plate. His face softened. "Yeah, you could say that. But I got out. Never did finish school, but it don't matter."

"You've been at the lodge a long time," Liz said.

Robert smiled for the first time that morning. "How did you know?" He allowed his eyes to connect with hers.

"Joe told me," she said smiling again.

"Yeah, I guess the only luck I've ever had is when the Strouts took me in and gave me this job and Joe helped me out."

"It must get pretty lonely up here. Do you have any friends?"

"Just Danny. He comes over sometimes on his sled and we smoke some, just a little." He flushed. "Well, you know. I mean the winter is really long up here, you know."

Liz got up and refilled his plate, pleased that things were going as planned.

Half-awake and half-asleep, Lee heard Liz's footsteps on the stairs. The door opened.

"Lee? Lee, I have your breakfast."

Lee was slow to move. "Here...set it here." He sat up and pointed in the direction of the nightstand.

Liz set the tray down. She smiled. "Let me tell you what I found out. Robert has a friend at Baker Lake who could get us across the border." She didn't wait for Lee's reaction. "He makes a lot of trips across. He's got some friends with the Canadian railway." She pressed on. "He could get us into Quebec City. One of Sam's friends could meet us there."

"Slow down. How did you find all of this out?"

"Well, I literally cornered Robert in the basement. Had to plead a bit, but I guess the idea of eating a meal prepared by someone else was too much for him to resist." She relayed Robert's story.

"So, let me guess Liz, Danny is the guy at Baker Lake?"

"Give the man a cigar," said Liz. "Very good."

"And why is dear old Danny Boy back-and-forth across the border so often?" Lee asked a question he was sure he knew the answer to.

"Well," said Liz "I think he's involved, as Robert says, in the import business."

Lee chuckled. "And let me guess, what is he importing? Drugs?" He shook his head.

"You could be right. But he's the only person Robert could come up with. Here, eat your breakfast before it gets cold." She offered Lee the fork.

He poked at the mystery meat on his plate. "Has anyone ever died of an overdose of Spam?"

Liz laughed. "It does taste better with the spices," she reassured. "Try it. You'll see."

Lee took a few more bites. "The eggs are good. This reminds me of my breakfast at Camp Liberty, the camp with the chains and padlocks on the doors."

"So what do you think? He can call his friend tonight." She waited. He didn't respond. "It will cost us, but I brought enough cash so that's not an issue."

"You know, Liz, I've been thinking," said Lee. "Thinking about a lot of things. Things I'm going to do that I have never done." He paused. "Finish some of the things that I said I was going to finish."

"Yeah, like finish painting the bathroom when you get back," she said smiling.

"No, I'm serious." He paused. "I'm going to finish that book. The one I've been working on forever." He found Liz's eyes. "I had this dream last night. I think it changed some things for me. I can still feel it." He closed his eyes. "I can still see it. I tell you something changed last night. I don't feel scared anymore."

"Well, I wish I didn't," she said as she began organizing the tray for her return trip to the kitchen. "Maybe you should. Joe says these FBI guys in Washington play for keeps."

"But scared is not going to help," Lee protested. "Look what fear has done to our country. Look at the crazy mess it has created in our lives." He was on his feet. "There is a part of me that has been afraid all my life. Fear has been an old friend. But like a bad relationship it's kept me from doing things I should have done." He had her attention. "From making commitments I should have made. You know what I'm talking about."

Liz nodded. "Oh yes," she said. "I certainly do."

"I've been like Robert in the last two weeks. Running from one hole to the next." His words came quickly, faster than he could say them. "No, I'm not going back to being that scared kid who hides his left hand in his pocket. The hell with that." He paused. "You know that stuff still effects me? I didn't realize it until now. I thought all that handicapped kid business was behind me." He shook his head. "But it wasn't. Isn't. Retirement just made it worse. What do they say? Are you disabled, or are you a person with a disability?" He paused. "There is still a part of me that's disabled.

"But I belong here. It's my home, North and South. It's my country. Remember that argument I had with Dave? We both agreed it wasn't about conservatives versus liberals and it wasn't whether the government was going to run our lives, it was whether the corporations were." Lee's voice rose. "Is 'Greed is Good' going to be our national motto? It's my country and I'm not leaving." His words were a mix of the anger of an adult and the stubbornness of a child. "Not because of a bunch of confused, little bow-tied bastards in DC, or wherever the hell they are. I'm not going to Canada." He was shouting now. "I'm going back to Portland."

Liz nodded as if to herself. "Lee, are you sure?"

"I'm sure. If I can finally understand and accept who I am, they will have to, too."

"I agree," she said. "It should work that way, but I don't think it always does."

"Well, maybe we will have to make it work that way," Lee said with resolve.

CHAPTER 22

Illness gave him strength and courage he had not had before. He had to think out the fundamentals of living and learn the greatest of all lessons...infinite patience and never-ending persistence. — Eleanor Roosevelt

Friday, April 5, 2013
The Lodge
Loon Lake, Maine
The Sabbath

Liz stayed busy exploring the lodge, talking to Robert. She found two candles in one of the bureaus in the dining room and later showed Lee her discovery. "We'll use these tonight for Shabbat prayers." When Lee responded only with a nod, she left to prepare for lunch, leaving him to his thoughts.

For the rest of the morning Lee stayed in the room, rocking in the chair by the window, looking out at the lake. He rocked, and rocked, and rocked. He needed to think, to think about the past two weeks, about the last sixty-six years of his life. What had happened had changed him, brought up old pain he'd thought had been resolved, or pushed so far inside he would no longer have to feel it. He understood things about himself now in a different way.

The world made the same demands on Lee that it made on everyone. To grow up and support yourself, to make a commitment to another person, to create a family. Important demands. But his defect—his hand, his disability—had caused him to question himself, stirring fear that held him back, stopping him. He had lost opportunities and people in his life he would never have again. Jean wasn't coming back. And Lee wasn't going there. Understanding and acceptance in your sixties can not give you back your thirties. That time was past.

Lee now understood in his heart how lack of acceptance and confidence in himself could be more disabling than the disability. This is what made the difference. Why some people with a disability make a life for themselves and others with a similar disability do not. He had understood all of this in his head for much of his life. But now he understood it in his heart.

He thought of Stella struggling with the pain of having lost her son, whom she believed she could not live her life without. Of Jim, fearing that the sins of his past could never be forgiven by others or by God, or more importantly, by himself. Of Robert, fearing the world outside of the county. Disabling fears that held them back. That stopped them.

He thought of Millie. A black woman. Older than the rest. In a wheelchair. But she seemed to Lee to be less disabled and more at peace with herself. Less driven by fear and more accepting of herself and her world than the rest.

Lee thought of himself. This mess he was in, this crisis, was really an opportunity. An opportunity to learn a lesson. And God was the teacher. A lesson in self-understanding and acceptance. A lesson in managing fear and anger so they did not manage any part of his life. This was something he had never been able to master by himself, not completely. Griff would say that this was God's grace helping Lee to do something he could not do for himself.

Lee had always done things for himself. He had always prided himself on his independence. But this time he was facing something he could not master without help. He had been forced to depend on others.

He heard Robert and Liz on the stairs. The door opened. "Lee, you've got to explain to Robert why you're calling Joe. He's afraid you're gonna get him in trouble."

Robert stood silently at Liz's side, staring at the floor.

"Robert, you know I'm in trouble with the police. I've got to talk to Joe."

Robert continued to look down at his feet and said nothing.

"You know how much he helped you."

Robert nodded.

"Robert," said Lee, "you haven't done anything wrong. You took us in." He tried to make eye contact, but Robert avoided his eyes. "We'll tell them you tried to talk us into giving ourselves up. That is what we're going to do when we call Joe. We just need to arrange it."

He waited. No response. "If you let us use the phone, they will come. Probably this afternoon or in the morning and we will be out of here." He paused. He wasn't sure what to say next. "They may ask you some questions, but they will let you go." He assumed they would. "You haven't done anything wrong."

Whether that mattered or not anymore, he wasn't sure. But he did know that the sooner Liz and he were out of there, the less trouble Robert would be in.

There was silence for a minute. "I'll do what Joe says," said Robert.

"Good. Can we call Joe?"

Without an answer, Robert left the room. Lee and Liz were alone. "Are you still sure this is what you want to do?" She wasn't sure what she wanted.

"Yes. I feel more certain about this than I did earlier this morning." The new energy, the force he felt from the previous night was still there.

"Alright, I guess," she said looking uncertain. "As I said, it's your decision."

Robert was back with the satellite phone. Lee placed the call. He knew that when Joe's office answered the Feds, with their global positioning system, would soon know exactly where he was.

Gail, Joe's secretary, sounded scared. He was in conference, but she would interrupt him.

Joe came on the line. He spoke first. "Lee, don't say anything. Just listen to me for a minute. The FBI wants to talk to you about some sort of deal. I'm not sure what they're up to. They want something from you. What it is I don't know. And why the hell did you leave the hospital? No, don't...don't answer that..."

Lee, breaking in, "I left because I wanted to have a choice. My choice is to come home. Deal or no deal."

"Well, I can arrange that," said Joe. "But I'm sure I'm not going to need to. By now they know where you are. But I will call them. Remember what I said about name, rank, and serial number."

"Sure, Joe. And Robert is here and wants to talk to you. He's worried about having to leave the county."

Lee put Robert on the phone. He couldn't hear what Joe said, but it seemed to calm Robert. He listened and, at the end of the conversation said, "All right," and hung up.

"Joe told me to go to my room and stay there. He said he would talk to them and tell them I had nothin' to do with you two." Robert hurried out of the room and that was the last time that Lee and Liz saw him.

"Well, are you hungry?" asked Liz.

"Starved, let's eat. Where's the Spam?"

She laughed. There wasn't much else to do but wait.

April 5, 2013
Agency Offices, Boston
1:00 P.M.

Jennings was at his desk thumbing through Jean Kudrick's file when Wright entered the office waving a cell phone.

"Doug. Brazil's attorney is on the phone. Brazil wants to turn himself in."

"Where is he?" said Jennings without looking up from the file.

Wright looked at the piece of paper in his other hand. "A place called Loon Lake Lodge in northern Maine. We just confirmed that from the tap on the attorney's phone."

Jennings closed the file and looked up. "Tell his attorney we will call him back. I'm going up there. I don't want this one screwed up." Jennings stood up and stretched. "Get me an Agency plane. Call our office in Bangor." Jennings started putting files in his briefcase. "I'll need a helicopter and someone who knows where the hell Loon Lodge is."

"Will do." Wright started for the office door.

Jennings quickly surveyed his desk. He picked up his dead partner Ron's old GPS "fountain pen" and shoved it in the breast pocket of his jacket, for luck. He glanced at the bay one last time before he followed Wright out the door.

The Lodge

Lee and Liz walked down the stairs, crossed the dining room and found their seats by the only kitchen window that looked out on the lake. Liz pulled out some sandwiches from the refrigerator that she had made earlier in the morning. Spam, of course. The sky was clearing, the sun bright on the snow. They ate and talked.

"Dru's new boyfriend," said Liz, "is in her program finishing his degree in oceanography this year."

"Do you think he's any different from the rest?" Lee asked. But Liz was still thinking about Lee's conversation with Joe.

"I think so. She thinks so," said Liz.

"Woodford. Is he the cousin of the old goalie for the Portland Pirates? Ouellet? That superstar with the Washington Capitols? Dru loved him. You sure she's not just dating him to get Ouellet's autograph?"

"I don't think so. Our daughter's not that shallow," she said grinning.

"Do you think he's ready to take on our daughter?" Most men had not been up to the challenge.

"Well, he's been there for her in the last two weeks. He wanted to come with her to The Cove but she wouldn't let him." She was starting to focus more on what Lee was saying. "I've met him. He seems to be pretty solid," said Liz.

"Well, he either cares about her or he's a fool. I guess we'll see. She's always had good taste in men. She loves me." Lee smiled remembering their breakfasts at McDonald's every Saturday for years. He stood up. "Why don't we take a walk? I'm not sure how much opportunity I'm going to have in the next few days to stretch my legs."

They put on their coats and slipped the borrowed snowshoes on. It was warm by northern Maine standards. In the thirties. They walked through the woods near the lodge. The snow from the night before was probably one of the last of the season. It was already starting to melt. Spring was in the air.

The sap was starting to rise in the maple trees near the lodge. Robert had tapped some of them. Lee remembered those Sunday mornings in early spring when he and his family, his mother was still living then, would drive out to one of the maple farms near Portland for a pancake and maple syrup breakfast. They would stay for some of the demonstrations on tapping trees and boiling down the sap. At least long enough to have homemade ice cream with maple syrup.

Lee and Liz stood for a long time on the dock watching the wind stir the snow on the peaks of Mt. Russell. They walked back to the lodge and their room and waited. They both drifted off to sleep on the four-poster bed. When they woke it was near sunset.

Liz arranged the two candles on the table for Shabbat. Lee stood behind her with his arms around her waist. Liz began the evening prayers. *"Baruch atah adonai elohenu melech haolum asher kidshanu b'mitzvotav v'tzivanu l'hadlik ner shel shabbat."*

Lee followed. "Holy one of blessing your presence fills creation, commanding us to light the Sabbath lights."

As they stared into the candlelight, they heard the low roar of a helicopter. It had not taken long for them to come. They watched quietly as the large green Army Reserve helicopter approached from the south, flying low over the lake and then over the lodge. It landed in a field to the north.

The side door opened and black-suited agents put on snowshoes and started to move across the white field toward the lodge. A tall man stood in the door of the helicopter. Lee recognized him. The way he stood. Arms folded against his chest. Special Agent Jennings.

Lee held Liz in his arms as tears welled up in their eyes. The next few days or weeks or...would not be easy. *But God's grace*, Lee thought, *is acceptance. The land of milk and honey. Home is not on the other side of the Jordan, or in a different state, or country, or world. It is in each one of us. A person walks uprightly when they accept themselves and are no longer disabled by fear. They reach home.*

Section II: Flight

Chapter Summaries, Discussion Questions and Author's Comments
Chapter 16 – 22*

CHAPTER 16

Chief Dutremble arranges for Lee to be evacuated by air to a Portland hospital because of his head injury. Liz, Lee's wife, goes with him. Lee and Liz arrive at the hospital where Lee is examined by a young intern. Lee decides to leave the hospital with Liz.

Discussion Questions

1. When they arrive at the medical center, Lee has difficulty accepting any help from anyone. He refuses to be helped off the plane by the EMT. What does this tell you about Lee's character? What is the upside and the downside in being "independent"? What role does independence play in resilience?

2. Lee decides to try to leave the medical center, saying, "At this point, what do I have to lose?" Is this an impulsive act?

Author's Comments

Lee has struggled all his life with the issue of independence. Many people like Lee may at times refuse help, even in situations where they need it for fear of being dependent upon others. Not necessarily the best idea. Lee is acting out of emotion, not reason.

Lee appears to have given some thought to what he is doing. He is, to quote him, "considering all the options." What would you do?

*Refer to pages 4 and 5 for a list of the Eleven Skills And Attitudes That Build Resilience.

CHAPTER 17

There is a disturbance in the ER, and Liz and Lee manage to sneak past the security guard and the police. Lee finds Betsy, an old friend retired from nursing, who is visiting the hospital. She is on her way to a lodge in northern Maine. She agrees to take them in her VW bus. The three manage to get through a roadblock, but the weather is closing in. It's snowing heavily by the time they reach the lodge.

Discussion Questions

1. Betsy is going through some major transitions in her life. What are they and how is she demonstrating resilience in dealing with them?

Author's Comments

Betsy has retired from a long career in nursing. She is returning to school. She is also dealing with a divorce and with conflicts within her family that have existed for many years. She is taking a very proactive role and is able to think on her feet as demonstrated in her interactions with the state police officers at the roadblock. She is a good communicator and asserts herself in situations, taking charge and being able to direct others when she feels she is the best person to give direction. She has clearly set goals for her life and is moving toward them. She still sees helping others as an important part of her life.

CHAPTER 18

The police are searching the hotels and inns along the Canadian border. Lee realizes he cannot stay at the lodge. They convince Ray, who runs the lodge and also operates a flying service, to fly them to Loon Lake Lodge, the remote inn where Lee's attorney had originally arranged for Lee to stay while they were negotiating with the federal agents. Ray flies them to the lodge and lands on the spring ice which is thin and dangerous.

Discussion Questions

1. In this chapter Lee's thoughts are about change: "But time and age change a lot of things." How is acceptance of change an important part of resilience?

2. In this chapter, Ray tells his story. How does his life illustrate the skills and attitudes that make for resilience?

Author's Comments

By definition, resilience is about change. It is about being able to adapt and deal with change. Being able to see clearly the things that are changing in your life and your world is important if you are to adapt to these changes and manage them. Age certainly does change a lot of things. Physical appearance and physical strength and endurance change with aging. Being able to accept these changes and value other things about ourselves is a critical part of "aging well."

Ray, like Jim, has survived the Vietnam War. He, unlike Jim, came through it "without a scratch." Throughout his life, Jim has demonstrated his ability to make plans and follow through with them and to set goals for himself. He is a good communicator and problem-solver. He is active and assertive in his interactions with others. He does not, however, appear to have a large support network. Although he may not appear to be a "religious" person, he clearly acts in terms of his values and beliefs. Like Lee, he has a sense of humor and uses it.

CHAPTER 19

Lee and Liz reach the lodge and convince the reclusive caretaker, Robert, who has cerebral palsy, to allow them to stay.

Meanwhile, Muqtada manages to see his brother, but his brother refuses to help him create the device that will spread the plague.

Discussion Questions

1. From what you see and hear of Robert in this chapter, what are your impressions of him as they relate to the issue of resilience?

2. On page 137, Ibraham, in talking with Muqtada, says, "My home is where I made it." How do you think about the issue of home and where your home is?

Author's Comments

Robert's communication skills are limited, and he appears to prefer spending time by himself and does not feel comfortable talking with others. His style of interaction is one that certainly does not encourage other people to communicate with him or to provide support. What other things do you notice about Robert?

CHAPTER 20

Lee becomes increasingly uncomfortable with Robert, whose way of dealing with his handicap reminds Lee of his own childhood. Robert has hidden most of his life from other people because of his disability. Lee feels like he has been behaving like Robert, acting out of fear and running like a rabbit from one hole to another. Lee weighs the options of leaving the country and going to Canada where his wife's family would assist him. Lee thinks of his friends at Pine Grove and how they must be suffering at present.

Muqtada plans the attack on Boston without his brother's assistance. He seeks the approval and support of a family friend who has served as a surrogate father for Muqtada.

Discussion Questions

1. To quote II Timothy, "God has not given us the spirit of fear, but of power and of love and of a sound mind." What is your reaction to this quote from the Bible?

2. Lee has more difficulty dealing with Robert than most of the other characters in this story. Liz asks Lee, "Why are you so down on him?" (page 140). Why do you think Lee is "down on Robert"?

3. Note that the goal of Muqtada's actions, and specifically Dr. Hazeem's, "…is not to spread the virus, but to spread the fear of the virus, to create a panic. That is what will bring down our enemy." Do you believe that fear could do this? How? Be specific.

Author's Comments

Robert reminds Lee of himself as a child hiding his hand in his pocket. Lee is confused about how to deal with Robert. Lee's self-image as someone who can relate to people like Robert, like himself, may be threatened by Robert's rejection of him. Do you think Robert is threatened by Lee? If so, in what way?

CHAPTER 21

In the night Lee has the recurring dream of falling and drowning. But tonight the dream is different. He dreams of himself as an old man who has finally dealt with his fear and no longer needs the hook to mask his disability. The dream convinces Lee to stay, to fight, to deal with his fear and the authorities.

Discussion Questions

1. "When God creates disability he seeks perfection, not in the disability but in the reaction to it." What is your reaction to this quote?

2. The dream sequence in this chapter has a major impact on Lee and his way of thinking about himself and his world. What is your reaction to the dream? Why do you think it is so significant to Lee?

Author's Comments

The dream is about self-acceptance. How accepting are you of yourself? How do you see yourself and how do you want others to see you?

CHAPTER 22

Lee calls his attorney, Joe, and arranges to give himself up. Lee understands for himself that God's grace is acceptance and that a person stands upright when he accepts himself and is no longer disabled by fear. Jennings and his agents arrive by helicopter and take Lee into custody.

Discussion Questions

1. Lee spends much of his time in this chapter attempting to understand the dream and trying to deal with all of its implications. How has fear held you back in your life? What would you have done sooner and more of if fear had not stood in your way?

2. How independent are you? How much do you depend upon other people in your life? How much do they depend upon you? What is the balance?

3. Re-read the last paragraph on page 151. Lee believes that God's grace is "acceptance...and that Home...is in each one of us. A person walks uprightly when they accept themselves and are no longer disabled by fear. They reach Home." What do you believe?

Author's Comments

Lee sees God's grace as God doing something for him that he could not do by himself: Accepting himself. Looking inside himself for a sense of peace and comfort, for home, is part of what comes with self-acceptance for Lee. He feels he is "no longer disabled by fear."

BOOK THREE: FIGHT

CHAPTER 23

And before honor is humility. — Proverbs

Lee opened his eyes. He was lying on his back. The room was dark. He turned his head toward the bluish light that came from a block of glass in the wall. He tried to sit up, but pain forced him back down.

He lay still again. Memory began to return. The pain began to melt. He remembered figures in black bursting through the door of their room. Lee had not moved quickly enough when he had been told to lay face down on the floor. One of them had shoved him down. Liz stood over him. A figure in black tried to push her away. Lee reached for her. He grabbed the form's arm. Then he felt the pain, and then came the dark.

Lee opened his eyes again. He could hear metal doors opening and closing. There was the sound of metal sliding over metal. A shaft of light shot across the room. Suddenly the room was filled with light. Lee's eyes burned. He closed them.

When he opened them, two figures in gray were standing over him. One of them spoke. "Wake up sleeping beauty. They want to talk to you."

Lee raised his hand, shielding his eyes from the light. "Who, who wants to talk to me?"

"Who do you think?" said the gray form, pulling Lee to a sitting position. In a flash the pain was back. Lee felt his head. It was completely wrapped in a bandage, like a turban.

"Where is it?" Lee asked, looking around, sounding confused.

"Where is what?" said the second form.

Almost shouting, "My hook."

"Hey, calm down buddy. We've got it," said the first.

"Where is it?" Lee asked again, feeling a wave of the old panic. He took a deep breath and tried to focus on what the gray forms were saying.

"You know you could hurt someone with that," said the second gray form.

"Don't worry about it. You'll get it back," said the first, pulling Lee to his feet. "Our little rag head is up."

"Let's go," said the second form.

They led Lee out of the room and into a hall. They moved quickly with one form on each arm. The hall was a green blur to Lee. They were buzzed through the heavy metal doors. Down one flight of steps with Lee's feet barely touching the ground. Through another door, into a short hall and into a room marked "Interview." They seated Lee at a long table in a small desk chair and left. There was the sound of the door, and then there was no sound.

Lee rubbed his eyes, trying to decide where he was. The room was dimly lit. There were four other chairs around the table and an observation window to Lee's left. The agents who had brought him to this place had, Lee was sure, flown from Bangor to the northern Maine lodge where they had arrested him. But he had no idea of where he was now and no sense of time either. Had days passed or only hours? Was he in Bangor or Boston, or someplace else?

Maybe he should have listened to Liz and left the country, gone across the Canadian border, left the craziness and paranoia behind. But he chose to stay, to not allow fear and paranoia to drive him out. He was no traitor, no threat to anyone, except maybe himself.

His ruminations were interrupted by the sound of metal sliding over metal. The door opened. A young man dressed in a dark gray suit entered the room and seated himself on the other side of the table. At first he said nothing, but busied himself thumbing through his stack of papers. He mumbled his name and something in the way of an apology about the system being down, again, and that being the reason for the stack of paper.

Lee watched him and said nothing. He felt more confused than scared. He was still trying to piece together the events of the last...he didn't know how long. Twenty-four hours?

"Lee Brazil?" the young man asked.

"That's right," said Lee.

"Well, you have been a very busy fellow over the last few weeks. Your trip to the Southeast was cut a bit short, wasn't it, by the explosion at Pine Grove?"

"Yes, I guess you could say that." *I'm sure you could say a lot of things,* thought Lee.

"You will be glad to know that things down there are under control now."

"I hope that's true," said Lee. After the explosion of the reactor and the evacuation of every living soul within one hundred miles, he assumed it would be a few thousand years before things got back to normal.

"Our people rescued you...rescued you."

Suddenly, Lee felt like he was in an echo chamber.

"Why did you leave the decontamination center . . .the decontamination center?"

"I don't know." Were things being repeated or were they just being repeated in Lee's mind? He didn't know.

"If you had been willing to work with us, we would have gotten you home...you home. Yet, somehow you managed to get yourself all the way to Boston . . .to Boston."

Lee nodded. He was having difficulty focusing.

"How?" The agent pressed on.

"I'm sorry. What's the question?" asked Lee trying hard not to show his confusion.

"What were you doing in Pine Grove?" The young man looked down at his notes.

"Working on my book," Lee asserted.

"We know about your book, and your friend, Angus. Quite a title, *Blueprint for Disaster."*

"It was just a book." That was true. It was just a book.

"So why did you run?"

"I didn't run. I just wanted to go home." That was true too.

"Well, it may be a long time before you see home again."

The anger flashed inside of Lee. "Look, I want to talk with my attorney." He started to rise but stopped himself. He knew he would be forced back into a seated position if his standing up threatened the young man. He took a deep breath. "Where am I? Where's my wife? And who are you?"

"As I said earlier, I am Special Agent Wright."

"I didn't hear you. Can you tell me what day is it?"

"You don't know?" The agent looked at Lee.

"No, I don't. And where is my hook? I need my damn hook!"

He raised his voice again. *Not a good idea,* he thought.

"We understand you're physically challenged, Dr. Brazil, and we --"

"Don't give me that politically correct physically challenged crap, I just want my damn hook!" He couldn't control the anger.

"I think you should calm down, Dr. Brazil."

"I am calm. I --" The sound of the door opening stopped Lee in mid-sentence. A familiar figure entered the room, balancing two cups of coffee.

"Take a break, Jim. I'll take over." Turning to Lee, "I'm Agent Jennings. Major Henderson introduced us." Jennings sat down across from Lee. "Look, I'm really sorry about your head. He shouldn't have hit you with that flashlight. You will get an official apology for that, I assure you."

He shoved one of the coffees in front of Lee. "Cream?" he said.

Lee nodded. As Jennings poured the cream, he mumbled, "That team from Tobacco and Firearms. Did I need them to take you down? Talk about using a sledgehammer to kill a piss ant. No offense intended." He smiled.

Jennings loosened his tie and folded his hands. "You know, they're all young kids now. Like Wright. A nice guy, but tight. You know what I mean?" Jennings smiled again. "All of the old guys like me are retiring. Getting the hell out. The money is in private security." He shook his head and thumbed through the files Wright had left on the table. "But as they say, we are not here to talk about me. We have business to do, Dr. Brazil, and we need your help to do it."

Well, now, that's at least a different approach from the one junior was using. Lee took a sip of the coffee.

"We need your help in locating Dr. Kudrick."

"What do you mean?"

"She never returned to her apartment after taking you to the waterfront."

Lee could feel the blood rushing to his face. *Something must be very wrong.*

"Are you okay, Dr. Brazil? "

"I'm fine." His ears were ringing. His head was starting to pound.

"You don't look --"

"I'm fine," Lee interrupted with as much force as he could muster.

"I don't know how to help you because I don't know where she is."

"Given your history with Dr. Kudrick, we thought the two of you might be planning...well..."

"We weren't planning anything. She's just an old friend. I shouldn't have gotten her involved in this."

Jennings was still smiling and nodding his head. "Now, Dr. Brazil, I think the two of you have been a bit more than friends over the years." Lee didn't respond. "Look, Lee, we know about your affair with Dr. Kudrick."

"What the hell does that mean? You're the friggin' FBI and you're threatening to what? Blackmail me?"

"No, no, no. Nothing like that." Jennings shook his head.

"I hadn't seen Dr. Kudrick in years and I wouldn't have if you SOBs hadn't forced me to contact her." Lee had just figured out that contacting Jean wasn't just his idea.

"That was good work on our part. Agent Wright came up with that. I will have to give him credit." He paused. "What I bet you don't know is that we knew about you from her."

Lee felt like he was going to black out. Jennings' words seemed to bounce off the walls of the room and come racing back at Lee. What was Jean doing? What was she involved in? Did she know they had been watching her?

"What do you mean?" Lee asked again.

"Are you sure you're okay? Just take a few slow deep breaths," said Jennings.

Lee knew he must be in bad shape if the FBI was giving him instructions on how to relax. He took a few quick breaths. He didn't feel better, but he would be damned if he was going to follow Jennings' instructions.

"I'm okay," Lee insisted.

"Good, good. As I said, we need your help in locating Dr. Kudrick."

"Why do you need to locate her? Her only involvement in this mess is the little bit of help she gave me."

"Dr. Brazil, you don't understand. We have been keeping tabs for some time on your good friend."

"Why? Why?" asked Lee, sounding like an old record player with the needle stuck.

"Well, I guess I'm not ready to tell you that, unless you're ready to be of assistance to us and to your country."

Here we go, waving the flag again, thought Lee.

"What does helping you find Dr. Kudrick have to do with helping the country? You lost me."

"We need her assistance in locating someone."

"You need my help in finding her, because you need her help in finding someone else?"

"Exactly," said Jennings.

"Why should I help you?"

"You know we will eventually find your Dr. Kudrick and you know we've got enough to detain all of you—Kudrick, your friend Griff, your wife, your attorney."

Lee looked away avoiding eye contact with Jennings. Yes, they would find Jean eventually. And given the present administration, jaywalking could land you in detention.

"And we believe Dr. Kudrick may be in danger."

Jennings had gotten Lee's attention again. Lee looked up. "What do you mean in danger? Who is the other person you are looking for?"

"Ibraham Hussein."

"Abe Hussein? Harmless-looking, soft-spoken Abe?" Lee turned the coffee cup in his hand. Jean had given him the nickname, Abe, since Ibraham was derived from Abraham, the father of both Arabs and Jews.

"It's pretty simple, Dr. Brazil. Other people who aren't as patient as we are also looking for him. We believe they think Dr. Kudrick knows where he is. And trust me, these are not very nice people," said Jennings smiling.

Lee looked down at the table, at his coffee and said nothing.

"Well, I'll give you a little time, to think about your answer." Jennings stood up and moved toward the door. "Damn coffee always does that," he mumbled. Jennings pushed the intercom button. The door opened and closed. Lee was alone again.

CHAPTER 24

Fear is the deadliest virus of all.
— Harry Eyres, "Slow Lane," *The Financial Times*

What was there to think about? Could he believe Jennings? If Jean was hiding from the Feds, she must have a good reason. Why would they be interested in Jean? Why would they be interested in her friends or the people that she knew? Lee was sure that this had something to do with her old lab. The West German lab where she had worked during the Cold War.

Lee remembered the first time they had talked about her work at the lab. It was the early 1980s. They were in London. Lee had flown over for a few days to visit Jean. It was Thanksgiving in the States. They were having their holiday dinner at Waltons. Nice, but not expensive. Lee mentioned an article he had seen in *The London Times*. The anti-war movement was accusing the lab of secretly working on the development of bio-weapons. The plague was specifically mentioned.

Jean laughed, yet seemed a bit uncomfortable. "We do a lot of things there that I don't know about or want to know about. I am not involved, at least not directly in anything like that. Abe may be. I don't know. I think he worked on plague control with the Soviets before he defected to the West. He never discusses it and I never ask."

The door opened. Agent Jennings was back. "If I help you locate Dr. Kudrick, what happens then?" asked Lee.

"Not much, unless you can convince her to help us."

"Why should she?" Lee pressed back. "On the negative side, a lot of bad things could happen to all of us if she doesn't."

"And on the positive side?" Lee wasn't sure there was one, other than not being held in detention for the next ten years.

"We could see that no one gets prosecuted, you, your family, Griff. We could even make you and Dr. Kudrick disappear for a while. For a few weeks or a few months, or for the rest of your lives.

"So what will it be? A deal you can't refuse. You've everything to gain if you help and a lot to lose if you don't."

Jennings waited. Lee considered the options. Jennings was right, there weren't any.

"So you want me to tell you where I think she might be?"

"Yes. Exactly," said Jennings.

"And the second part is to convince her to work with you?"

Jennings nodded.

"And what about that thing about disappearing?"

Jennings looked down at the file and scribbled something on the corner of one of the pages. "Oh, sometimes people want a chance to have what they have missed."

Jennings thought about his wife, now ex-wife, Margaret. "Timing is everything they say." Jennings' timing with Margaret hadn't been that great. Weeks away from home on assignment. But he was right about Lee and Jean. Right person, wrong place, wrong time had been the story of their relationship.

Lee stared hard into Jennings' eyes. "How do I know you'll keep your word?"

Jennings smiled. "You don't, but I usually do."

Lee realized that he wanted to trust Jennings. Why, he didn't know.

"Well, when do we get started?" asked Lee.

"Now," said Jennings.

"Okay." Lee thought for a moment. "There is an old inn near her home town. We stayed there a number of times over the years. A friend of hers from high school runs the place, or did. I guess it's still there. The Yankee Piper."

"Okay, Jim, you can come in and bring him his prosthesis."

"My hook," Lee corrected him.

The door opened and Agent Wright and the hook appeared. Lee slipped it on quickly.

"Here's a map of the area," said Wright. "Show us where the Inn is."

"Before I show you anything, you've got to tell me where the hell we are."

"We're in Boston. It's 8:13 on Saturday morning, the sixth of April, 2013," said Agent Wright.

"Where are my wife and daughter?"

"They're in Portland. They surrendered their passports and agreed not to leave town." Jennings stood up, walked over to the file cabinet and opened the top drawer. "We haven't charged them...yet."

"I can speak with them?" asked Lee.

"No," said Wright.

Lee wasn't surprised. The fewer players with the least amount of information made their jobs easier.

"And my attorney?" asked Lee.

"I believe he's in our custody in Portland. Aiding and abetting, you know what I'm talking about," said Jennings.

"Oh, that's convenient. So I don't have an attorney?"

"If you work with us," said Jennings smiling again, "you won't need one."

"Now are we finished with the twenty questions? Can we get back on track?" asked Wright sounding irritated.

"Forgive me for interrupting the process with concerns about my family and what used to be known in this country as a person's civil rights."

April 6, 2013
I-90
Boston

Traffic was light for a Saturday morning in Boston. Wright drove. Lee sat in the back. Two other agents followed. The air felt unusually warm for early spring and smelled of rain. The sky was a pale gray.

Agent Jennings talked most of the way. He complained about health benefits being cut and not getting a raise in three years. No one had. Lee was feeling more anxious as he thought about his conversation with Jennings and the prospect of seeing Jean again. Disappearing, a second chance.

Lee broke into the conversation. "I was thinking about Abe. The last I knew he was working for a research institute in Boston."

"We know. He disappeared from our radar the same day as your Dr. Kudrick."

"You think that's more than a coincidence, don't you?" He was sure they did.

"Wouldn't you?"

"I don't know. You're the super cop. Do you think they're together?"

"We're not sure. But let's just take one thing at a time. Let's check out the Inn."

"If Jean is there, how am I going to convince her to turn Abe in? I met the guy years ago. Right after 9/11. After he had lost the university appointment, I assume because of the fact that he was Arab." Lee recalled that Abe seemed to take it all in stride. No bitterness. "Why are you looking for him?"

"He has information that our enemies desperately need to carry out their plan."

164

"What plan?"

"Let's just say a plan to kill a lot of people."

"I don't think Abe would do that. Besides, I'm sure Jean will think this is just more of the government's paranoia and hysteria after Pine Grove."

"We were working on this a year," asserted Jennings, "before Pine Grove happened."

"I think you're goin' to have to tell me a lot more about this if I'm goin' to convince Jean that Abe would help terrorists commit mass murder."

"We believe they have a way of forcing him to help them." Jennings stroked the scar on his left hand. "His older brother is part of the group. He's the leader of the cell."

"Oh great!" exclaimed Lee. There was silence in the car.

"Are you with us, or are your feet getting cold?" asked Jennings, staring at Lee.

"I told you I would help you."

"How much do you know about Hussein?" asked Jennings.

"Not much. I know he defected to the United Kingdom in the Seventies from the Soviets and that he had been a scientist in one of their labs that supposedly worked on controlling outbreaks of the plague."

"He was," asserted Jennings, "one of the original bio-weaponeers. He worked with Domaradskij at Obdensk in the old USSR labs near Moscow. He was involved in developing a method of rapidly spreading the plague."

"Pardon me," said Lee, "for not understanding what you're talking about."

The traffic was getting heavier as they approached Framingham.

"The Black Death is what we're talking about, Dr. Brazil. It killed a third of Europe during the Middle Ages."

"But the plague has been under control for years, hasn't it?" asked Lee. "When there is an outbreak, don't most of those infected survive because we can kill the bug with antibiotics?"

"Yes," agreed Jennings. "But the Soviets created a germ that can't be killed with an antibiotic and, thanks to Dr. Hussein, can be rapidly spread through the air without the victim having to be bitten by an infected flea or rat."

"So someone could spread it through a subway or stadium?" asked Lee. "Produce a mass outbreak that couldn't be controlled with antibiotics?"

"Exactly."

"And they need Abe to help them produce the germ that resists antibiotics?" asked Lee, still confused.

"No, we think they already have the germ. What they need is his expertise in building the device that can spread it." Jennings paused to let Lee absorb the information. "Is it starting to make sense why we need to find this man?"

"Yeah, but why now?"

"We think they will stage an attack before summer," said Jennings. "The plague germ does better in the cold. We also know that his brother, Muqtada, is in this area."

"This is it," said Lee. "Take this exit." They left the interstate and drove south on an old state highway. There was no traffic. "Pretty dead out here, right?" said Jennings.

"Yeah," said Lee. "Both the interstate and the turnpike bypassed this place in the 1970s and 1980s. Most of the businesses that depend on traffic closed." He paused. "But Jean's friend hung on. I guess the place has been in her family for a long time."

The Inn sat on a hill overlooking the highway. The main building was a two-story, white frame Colonial with columns. A string of tourist cabins formed a crescent with the main house at the center.

"Just one way in and one way out. I like it that way," said Jenning as they approached the main house. It was midmorning. The housekeeper's cart was stationed outside a cabin. Three cars were in the lot. Two in front of the main building and one parked in front of a cabin.

"Any of these match the description of her rental car?" said Jennings.

"No," said Wright.

"Frank," said Jennings into his headset. "Drive around back and check that garage. Juan, see if you can find the maid that goes with the laundry cart."

Lee and the two agents waited. It only took a few minutes, but it felt longer to Lee.

"Okay," Jennings spoke into the headset. Turning to Lee, "The tag on the car in the garage is a match and the maid says there's a weekly in cabin six that matches Kudrick's description. The maid thinks she's still in the cabin."

"All right guys," said Jennings into the headset. "Just hold your position and keep your eyes on cabin six. Wright and I are going to talk with the desk clerk. I'm going to turn on the jamming device so that no calls come in or go out of here in the next few minutes. Going visual." Turning to Lee, "Stay here." And with that Jennings and Wright disappeared into the main building.

Lee wondered what was he going to say to Jean? "Hi, just dropped by to tell you that I am not blowing up nuclear reactors this week, that was last week. This week I'm here to warn you that your good friend, harmless Abe, is a terrorist and by the way you need to turn him in so that he and his wacko brother won't release the Black Death on the residents of a major U.S. city."

Jennings opened the back door of the car. "Hop out," he said. "It's your turn. Dr. Kudrick is in cabin six. We'll be waiting."

Lee got out of the car. "What do I say to her?" asked Lee. He felt he had no idea what he was doing.

Jennings shook his head and glared at Lee. "I don't give a rat's ass what you say, but you had best convince her to help us or it's not going to be a pretty picture for anyone, especially you."

"Do you guys know any way to motivate people other than to try to scare the hell out of them?" asked Lee.

Jennings didn't respond.

"Do I tell her you guys are waiting out here?"

"Sure," said Jennings, "have her look out the window and I'll wave." Lee waited for a real answer. "You're wasting time," said Jennings. "You're a smart guy with a Ph.D. You'll figure it out."

CHAPTER 25

North Field, Massachusetts

Lee took a deep breath and looked back at Jennings and Wright. He knocked. There was no answer. He knocked again. He could hear footsteps in the cabin and then silence. Suddenly the door opened. Jean grabbed Lee's arm and pulled him inside.

"The paper said you were probably in Canada, but no one knew where you were. What are you doing here?"

"Well, I'm obviously not in Canada, although at the moment I wish I were."

"Who are those guys in the parking lot? "

"The FBI."

Jean put her hands on Lee's shoulders and her face directly in his. "How did they find you?"

Lee hesitated. "Well, they didn't. I found them."

"But why?" asked Jean.

"I had this dream."

"Oh God, you and that divine sign thing." Lee knew she wouldn't understand. A good Catholic girl, but not a fan of his divine intervention dreams.

"Look, Jean, I decided that this was my country, my home, and I wasn't leaving."

"Great, Lee. Hooray for the red, white and blue." Jean was angry. She let go of Lee's shoulders and turned facing the wall. "Are you under arrest?"

"No. I don't think I am." He paused. "To be honest? I don't know what I am."

Jean began to pace. "Do they still think you and Angus were involved in creating the explosion at Pine Grove?"

"I don't think so. I don't know," said Lee.

Jean was staring at the floor and pacing back and forth in front of Lee. "So why haven't they released you?"

"They want my help."

Jean's pacing increased in speed. "What kind of help?" She sounded angrier than before.

"To find you and convince you to help them find someone they're looking for."

"What do you mean? Find me?" She was silent for a moment. She stopped pacing. "Who are they looking for?"

"Abe."

"Oh no." Jean shook her head and gestured with her arms to emphasize the point. "They have harassed that poor man since 9/11. They follow him around. Tape his phone calls." She glared at Lee. "He almost lost his current position a few weeks ago because they were snooping around the institute where he works."

"Well the boys out in the parking lot say he disappeared on the same day that you disappeared, and they are sure it wasn't just coincidence."

"I didn't disappear." Her voice was rising. "Can't someone visit a friend? I just thought I would stay out of the way until they figured out that you weren't Public Enemy Number One." She began to pace again. "I have no desire to spend time in one of their detention centers. I think those little cells with those little windows," she gestured, "would drive me a little crazy."

"Well, they don't see it that way." He paused. "They think you and Abe, and his brother are involved in some kind of...I don't know what, involving the plague."

She stopped pacing and faced him. "Abe was involved in that research years ago. He has publicly disavowed his involvement in the project." She paused. "He has worked for years with the Peace Movement and the Muslim community in Boston to encourage dialogue with Jewish and Christian communities," she pleaded.

"Well," said Lee, "the FBI probably thinks all of that is some kind of front."

Jean's voice was much louder now. "I know Abe, and it isn't."

"But you know where he is?" asked Lee.

"Maybe." Jean hesitated. "I ran into him a day or so before you arrived in Boston." She looked away. "He said they were following him that day. He said he was tired of the city. Tired of being followed and was going to visit a friend."

"Do you know which friend?"

She looked at him.

"Well, do you know which friend?"

"Maybe." She hesitated again. "But why should I tell them?"

Lee's head was throbbing again. This wasn't going very well.

"You look awfully pale...and your head. What happened?" She pulled a chair from the table. "Come sit down." He sat. "Lee, I don't believe you're thinking clearly about this. They're just trying to scare us into cooperating. You haven't done anything wrong. We haven't done anything wrong."

"That doesn't seem to matter anymore. What's to keep them from locking both of us up in a detention center for the next few months or the next few years?" asked Lee, pushing down the fear that was starting to rise inside.

"I suppose nothing," said Jean.

"So where is he?"

"Lee, I can't tell you. Your friends in the parking lot are probably listening to our conversation right now."

"So why don't we just ask them to come in?" said Lee in frustration. "Maybe they can explain this better than I can. I don't think they are going to give up and go home." He stood up and walked to the window.

"I suppose not," said Jean.

"Look, Jean, I am sorry," said Lee catching her eyes. "I was worried about you and these guys are...well, convincing."

"I'm sure they are," said Jean breaking eye contact with him.

With some hesitation, Lee opened the door of the cabin and motioned for Jennings and Wright.

At first they looked a bit surprised, but their surprise quickly turned to irritation. Jennings stepped out of the car and motioned for Agent Wright to follow. Jennings brushed past Lee. Wright followed. Lee closed the door. No one spoke. Wright took stock of the room while Jennings stood with his arms folded, facing Jean.

"I take it you're not from the INS," said Jean.

Jennings smiled and shook his head.

"Do you have a search warrant?" asked Jean as she followed Agent Wright with her eyes.

"We don't need one," said Jennings. "You asked us in, didn't you?"

"You have been listening in the whole time, haven't you?"

"The miracle of modern technology," said Jennings smiling.

"So what can we do for you?"

"I think the question, as I understand it from Dr. Brazil," she looked at Lee "is what do you expect me to do for you?"

"As I believe Dr. Brazil explained, we need your help in locating Dr. Hussein."

"You guys have been following him around for years. What happened?" asked Jean. "Did the miracle of modern technology fail you?"

"No one is perfect, my dear."

"Don't 'my dear me' you —"

Lee broke in. "Can we get back on track? I am sure Dr. Kudrick will do what she can to help you."

Jean was still boiling. "I didn't say I would or that I wouldn't. So far, no one has explained to me why I should." Jean walked to the other side of the room.

"The lives of the residents of our largest cities are being threatened," said Wright.

She looked out the window. "As long as that cretin you guys elected president is in office, no one is safe."

"Now, let's not digress into politics, Dr. Kudrick," said Jennings. "Let's talk about what we do know. Dr. Hussein may not want to help his brother, but he most likely will. Family loyalty— honor will be the issue. Muqtada has enough of the antibiotic-resistant strain of the plague to create a national panic. This on top of the accident at Pine Grove? Well, you can imagine what will happen. It will be a one-two punch for our nation."

"How do I know you're not just making this whole thing up as a way of tricking me into helping you capture his brother?"

"You don't," said Jennings looking at the scar on his left hand.

Jean wasn't sure what to say or do next. She was staring down at the floor. She had begun to pace again.

"Well I can see," said Jennings growing impatient, "you need time to think this through."

Jean nodded. "Yes, I do," she asserted.

"That's fine," Jennings nodded, "but you will be spending that time with us."

"What are you talking about?" asked Jean.

"I mean," said Jennings looking at Wright, "Uncle Sam is going to be taking care of your room and board for the next few days or weeks or whatever."

"You can't do that," Jean protested.

"Oh, yes we can." Jennings turned to Lee. "Ask your friend, Dr. Brazil. The new provisions that were added to the Patriot Act allow us to hold the two of you in protective custody for an extended period of time." He paused. "We will give you a few minutes to get your things together."

"Frank," speaking into his headset, "drive her rental car back to Boston." He looked at Lee. "As Dr. Brazil knows the late charges can be murder." Extending his hand, "Your keys, Dr. Kudrick."

"You're serious, aren't you?" Jean was beginning to grasp what was happening.

"As serious as a heart attack," said Jennings again smiling.

"You can ride with Agent Gomez. Let's go."

CHAPTER 26

Now Cain talked with Abel his brother and it
came to pass when they were in the field, that Cain
rose up against Abel his brother
and killed him. — Genesis

The drive back to Boston seemed longer to Lee than the ride up. The conversation in front again focused on Jennings' plans to retire and how he had been unfairly treated and passed over for promotion. Lee shook his head. One minute Jennings sounded like a patriot ready to lead his troops into battle to save the nation, and the next minute he was a whining bureaucrat complaining about his benefits package.

But this was the least of the things that Lee felt confused about. Why had he stayed? He was feeling much less confident in that decision and why had he led them to Jean. These guys were just going to put her in a cell. They seemed in no hurry. All of their talk about wasting time and an attack. What were they doing about all of that now, as they drove slowly back to Boston through the afternoon traffic?

Lee did not see Jean again that day. It was after dark when they arrived at the detention center.

"Okay, Jim, let's drop this one off," said Jennings. Jim pulled the car through the security checkpoint and up to the sallyport.

"I'll take him in," said Jennings. Jennings opened the door but said nothing to Lee. Lee slid out. They were buzzed in.

"Here you go, boys. Put this one back on ice for the night."

"Okay, Doug. Brazil, right?" said a voice over the intercom.

Jennings nodded. An officer appeared at the door. Lee was buzzed through. Jennings was buzzed out.

The officer escorted Lee down the hall and up the stairs and through the doors to his cell. The route was becoming all too familiar.

"You hungry?" asked the officer.

Lee nodded.

The officer left. Lee sat on his bed for what seemed a long time. He didn't move until he heard the heavy metal doors in the hall outside opening and closing. He stood up and stepped toward the door. Then a voice said, "Stand away from the door."

Lee complied. The door opened. An officer carried in a tray of food and set it on Lee's bed. He said nothing, turned and left. The door slammed shut. Lee was alone again. He ate very little. A sandwich of mystery meat. Chips. Coffee, cold like the sandwich. No silverware. They couldn't risk that, but they apparently had decided he could keep the hook with him. Crazy. Crazy. But Lee certainly wasn't going to object.

Lee had thought the old motel room he had been locked in at Camp Liberty was bad. But this was a few dozen times worse. There was nothing in this place. Just him, a metal bed with a blanket, a metal sink, a metal toilet and, oh yes, a small roll of toilet paper. He had never seen one that small.

Lee lay down on the bed and closed his eyes. His head still throbbed. He thought of his wife and his daughter, and wondered if he would ever be home with them again. He thought of Jean. Of second chances. Of disappearing. He fell asleep.

In his dream it was late August. The sun was high in the summer sky. The air sweet and heavy with the smell of honeysuckle. Jean and Lee stood in a field of corn just before harvest. Walking. Running. They were young. Excited. Talking. Laughing. Planning. Planning a trip to the islands. A trip they had each agreed not to take without the other. A trip they had put off many times. But today, in the warm afternoon sun, they knew they would finally go. They could see the white sand and the blue Pacific. They could smell the cool, salt air.

But voices intruded—angry voices. They walked toward the voices. On the edge of the field they saw two men. They were quarreling. One man held a sheep that was bleeding. It's head had been gashed by the hoe that the other man held. The farmer was saying that the sheep had broken through the fence and eaten his corn.

As Jean and Lee listened, their confrontation escalated. The man with the hoe threatened to kill the sheep. The shepherd shielded the animal with his body. The farmer raised his hoe.

"Stop!" Lee screamed and sat up in bed. He opened his eyes. He was drenched in sweat. His head was pounding. The room was quiet. There was no sound. Lee banged on the bed frame with his fist. He clapped his hand against his thighs. He hummed. But his sound was swallowed up by the silence and the dark. He lay back down.

Fear. His fear was starting to build again. He felt lost again. Is this why he stayed? God knows how long he would be here. How long Jean would be here. They knew he was not involved in the accident at Pine Grove. They hadn't said it straight out, but they knew. "Why are they holding me?" he said aloud. "Just because they can," he answered himself.

"Maybe they have something else they want to blame on someone. Maybe I'm 'it,' like Jean said. If they're interested in Abe, they've found Jean. Why don't they let me go? They're angry with me because I didn't convince Jean to help them find Abe."

Talking out loud seemed to help. "She's right about Abe. But are they right about Muqtada? Or is this just more of their scare tactics?"

Lee's thoughts rolled around in a ragged circle like those pictures of hurricanes on the weather channel. And just like a hurricane, they produced total chaos.

"Stop, damn it," said Lee out loud. "Refocus. Breathe. Slowly, deeply. Very deep, very slow. Let the tension go. Let the fear slip away. Slow. Deep. Very slow. Very deep."

Lee rolled onto his side and continued to breathe deeply and slowly as he drifted into sleep. He thought of the beach and the ocean as he finally relaxed and fell into a deep sleep.

The door opened. The lights were switched on. Lee rubbed his eyes trying to push away sleep.

"Come with us, Dr. Brazil" said a guard standing by his bed. He turned and moved into the hallway.

"Where are we going?" asked Lee. There was no response.

Lee didn't need to dress. He was still wearing the street clothes that Jennings and Wright had provided.

"Follow us," said a second guard pointing to the door. Lee complied. He stumbled through the door into the dimly lit hallway, through the first security door and down the stairs. They were buzzed through a second and a third set of security doors until they reached the entrance to the detention center, the sallyport.

A car was waiting. The first guard opened the door. "Get in" he said. Lee complied again. The car was a black, non-descript limousine. A small courtesy light illuminated the cold, black leather seats. There was no one else in the back of the limo but Lee. It was still dark out.

"Where are we going?" asked Lee. Again, there was no response. The door was closed.

The car pulled away from the curb. Lee tried to look out, but the privacy glass only let in a gray light and blurred images as they moved past streetlights and passing cars. Lee made a vain attempt at opening the car door, but it was locked. He leaned back and closed his eyes. "Where are we going?" he mumbled to himself.

The car was moving faster now. They were on a turnpike or interstate. Lee dozed off. He was awakened by the car slowing and turning. "An exit. But where?" he thought. In a few minutes the car stopped. He heard voices and the sound of a metal gate opening and then closing. The car proceeded slowly through. It turned again and then stopped. The car door opened.

"Get out, Dr. Brazil." The voice was familiar. It was agent Wright.

They were standing in front of a Lear Jet 60XR, a fast and comfortable plane that can accommodate five passengers and a crew. "Are we going somewhere?" asked Lee. Wright didn't answer.

A second black limo pulled up. "Ah, Dr. Kudrick is here," said Wright. He quickly opened the door and helped Dr. Kudrick out.

"Lee, are you okay?" she said with concern.

"I hope so. I'd feel a lot better if I knew what the hell was going on."

Jennings appeared out of the darkness. "Why don't the two of you go aboard and get settled?" He pointed to the stairs of the plane. "The plane's warmed up and ready to go. We will be in the air in a few minutes." Jennings turned away and began to talk with another agent.

"The visibility isn't good enough to fly tonight, is it?" asked Lee.

"It's going to clear off very soon," replied Jennings with a chuckle in his voice.

With some hesitation Jean and Lee climbed aboard. Lee surveyed the interior of the plane. "Our government employees do travel in style, I guess." He walked down the aisle of the plane. Television, a wet bar, and a lavatory. "I haven't been on one of these in years," said Lee shaking his head.

Jennings came aboard. The cabin door was closed. "Buckle up," he said as he opened the door to the flight deck. "We'll be taxiing out in a few minutes."

The plane moved quietly down the runway, took its position for take-off and within a few minutes, was in the air. It headed into a heavy fog. They quickly gained altitude. As they broke through the fog, the moon was rising and almost full. In a few minutes they were over a large body of water. Lee assumed it was the North Atlantic.

Jean thumbed through a magazine as she settled into an overstuffed leather flight seat. "Are we being taken to another interrogation center?" she asked with anger in her voice.

"I'm sure there are others," replied Lee "but I guess we should just sit back and enjoy the ride." He took a deep breath.

Lee tried the remote control for the television but it wasn't working. He pushed the call button. The light flashed but no one came. Lee found a stray sprig of parsley by the game table, a garnish that had been missed when the cabin was cleaned. He turned it between his thumb and forefinger. "Karpas," he said to himself. "A symbol of peace." He continued to turn it between his thumb and forefinger.

"Lee, what are you doing?" asked Jean sounding irritated. "You could drive me crazy with those nervous habits."

"Sorry. I was just thinking about…well, the future."

"I've been thinking about the future too," said Jean "A physician friend of mine was talking about her terminally ill patients. She says it's their fears and regrets that keep them from finding peace in the last months of their lives."

"You're not…" said Lee.

"No, Lee," she snapped. "God, are you morbid tonight." She shook her head. "But what she said, I think, applies to relationships."

"Yes," said Lee with hesitation. "I guess it does, sometimes." Neither knew what to say next. Lee stared out at the moonlight on the water. He changed the subject.

"Shouldn't we be higher? My God, I can see whitecaps" he said with alarm.

"Oh relax, Lee." She thumbed through the magazine.

"No," he insisted. "Look out the window."

Jean leaned across him. "You're right," she said with surprise. "Something is wrong." The plane was losing altitude and the air speed seemed slower.

"Where's the intercom button?" Lee fumbled with the call station and phone again. The door to the flight deck opened. Jennings appeared.

"That won't be necessary," said Jennings. "I'm afraid our flight is going to be declaring an emergency in just a very few minutes."

Lee started to rise.

"I think you should remain seated, Dr. Brazil, and keep your seatbelt firmly tightened around your waist," said Jennings gesturing with his hands. "In fact," his voice rising, "I think I have something that will assure that both of you remain seated for the duration of your flight." He raised his left hand again. He was holding a giant roll of duct tape.

"What the hell are you talking about?" said Lee unbuckling his seatbelt.

"I'm talking about when and how you want to die."

In the other hand Jennings was holding a pistol that he pointed at Lee. "Now, the first thing you're going to do," said Jennings throwing the roll of duct tape at Lee, "is to secure Dr. Kudrick's arms and legs to her flight seat."

Lee started to speak.

"Shut up," shouted Jennings. "Do you want to die right now?" he raised the gun. "Just start taping. You two have been tying each other up for years, haven't you?" he chuckled.

"This is a joke, isn't it?" asked Jean.

"Oh no," said Jennings smiling, "I'm afraid it isn't. The plane is going to crash into the sea in about one hour. The crash will be preceded by a devastating explosion that should instantly kill anyone aboard." He looked at Lee. "So don't worry about drowning, Dr. Brazil."

"Why are you doing this?" asked Jean. "You're going to kill us all?"

"No," replied Jennings "just the two of you."

"So, what are you and the pilot going to do?"

"Oh, there's no one else on this plane except the three of us. I am the pilot and I brought a parachute." He paused. "But, unfortunately, the two of you didn't."

"So you're going to bail out?" asked Lee.

"Exactly. The plane is on automatic pilot. The self-destruct mechanism is set. We are flying below radar."

"Why are you doing this?" asked Jean with fear in her voice.

"You know why," said Jennings with a wink. "The two of you wanted to disappear, didn't you? A self-destruct mechanism is an excellent invention." He laughed. "You two do remember *Mission Impossible*?"

Jennings began to strap his parachute on, but he stopped suddenly. His face was turning red. "Jeez, it's hot in here," he mumbled to himself." He stumbled as he reached for a button under the game table that opened the mid-cabin door. Jennings gripped his left arm and chest. "I don't know what's happening." He leaned against the cabin wall. "Boy," he said as he dropped to his knees and began to vomit.

"He's having a heart attack," Jean sounded with alarm. "Pull that damn tape off. Hurry!" she screamed, "before he gets through the escape hatch."

Lee fumbled, digging with his fingers at the tape.

"Lee," she said with irritation, "what's taking so long? What's the problem?"

"Jean, what do you think the problem is?" Lee said taking a deep breath. "For one thing, I have no fingernails."

"Well," she snapped, "you shouldn't have bitten them."

"Thanks for telling me now," Lee said with sarcasm.

"Well, just try to tear it." Jean was sounding increasingly desperate.

"Jean, I'm working as fast as I can. Don't yell at me. Yell at Mr. 'Your security is our business'" lying face down in his own vomit."

Lee managed to peel the tape from his left arm. With his hook now free, he ripped the tape from his ankles and legs. He turning to Jean and tore the tape from her right arm and hand.

"Here," he said, pulling off his hook and shoving it into her hand. "It's always worked great on duct tape."

Lee rolled Jennings over on his back and felt for a pulse. There was none.

"There must be a defibrillator on this plane somewhere," said Jean. "Can we revive him?"

"I don't want to seem like I'm not a compassionate humanitarian, but this guy was going to kill us, and may still."

Jean placed her fingertips on Jennings carotid artery. She looked into Jennings cold, dead eyes. "I'm afraid you're quite dead." Jean reached into Jennings' coat pocket and retrieved the gun. "We've got to get in there" referring to the flight deck. "We've got to get control of this plane." Jean pointed the gun at the cockpit door.

"Jean, what are you doing?" She fired two times. One bullet ricocheted off of the door and knocked a cabin window out. "Stop it," yelled Lee. "Give me that gun before you shoot the plane down with us in it." Lee, with some difficulty, pulled the gun out of her hand and pointed at the door. "Jean, look. You haven't even damaged the latch with two bullets at close range."

"Well, you got any brighter ideas?" She started to pace.

"What can we do even if we get in there?" asked Lee, his voice rising.

"I don't know. I can't fly this plane and neither can you."

"Well," said Lee looking at the escape hatch, "we've got one parachute, but I don't know how to bail out."

"That's it," said Jean. "We can strap ourselves together and bail out together."

"How will we do that?" asked Lee sounding skeptical.

"We'll use your belt and Jennings belt…and the rest of the duct tape." Jean said with renewed energy.

"Okay," Lee said slowly, "but what do you know about bailing out?" Lee was still unsure he wanted to follow Jean's direction.

"Enough" snapped Jean. "I took a skydiving course years ago. The problem, though," said Jean sounding less confident, "is that we're flying very low."

"Flying low is a problem?" asked Lee.

"Yes. With one parachute and two of us, it is."

"Let's take a look at it." They finished unbuckling the parachute from Jennings' body and examined it carefully.

"Yeah," she said with certainty, "I can do it."

"Do what?" asked Lee. He was starting to think about actually bailing out of the doomed plane.

"Guide us down. Let's do it. We have no other option if we are to survive."

"If you're steering, I assume you're the one wearing this," said Lee as he handed the parachute to Jean.

She nodded and quickly slipped into the harness. They connected the belts and ran them through the two straps on the parachute. Lee insisted on putting on a life vest and inflating it. "Padding" he said, "for when we hit the ground."

Sitting on the cabin floor, they wound the tape tightly around their bodies, pressing their hips and thighs together.

"How come we never tried this when we were dating?" Lee wisecracked.

Jean ignored the comment and finished wrapping the last piece of tape around their thighs. "Now you've got to keep your legs up until," she said with emphasis, "I tell you to put them down. We may need to land on our butts."

"Are you right about this?" asked Lee looking for some reassurance.

"Of course, Lee." Jean rolled her eyes. "I do this sort of thing all the time."

"Okay, okay. It's the only option we've got." Lee sounded resigned to what they were doing. "I would certainly prefer being strapped to you and dying than being blown into fish food."

"Well, what does it look like down there now?" He strained to see what was below them but couldn't. "Are we over land or still at sea?" asked Lee.

"Looks like pastures, crops of some sort," said Jean. The moonlight reflected over farmland below. "But, a couple of stone walls that we will need to miss. No high voltage lines that I can see."

"Good," said Lee trying to sound confident about what they were about to do.

"We need to go, now" she said nudging Lee forward. "Put your legs and feet out first. I'll count to three and push us off." She bent over and looked at Lee. "I'll open the chute as soon as we clear the plane."

"Do we need to go right now?" asked Lee, fear pushing up inside.

"This is," said Jean, "as good a place as any."

"One," she began to count.

Okay, you're the guide," said Lee.

"Two."

"I'm just along for the…"

"Three."

"…ride." Lee's stomach, along with all the blood in his body, rushed into his mouth and head. At least it felt that way. The ground came up fast. The chute popped open. They were floating.

"Too fast," screamed Jean. But, suddenly, there was a blinding flash of something white in the moonlight. An updraft pulled them away from the ground and slowed their descent.

"It's a cornfield," yelled Lee.

"Keep your legs up," shouted Jean.

They were still moving fast. The wind rocked them forward and Lee's feet caught the top of the stalks of corn. They began to spin. Then tumble. The ground was soft and wet. When they came to rest they were face down in the mud and partly covered with the parachute and the cornstalks.

"Are you okay?" asked Lee.

"Badly bruised, I'm sure, but I'm always alright no matter how hard I hit the ground, right Lee? You should know that," said Jean. "How 'bout you?"

"The same…but can you roll over? I'm sucking mud down here."

"I always do, don't I?" said Jean. "But give me some time. And please tell me why you had to scream Geronimo all the way down? I'm deaf enough."

"I stopped screaming when that white thing…what was that?" Lee was having some success in pulling off the tape.

"I don't know," replied Jean, half listening "Smoke, I guess."

"But," Lee persisted, "from where?"

"I don't know, but Lee," she sounded irritated, "don't start with me, on that angel business."

"Okay. Whatever it was…" Lee wasn't thinking just about angels. He was thinking about Howard and the ball of light that had hovered over Tyson Park the night he had left Tennessee for the last time.

Jean interrupted. "We don't know what it was. Let's just get out of this tangled mess," she said with a shiver, "and see if we can find some shelter for the rest of the night. The wind is picking up and I'm cold."

They continued to slowly unravel themselves from the parachute and tape and began to walk in the direction of the setting moon. In the failing light, Lee could make out a structure in the distance.

"Look over there, Jean" Lee pointed. "There's a building." They walked toward it. As they got closer, its shape reminded them of an old airport control tower. They continued to walk until they were standing in front of it.

In the moonlight they could see a faded sign over the entrance. It read "Keep this show on the road. Grafton-Underwood 384th BG."

"Jean, can you make out what those numbers are at the bottom?"

"I'll try." She peered at the faded and peeling paint. "It looks like 384."

"The 384th," said Lee with excitement. "Glenn!"

"Glenn?" echoed Jean.

"You remember my uncle. He served in the 384th. He was the tail gunner on a B-17. The only survivor of the Saint. This must have been his base" he paused. "We're in the midlands of England?" asked Lee with disbelief.

"We're on an Air Force base?" asked Jean. "In England." She sounded bewildered.

"No, it was closed a long time ago. All that's left of it are decaying buildings like this one and a memorial."

Jean pushed the door to the control tower open. "I don't care where we are now. It will be better than where we have been. At least it will keep the cold wind off us."

They dragged the parachute in and found the driest corner.

"I'm sure there's a home around here," said Lee.

"Lee, let's just take a break. I don't think I can go any further." They curled up and covered themselves with the parachute and an old tarp left by the military and drifted off to sleep. They were together again, but Lee could see that it was somehow different. Their feelings for each other from the past were still there, but that was all. They no longer felt any pressure for it to be anything more than what it was. They'd had a good run. They'd kept the show on the road. But the road had divided years before. They had been living separate lives and would continue to do so. Acceptance of this without all the fear and regret they had carried for years seemed to be the only way out. Like Lee's uncle, they had bailed out and survived.

The door opened with a clang. Two guards entered the room and shook Lee awake. "No, no," Lee muttered.

"Rise and shine. It's talk time again," said the first guard.

"What? What do you mean? Where's Jean?" Lee rubbed his eyes and tried to focus.

"Get your ass up or we will get it up for you," said the second guard. Lee got to his feet. It was a dream. But there was no time for dreams now.

"Because you cooperated, you get a shower and clean clothes," said the first guard.

"Move it," said the second guard.

Lee was escorted down the hallway and through two security doors, and into a stainless steel shower room.

"You get five minutes of water from the time we turn it on. Now strip."

Lee complied. This was not his idea of a shower. Once under the water, one of the officers sprayed a harsh-smelling soap on Lee's hair, back, belly, and legs. The water was lukewarm. The five minutes passed quickly. The water was shut off. Lee was given a small hand towel.

"Dry yourself and get dressed."

"Can I shave?"

"Not today. Maybe tomorrow. It depends on you."

Lee dressed in the orange prison pajamas he was given.

"Okay they're waitin'. Let's go." The first guard led the way. Lee followed.

CHAPTER 27

And Cain said to the Lord, "My punishment is more
than I can bear!...I shall be a fugitive and vagabond
on the earth. — Genesis

Sunday, April 7, 2013
8:30 A.M.

It was the same interview room. But this time it was not empty. Jean sat in the seat that Lee had occupied the day before. She looked tired, pale, as if she hadn't slept. She was still wearing the same blouse and slacks from the day before. Lee made eye contact with her. She gave a weak smile. Her confident air from before was gone. Jennings sat next to her. Wright, directly across from her. Two other agents sat at the end of the table. Both men. Both early forties. Brown skin. Middle Eastern, Lee thought. Lee was placed in a chair between one of the men and Jennings.

"Okay ladies and gentlemen, we are here to discuss the fate of your close friend Ibraham Hussein. It appears Dr. Hussein is missing. We would like to locate the good doctor before his brother does."

"And have him lead you to his older brother?" said Jean looking down at the table.

"That would be useful," said Jennings to Jean. "I do not understand, Dr. Kudrick, why you seem to have such a problem with this request."

Jean raised her head and faced Jennings. "I think Dr. Hussein has been harassed enough by your agency."

Jennings smiled. "Maybe we have been a little tough on him. But this is an opportunity for him to be rid of us."

Jean persisted. "By turning in his brother?"

"In a manner of speaking," snapped Jennings. "His brother is the main reason Dr. Hussein has been a person of interest to us. We knew his brother would eventually ask for his help." He shoved a file in front of Jean. "Dr. Kudrick, why don't you take a close look at the person you are protecting. Muqtada Hussein."

The file was filled with newspaper clippings and e-mails. There were pictures of bombed out buildings, burning cars and maimed bodies. The headlines declared that Muqtada Hussein had masterminded at least three attacks on U.S. interests in the Middle East. Over one hundred people had been killed. Hostages had been taken in one of the attacks and later killed.

Jean took her time examining the file. "How do you know for certain he was involved in all of this?"

Jennings smiled again. "We don't. But we would be very surprised if all of these reports were wrong." Jennings waited. "So are you still interested in protecting this person?"

Jean closed the file and then her eyes. She folded her hands and sat quietly as if deep in thought.

While waiting for her answer, the group was interrupted by another agent who entered the room to hand Jennings an e-mail.

Dr. Kudrick began to speak, but Jennings waved her off. The room was silent as Jennings read the e-mail. His complexion appeared to become darker, as did his mood. Beads of sweat appeared on his forehead and he pulled at his collar.

"Here, Dr. Kudrick, if you need anything more to convince you to help us." He placed the e-mail in front of Jean. "Apparently we are the target," said Jennings rubbing the scar on his left hand. "Boston...the T...the Garden. The opener for the Red Sox. We don't know when. With the increase in activity of the cell, we do know it will be soon." He waited. "But we don't think they can pull it off without the help of your friend Ibraham."

"If Jean helps you find Dr. Hussein, what happens then?" asked Lee trying to push himself into the conversation. Jennings ignored his effort and pressed harder.

"Dr. Kudrick, we need your help."

"Okay, okay. But what will you do when you find Abe? What if he refuses to help you? You're asking him to...if he helps you find his brother..." Jean was looking for the right words but couldn't find them. "It will be a death sentence for his brother, won't it?"

"Look Dr. Kudrick, it' a free country."

Lee tried to deflect the pressure. "So they say!" blurted Lee.

Wright looked at Jennings as if to say, Do you want me to get this guy out of here?

"As I was saying, he is free to decide if he helps us or not." Jennings knew that was a lie. He tried again. "If he wants the blood of innocent people on his hands, that's his choice."

"You do have a way with words," said Lee sounding more cynical than before.

"Okay, that's enough," said Agent Wright, rising to his feet.

"It's okay, Jim," said Jennings, sounding in control. "Dr. Brazil is entitled to his opinion."

"It appears to be one of the few things that I am entitled to these days," mumbled Lee.

Jennings ignored Lee and turned to Jean. "Why don't you let Dr. Hussein make his own choice?"

Jean was responding to Jennings. "You're not planning on arresting him?" asked Jean, searching, for what she wasn't sure.

"We have no reason to arrest him," said Jennings. "We just want to talk to him."

They were almost there. They almost had her.

"All right. I think I know where he may be."

"Thank you, Dr. Kudrick," said Wright. "You won't regret this."

"I hope not," said Jean. "But with conditions."

Good move. Conditions, thought Lee.

"First, I will show you where he is. Second, Dr. Brazil goes with us."

Okay. Where is Dr. Hussein?" said Wright. He had read the e-mail.

"We can reach him by car in a couple of hours."

Yes," said Wright impatiently. There was no time for dead end streets.

"You weren't listening," said Jean. "I will show you. I am not going to tell you."

"Dr. Kudrick," said Wright in an angry tone, "we are not interested in playing games."

"It's okay, Jim." Jennings turned to Lee. "We will let Dr. Kudrick show us the way."

The medication that Dr. Rodriguez had given Jennings to help control his temper was working. *Margaret was right about the medication,* thought Jennings. *She was right about a lot of things.*

"Dr. Brazil will enjoy the ride. Give him street clothes, Jim. We will leave in fifteen minutes."

CHAPTER 28

And dispute not with the people of the Book
except with means better than mere disputation, unless
it be with those of them who inflict wrong and injury....
Our God and your God is one; and it is to Him
we bow in Islam. — The Qur'an

The two-car convoy drove north, crossing the Tobin Bridge, heading toward New Hampshire and Maine. Agent Wright drove the lead car with Jennings. Jean and Lee shared the back seat. Agent Gomez and Clark followed. Rush hour was over, and the traffic moved easily.

"Continue north until you reach the Maine Turnpike. I'll give you directions from there."

"Yes, ma'am," said Wright. Little else was said until they were outside the city. Jennings turned so he could face Lee and Jean.

"Muqtada is a very interesting fellow. He is the oldest, a few years older than his only brother, your friend Dr. Hussein. I am sure you know, Dr. Kudrick, that his father was a player in the Shah's regime. He apparently had a number of close friends in the Nixon and Ford administrations. When things started to fall apart in Iran, he moved his family to the States. He sent his youngest son, Ibraham, to MIT --"

"Yes, I know," said Jean avoiding eye contact with Jennings.

"-- and Muqtada to the University of Massachusetts, although he apparently never completed his degree. In horticulture, I believe. Your friend, Ibraham, took the best education U.S. dollars could buy and moved to the USSR in the mid-1970s. He later realized the error of his ways, defected to the British, and came to work in your lab in West Germany."

"Yes. Your point?" asked Jean sounding uneasy with the conversation.

"Just some history I thought we might review. It seems Dr. Hussein was the fair-haired child of the family."

"That's an interesting turn of phrase," said Lee. "Given that he's Arab."

Jennings looked a little irritated but continued. "His old man apparently never got over losing his youngest son to the Soviets. Muqtada tried returning to Iran in the late 1980s after the old man's death and a couple of failed business ventures in the States. But he was never accepted by the young fundamentalists loyal to the Ayatollah who ran the country after the overthrow of the Shah. They never trusted him. Muqtada traveled throughout the Arab world in the late 1990s and apparently made the acquaintance of Bin Laden. According to one report Muqtada was seriously injured in an explosion. You and he, Dr. Brazil, have something in common. You are both amputees. He lost his left hand and part of his arm."

"I'm not an amputee," said Lee forcefully. He still found himself feeling irritated when he had to correct people's assumptions about the hook.

"Oh yeah, that's right, you were born that way."

"Yes, I was born this way," said Lee in a more relaxed tone.

Do I have to keep correcting people for the rest of my life? Maybe not. Maybe I can let it go and really feel okay about it. That would be new for me. To let go.

He remembered the dream at the Lodge. He could still feel it. He could still see it. The pictures of things that had never been because of fear. The Lee that didn't need the hook. Proud. Confident. Sure of himself. Accepting of himself. He sensed that something that night had changed. The weight of fear had been lifted.

Lee tuned back in. They were crossing the bridge at Portsmouth. The sign read *Maine—The Way Life Should Be*. Lee had always felt a sense of relief when he had crossed the center of the bridge and was back on the Maine side. Today was no exception. Lee had no idea what lay ahead, but he was sure he could handle it here better than someplace else.

"Anyway," said Jennings, "he apparently got into the terrorist business as a way of redeeming himself with the Arab world and reclaiming the family honor."

"So we have to find Abe before his brother does," said Jean not feeling sure of her decision.

"Exactly. So where are we going?"

"You will find out soon enough," said Jean.

"I think I already know. You are taking us to a farm his family owned in the 1980s and 90s, and sold in the late 90s to another Iranian ex-patriot and his American wife. Gomez and Clark checked the place. As of two days ago, no one has seen Dr. Hussein."

"Well, that is where he told me he was going," Jean insisted.

"He has been friends with the Hazeems since the farm was sold."

"I hope you're right, Dr. Kudrick," said Jennings. He and his agents had no other leads to follow in locating Dr. Hussein.

They took exit 2 off of the Maine Turnpike and followed Route 109 to Route 9. A few miles outside of North Berwick, they turned onto a private road that took them to the farm.

The farm consisted of white clapboard buildings. The fields were still covered with snow that had begun to melt in the afternoon sun. Outcroppings of rock shone through. A white Volvo blended in with buildings and snow, except where the salt had eaten away paint and exposed metal. Another Volvo, a newer model, dark blue, was parked near the garage. The couple was apparently home.

"Gomez, you talked to these folks on Friday?" asked Jennings on the headset.

"Yes sir. And they said they had not talked to Dr. Hussein in weeks."

"Wright and I will confirm. Hold your position and keep an eye on our two friends in the backseat."

"Affirmative."

Jennings and Wright approached the house. They rang the doorbell and waited. A woman in her late fifties opened the door. An older man stood behind her. After a brief conversation, Jennings and Wright returned to the car.

"Other than being a bit irritated that we were here again asking the same questions, they had little to say. Hussein was here in early February but they have not seen him since." He waited for Jean's response. "So what other ideas do you have, Dr. Kudrick?"

"They must be lying," insisted Jean.

"Why would they lie? They have lived here for years. Upstanding Maine citizens like your Dr. Brazil." Jennings turned to Wright. "What do you think, Jim?"

"Why is it so quiet?" Jean said suddenly.

"What do you mean?" asked Jennings.

"The sheep. Where are the sheep?" She sounded puzzled. "They raise sheep. Abe talked about the sheep. He loved that part of coming here."

"In the barn, I guess," said Wright sounding disinterested. They had just wasted the morning. Precious time they didn't have.

"No," rolling down the window and listening. "If they were in the barn we would hear them," said Jean "It's lambing time, it's spring. With their new babies there should be a lot of noise and activity around the barn and there isn't." She was sure of it.

"Gomez," said Jennings on the headset, "did you and Clark check the barn when you were here?"

"No, we didn't have a search warrant."

"Damn it, Gomez, I told you to do a thorough search." Jennings' temper was back. He was shouting into the headset. "If you thought you would need a friggin' search warrant, why didn't you get one? You know they're not that difficult to obtain these days."

Turning to Agent Wright. "These guys couldn't find their ass with both hands and a map." Speaking into the headset, "Okay boys," Jennings took a deep breath trying to calm himself, "Wright and I will do it. It's mud season and I wouldn't want you to get your shoes dirty." Turning to Lee and Jean he added, "I picked up a search warrant for this place this morning, since I thought we might be here before the day was out. I came prepared, unlike my two Ivy League boy scouts. Wait here."

"Doug, don't you think we should..."

Jennings glared at Wright. "We should what, Jim?" Jennings' face was turning an even brighter shade of red.

"Nothing," said Wright and opened the car door.

Jennings and Wright stepped out of the car. Jennings muttered something under his breath and slammed the car door. The two disappeared around the corner of the garage.

Lee and Jean waited. Five minutes turned into ten and then fifteen. They heard the doors on Gomez and Clark's car open. They turned. Gomez was reaching into his pocket when the first shot struck him in the forehead and threw him back against the car. The second shot struck him in the chest. Agent Clark turned toward the car and managed to open the door on the passenger's side before a burst of automatic weapon fire struck him in the back and drove him to his knees. He collapsed into the muddy tracks of the driveway.

Lee and Jean watched all of this with disbelief, like watching an old 007 movie that you had seen a number of times before, but now you were suddenly part of the action. But this was no movie.

Jean looked at Lee and started to climb over the front seat. Lee grabbed her and pulled her down just as another burst of gunfire exploded the car's windshield.

"Get down, Jean, you want to be next?" shouted Lee.

"We have got to help them," she yelled.

"I'm afraid it's a little late for that," said Lee.

Lee had only been shot at once in his life. He had his life threatened a few times by some of the folks he had committed to the state hospital, but they had never tried to act on their words. The shooting occurred when he was working with the Sheriff's Department in the Cherokee Mountains. He was doing a ride-along with the chief deputy, Carson Brown. It was part of a training program in domestic crisis intervention. It was Saturday night. They had gotten the call from dispatch.

"22 … got a call up on Ridge Road," said the dispatcher.

"Let me guess," said Carson. "Billy and his old lady are at it again."

"Yeah, their daughter called," said the dispatcher. "He's drunk as usual. Beat Mary up pretty bad this time. Scared the hell out of the kid."

"Okay, we'll take it." Carson looked at the young psychologist with his long hair and double-breasted suit.

"You ready for this, Brazil?"

"Sure," said Lee trying to sound confident.

"This is a good one for you," said Carson as he flipped on the siren and the lights. "We have been up there three or four times in the last six months. Usually we can talk to him." He sighed. "She never presses charges."

But there would be no talking. They turned off the main road and headed up what was referred to in the mountains as a pig path that ran straight up the mountain. A mobile home, which had seen better days, was perched on the top of the ridge. Carson pulled in slowly. As he turned off the ignition, the door of the trailer opened. A man carrying a shotgun stumbled onto the porch. For a moment he looked disoriented.

"Get out and get down," barked Carson.

Lee pushed the door of the cruiser open and crouched behind it.

"Get off my property!" ordered the man.

"Billy, we just want to talk," yelled Carson. Before Carson could say more, the man fired the gun at the windshield of the cruiser. Lee took a deep breath and waited for Carson.

"Bill, you know you shouldn't have done that."

"Go to hell!" yelled the man and threw the gun in Carson's direction. He bolted for the woods.

"Okay Brazil, looks like we got to catch this one before you can talk to him." As they pursued the man into the woods, his wife yelled from the porch, "Be careful, Carson! He's got that huntin' knife with him."

Lee felt the same confusion and fear now as he waited with Jean. What was going to happen next? That night in the Cherokee Mountains, the man escaped. He knew the mountains better than the deputy and Lee. But there would be no escape for Jean and Lee. They heard voices and footsteps. The back doors of the car were pulled open, the barrel of an assault rifle was shoved in their faces and they were dragged from the car and pushed face down into the cold, wet driveway.

"So, my friends, you have come to save Ibraham from me? I'm afraid you're a bit late. My brother chose not to save himself and honor his family."

"He's dead?" cried Jean. "You killed him? You-"

"Shut up, Jean," said Lee in a half-whisper.

Muqtada pressed his knee in Lee's back. "I will choose who talks and who does not. Do you understand?"

Lee nodded.

Muqtada turned to Jean. "You were asking a question, which I will be happy to answer. But first we must go inside before our activities attract the attention of our neighbors." Turning away from them, directing the others, "Amon, Bassin put the agents and their cars in the barn. The woman comes with me. Put him in the basement."

Bassin and Amon pulled Lee and Jean to their feet and pushed Lee toward the bulkhead of the house, while Muqtada escorted Jean toward the front door. The stairs were dark. Lee missed one and slid the rest of the way into the basement.

"You stay," Lee's captor said as he fumbled for a key. Finding it, he unlocked the metal door. He slid it open and motioned with his weapon for Lee to enter the room. On the floor with his feet and arms tied was Jennings. He pushed Lee toward a metal pole. He clipped one end of a handcuff around the pole and the other around Lee's right hand. He made sure Lee could not reach Jennings. He left, locking the door behind him.

"Well," said Lee, "what do we do now?"

"Where are Gomez and Clark?" asked Jennings. "I heard shots."

"They're dead," said Lee showing no emotion. Jennings closed his eyes. "So is Jim." Jennings' body stiffened. He didn't move. He didn't speak, but he couldn't stop thinking. He knew he was not responsible for what had happened to Ron, his partner. It had been an accident. A high-speed chase. That's where he had gotten the scar on his left hand. It wasn't Jennings' fault. They were following procedure. But this time he wasn't. Three agents were dead because of his anger. Wright had tried to stop him, but Jennings hadn't listened. Lee waited.

"Where's Kudrick?" asked Jennings.

"With him," said Lee accepting that there was little he or Jennings could do about it.

Their conversation was interrupted by the sound of footsteps on the basement stairs. The door slid open. Muqtada stood in the doorway, his form illuminated by the late afternoon sun that shone through the small basement window. The shades of red and yellow made him appear even more menacing.

Muqtada spoke in a calm and confident tone. "Agent Jennings, I require your assistance. Dr. Hazeem has agreed to aid me in obtaining your cooperation, but I must first thank you and your fellow agents for helping us to locate my brother's plans for the device. The copious notes that your agents made regarding my brother's activities and relationships have been very useful."

"Glad we could help," muttered Jennings under his breath.

Bassin untied Agent Jennings' feet and escorted him out of the room. Jennings did not resist. Muqtada neither spoke to nor looked at Lee. The door was closed and locked. The last rays of the afternoon sun faded as day turned to evening.

At the top of the stairs Muqtada turned to Bassin, "Take Agent Jennings to Dr. Hazeem and Amon. Tell them we will join them in a few minutes. I will be waiting in Dr. Hazeem's study."

Muqtada seated himself behind the large mahogany desk. For the first time he felt sure of himself. He felt in control of what was happening. He was not the one being lectured to. He could give a lecture if he chose. He was sitting behind the desk.

Bassin entered the room and seated himself in the high winged chair in front of the desk. Muqtada folded his hands and looked at him. "We must now decide our next step. By an Act of Allah we have traced my brother's plans to his friend, Mark Johnson, who is staying on a boat in the harbor, *The Flying Dutchman*." Muqtada's tone was calm and direct. "Dr. Brazil and Dr. Kudrick are friends of Mr. Johnson. They could be useful in obtaining his cooperation."

But Bassin appeared anxious. "Yes, yes I think so. If we kill one of them in front of Mr. Johnson, he will know we are serious."

Muqtada hesitated. "Yes, that was my thinking." Muqtada did not enjoy the thought of killing these two people. But, of course, it would have to be done.

"And the federal agent?" asked Bassin. "Should we kill him now?"

"A hostage can sometimes be useful. With our change in plans, we may need Agent Jennings. Unfortunately, we will have to use Dr. Hazeem's system for distribution and delivery. But we will have my brother's plans for the device for the future."

"Should we change our plans at this point?" asked Bassin, fearing his leader's response. "We will not be able to leave Boston as we have planned." Muqtada did not respond well when his followers questioned his decisions.

"Yes, but we will be at the marina and we can arrange to be picked up there." Muqtada was becoming irritated and Bassin sensed it. But Bassin pressed on.

"It is more risky, is it not?" asked Bassin. Muqtada ignored his question.

"But I, of course, will follow your direction." Bassin had little choice but to comply.

"Yes, my friend, if we are to have the plans we must take this risk." Muqtada knew his old friend was right, but he too felt he had no other options. This was his opportunity. He must take it.

CHAPTER 29

Fight for the sake of Allah those that fight against you,
but do not attack them first. Allah does not love
aggressors. — The Qur'an

Sunday, April 7, 2013
North Berwick, Maine

Lee listened but there was no sound, other than the occasional roar of the furnace turning on, running for a few minutes, and then shutting off. He assumed they were giving poor Jennings the third degree, with God knows what kind of "medical assistance" Muqtada's friends might provide. What the point was he didn't know. Where was Jean? What were they doing with Jean?

If he had just stayed put at the lodge he would not be dealing with this. He was sure that he should not have involved Jean in this again. Poor Abe was dead, probably dead when Lee had made the decision to take Jennings and Wright to Jean. Lee had chosen not to leave. To stay. But what for? To be killed by a group of terrorists, or to somehow stop them from carrying out their plan? The first was easy. Do nothing and they would kill Lee when he was no longer of benefit to them and their plan. The second seemed impossible. How to stop them?

The pain in Lee's head was back. He closed his eyes. He dozed. Thoughts of Maine, of the ocean, of his daughter and wife, of the Cherokee Mountains floated through his head.

The sound of Lee's captor's key in the door lock yanked Lee back to the present. Light from the hall flooded the room. Lee turned to rub his eyes but his captor was busy trying to unlock the handcuff. "Stop," he said. "On your feet." Lee complied.

"Come." He shoved Lee into the hall and in the direction of a set of steps that Lee assumed led to the main house. At least he assumed that's where he was being taken. Maybe he was being taken out into the woods to be shot.

At the top of the stairs Muqtada greeted him. "Dr. Brazil, Agent Jennings has been very cooperative this afternoon. I trust you and Dr. Kudrick will be equally helpful." Muqtada led Lee into the study and seated himself behind the large desk. Amon seated Lee in the winged chair. Muqtada continued. "You and Dr. Kudrick have a friend in common with my brother. Mark Johnson. I would like your and Dr. Kudrick's assistance in obtaining Mr. Johnson's cooperation."

Lee hadn't seen Johnson in years. Like Ibraham, he had worked at the German labs with Jean.

"What do you want us to do?"

"Accompany me to Mr. Johnson's boat," said Muqtada.

"I assume we have no choice." Lee was certain of that.

"You could resist, but we would be forced to take your life."

"You're planning on letting us live?" *An unlikely outcome,* thought Lee.

Muqtada hesitated and smiled. "As I understand from reading Agent Wright's notes and from my conversation with Agent Jennings, you are in serious trouble. They suspect you of being a terrorist or at least a sympathizer with our cause."

"If you're asking if I agree with the policies of my government in the Arab world, I do not. I can sympathize with your cause, but not with your methods." Lee paused and looked away. "I do not agree with the violence."

"It is a terrible thing we do, but necessary. We are not the aggressors." He tried to make eye contact with Lee. "It is your government and your corporations that are the aggressors."

Lee avoided Muqtada's eyes. "If you looked at their notes, you know that I could have left this country, but it is my home." He faced Muqtada. "I chose to stay. To try to change things, to try to change my country's direction." He paused. "Mass murder will not change things for the better." His tone was forceful. "It will only provoke my government."

"You sound like my brother. He was corrupted by your government." Muqtada shook his head and looked down at his hands. "Even when he was dishonored by them, he would not strike out against them."

"Abe didn't believe that was the answer."

"Greed and money drive your government." Muqtada's voice grew louder. "To those who worship other things than Allah, hard is the way to which Allah calls them."

"I do not disagree," said Lee in a reassuring tone.

"Well, if you do not disagree, then you understand that the only way to stop your government is to destroy the corporations and your economy." He paused and cleared his throat. "We must create so much fear and panic in your country that your economy will collapse and your government will be forced to stop their aggression."

"I do not believe that you can justify mass murder," said Lee, his voice rising. "There are other ways."

"I have lost much in my life," said Muqtada trying again to make eye contact with Lee. "I believe you understand how it feels to lose a part of yourself. I, like you, have lost a part of my body, but of more importance, I have lost my home. Home is everything." Muqtada looked away and then back at Lee. "I must reclaim it, and to do that I must reclaim my family's honor."

"The people of Boston are innocent," pleaded Lee. "Doesn't the Qur'an prohibit the killing of innocent people?"

"Yes, but the people of your country are not innocent," Muqtada insisted. "They have inflicted wrong and injury on us." He paused. "Do they not pay the taxes your government uses to buy the weapons that kill my people?" His tone was sharper now. "Do they not own the stocks of the companies that rob us of our resources?" he asked. "Do they not buy the products these corporations produce?" He was shouting.

"Yes, but they —" Lee attempted a response but Muqtada allowed none.

"Well, then, you see they are not innocent. They are as wrong and as corrupt as my brother, Ibraham."

"I don't think you understand," said Lee, his voice rising to match Muqtada's. "There are other ways to accomplish your goals."

"I think you are mistaken. I do understand," said Muqtada with force. "But we have not time now to continue our debate." Shaking his head and turning away from Lee. "Bassin take Dr. Brazil back to the basement. Agent Jennings will join you shortly."

Lee was escorted back to the basement room he had spent the last two hours in and handcuffed again to the pole. The door was closed and locked, and he was once again alone in the dark.

Muqtada had all he needed now. He was ready. In the bedroom that Hazeem had provided for him, Muqtada gathered his belongings: clothing, toiletries, identification cards and passports—all forgeries—and some photographs of his family. Out of the corner of his eye he saw the barn. The doors were open. Amon was preparing the truck for the trip to Boston.

Muqtada's thoughts flashed back to a late afternoon in April many years before. He was with his brother. They were in their teens. They were in the barn, pushing and shoving each other. His brother was chasing him with a hoe. Ibraham struck at Muqtada in play. But Muqtada tripped and a blow landed on his back. Muqtada was furious. He grabbed the hoe from Ibraham and raised it to strike his brother. Suddenly their father was there. He pulled the hoe from

Muqtada's hands and slapped him across the face, knocking him to the floor of the barn. He picked up Ibraham to see if he was hurt. Muqtada was bleeding. His father did not notice.

Muqtada looked out again at Hazeem's barn. In the barn only a few days before Amon had taken a hoe from Muqtada's hands. The blade was covered in blood. Ibraham lay on the floor of the barn, bleeding profusely, not moving.

Muqtada could not recall what had happened. He remembered that they were talking. About the farm. About their father. He remembered the rage building inside him, but nothing else. He had blacked out before when he was angry. In recent years the blackouts had been more frequent. He had killed before, but not in rage, not his brother.

"No time for this now," he said to an empty room. "What's done is done." He grabbed the bag and hurried down the stairs. Bassin was waiting.

Muqtada was right. There was no time for debate. There was only time for action and apparently not much time left for that. Lee felt totally helpless. He heard footsteps on the stairs and the sound of Jennings' voice. The door opened and Jennings, being partially supported by Bassin, was dropped on the floor next to Lee and handcuffed to the same pole. The door was closed and locked. Lee could not see Jennings, but he could hear his breathing, heavy and irregular. The sound was muffled, perhaps by his hand or arm. It almost sounded like he was crying.

"Are you okay?" asked Lee. "What the hell did they do to you?"

Jennings' replied slowly. "They gave me some type of drug. Amobarbital, I think." He paused, catching his breath. "I told them everything. I couldn't stop myself. I just went on and on. I couldn't stop. I just couldn't stop."

"It's okay," said Lee in a comforting tone, but his words weren't that comforting. "I assume they are going to kill us anyway, so what does it matter?"

"This wingnut has figured out some way to distribute the plague in Boston without having to use his brother's invention, the atomizer," said Jennings stroking the scar on his left hand. "I was certain he had to have it and without his brother's help he couldn't pull it off."

"Your office knows where you are and they will be looking for you, for us, won't they?" asked Lee in a hopeful tone.

"They know where we are, but Muqtada e-mailed them from my car saying we would not be returning to Boston before tomorrow morning." Lee rolled his eyes. "I doubt anyone will be looking for us before midmorning tomorrow." He paused. "The Bureau has put most of its resources into the mess at Pine Grove. It took all I could do to get them to free me and three other agents to work on this." Jennings sounded apologetic. "The people at the top aren't convinced a bio-terror attack is that likely."

"Apparently our friend Muqtada thinks it is."

"But how?" Jennings still believed it couldn't be carried out without the device to spread the disease.

"I remember my wife's mother, who was in Shanghai during the war, talking about Japanese planes dropping canisters filled with plague infected fleas on Chinese cities during World War II."

"What? They're going to bomb Boston with canisters of fleas?" said Jennings sounding irritated and more than skeptical.

"Well, apparently it worked. It spread the plague throughout southern China and thousands died. They still have an occasional outbreak of plague even to this day, seventy years later." The two men sat in silence.

"What was in the barn?" asked Lee out of curiosity and trying to make conversation.

"Dr. Kudrick was right, there weren't any sheep, just a soft drink delivery truck and stacks of some off brand cola."

"What else?" Lee pressed.

"There were vats with some concoction in them, but before we could check them out they shot Wright in the back of the head." Jennings stopped and then continued. "It happened so fast. I turned around just in time to get whacked in the side of the head with something." Tears welled up in his eyes but both men ignored them. "The next thing I knew I was tied up and lying on my back down here."

"So what are they going to do with a cola delivery truck?" asked Lee.

"I assume that's their transportation to Boston."

Their speculation ended when they heard a truck being backed into the driveway and the bulkhead being opened. A few minutes later the door was opened and they were ordered on their feet by Amon. They were handcuffed together and marched to the truck.

"You mean our transportation," said Lee.

"Shut up, big mouth," said Amon. Pointing to the truck, "Get in." They climbed in the back of the soft drink delivery truck.

"Go to the back," he said shoving Lee. In the dark behind a stack of cola Lee tripped over something lying on the floor.

"Jezum, watch it," said Jean. "I'm in here, too. You always were a klutz." Lee smiled.

"Shut up and sit," said Amon.

"Yes, master," mumbled Lee under his breath.

"Lee," said Jean in a warning tone. Amon placed an extra handcuff on Jennings left hand and attached the other cuff to a support brace on the side of the truck.

Muqtada and Bassin appeared at the rear door of the truck wearing green uniforms sporting the logo of "Rave Cola."

"Now my friends," said Muqtada, "we will be leaving. Do not waste your energy crying for help. No one will hear you. The truck is well insulated."

With that, Bassin closed the truck's rear door. The engine started and they assumed they were on their way to Boston.

Section III: Fight

Chapter Summaries, Discussion Questions and Author's Comments
Chapters 23 - 29*

CHAPTER 23

Lee is taken to a detention center in Boston. He is interrogated by Jennings and his partner, Wright, and learns that Jean is missing. The agents request help in finding her, saying that she may have been taken captive by Muqtada.

Discussion Questions

1. In this chapter, Lee is again injured, disoriented, confused and experiencing considerable physical pain. Fear and panic appear to descend upon Lee again. A few pages before, Lee was confidently saying that he was "no longer disabled by fear." He appears to be questioning his decision to stay and "fight." How do you explain this?

Author's Comments

Managing strong emotion and stress and being able to stay with changes in behavior and attitude is a difficult process for all human beings, including Lee. The process is often two steps forward and one step back, a fairly normal part of the change process. In this chapter, Lee is clearly not in control of what is happening, and those in control are trying to manipulate Lee with fear.

*Refer to pages 4 and 5 for a list of the Eleven Skills And Attitudes That Build Resilience.

CHAPTER 24

Lee is convinced by Agent Jennings to help the FBI locate Jean. He learns that they are looking for Ibraham Hussein and that Ibraham has been involved in developing bio-weapons in the past with the Soviets.

Discussion Questions

1. In this chapter, the interrogation of Lee proceeds with efforts by the agents to manipulate Lee with fear and threats. On page 163, Lee realizes that he wanted to trust Jennings. Why?

Author's Comments

Agent Wright and Agent Jennings are playing the traditional "good cop and bad cop" with Lee. Trusting Jennings would be a way of resolving the dilemma: Deciding that he, indeed, was the good guy and really trying to help Lee and Jean. Lee finally decides to work with Agents Jennings and Wright. What do you think about his choice? What would you have done in this situation? How would your resilience determine what you would have done in this situation?

CHAPTER 25

Lee helps the federal agents locate Jean at an inn near her hometown, but he cannot convince Jean to assist the agents. They take Jean into custody and return Lee to detention.

Discussion Questions

1. In this chapter, both Lee and Jean appear to have great difficulty managing their emotions and dealing with the situation that they are in. The federal agents continue the pressure on both. Jean becomes quite angry at Lee, the federal agents, and at the government in general. How is she using her anger?

Author's Comments

Jean may be using her anger as a way of dealing with her fear, as a way of controlling it. She appears to be quite frightened of what is happening in this situation but does not talk about or deal with her fear directly. Why not? Anger can suppress fear and, in some situations, this may be a good strategy. What do you think?

CHAPTER 26

Lee has returned to the detention center. He can sense his old friend, fear, returning. His sleep is troubled and his "thought's roll around in a ragged circle like those pictures of hurricanes on the weather channel." And just like a hurricane, they produce total chaos." He dreams of Cain's betrayal of Abel, and of Jennings' offer to help Lee and Jean "disappear."

Discussion Questions

1. Lee is back in detention again. He has been isolated and ignored by the federal agents on his return. As indicated on page 171, "Fear, his fear was starting to build again." What does Lee do to contain his fear and manage it?

2. What is your interpretation of the Cain and Abel dream?

3. The dream of disappearing focuses on acceptance of what is. How is acceptance different from giving up?

4. In their escape from the doomed plane, what resilience skills did Jean and Lee practice to save their lives?

Author's Comments

As seen on page 171, Lee makes use of breathing exercises as well as again trying to think and use his head to control and vent the feelings that are building inside. Managing your feelings plays a major role in resilience.

The dream sequence begins with Lee's fantasy of being able to escape with Jean to a paradise of white sand and the blue Pacific. But, "voices intrude – angry voices." The dream focuses around the temptation of withdrawing into fantasy to avoid the conflict that Lee finds himself in which is symbolized by the conflict between the brothers, Cain and Abel.

Lee is beginning to accept the reality that "disappearing" with Jean is not possible and that he and Jean have been leading, and will continue to lead, separate lives. Some things must be accepted whether or not they are really understood. Reality is reality, whether he likes or wants to accept it.

Lee and Jean, again, work well together as a team. They communicate well, listen to each other, problem solve together, show flexibility and continue to make use of humor as a way of dealing with their situation. They demonstrate a number of times their faith in their own abilities as well as the abilities of the other person and, at least on Lee's part, a recognition that some things, such as the updraft at the right moment, could be more than luck.

CHAPTER 27

Jean is finally convinced by Jennings to lead the FBI to where she believes Ibraham is staying. She agrees to take them there with Lee, but will not tell them where she is leading them.

Discussion Questions

1. Jean agrees to assist the federal agents. Her way of dealing with them is quite different from the day before. Why?

2. Jennings appears in better control of his emotions. He attributes this to medications that he is taking. How do you feel about the increasing reliance that our society seems to have on using psychotropic medications to manage emotion? What do you think is the upside and the downside?

Author's Comments

Jean is tired, pale, and has not slept. She is still wearing the same clothes from the day before. "Her confident air from before is gone." Lack of sleep and physical stress as demonstrated throughout the novel can have an extremely negative impact on an individual's sense of confidence in themselves and their ability to deal with adversity. After making a decision to work with the federal agents, Jean appears to bounce back some and gain some control over the process, adding "conditions" to her decision to help the federal agents.

A number of psychotropic medications certainly "work" in terms of their ability to decrease anxiety, at least temporarily, and to decrease the frequency and the intensity of depressive symptoms and outbursts of anger. Many, however, would argue that there is a downside to our society's increasing reliance on these medications to regulate and manage our emotions. Most human beings can learn ways of managing their emotions. This may take more time and effort than taking a pill, but in the end we are doing this for ourselves, not depending on a medication. This is certainly less expensive for us, and the healthcare system, in the long run. What do you think?

CHAPTER 28

Jean leads the agents to the farm in southern Maine where Ibraham and his family lived. The federal agents do not know that Muqtada and his allies are staying with the couple who own the farm. Their check of the farm a few days before was inadequate. The party is ambushed by the terrorists and three of the agents are killed. Jennings, Jean and Lee are captured. They learn that Ibraham is dead and that, from the computers of the federal agents who were killed, Muqtada has learned the whereabouts of the plans for the device that his brother created.

Muqtada decides to follow through with the attack on Boston without the device but through other means. He also wants Jean, Lee and Jennings to assist him in finding his brother's plans. Muqtada recalls killing Ibraham when in a blind rage.

Discussion Questions

1. In this chapter, three of the federal agents are killed by the terrorists. Jennings later blames himself for their deaths Was he responsible?

2. Muqtada decides to alter the plans that he and his fellow terrorists have made and to attempt to obtain the plans for the device to spread the plague. "This was his opportunity. He must take it." How is Muqtada's thinking being affected by his emotions?

Author's Comments

Law enforcement officers can make mistakes, sometimes fatal ones when they act out of anger or emotion. Jennings' anger caused him to not listen to his partner, Jim, and to act impulsively (page 181). Should he "blame" himself? Is taking the blame and taking responsibility different? I think one can hold themselves and others accountable without the heavy dose of negative emotion that blame adds.

Muqtada, like Jennings, is clearly acting out of emotion when he decides to suddenly alter plans that have been made and well practiced and to not hear the concerns of those closest to him and "the mission," like Bassin.

CHAPTER 29

Jennings is interrogated by Muqtada. Lee engages Muqtada in a confrontation in which Muqtada tries to justify terrorism. Muqtada complains of the imperialistic attitude of the United States and the greed of the corporations. Lee agrees with his logic but not with his means.

Jennings and Lee begin to piece together Muqtada's plan. They are loaded into the back of a soft drink delivery truck along with Jean. Muqtada and Bassin, who are driving the truck, leave for Boston to begin the attack.

Discussion Questions

1. On page 185, Muqtada says to Lee, "Home is everything." Contrast your view of home with that of Muqtada.

2. In preparing for the trip to Boston, Muqtada recalls the death of his brother but concludes by saying, "No time for this now...what's done is done." This is a strategy that many people use to deal with distressing and disturbing events. As it relates to resilience, what is the upside and the downside in using this strategy?

Author's Comments

Getting through a difficult and stressful time requires focus. Being able to set aside strong feelings and concentrate on what needs to be done is a strategy that is frequently used by police and those in combat situations or in emergency medical care units. The problem is that people frequently never get back to dealing with the strong feelings that have been evoked by the situation and set aside. Human beings need the opportunity to be able to discharge these feelings and to "process them." This means being able to vent the feelings, e.g., talk about them, cry about them, get them out in some way, etc., and to spend some time trying to understand them and understanding where they fit in the person's life and how they can be dealt with in the future. This does require time, a support network, the ability to communicate and the opportunity and support to find meaning and direction from these feelings, primary factors in resilience.

BOOK FOUR: HOPE

CHAPTER 30

The only thing we have to fear is fear itself...
— Franklin Roosevelt, 1933

...and those who would use fear to control us.
— The Author

The truck rolled along the back roads of southern Maine. Lee assumed that Muqtada would avoid the turnpike and enter I-95 just north of Portsmouth.

Jean spoke first. "Caroline, Dr. Hazeem's wife, told me she and her husband were going to cross the border into Canada tonight." Jean paused. "She is scared out of her mind. She liked Abe, just like I did. She seems not to understand any of this." Jean wiped tears from her cheek. "But one thing is certain, she will not say no to her husband, the good doctor, or to Muqtada. After what happened to Abe she knows what would happen to her." She paused. "I just have a really hard time believing that Muqtada could do that to his own brother. Abe was a good soul." The tears came again.

"Cain and Abel," said Jennings, sounding as if he thought that explained the situation.

"At any rate she did tell me Amon is going with them. I guess to make sure they get across the border and that no one gives away their plan. She says he will kill all three of them before he allows them to be captured."

"Nothing like a good friend," said Lee with sarcasm.

"So what do we do now?" asked Jean.

"There must be a light in here." Lee ran his hand along the wall of the truck.

"I'm sure there is," said Jennings as he pulled a small pen light from his breast pocket.

"It is probably by the rear door," said Jean. "Shine the light over there. Yeah, there it is, about halfway up the door on the left."

"Maybe I can reach it," Lee said as he wiggled and stretched out his arm.

"Try," said Jean.

Lee's left ankle was cuffed to the support brace of the truck, but his arms and hands were free. "My reach just isn't long enough. But if I slip off the hook," concentrating. "And use it to extend my reach," straining, "almost got it." Lee holding the hook in his right hand took another swipe at the switch. "Got it! And then there was light," said Lee.

"Would you cut the routine?" asked Jennings.

"He does that when he's nervous," said Jean.

"Well, it's irritating," said Jennings.

"I always said you guys had no sense of humor," said Lee. "If I am going to die in the next few hours, I want to have a couple of laughs before I go."

"Okay, let's see what we have here," said Lee examining the rack of cans nearest him. "Rave Cola. Rave Cola," he said as he picked up one of the cans. "Something about these cans seems just a little different. Looks like cola, but it doesn't feel like cola. It's too light." He shook the can. "And it doesn't sound like cola. It sounds like it's full of sand."

"Or fleas!" screamed Jean.

Lee almost dropped the can.

"Let me see it," she said. Lee carefully handed her the cola can. "Look at this. There are two chambers in the can. The top portion can be turned." She paused. "A release mechanism, maybe?" Jean nodded to herself. "Yes, it must release the fleas into the upper chamber."

"That's impossible. The whole thing is impossible," said Jennings with a snarl.

"It's not impossible," Lee glared at Jennings. "Here's how it could work. Imagine this. You are a member of the cell. Your job is to spread the disease. You have been given cans of the cola to place across the city. On the subway, you open the top of one of the cans and appear to be drinking." Lee sounded confident in what he was saying. "As the train rolls into a station you place the can next to your seat." Lee places an imaginary can of Rave Cola on the floor of the truck. "As you rise to exit the car you twist the top of the can." Lee twists the top of the imaginary can. "You have released the fleas into the upper chamber. By the time you exit the car, the fleas will have found the opening in the top of the can and will be looking for a host. The subway car doors close...." He draws his hook and his right hand together.

"Thousands of people carrying the disease into homes and workplaces across the city. The state. The country. Instant plague. Instant panic."

"Oh my God, Lee, you're right," said Jean.

"Oh, God, I am," said Lee as he realized the implications of what he had just acted out. The country had survived the Bird Flu panic of 2012. But this? The Black Death?

The silence was broken by Jennings. "Muqtada and the Hazeems must have filled the cans with infected fleas they had been raising in those large vats we saw in the barn." Jennings was beginning to understand and accept what was happening.

"They got rid of the sheep," said Jean, "to make room for the vats and the canning equipment." Fear was in her voice. "They must have filled these cans in the last twenty-four hours. How the hell they did it, I still don't understand. Oh God," said Jean. "This could work." She tried to stand, but the cuff jerked her back down.

"Yes," said Jennings. His tone was dark. "At least, it could scare the hell out of people and create a panic."

Lee still hadn't spoken. Jean's complexion had turned a strange shade of white. "How many cans like this are there?" asked Jean, looking at Lee.

Without saying anything, Lee stood up and began a quick count. Cases with the special six-packs were marked with an X. "Looks like there are eight cases, each with one six-pack, forty-eight cans."

"I'm sure he's planning on dropping cases of the cola off at different points in the city," said Jennings. "Convenience stores. Shops operated by the cell. Members of the cell will go to these stores in the morning, pick up the cans and begin the process of placing them across the city." Jennings could see the whole thing clearly now.

"Who's going to be suspicious of a can of cola?" said Jean. She shook as she spoke. "Who's going to notice it in the garbage can at the Garden or Fenway or under the seat of a car on the T?"

"Well, we can keep up with where they are dropping the cola off," said Jennings with authority.

"How?" said Lee sounding skeptical.

"GPS," said Jennings.

"Since when do we have global positioning?" asked Jean.

"Since my old partner, Ron, left me his." Jennings pulled the fountain pen from his breast pocket.

"007 strikes again," said Lee.

It was time to focus on what they could do. Jennings studied their position. "We are heading south on Route 9, about 10.3 miles from York Village."

"But what do we do with this information?" Lee paused. "How do we let your office know what's happening, Jennings? Do you happen to have a cell phone or radio transmitter that looks like a pencil?"

"No," said Jennings, almost smiling.

"Which means we have to escape," said Jean coming back now with force. "They're going to kill us anyway. What do we have to lose?"

"Nothing," said Lee agreeing. Jennings shrugged.

"We've got to use our heads," she said.

"Good, you two Ph.Ds put your heads together and come up with a miracle," said Jennings sounding hopeless again.

"Okay," said Jean. "We've got to use surprise." She paused. "But how?"

The three argued back and forth about attacking Muqtada and Bassin at one of the stops, but decided that wasn't smart, since they didn't know who else would be there. Maybe they would be taking on five people, rather than two. At Jennings' insistence they decided they would wait until they were at the marina, and Muqtada and Bassin unhooked them from the truck. They would wait until they were off the truck. Jennings would appear to fall. Jean would come to his aid. While Muqtada and Bassin were distracted, Lee would use his hook like a club against Bassin. Jean would punch Muqtada in the groin while Jennings attempted to disarm him. It was the best they could come up with. They would only get one chance. They rehearsed the plan a number of times.

Jennings checked his GPS unit. "We're crossing the Tobin. You better turn off the light. They could be stopping anytime now."

After a couple of tries with the hook, Lee flicked the light off. The truck speed slowed. They stopped and began backing up.

"First stop," said Jennings looking at the GPS. "Canal and Market."

The side door of the truck was rolled up and two cases of cola were unloaded. Jean, Lee, and Jennings were tucked far away in the back of the truck, out of sight and earshot of passersby, of which there were few. The door was rolled shut and they were soon on their way to the next stop.

"Boylston and Jersey," Jennings noted.

The routine for each stop was the same. The truck made eight stops. They were near entrances to the T, the Boston Garden, Government Center, Fenway Park, and Faneuil Hall.

"They have practiced this run," said Jennings with confidence, "a number of times."

"But there is one thing they haven't practiced for," said Jean. "The marina."

"But if we get as far as Mark's boat," said Lee, "we're dead. We have got to make the plan work as soon as we're off the truck."

The truck picked up speed.

"We are heading in the direction of the marina," said Jenning staring at the GPS display screen.

"Where do you think we're going?" asked Lee.

"Where the fewest number of people are," said Jennings. "This time of year and this time of morning on a Monday it won't be hard."

"What time is it?" said Jean yawning.

"Four A.M.," said Jennings.

"He's going to drive around some. Maybe park at a station. He will wait until it is light. Get some sleep," said Jennings, trying to sound in command of the situation. "I'll take the first watch."

CHAPTER 31

So peace is upon me the day I was born, the day
that I die, and the day I shall be raised up
to life again. — The Qur'an

Monday, April 8, 2013
4:00 A.M.

Lee and Jean dozed for the next two hours. When Lee awoke it was quiet, a time to think, to put things in perspective. At least that's what he thought. The calm before the storm. And to feel Jean once again close by, even under these conditions, felt good. But why had he given into the pressure from Jennings? If he had just left her out of this, she would be safe.

Lee had thought about his life ending before. He had made the arrangements. The will, the letter to his family, arrangements regarding the practice and his partners, the funeral. He had busied himself with all of this when he thought he might have lung cancer.

But now it seemed different. There would be no benign death with family at his side, with a physician grimly telling him how long he might have.

No, if he were to die today, it would be this morning in a struggle with a man that in some strange way he felt sympathy for. And not on sterile white sheets in a warm bed, but on the cold dirty pavement of a parking lot or a pier, with steam rising from his blood as it drained out of his body.

No! Stop, he said to himself. *Stay positive. If anyone's blood is going to be shed, it must be Muqtada's. This is not just about you and those you care about. It is about all of those unsuspecting people asleep in their beds that will be dead within a few days if you and Jean and Jennings can't stop this madman.*

But was Muqtada a madman? No. He was not insane. He was acting on his beliefs. Granted they were very different from Lee's. But he was trying to stand upright. He was in search of his home, a home that he believed had been taken from him and his family by greed and racism. Jennings was right. Lee and Muqtada had some things in common, most visibly the handicap, the disability. But beneath the skin, not as easily seen, there was more.

So now it came down to kill or be killed. Since the dawn of time many had waited, like Lee, for the sunrise knowing the day would bring their death or the death of their foe, and often understanding that they shared much in common with the person they would kill or be killed by. Muqtada, Lee thought, sensed all of this. But would he hesitate in taking Lee's life? No. Lee was certain of that. The question was more whether Lee would hesitate in taking his. Lee had had a couple of glimpses of death before, that night in the Cherokee Mountains, the time he thought he had lung cancer, but he had never taken a life. He had spent much of his life trying to prevent people from taking their own or someone else's.

Dueling gimps, thought Lee. God or Allah does have one hell of a sense of humor. Had he placed Lee and Muqtada here at this moment in time for a reason? Did Lee believe that? Muqtada clearly saw it that way. He was willing to be a martyr for his faith, an avenger for his family and his people. Was Muqtada wrong? Was Lee placed here to stop him? The opportunity to save countless lives was here, in front of him, but it would most likely require taking Muqtada's life or surrendering his own in the process.

"Wake up," said Jennings, "we're at the marina."

The doors of the truck's cab were opening and closing. The rear door to the truck was rolled up and Bassin climbed in while Muqtada scanned the parking area. Bassin unlocked Jean from the floor of the truck. He then unlocked the cuff that attached Lee to the truck, but he did not release Jennings' cuff from the support brace of the truck.

"Dr. Kudrick and Dr. Brazil, please come with me," said Muqtada.

"Hey," said Jennings. "I thought I was going too."

"No you will stay with Bassin and the truck. I will take Dr. Kudrick and Dr. Brazil to meet their friend." Turning to Bassin, "I will call you, Bassin, when we are safely aboard and direct you to the boat, and you and Agent Jennings can join us." Bassin handcuffed Lee's right hand to Jean's left and herded them off of the truck.

"I need a bathroom," said Jennings.

"Bassin will give you your privacy to do whatever you must," said Muqtada. Bassin closed the door.

Turning to Bassin, "Wait in the truck's cab. I will call you within twenty minutes. If I do not call you, kill Agent Jennings. Come to me. I know you will not allow yourself to be captured." He put his hand on Bassin's shoulder. "Goodbye, my friend."

"Now Dr. Kudrick and Dr. Brazil, will you be good enough to accompany me? Please walk in front." He shoved Lee. "Be assured I will not tolerate any disobedience on your part," said Muqtada holding a snub-nosed .38 with a silencer against Lee's back.

Muqtada and Bassin had parked the truck in a small parking area overlooking the marina. Bottles and cans that had been covered by the snow littered the park. The sun was just coming up. The wind off the bay was strong and cold. The sky was steel gray, as was the water.

"Show me the boat," said Muqtada.

"It is the large one over there," said Jean pointing. "A two-master. *The Flying Dutchman*."

"Yes," said Lee. "*The Flying Dutchman*."

They reached the main dock. The wind was stronger now. Coming in gusts. The large boats rocked in their berths. No one was around. Six-thirty in the morning was still early for the people who used this marina. Lee knew they were running out of time and they had no plan.

"The Flying Dutchman," Lee mouthed to Jean.

As they neared the boat Jean appeared to trip on one of the planks and pulled Lee down with her.

"Get up! Quickly," shouted Muqtada.

"The Flying Dutchman!" Lee yelled against the wind.

Jean nodded. Lee came up first. He spun around on his left heel and struck Muqtada in the face with his hook. Muqtada stumbled back. At the same time Jean grabbed Lee's right arm with both of her hands and Lee threw her toward Muqtada knocking the gun from his hand and forcing him back against the wood railing. As Muqtada scrambled to pick up the gun, Lee swung Jean around a second time. Both of her feet struck Muqtada in the chest and forced him through the railing and into the water. The tide was out and Muqtada dropped thirty feet before hitting the water.

The impact of Jean striking Muqtada caused Lee to lose his footing. He fell backwards. Jean hit the planking with a dull thud and slid across the walkway and through the railing, dragging Lee behind her. The old dream of falling flashed through Lee's head as he grabbed at the planking, finally catching hold of the railing with his hook as he slid through. With effort he found footing with his right leg. The two were no longer sliding into the sea, but Jean was hanging by her left hand, the handcuff being her only link to dry land.

Lee began to pull her back. It was a slow and painful process for both of them. He pulled her hands level with the bottom of the planking, her legs dangled in the air. She found a grip with her right hand and then was able to find a foothold with her left foot. She was able to push her upper body onto the walkway. Lee put his left foot on another part of the railing and pushed with all of his strength. Slowly Jean was able to pull herself onto Lee and the walkway. The two collapsed from exhaustion.

A minute passed before they felt footsteps on the walkway. Lee opened his eyes expecting to see someone from one of the boats who had heard or seen the commotion on the dock and was coming to their aid. But to his surprise, he heard a familiar voice. "You thought a man with only one arm could not swim or climb the ladder from the sea?" shouted Muqtada. Lee and Jean rolled over on their stomachs and started to stand up.

"No, no," yelled Lee. "I thought the fall would have killed you." He looked for the gun as he spoke. He saw it lying a few feet from Muqtada.

Muqtada's eyes were also scanning the walkway. His hair and beard were matted with sand and saltwater. He looked like the crazed killer he had been portrayed as.

"Now," screamed Jean pulling Lee forward in the direction of the gun. Jean dove on top of the gun as she pulled Lee down with her. Muqtada stumbled across the walkway and reached for the gun. He fell onto Lee's back. Lee tried to force Muqtada off by rolling onto his side, but Muqtada grabbed Jean's arm and then her hand. The gun discharged. Muqtada collapsed onto Lee. Blood poured out of his chest. Steam rose from the tangle of bodies and blood. Lee pushed Muqtada off his back and onto the planking.

Jean ripped a piece of material from Muqtada's shirt and made a compress. "Here," she shouted over the wind.

"I know. Pressure on the wound," said Lee, as he shoved the compress into Muqtada's chest.

"We have got to call for help," said Jean, scanning the shore.

"How the hell are we going to do that? This wind is so strong no one can hear us," said Lee. "One of us has to stay with Muqtada. Bassin may try to come to his aid."

"Well, then," said Jean, "we will have to get these handcuffs off. He must have the key." They quickly searched his pockets, but there was no key. "Well, I guess we'll just have to blow them off. Put your hand down here," she pointed to the walkway.

"Don't forget it's the only one I've got."

"Shield your eyes," said Jean as she aimed the gun at the chain linking the two cuffs. She fired. "Missed. Damn it!" She fired again and the chain was severed. She handed the gun to Lee.

"Go! There should be someone in the office over there." He pointed to a repair shop.

"Okay, okay," yelled Jean. "Just watch for Bassin." And then she was gone.

Lee turned his attention to Muqtada. He had not spoken or moved since the gun discharged. Lee took his jacket off and placed it over Muqtada. Muqtada opened his eyes and with a weak voice said, "Now, my friend, despite your best efforts I fear I am dying. The terrorist who would kill thousands is dying. Let me ask you, your President Truman, who ordered the atomic bombs dropped on Hiroshima and Nagasaki that killed thousands of innocent people, was he a terrorist?"

Lee said nothing.

"You Christians and Jews. You people of the Book are full of contradictions." Catching his breath again, "You will make a great effort to kill us, but then you will make an even greater one to try to keep us alive." He coughed again. "I believe you are very confused people."

"About that I believe you are correct," said Lee.

Muqtada smiled. He rolled his head to the left.

"Save your strength," said Lee, not knowing what else to say.

Muqtada's breathing slowed. He coughed again. He opened his eyes for the last time, and was home.

CHAPTER 32

You'll learn to see, to find the man behind the monster.
— The Phantom of the Opera

Monday, April 8, 2013
The Marina
Boston Harbor

Lee heard the sirens. He thought he heard gunshots, but he wasn't sure. The wind was still strong and blowing in from the sea. Two police officers arrived first, took the gun and told Lee he could stop applying pressure to Muqtada's wound. They moved Lee to a bench on the pier. Someone, an EMT Lee thought, put a blanket around his shoulders.

Other people were arriving. Lee tried to tell them about Agent Jennings. They said they were handling it. A half an hour passed. Two men who identified themselves as federal agents arrived. They quickly took charge. Muqtada's body was removed from the pier; Lee was taken to a police van. Jean did not return.

Lee could see news crews arrive and be ordered by the police to leave. After an hour, Lee was taken back to the detention center. He was placed in an interview room, given a sandwich and a cola. But no one seemed interested in talking with him. After another hour, he was taken back to his cell. Lee was allowed to shower and shave. This time the water was hot and the guard allowed the shower to run as long as he wanted.

Muqtada's blood had dried and was hard to wash away. *Perhaps*, Lee thought, *if the blood of those we had killed was harder to wash away, we would not be, as Muqtada put it, "so confused."*

Lee was again taken back to his cell and given dinner, a sandwich with tomato soup and coffee. He had no idea what was happening outside the center. When he asked the guards, they reminded him that there was a news blackout in the facility.

He assumed Jean was okay, although no one would tell him where she was or how she was.

He lay on his bed. He could barely keep his eyes open. He wasn't sure why he should. He finally gave into fatigue and closed his eyes. *The sleep of the dead,* he thought, as he lost consciousness. Lee slept for twelve hours. He heard no one. No one bothered him. When he awoke, it was light out. He had lost his watch somewhere in his travels, the watch his daughter had given to him. But now he thought of it as only a watch. It was still important, but he didn't need it as before. He didn't need it to help him control his fear of losing a person he loved so much, his daughter.

A lot of things seemed less important now—like the bickering with Liz over subjects they couldn't even recall the next day. He thought of her, of Liz. He might not see her or even talk with her for...he had no idea how long it might be. But she was there. He assumed she would always be there. He could feel her with him, even in this God-forsaken place.

Lee lay back down and drifted back into a light sleep. In his sleep he heard the metal doors opening and closing. He sat up. The door opened. Two guards entered his cell. He remembered one of them from his first night here.

"How 'bout some coffee? The boys downstairs want to talk to you."

The second guard, a younger man, looking a bit unsure of himself, shoved a cup of coffee in Lee's direction. Lee took it and smiled.

"Would you like to clean up a bit before we go down? We can stop at the shower for a minute or two," said the first guard.

202

"Yes," said Lee. "I would like to wash my face...and my hands"

After a short detour through the shower room, Lee was taken down the steps, through the metal doors and short hallways, and placed in the now familiar interview room. Coffee in hand, Lee waited. The door buzzed and Jennings entered the room alone.

"You're alive," said Lee relieved. "And Jean? Where is Jean?"

"She's fine. I'll get to that."

"And the soda? The fleas? Is Bassin in custody" Lee wanted to know everything.

"Actually, it was Jean who gave the agents the locations of the cases of Rave Cola as well as an exact count of the number of infected cans. The agents sealed off and evacuated the areas." Jennings stroked his scar. "When the police arrived Bassin fired a few shots at them and then killed himself. Dr. Kudrick tells me he had been ordered to kill me if Muqtada did not return or call him. But he didn't. I'm not sure why."

Jennings stood up and walked to the other side of the room. Keeping his back to Lee, he pretended to be looking for a file in the cabinet. "But I'm alive, which is more than I can say for three other people. Wright was single and so was Gomez. Frank had a wife and a young daughter."

"I'm sorry," said Lee trying to sound more sympathetic than perhaps he felt.

Jennings changed the subject. "Look, we have got to talk about what we are doing with you and Dr. Kudrick." Jennings returned to the table and faced Lee. "Command has decided that you will stay with us at least a few more weeks, maybe a month or two."

"Why?"

"Because this whole thing has to blow over. The plague canisters were recovered, at least we think we have gotten all of them. A couple were opened, but according to the CDC the outbreak has been contained." He stared at his hands and stroked the scar. "The media will report any deaths as due to Asian flu, the garden variety type. Not bird flu," Jennings assured Lee. "The initial symptoms are similar."

"But, does the turning black part just before you die and vomiting blood go along with a bad case of the flu?" asked Lee, being cynical.

"Yeah, well we will leave that to the CDC to worry about," said Jennings. "Look, there hasn't been a word said about the plague and we want to keep it that way. The country couldn't take worrying about that right now."

"You mean," Lee's tone was sarcastic, "the stock market couldn't take it."

"Well, yes," Jennings agreed. "You saw the drop after Pine Grove. Worse than after 9/11 and the crash of 2008. You think we want this out now?" Jennings thought about the rest of his retirement evaporating.

"No, I'm sure they don't," said Lee, sounding more accepting.

"So that's the main reason for keeping you here." He paused. "We can make you more comfortable. A different cell. Maybe even a room with a view," he smiled.

"They're afraid I'll talk about this if I'm released?" asked Lee.

"They," snapped Jennings, "want to be certain you don't."

"What about talking to my family or my attorney? That won't be possible either, right?"

"Exactly," said Jennings.

"So how long do I get to enjoy the hospitality of the federal government?"

"That depends on you," said Jennings looking at his watch. "They have to be convinced you are going to cooperate when you are released and that things are settling down outside, getting back to normal."

"Well, at Pine Grove..."

Jennings knew what Lee was going to say. He cut him off. "Yeah, yeah. It will take thousands of years. You know what I mean, relatively speaking."

"And Jean? What about Jean?"

"They have decided that Dr. Kudrick will return to Europe in the next few days. Detaining her longer would only arouse suspicion." Jennings looked at the file he had taken from the cabinet, avoiding Lee's eyes. "We have already talked to her and explained that the length of your detainment is contingent upon her cooperation."

"In other words, if she talks to anyone about this, I could be spending a hell of a long time in here?"

"Exactly."

"God, that is an annoying word," said Lee sarcastically. Jennings smiled. "So, no disappearing for us?"

"No, I'm afraid not."

"I guess making three federal agents disappear was enough for the 'they' you've been talking about."

Jennings looked down at the table and said nothing.

"Okay, that was a cheap shot," said Lee.

"It has been explained to the press that the three agents died in a gun battle with two suspected terrorists, and that both of the terrorists were killed."

"They didn't tell the press the whole story about where or how they were killed?" Lee was sure they hadn't.

"No. It's classified. I believe the administration has made it clear to the major media outlets that we expect their cooperation in matters of national security." Jennings cleared his throat. "I think they have learned their lesson." Jennings was referring to an incident two years before when the media was blamed for the death of four federal agents. The networks involved were fined and the reporters prosecuted under the amended Patriot Act. They had just begun to serve their sentences in federal prison.

"Our three agents will be buried on Friday. The President plans to speak at the funeral."

"I'm sure he wouldn't want to miss that opportunity," mumbled Lee. "When is Jean leaving?"

"Tomorrow evening."

"May I see her before she leaves?"

"That I can arrange," said Jennings, really smiling for the first time in the conversation.

"When?" pressed Lee.

"Tomorrow afternoon. Now I would suggest you get some rest. You look like hell."

"I feel like hell. I'm getting too old for this stuff," said Lee. His head still ached, although not as bad. Some of the swelling had gone down and the bruises were starting to fade.

Lee took Jennings' advice. There was nothing else to do. He slept away the afternoon.

Evening came and the guards brought dinner. He wasn't hungry. He sat on his bed and stared at the wall. His body and his mind felt used up. Empty. He finally lay down again and fell into a dreamless sleep.

He woke early the next morning before it was light out. He was going to see Jean. At least that's what they said would happen. What "they" would allow. It appeared that "they" were even in control of his relationship with Jean.

But what did he have to say to her that he hadn't said before? Lee felt that old mix of emotions he had always felt when Jean was leaving. The fear of her not returning. The anger that they were separated by an ocean, a sense of futility. What did it matter what he said. She was leaving. Just like he had predicted at the Parker House. Saying goodbye in a police station, but absent the trip to the South Seas she had talked about.

What if they had had that time together? If Jennings could have arranged for them to disappear for a while? If they had gotten that second chance that people talk about? Would he have taken it?

No, not now. That time had passed. Lee finally understood that he could no longer go back to a place or a time or a person in the past to avoid dealing with the problems of the present. He had created a home and a family with Liz. It was where he felt he belonged, and not on the other side of the world. It would be different now that Dru was out of the house. Could they create a new home together without their daughter? He wasn't sure. He had begun to feel a new energy for their relationship after that night at the lodge. After the dream. And he was certain that he would not continue to avoid trying to work their problems out because he was afraid of failing. He was ready to go home.

Lee heard voices in the hall and knew breakfast was on the way. He at least had an appetite this morning. Scrambled eggs with sausage links. Lee thought it tasted good. His standards around food had definitely dropped over the past three weeks.

He thought he might actually be underweight. The first time since he was five, when he had almost died of a respiratory infection. His fear of not being able to breathe went back to that time. To his bouts with asthma, when he had to struggle for every breath. He had been sick as a child. Very sick. When the asthma attacks came on, he drove everyone away. If anyone tried to comfort him, he felt he was being smothered. He was sure there was some deep psychological meaning in all of this, but he had never fully understood it. As he thought of seeing Jean, some of that old tightness in his chest returned. He had to force himself to take deep breaths.

He lay back on his bed and tried to remember the days at the university when no one had to leave, when five years of graduate work seemed as if it would take forever. When time stretched out in front of Lee as far as he could see. When the future was yet to be determined.

Time moved so much faster now. As he had told Jean, he could see the end approaching. More doors were closed now than were open. The future would be shorter than the past. How long would he be kept here? How much of his precious time would be wasted sitting in this cell?

Lee heard the metal doors opening and closing. He assumed it was time to talk to Jennings again. To hear what the government had decided his life would be like today.

CHAPTER 33

The Lord will give grace and glory. No good thing
will He withhold from those who walk upright.
— Psalms

Wednesday, April 10, 2013
Agency Office
Boston

This time Jennings was waiting in the interview room. "Come in." Jennings stood up. "We can move you up to a better cell this afternoon." He paused. "Are you getting bored? I'll be glad to get you something to read."

"The newspaper would be nice," Lee said as he took his seat at the table. "You know," said Jennings as he sat back down, "there's a news blackout within the facility."

"How about some writing material?" asked Lee. "A couple of legal pads, a pen or two."

"You know you can't write anyone," said Jennings staring at his hands.

"I know. I know," said Lee sounding impatient. "I am not planning on writing anyone." *God forbid*, he thought.

"Well, sure," said Jennings and he smiled. "I can get you some writing paper and pens."

"History," said Lee. "I enjoy reading history."

"I thought you might. What do they say? We are doomed to repeat the mistakes of the past unless we understand them. Churchill, right?"

"I'm afraid our country has a very short memory," said Lee, giving Jennings a look of half worry and half disgust. "Vietnam followed Korea. Iraq followed Vietnam. Iran followed Iraq."

"Well," said Jennings with a chuckle, "you best hope our society continues to have a very short memory, otherwise you could be spending a lot of time in here."

"Well, I guess that's a more positive way to look at it," said Lee and he smiled.

"I arranged for Dr. Kudrick to be brought to this room at noon. You will have thirty minutes. We will give you as much privacy as we can."

"No one behind the glass?"

"No one behind the glass," Jennings assured.

"No recording our conversations?"

"No, we won't be recording your conversation." Jennings smiled again. "We have very little interest in your conversations now."

"It sounds like your superiors feel they have things under control."

"The media," asserted Jennings, "has been cooperating."

"These days the media has more interest in protecting the stockholders of their parent corporations than in actually reporting the news," said Lee with a smirk.

"I assume it could effect their coverage sometimes." Jennings sounded increasing ill at ease with the conversation. The intercom buzzed.

"Well, I think that means that she's here," said Jennings looking at his watch.

Jennings had Dr. Kudrick buzzed in and excused himself. Jean took a seat next to Lee and took his hand.

"How are you?" asked Lee, noticing a large bruise on her left arm.

"Okay for an old girl. A bit sore, but okay I guess. And you?"

"The same minus the 'old girl' part."

"Muqtada died, didn't he?" asked Jean. "They wouldn't talk to me about it."

"Yes," said Lee. The image of Muqtada smiling as he slipped into death flashed into Lee's head.

"I didn't pull the trigger. I know I didn't," she said. "He must have." She paused. "Maybe he wasn't thinking clearly after the fall off the pier. Shock will do that."

"I don't know, Jean. I think he knew what he was doing." Lee stopped. The image came back "You know, he said something just before he died that I have been thinking about. He said we were confused." Lee paused. "I agreed with him."

"I don't think he was an evil man," said Jean, seeming almost ashamed to make such a statement.

"Many people thought he was," said Lee, "but when I talked with him he sounded like...well, President Truman when he was justifying dropping the atomic bomb on Hiroshima. He said it was a terrible, but necessary thing that he was doing." Lee paused. "Truman believed the Japanese had to be stopped. Muqtada clearly believed America has to be stopped."

"I can understand," said Jean, "why much of the Arab world sees Muqtada as a hero and not the angel of death." Lee nodded. "Our perception of evil and good has a lot to do with where you're standing. Here or in Iraq."

There was an uneasy silence. "Jennings says they're forcing you to fly back today."

"Yes. Well, frankly, I will be glad to get back home," said Jean, avoiding Lee's eyes. "I don't think I can do anything by staying here. It would only complicate things."

"I guess you're right," said Lee not knowing what else to say. "I should be home soon. They can't keep me forever. At least I don't think they can." He wasn't sure.

There was silence again. Neither knew what to say.

"Well," said Lee, "what will you do when you get back?"

"Oh, you know me, I'll probably take . . . Oh, hell, Lee, I don't know what I'm going to do." She stopped. "Let's cut the small talk. Who knows what anyone is going to do. Both our lives have been turned upside down in the last few months." She stopped again. "I'll try . . . Well, I don't know what I'll try, but I will try. I will have my friends." She paused. "What will you do? They'll release you within a couple of months." She wasn't sure either. "Well, I assume they will. You'll be back at home with your family and your friends soon." She certainly hoped he would.

Lee leaned back in his chair and closed his eyes. "You know, I feel different now. I took on some things I've avoided all of my life. Some of it finally feels finished." He looked at Jean. "It feels like a lot of that old fear and anger is gone. The old hurts don't seem to pain me as much as before. I was thinking," said Lee with hesitation, "about successes and failures in my life last night and I thought about us. I don't know what box to put us in."

"Maybe you don't need to put us in any box," said Jean looking into Lee's eyes. "Even though we're getting a little old, maybe we are still a work in progress."

"Yeah, maybe we'll end up pushing each other's wheelchairs around the nursing home," said Lee.

They both laughed.

"If Jennings could have done his thing," asked Lee, taking a deep breath, "about making us disappear for a while, would you have....Well, you know what I mean."

"I don't know," said Jean. "I'm not sure I would want to disappear if I couldn't take home with me." She could see that Lee's face was starting to flush. "But I wish we would have had the choice. And you?"

"The same," he said and looked away. His face was getting redder. He changed the subject again.

"Jennings talked about possibly needing 'our assistance' in the future," said Lee.

"I assumed he was making a joke. He does seem to believe we should feel indebted to him for releasing us and not prosecuting." She paused. "He said the statute of limitations on the 'things we did' doesn't exist anymore under the new Patriot Act."

Lee shook his head and laughed. "All I know is that for me it is over and I am not going to worry about what might happen in the future." He paused. "Hey, that's a change for me, isn't it?" He put his arms around Jean. She put her head on his chest. They closed their eyes and went back in time to that first summer at the university so many years before.

When their thirty minutes was up, Jennings buzzed the door open. "Dr. Kudrick, it's time to go. I know you have some packing to do and you can imagine what a hassle airport security is now."

Lee felt that old tightness in his chest. He held onto Jean's hand. He tried to speak, but couldn't. Soon there would be thousands of miles and thousands of minutes between them...again. That was certain. The future's they would create for themselves would be on different continents.

"I'll keep up with you and with what happens." Her eyes were filling with tears.

"I'll see you in the morning, Dr. Brazil" said Jennings. Lee nodded. He let go of Jean's hand. Jennings ushered her through the metal door. She was gone.

Jennings delivered Jean to a young agent, Clark's replacement. He would escort Jean to her flight. Jennings shook Jean's hand, wished her well. Assured her that he'd do his best to get Lee released within the next few weeks. She nodded, but didn't or maybe couldn't speak. He had the strange feeling he would be seeing her again. Why or how he wasn't sure.

He returned to his office. To his surprise it felt empty without Wright. He pulled his chair to the window that looked out on the bay. He had nothing left to do. Tomorrow he would be placed on leave for a month. The leave really wouldn't be leave. Command had decided that he was to be a hero. He would receive a commendation and shake the President's hand on Friday. Of all the things he had been involved in with the Agency, he would be recognized for what he felt least proud of, this assignment.

But the Agency didn't want to hear the details. Angry outbursts, resentment, stupid impulsive actions. No, they knew what the details had to be: calmness under fire. Confident, calculating, intelligent behavior. *What a crazy world,* he thought. But his fame would not last. Their fame never did. In recent years other agents had played the same role. The country needed heroes weekly or at least monthly, real or imagined. In a few weeks things would get back to normal. At least he hoped they would. The public would have been entertained. The media would have gone away.

Jennings watched the bay change colors from a dark blue to a reddish gold as the afternoon sun disappeared behind the Boston skyline. He thought of other sunsets, of the village on the North Sea, of Margaret, of maybe someday.

That afternoon Lee was taken to a new cell. It had, indeed, a view—a view of the bay through a small window above the bed. Lee thought about Howard and wondered if he had reached home. Of the home Millie had made at Bambi's, and the one Jim and Ben had made on the road. He thought about Muqtada. He knew Jean was somewhere over the Atlantic, heading to the home she had made. He thought about his wife and daughter and his home.

He felt good about himself. With God's grace he had stood upright, had accepted himself for who he was. He was no longer disabled by fear. He had reached home and finally moved in. Home had been within him all along.

Dinner was brought to his room at six o'clock. Along with the meal, the guard brought two legal pads and two pens. Lee started writing soon after he finished his dinner. The food was still miserable.

Epilogue

May the source of strength who blessed the ones before us
help us find the courage to make our lives a blessing…
— Mi Shebeirach

My grandfather remained in detention for a number of months while Joe tried to obtain his release. Grandmother and Mother called everyone they knew in Washington and many they didn't know. But Grandfather, they said, seemed to take it all in stride. He complained about the food and being away from his family and friends, but he said he enjoyed the opportunity to finally have time to write. We never knew what he had written during those months, but we now assume it was this story.

Those who helped Grandfather, like Griff and Jean, were never prosecuted. People said that Grandfather's release and the failure of the government to take any action against his friends and family was part of some deal that Grandfather worked out with the FBI. He refused to talk about it. But after we found his manuscript, we understood that they were right.

As for the people Grandfather had met on his Passover journey, Howard was never found. Grandfather made a number of efforts to locate him, but given the collapse of the infrastructure in that area after the disaster it wasn't possible. "Maybe he finally found Home," Grandfather would say.

As for Stella, Grandfather had Mother send Stella the money from the sale of her truck while he was still in detention. He heard from her a few years later. She had returned to the area where she had grown up to stay with one of her sisters who had developed cancer. Her family, you will recall, lived near Pine Grove and just on the edge of the "Dead Zone" the government established after the disaster.

Millie, well, she finally got to retire. Bambi's burned to the ground one Sunday morning. Millie had saved enough that she didn't have to work again. She is in her late 90s and still going strong. And Bird, according to Millie, she just left Vinnie's one morning and never came back. She hasn't been heard from since.

Jim and Ben visited Grandfather once when they were pulling a load to Bangor. Jim continued to drive until the pain in his legs stopped him. He lives in Florida now and works part-time as a bartender. Ben is still driving, but thinking about retiring to Florida and living with Jim.

Griff continued his work for the funding of AIDS research. Grandfather and he spent a lot of time together before Griff's death. He died the way he always said he wanted to. He took the *John Wesley II* out one stormy morning in late winter and never came back. Sadly, the AIDS epidemic has continued to grow.

Betsy finished seminary and became a minister. She settled into a church in Massachusetts. And she finally found a life partner. It wasn't Ray, but a woman named Sherry. Over the years they visited Grandfather and Grandmother a number of times. Betsy spoke at the memorial service we had for Grandfather. She quoted a passage from Romans, "And we know that all things work together for good to those who love God, to those called to God's purpose."

She said she thought Grandfather would probably have said he "hoped that's the way it worked." And that he "had sort of counted on that."

Ray continued his life at Flying Fish Lodge. He flew Alvin well into his seventies. But his health failed him in his early eighties. He refused to move to assisted living. Things got worse. The Sheriff told me that when the adult protective worker went out with one of his deputies to move Ray into a nursing home, they found a note. "Gone for a walk." It was the middle of January in northern Maine. Where an eighty-five-year old man on oxygen had walked to they didn't know. They searched the lodge and the surrounding woods, but they couldn't find Ray. They thought they would find his body in the spring when the snow melted. But they never have.

Robert still lives at the Lodge on Loon Lake. The Strouts died in the 2020s and are buried near the lodge. Their children decided to keep the lodge and Robert. He has never ventured out of the country again.

Joe closed his practice a few years after Grandfather was released. He took up real estate development and, they say, made a lot of money. Grandfather and Joe remained close friends. Joe lives in a house he built on Sebago Lake. He continued to compete in water ski competitions well into his eighties. He is in his nineties now and still swims every day. He says he would still water ski, but he can't find anybody he would trust to drive the boat.

Dr. Hazeem and his wife, Carolyn, disappeared. I could find no one, including Carolyn's family, who knew anything about them.

Special Agent Jennings retired from the F.B.I. a number of years ago. He is supposedly living somewhere in Europe. Whether he and his ex-wife Margaret ever got back together again, I do not know. I could find no address for her in Boston.

When Grandfather was released, he told everyone he was going to practice gratitude for the next ten years. And he did. He got to practice a lot of it on me. I came along four years after he was released. He spent much of his time with mother, grandmother and me. I saw more of him than my father, who was often away. My parents were Oceanographers. They were involved in studying global warming. Grandfather was there for Mother and me when Dad didn't return from one of his trips. His small research vessel was no match for one of the most severe Nor'easter's the coast had ever seen.

In the last years of my grandfather's life, he seemed more at peace and more hopeful. He said he loved being with Grandmother and with us. He was no longer angry, Grandmother said, except with me sometimes…and the Republicans. He never returned to the south. He said he didn't need to.

A few years ago, some material from the nuclear accident at Pine Grove was declassified. We found out that Jennings was right. A technician who had no connection with Grandfather or with his friend, David, or for that matter any kind of terrorist group, was blamed. An investigation revealed that the technician was going through a divorce and a custody battle with his wife. He was reportedly depressed and had been drinking heavily in the weeks prior to the accident. Whether what happened was an accident or suicide has never been determined.

The Labs had been experimenting with a new method for processing nuclear fuel pellets. The process involved mixing uranium with nitric acid and water. Apparently the employee mixed twenty or thirty times as much uranium with the nitric acid and water as he had been instructed to do. A chain reaction occurred and a huge amount of radiation was released, most of it through radioactive gasses. The blue flash was caused by the initial chain reaction, which could have been brought under control in time.

A similar accident has occurred at Japanese Fuel Reprocessing Plants and has been contained within twenty-four hours. Apparently the terrorist cell that attacked the labs at Pine Grove understood that this was a major opportunity and they moved quickly. When their plane, loaded with explosives was able to destroy the control center for the plant and part of the old containment building, the chain reaction spun out of control. Presto. Chernobyl. Nuclear disaster.

The lawsuit that Grandfather had been involved with regarding birth defects and injuries to residents living around Pine Grove in the 1950s and 60s ended a few years after the Pine Grove disaster. The companies involved with Pine Grove Labs filed bankruptcy and it was all over. But Grandfather lived a longer and healthier life than he ever thought he would. He continued his work until his death. He died peacefully in his sleep one night in the spring of 2037. He was 90.

Grandmother is still alive. She complains a lot about her health, but I think she's in amazingly good health for a woman of 96. I think she misses Grandfather. When she realized I was serious about publishing Grandfather's manuscript, she allowed me to reprint the letter grandfather had written her years before his death. Grandmother wasn't the sentimental type so I knew her keeping the letter meant that it was important to her.

September 18th, 2018

Dear Liz:

I wanted to put on paper some of the things that I know I should have said more often. I realize I allowed the tension between us, especially in the early years of our marriage to keep me from saying, and more importantly showing you how strong my love for you was and is.

Over all these years of marriage, much has changed and I think most of it for the better. I, like you miss our youth. I'm not sure I've aged gracefully, if anyone does but I am sure I have not been the easiest person to live with or grow old with. Putting closure on my relationship with Jean, settling it in my mind has, I realize now, made things better between us. I know that comes as no surprise to you. I appreciated your patience and your persistence. Many women would have had neither. I assume much of that comes from the confidence I believe you've always had in yourself and in our relationship.

But I must tell you that for much of the change in me, I think I owe a debt to one of the first couples I worked with when I returned from Boston and restarted my practice. They immediately reminded me of us. The woman was Jewish and the man Protestant, and he like me, assumed that his wife should understand what he felt or needed without him having to tell her. For him it was a "logical" assumption, that since they had been married for so long she should know. Like me, he knew it really wasn't logical or realistic to expect but like me he continued, on good days to feel disappointed and, on bad days to feel angry and resentful.

It quickly became clear to me that if I was going to help him make changes in his thinking, I would have to make changes in mine. I thought about referring them to someone else but decided that this was finally an opportunity to take a different route out of the rut that I had been in for years. After all that time, I knew the contours well. I was able to finally change my thinking about us, which allowed me to provide coaching that was helpful to him and their relationship.

I am sure that because of my work with them, I began to look at our arguments in a different way, as opportunities to talk about what was important to me. I began, I am sure you remember, to reign in some of my humor which really wasn't humor, but sarcasm. Something you had been asking me to do for years.

Perhaps most important, I stopped seeing our disagreements as mortal combat where there had to be a winner and a loser. Instead of fighting on or giving up, I began to accept that saying things again in a different way, some things I might have said many times before, was a necessary step to making things better between us. I guess you could say I finally took my own advice. A small shift in my thinking, I believe, made a major shift in the way that I feel toward you and treat you.

Things can always get better if you try in a different way, a tired expression, I know, but one I think I understand better now than I ever have.

So, my dear, I just wanted to make sure I said these things before I slip out of this life.

With all my love,

Lee

They had fifty years together. That anniversary was a grand celebration for them and the family. Grandfather died late that fall.

Mother met the second love of her life two years ago. I think they both work too much. She says she likes to stay busy. She teaches a full load at the university and continues her research and her trips.

And Boston, over the last twenty-five years, has reported a number of mysterious deaths with the victims experiencing symptoms resembling the plague. The CDC and the federal government continue to deny that the plague virus was released in Boston. They have, however, confirmed that Muqtada Hussein and an accomplice planned such an attack, but that the plot was foiled and the terrorists killed in a gun battle with federal agents. They denied that my grandfather or Dr. Kudrick were involved in any of it. Dr. Ibraham Hussein is still listed as a missing person with the Massachusetts State Police.

As for Pine Grove, the "Dead Zone" after the second explosion was extended to a one-hundred-mile radius around the Labs. Pine Grove and the surrounding communities like Bourbonville and White's Fork were abandoned for many years. The Dead Zone has recently been reduced to twenty-five miles and some people — some refer to them as nuclear pioneers, others as fools — have moved back into the area. It is a difficult life. You cannot eat anything that grows in the local soil. Closed, raised gardens are used. Water for drinking and bathing must be trucked in daily. Much of the area has returned to wilderness, although wildlife of any kind is rare. The death rate and rate of birth defects among animal life is very high, just as it is for humans in the area. But some "wildlife" seems to do quite well. Kudzu and very large brown cockroaches to name two.

The cleanup of Pine Grove continues, but as you know, there is less and less money each year to fund the effort. The politicians say there will be more money when the economy improves. The world economy remains depressed. Pine Grove is like many other areas of the world today. After the use by our government of tactical nuclear weapons and the nuclear terrorism that went on in the 2020s, a number of cities remain ghost towns. The fundamentalists thought that the world would end in the 2020s. Armageddon, they said. I think they were somewhat disappointed with the outcome. The world may go out with a whimper rather than a bang.

The power centers of the world economy are in Europe and China, with the French — who have had no nuclear disasters, at least not as of this date — appearing to have the strongest economy. Our country once again has returned to a policy some would call isolationism. I believe our people have been humbled by the events of the last twenty years. Gone is the arrogance and the evangelism for "our way of life," replaced by a new tolerance and a willingness to live and let live.

And Jean. I do know she returned to Europe. She is still living in a small village near Amsterdam. Grandfather wrote her frequently and she would write back. He would give me the stamps from her letters. I still have them. She would send him tulip bulbs each spring, which I would help him plant. Grandfather and I had quite a tulip garden, which I still care for. Grandfather continued to travel. Many of his trips were to Europe.

Exactly where this last piece of my grandfather's writing fits in his story, I am not sure. But I think he would have wanted me to include it. It gives a glimpse into those years after grandfather returned from detention and it may explain, in part, his trips to Europe even after the travel restrictions were imposed.

Thursday, December 15, 2016
Paris, France

At 4:15 Lee took his leave from the professional meeting he was attending. He wasn't really there to attend the meeting but to deliver a package. The French say that good things come in small packages. Lee just knew that he had to deliver this one before he would be allowed to return home. He turned left on *Boulevard Haussman*. The sun was low in the sky. The shops were starting to close. The people of Paris were on their way home for the evening. He walked toward the Opera House. The wind was stronger and the sky darker. A light rain began to fall. As he turned off *Boulevard Des Italiens*, the Opera House came into view. A massive structure, the Opera House was designed and built by Garnier in the early 1860s. Lee remembered the tour brochure's description of the façade as resembling a dresser full of curios. On this dark December afternoon, the newly restored façade of red and green marble and bronze only appeared black and white.

Lee's pace quickened as the rain became heavier. He climbed the steps into the Opera House, found the ticket agent in the gift shop, purchased one self-guided tour as directed and looked up. The great staircase, often referred to as the monument within a monument, the set for the performance of Masquerade in Webber's *Phantom of the Opera*. Lee climbed its marble steps, slowly into the anti-hall, with its large arches that open into the Great Hall. He stopped and gazed up at the ceiling paintings, trying to forget his purpose in being there. He had been overwhelmed by the beauty of the house years before. For a moment he felt no different but today was different. He walked on.

The auditorium is horseshoe in shape. Red and gold décor, with the centerpiece being the main light and the ceiling painting. The light is two stories in height, gilt, bronze and crystal with five crowns and hundreds of lights. The ceiling painting is by Chagal and had been completed in 1964. Lee had not liked it the first time he had seen it and he still felt it was out of place. The best seats in the house are in the orchestra, the balcony or the ground floor boxes. Boxes cover the walls, superimposed over five floors.

Lee made his way to the orchestra. He found the small door to the stage house. He was alone. He backed up to the door, put his hand behind his back and tried the latch. It was unlocked. He surveyed the auditorium again, listening for voices. He quickly opened the door and slipped through it.

Suddenly, he had passed from a world of light and color into a world of shadows and darkness. He reached for the door latch to lock it but hesitated. Lee felt he was being watched. He turned on his heel but no one was there. He waited. He heard voices in the auditorium. He locked the door.

He placed one foot on the stage step immediately in front of him and felt for a railing, which he found with some difficulty. He placed his other foot on the next step and began to ascend the stairs slowly and quietly. At the top of the stairs was a florescent bulb covered by a metal guard overhanging a bank of levers and switches.

Lee could see better now as his eyes adjusted to the dark. The stage house was huge, 40 – 50 meters in length and 20-30 meters in width. Above him was a sea of ropes and pulleys. Below him he knew were five levels of trap rooms. He waited.

It was approaching 5:00 P.M. The Opera House would close for the evening. There were no performances scheduled. He again felt he was being watched. He turned quickly but he could see only the dark. He waited as he had been instructed.

He heard creaking floorboards and a swishing sound as if a cord of rope or a cable was being unwound but he could not identify where the sound was coming from nor could he see anything. He knew that somewhere in the stage house floor there was a trap door that led to an underground reservoir. There had been rumors in Garnier's day of an underground river and lake that had inspired both Leroux and Webber in their story telling.

He waited. He wanted to sit down, but he remained on his feet. He did not move. It was now twenty minutes after the hour.

"Dr. Brazil," said an unfamiliar voice to Lee's right, somewhere in the dark.

"Yes," replied Lee.

"You have brought the package?"

"Yes." He again stared into the dark but could see nothing.

"Please place the package on the floor in front of you and withdraw to the stairs from which you entered the stage-house."

Lee complied by backing slowly away until standing next to the bank of levers and lighted switches at the top of the stairs. Lee again heard the creaking of floorboards and the swishing sounds that now seemed to be coming from a number of different directions. There was a sudden flash and the stage house lights came on. Directly in front of Lee, 20 feet away was a small man, late 50s or early 60s, overweight, balding, who looked quite confused and frightened, holding the package in both hands.

To the man's right, Lee recognized Jennings, even with night vision goggles. He was accompanied by a large man holding a weapon of some kind that was pointed directly at the small, nervous man. To the small man's left were two other men of average build, both wearing brown raincoats, one carrying an umbrella. Both were pointing weapons at the small man.

"Louie," said Jennings addressing the nervous little man who was now perspiring heavily. "We are very disappointed in you." The little man said nothing.

"Bob, please escort Louie downstairs. I will be with you in a few moments," said Jennings. As they passed, Jennings pulled the package from Louie's hand.

"And how are you this evening, Dr. Brazil?" Jennings said extending his hand. Lee hesitated but shook it.

"I'm sorry for the inconvenience. We're not quite finished here. But don't worry, we will be very soon and you will be on your way back home." Trying to sound sincere. "We do appreciate your assistance in this matter."

"That's fine," said Lee quickly. "I really don't need to know the details. I just want to finish this business." He looked away.

"And that you shall." Jennings examined the package without opening it. "This little favor should be the first and the last time we ask your assistance. I suggest you wait for us across the street." He looked at Lee. "You can have something to eat and drink while you wait. The *Café de la Paix*. Have you been there?"

"Yes. I was planning on meeting someone there this evening," said Lee looking away again.

"Our mutual friend, Dr. Kudrick?" asked Jennings smiling.

"Well, yes," said Lee avoiding Jennings' eyes. "How did you know?" But before Jennings could speak Lee caught himself. "Never mind. I don't want to know," said Lee with resignation.

"Well," said Jennings gesturing a salute, "give my regards to Dr. Kudrick. I will see you later this evening" Jennings looked up from the small computer he was holding. "I will not be interrupting anything, will I?" asked Jennings again with a smile.

"No," replied Lee with force, "I don't think so."

"The café is a very popular place," said Jennings. "Great for people watching."

They walked through the darkened Opera House and down the great staircase. Out of the shadows stepped another man.

"Phil," said Jennings, "take Dr. Brazil over to the *Café de la Paix*." He looked at Lee. "Your evening will be at our expense. Try the onion soup. It's great." Lee didn't respond.

"This way, Dr. Brazil." Phil opened the door and ushered Lee onto the steps.

The *Café de la Paix* was only a few yards away in Le Grande Intercontinental Hotel, one of the oldest cafés in Paris. Like the Opera House, it had been designed by Garnier and, in many ways, was as elegant and beautiful.

Lee requested a table by the window. The waiter was friendly and Lee ordered a cup of coffee. He glanced at the menu. "Ten euros," he mumbled under his breath. "I'm glad they're paying for it." Lee told the waiter he might order a meal later. Lee waited.

It was after 6:00 as Lee peered out the window at the intersection, watching motorists and pedestrians jockeying for position. Legend has it that if you sit at the *Café de la Paix* long enough, you're bound to run into a friend or an acquaintance.

It was raining heavily now. A number of tourists had taken shelter under the café's awning. Lee noticed one woman in a beige raincoat with a bright red umbrella, fighting the wind as she walked in the direction of the Opera House. Of all the people on the street, why she had caught Lee's eye, he wasn't sure. He assumed it was the umbrella. He watched her until she disappeared into the dark and the rain.

Time passed slowly as Lee sipped his coffee and waited. He had thoroughly surveyed the restaurant's décor and had counted the number of wine glasses hanging over the bar three times. Finally an English couple sitting at a table near him attracted his attention. He could not hear the conversation but their body language told the story. They were young and in love. In Paris. Perhaps for the first time ordering glasses of Kir Royal to celebrate Paris. They were talking of their future together, that lay before them broad and wide, with no end in sight. They would come back to Paris every year. Maybe they would live here someday. Maybe retire here.

Lee had lost track of time when he suddenly realized that a woman in a beige raincoat, soaked through, holding a bright red umbrella was standing at his table. It was Jean.

"Sorry I'm late." she said and gave no explanation.

"Well our timing always was terrible," said Lee sounding a bit nervous. They laughed. She sat down.

"How long have you been in Paris?" asked Jean.

"I just came over on the Eurostar yesterday and unfortunately," Lee sighed. "I'll be going back tomorrow."

Jean frowned. "Why such a short trip?"

"Well, I'm afraid I'm doing a favor for one of our mutual friends."

Jean hesitated. "You don't mean Jennings do you?" she said in a low voice.

Lee smiled a nervous smile. "Well, you do remember our agreement with him."

"I'm afraid I do," said Jean looking down at the table.

Lee shook his head and smiled. "A delivery boy at my age," he sighed again. "but it was better than spending more time in Boston." His voice dropped: "I'm not sure what I was involved in tonight" he said with frustration. "I don't know that I want to. Some poor bastard, Louie, was…" Lee stopped.

"I'm not sure we should talk more about this."

Jean leaned closer. She was paying close attention to what Lee was saying.

"You know I want to trust Jennings." He paused. "I want to trust our government again. Maybe this little favor as Jennings called it is important," he paused, "to the world." Lee was struggling to explain a feeling he had that he didn't understand.

"I'm feeling more optimistic these days," sounding more certain of himself. "I've stopped being afraid of the future. I think things are starting to change… for the better."

"Well, I don't know, Lee," she sounded doubtful. "We're so far behind the curve on so many things, the economy, health care, global warming." She started to list them.

Lee nodded. "Yes, yes I know Jean."

"And the trouble in the Middle East," she said with disgust. "It just goes on and on. God, I'm tired of it."

"Yes," said Lee with impatience. "But we're good problem solvers. The New Deal, The Marshall Plan, the moon landing. We get things done," said Lee, "when we get on the same page and support each other. We love pulling it out in the bottom of the ninth."

"Well, let's just hope we don't strike out. Our batting average hasn't been that great lately."

Lee persisted. "Things are changing," his voice was rising. "We're in a race for the future. You can feel it." He paused. "I think," he asserted, "we're finally focusing on ourselves rather than on the other guy. Maybe we're finally getting away from all the damn blaming and scape-goating and realizing we're all in this together."

"Aren't you the optimist," said Jean sounding surprised.

"Yes, finally," said Lee agreeing. "I believe the promise of America is still alive."

"Well, hooray for the red, white and blue," said Jean looking away and appearing uncomfortable with the conversation.

"Well," his voice trailed off, "I guess we'll see." He was remembering the red umbrella in the rain and the woman who was wearing a trench coat like Jeans.

"Jennings hasn't asked you for any 'favors', has he?" asked Lee.

"Oh no," said Jean avoiding Lee's eyes.

"Did you walk past the café tonight?" He paused. "I mean in the rain you might have had difficulty seeing it."

"Uh, yes," said Jean quickly. "When I reached the Opera House I realized I had missed you and I turned around." Her words were rushed. "Why?"

"I was just wondering." Lee waited a moment and then tried again. "Jennings told me if I cooperated they wouldn't ask you."

Jean didn't respond.

"He knew I was meeting you here tonight. He even seemed a bit pleased I was going to see you." He paused. "He told me to give you his regards."

Jean smiled again but, for whatever reasons she had, she was not going to say more. There was a long pause in the conversation.

"Well, my dear," said Lee with a broad smile and a wave of his hand "there is still time for us to 'have Paris,'" referring to a line from *Casablanca.*

Jean smiled directly at Lee. "Well, Rick, an aging Ilsa thanks you, but our timing, as usual, is a bit off."

"I would say by at least thirty or forty years," Lee quipped. They looked at each other and laughed and the tension went away.

"I'm glad you could come over on such short notice," said Lee sounding apologetic.

"I wanted to see you," said Jean. "Your letters say so little."

"I know, I know," said Lee shaking his head. "It's been a long time since we've really talked."

"You look good, Lee." Her eyes met his. "God, it's been over three years. What have you been doing?"

"Restarting my life. It took a while. The time in Boston wasn't easy but explaining why I was away for seven months was harder. People's imaginations." He shook his head and smiled. "Small town rumors. You know."

Jean nodded. She had grown up in a small town. She understood.

"But things have settled down," he said in a reassuring tone "I work part time. Liz spends a lot of time doing her art. Painting mainly." He moved on quickly. They had never talked very much about their partners but they did talk about Dru.

"She's still in graduate school working on her doctorate in Oceanography." Lee sounded like a proud father. "And, she's had a serious boyfriend over the past few years."

"Marriage?" asked Jean.

"Well, yes. It's starting to sound like that," said Lee slowly. "I don't know if I'm ready for that."

"You never were," snapped Jean with a smile. Lee, with some hesitation, returned the smile.

"And she wants kids," said Lee with a tinge of panic in his voice, "before she gets too old."

Jean nodded. "That may be a good idea. Some people wait too long."

"But Jean, she's only twenty-six." Lee stopped and looked at Jean who was starting to laugh. Lee joined her.

"And you?" Lee realized he had been talking about himself and hadn't asked.

"Oh, I have a busy life," she suddenly looked nervous again. "You know, with my friends and music…and some, well major changes since I saw you." She looked away again.

"Major changes?" echoed Lee. "You didn't say anything about major changes in your letter," his voice rising with concern. "Is it your health?" he quickly asked. "I mean, you did smoke for a long time." Lee remembered his cancer scare.

"No, no, Lee, my health's fine." She paused. "Well," she said loudly, "I've been thinking about getting married again."

"You're okay. That's good." Lee appeared not to have heard what she had said.

Jean smiled nervously. "His name is Karl. He was a dear friend of Ian's. He lost his partner three years ago" She began to explain in detail. "When I got back, he would come around. We started going out to dinner." Jean's face was starting to flush. "You know, once or twice a week and, well…" She was searching for words. "I've known him for years." She paused. "He's a good man."

"I'm sure he is," said Lee trying to catch a second wind.

"You look shocked."

"No, no, I'm not shocked," he lied. "I'm just a little surprised, but I'm glad you've found someone…you love and who," he said quickly, "loves you". He paused. "I mean this is not just about not being alone?" Lee looked concerned again.

"No, no, Lee," she sounded irritated. "I'm almost seventy and I don't want to be alone, but," she said with force "I wouldn't do it for that reason."

Now Lee's face was starting to flush. "I'm sure you wouldn't," he said apologetically. "I didn't mean to imply…"

Jean took Lee's hand. "I understand. I'm not sure what I will do." She paused. "There's no rush." There was silence.

"Enough said…So, Dr. Brazil, the man said the meal was on Uncle Sam, right? What should we have?"

"How did you know that?" asked Lee.

"Well, I'm sure," she said with a half smile "the least they could do is pay your expenses."

Lee continued to look puzzled but had no response. He motioned for the waiter. "A menu for Madame."

"Oui, Monsieur."

"I was thinking about the *croquette, monsieur*." He paused. "The waiter tells me that's a ham and grilled cheese sandwich which is apparently very popular. Jennings recommended the onion soup."

The waiter brought the menu. Jean perused it.

"How about the haddock with sauerkraut in a cream sauce? I'll have that and a Grolsch. Beer, yes, definitely beer," she said continuing to study the menu. "These prices are something else."

They ordered. "I think we offended the waiter" said Lee. "Coffee, beer, no wine."

They continued to talk about the past. The good and the bad. The food came. The onion soup was especially good. Jean enjoyed the haddock, but Lee had a hard time understanding how anyone could put a sauerkraut cream sauce on a good piece of fish.

Lee called Jean's attention to the young British couple. They were on their second, or was it their third glass of Kir Royal.

"So young," said Lee with envy.

"We were once," Jean asserted, "and we're still here like a rock." She smiled. "Time and distance may wear us down but it hasn't destroyed us."

Lee felt, for a moment the old sadness and a flash of anger. But just for a moment.

"Unfortunately," he said in a soft voice, "a rock may be strong and permanent but it can't grow and change."

Jean objected. "But," her voice rising, her eyes searching for his, "I don't feel like we're that cold and lifeless tonight, are we?"

Lee had looked away.

"Lee," she said as she touched his hand, "my dearest friend."

"Yes," said Lee finally turning to face her.

"Friends are what we are," she said, "not partners, not lovers anymore."

"And," Lee said, "that was true a long time before Jennings entered our lives. In many ways nothing has changed. But," he said with emphasis, "staying dear friends through the storms we've weathered in this relationship is no small feat."

"So," said Jean with energy, "I propose a toast."

Lee caught the waiter's eye. "Two glasses of Kir Royal."

They were brought out and the waiter smiled.

"I propose a toast to us," said Jean raising her glass. "To our past and to our future."

"To," Lee added "the separate lives that we lead." They touched their glasses and took a sip.

Some things, Lee thought, *have to be accepted even if they are never to be understood.*

A few months after Grandfather's death, I went to the cemetery to tend his grave. I found a beautiful vase on his grave with tulips. They must have been there for a few days. They had wilted in the summer sun. Attached to the vase was a note, water stained, difficult to make out. I have the vase in my workshop. When our tulips bloom this year, I will pick some of his favorites, place them in the vase and put them on his grave. I think he would like that.

As for Maine, the winters come earlier and are colder. The lobsters shed later every summer. Mother still says a new Ice Age is coming. The fishing isn't as good as it used to be. But Maine doesn't change very much. There is good and bad in that, but I think most of it is good.

And me, I enjoy my life. My world is relatively small. But I am at home with the ocean and with the Maine winters and with my family. I can wait. I am an optimist. Grandfather used to say that the human race grows smarter and stronger each time the cycle is repeated. Let us hope he is right and that his favorite prayer, "Dear Lord, save us from us," is answered.

Benjamin Brazil-Woodford
Winter Harbor, Maine
September 3rd, 2042

Section IV: Hope

Chapter Summaries, Discussion Questions and Author's Comments
Chapters 30 - Epilogue*

CHAPTER 30

As they talk, Jean, Lee and Jennings realize the back-up plan that Muqtada is using to spread the plague involves plague-infected fleas that have been packed into empty cola cans. The cans will be distributed throughout the city of Boston and opened in places like Fenway Park, the Federal Office Buildings, and the Garden. They arrive in Boston, and Muqtada begins the delivery of the cases of cola. Jennings, who has managed to retain a GPS device, is able to track the locations of the deliveries. After they finish the last delivery, Muqtada and Bassin drive the truck to the marina where Ibraham's friend, Mark, is staying on a boat, *The Flying Dutchman*. They will wait until sunrise before they approach the boat.

Discussion Questions

1. In this chapter, Jean, Lee and Jennings understand that Muqtada's plan might work. They are also dealing with the realization that they will most likely be killed by the terrorists when they are no longer of use to them. How do they deal with these realities? Think again about the attitudes and skills involved in resilience.

Author's Comments

Lee attempts to deal with much of his anger and fear through sarcasm and humor, at least initially. Jean tries to deal with her feelings through asserting herself and thinking, coming up with a plan for survival. Jennings, who is still in shock regarding his loss of control over the situation, is having a difficult time deciding what to do. He vacillates between trying to provide leadership and "sounding hopeless again" (page 198). By the end of the chapter, Jennings has reasserted himself and is giving direction to Jean and Lee. "Get some sleep...I'll take the first watch." These are old patterns of coping for all three characters, which is usually what we fall back on in a crisis.

*Refer to pages 4 and 5 for a list of the Eleven Skills And Attitudes That Build Resilience.

CHAPTER 31

In the hours before sunrise, Lee contemplates his death and the possibility of killing Muqtada. The three have concocted a plan to try to overpower Bassin and Muqtada, but Muqtada frustrates the plan by leaving Jennings with Bassin and ordering Bassin to kill Jennings if Muqtada does not return.

Muqtada takes Lee and Jean with him since they know Ibraham's friend, Mark Johnson. As they approach the boat, Lee confronts Muqtada. There is a struggle on the dock and Muqtada is knocked into the sea. Jean and Lee almost fall from the pier into the water, but Lee is able to pull them to safety. Muqtada manages to climb back onto the pier. The three struggle for the gun. The gun discharges, and Muqtada is shot. While Lee stays with Muqtada, Jean alerts others and calls for help.

Discussion Questions

1. In Chapter 31, Lee demonstrates again a number of the skills and attitudes of resilience. What are they?

2. To Lee personally, what is the significance of the scene on the pier where Lee catches himself before falling into the sea and manages to pull Jean back on to the pier (page 200)?

3. How does Muqtada exhibit resilience?

Author's Comments

While waiting for dawn to come, Lee takes the opportunity to think again. He looks at the big picture and his thinking to some degree is optimistic. He tries to make sense of what is happening on a much broader scale than the impact that it will have on his life individually.

In the scene where Jean is dangling from the edge of the pier, Lee finally deals with his fear of falling and drowning. It requires every ounce of physical strength and skill that he has, but he is able to "catch hold of the railing with his hook as he slides through...the two were no longer sliding into the sea." With great effort, he manages to "pull her back. It was a slow and painful process for both of them."

Muqtada certainly exhibits resilience in being able "to climb the ladder from the sea." It should also be noted that Muqtada, as he is dying, asks Lee a question that Lee cannot answer, "Your President Truman, who ordered the atomic bombs dropped on Hiroshima and Nagasaki that killed thousands of innocent people, was he a terrorist?" I am sure most of us have never entertained this idea. Why does the question seem like a logical one to Muqtada, but not at all logical for most Americans?

CHAPTER 32

Muqtada dies from his wounds. The plague-infected cans are retrieved by the federal agents. Most have not been opened. Lee is returned to the detention center. Federal agents frustrate news coverage of the event and concoct a cover-up that involves the death of the terrorists and the three federal agents but makes no mention of the plague or of Lee and Jean.

Jean is to be sent back to Europe the following day. Lee will be detained for a few more weeks or months until things "get back to normal." Jennings tells Lee that neither he nor Jean can ever talk about what happened. Jennings explains that Lee's time in detention is contingent upon his and Jean's cooperation.
Jennings arranges for Lee and Jean to meet.

Discussion Questions

1. In his travels, Lee has lost the watch that his daughter gave him. He says it is "still important but he didn't need it as before." What is Lee trying to say?

2. There is an awkward interaction between Lee and Jennings on page 203 similar to the one between Lee and Jennings when Jennings is returned to the furnace room after being interrogated by Muqtada (page 186). What's going on with Jennings?

3. In this "fictional" account of the future, Jennings, on page 203, talks about how the media is being managed by the federal government. What do you think the role of the media should be in a free society?

4. On page 204, bottom of the page, Lee says that he "finally understood that he could no longer go back to a place or a time or a person in the past to avoid dealing with the problems of the present." Avoiding or denying the present is a very human thing to do. How often have you done this in your own life?

Author's Comments

Lee realizes on an emotional level that watch or no watch he is and will continue to be connected with his daughter and that this cannot be taken from him or lost.

Jennings appears in both scenes to be affected by emotions that he prefers to avoid dealing with directly and tries to prevent Lee from being aware of these feelings. Men in our society in particular are taught that being angry is more acceptable than being sad or scared. Jennings has learned the lesson well.

Although it is very human to "go back to a place or a time or a person in the past to avoid dealing with the problems of the present," it usually does not serve us very well. This can be a short-term strategy for dealing with hard times, but "going back" should not be a means of solving the problems of the present.

CHAPTER 33

Jean sees Lee. They say their good-byes and talk about Muqtada. They discuss the fact that Muqtada may not have been an "evil" man, at least not to those who saw the world from the place where he was standing. Lee accepts the fact that Jean is returning home to Europe. Lee begins to write what becomes this story. With God's grace he feels he has stood upright. He accepts himself. He no longer feels disabled by fear. He has found home and moved in.

Discussion Questions

1. In this last chapter, Jean and Lee discuss the concept of evil. In your own life, do these concepts help you make sense of the world and world events? If so, how?

2. Jennings is recognized as a hero. "The country needed heroes weekly or at least monthly, real or imagined." Why?

Author's Comments

The concepts of good and evil have been used for thousands of years to explain human behavior. They are the centerpiece of many religions and religious practices. Some people would argue that trying to understand another culture or a society's worldview that is different from our own is more easily done without applying these concepts.

When people are afraid, they may look to others for answers and for examples of heroism and courage. We all possess these. We just need to "walk upright" and to look inward.

EPILOGUE

In the Epilogue you find out what has happened in later years to the different characters in *Reaching Home*. Benjamin also recounts events that many of you may find quite disturbing. For example, he talks about the use "by our government of tactical nuclear weapons and the nuclear terrorism that went on in the 2020s, with cities of the world remaining "ghost towns." It would also appear from his account that the world has done little to deal effectively with the AIDS epidemic; that our country once again has returned to a policy some would call isolationism, and that global warming is continuing.

Discussion Questions

1. The relationship between Liz and Lee improved in the later years of their marriage. Why?

2. Do many of the tragedies, such as global warming and the use of nuclear weapons, described in the Epilogue have to befall our world?

Author's Comments

His relationship with Liz has improved, in part, because Lee has been more open with her, has put closure on his relationship with Jean and has begun to think about their problems in a different way. Decreased tension and a willingness to see (and think about) the relationship in a different way can do a lot to improve all facets of any relationship.

There is still time for us to solve many of our problems, such as global warming and the economy. Accepting that we are citizens, not just of this country, but of the world, whether many of us like that fact or not, is a necessary step to our and our nation's survival. Continuing, as a people, to behave as if we believe there are only two options—the world plays by our rules or we pick up our marbles and go home—will not work any longer, if it ever really "worked" before. Unfortunately, much of the world sees us now as an arrogant, spoiled brat who doesn't play well with others. It will be increasingly to our advantage in the future for our fellow citizens of the world to see us as a member of a group who will take turns and listen to others whether we like what they say or not, as a nation who accepts it's limitations as well as its strengths and does not always have to be the leader of the band.

Our leaders' attitudes and behaviors certainly have much to do with how we are seen in the world but any leader will fail if the expectation is that he or she will fix our nation's problems. We must do the fixing. Each one of us needs to accept our responsibility for changing our behavior and our nation. We must work together. We will not reach home without the help of others who may be quite different from us in their beliefs and behavior. We can do our part to fix the oil crisis, the problems with health care, global warming, the economy, etc. We can demonstrate resilience by:

- Driving less, taking the bus, buying more fuel efficient cars, etc. (Flexibility)
- Being less focused on having more! Spending our money wisely. Saving versus spending. (Manage strong feelings, problem solve)
- Paying attention to what our federal and local leaders are doing and let them know what we would like for them to do. (Communication)
- Changing our attitudes about difference and diversity, welcoming it rather than always being suspect of it. In short, we can practice inclusion rather than the easy path of exclusion. (Connect with others)
- Becoming better problem solvers when it comes to insulating and heating or cooling our homes. (Problem solve)
- Tolerating a little more discomfort in our lives rather than trying to immediately avoid it or relieve it. (Manage strong feelings)
- Beginning to believe that better days are ahead and that together we can ensure that they come faster. (Optimism and self-confidence)
- Getting better at acting on and practicing our values and not our fears. (Sense of purpose and belief)
- Focusing more on helping others and not just taking care of ourselves. (Helping others)
- Lightening up, laughing. If we think we're about to go over the falls, we should at least enjoy the ride down. (Use of humor)
- Cutting our health care costs by taking better care of ourselves, losing weight, exercising, etc. (Care for self)

And there are a lot of others that you can add to the list. America is still a work in progress. As John F. Kennedy suggested, we must not ask what our country can do for us, but what we can do for our country. And right now, that's a hell of a lot. And the only way it will be done is if we do it, each one of us.

Let's practice the skills and attitudes that build resilience in ourselves, our family members and our community and let's stop expecting that our world will change for the better unless we are willing to change for the better.

Our leaders cannot do it alone. Bounce back, America.

Yes we can!

Module IV

Developing A Plan For Building Your Resilience

This section will give you an opportunity to think about the concepts and skills that we have been discussing. Putting a plan down in writing and reviewing it periodically, e.g., on the first Saturday or Sunday of January, April, July and October, would be well worth your time and energy. As you review the plan, you can also review your readiness in other areas. Having a readiness kit with duct tape and other items that you will need in the event of an emergency is a good investment of time and energy. Information about the items that should be in this kit and how they should be maintained can be found on the web at **www.ready.gov**.

But as we have pointed out throughout this guide, duct tape is not enough. Building resilience long before it is required is something you should be thinking about and doing on a daily basis. It can certainly help you to lead a longer and healthier life. So as you develop and write your plan for building resilience, ask yourself the following questions:

1. **How can I strengthen and build my connection to others?** As pointed out throughout *Reaching Home*, having a support network is critical to adapting well to difficult times. Who's yours?

2. **How should I change my thinking?** Can I become more optimistic? More into seeing things in my life as temporary, both good and bad, rather than permanent? More into seeing things that happen as having a specific effect on certain areas of my life rather than having a pervasive effect, good or bad, on my life in general? Less into playing the blame game, blaming myself, or others, for adverse events, while remaining accountable?

3. **How can I improve my planning and decision-making skills?** Do I need to work on being more decisive?

4. **How am I taking care of myself each day?** Diet? Exercise? Financial? Getting things done today rather than putting them off to tomorrow?

5. **What can I do to feel more confident and self-assured?** Self-confidence is one of the best buffers against anxiety.

6. **How can I practice flexibility on a daily basis?** As demonstrated throughout *Reaching Home*, flexibility, by definition, is a key element of resilience.

7. **What are my goals for the future?**

DEVELOP SMART GOALS

SMART goals are:

- Specific: what exactly are you going to do?
- Measurable: will you and others know when you've reached the goal?
- Attainable: are you capable of reaching the goal? Do you have the ability? The resources? Time?
- Realistic: are you willing to commit the time, resources, etc. to reaching the goal?
- Time specific: exactly when are you going to start? What are your timelines? When should the goal be reached?

Goals can push us and pull us forward, especially in bad times. You need to be persistent in trying to reach your goals but not rigid. Ask yourself how you would change your goals if your life suddenly changed due to illness, death of a loved one, a national crisis or a natural disaster.

A Plan For Building and Maintaining My Resilience

1.

2.

3.

4.

Module V

Building The Resilience Of Your Family And Community

How can you integrate the skills and attitudes that you are learning as part of this program into your life outside of work, into your family life and personal life? Take a few minutes and give this some thought. **Exercise One:** Try to come up with at <u>least five ways</u> in which you can do this. If you are participating in a workshop, you will most likely be working in a group. Discuss these ideas with your fellow group members.

Here are some other ideas:

Share the book and materials with your family. Discuss what you have learned. Approach your church, civic group or club about doing a program focused around resilience, at least a discussion group that you might lead on the topic. If they are interested, you may want to follow up with a workshop or a program specifically for your organization. If you are part of a book club or reading group, suggest that they select books that focus on resilience. In Appendix V you will find a list of other books in addition to *Reaching Home* that your group might consider.

Since we spend much of our life at work and this, for many of us is our community, think about how you can integrate these skills and attitudes into what you do on a daily basis at work. Take ten minutes, think, and make some notes. Be prepared to discuss them if you are doing this program as part of a workshop. Think about a different attitude, e.g., optimism, you can take toward work, what you might do differently, e.g., take time to make a connection with some of your colleagues at work. **Exercise Two:** See if you can come up with <u>five ways</u> in which these skills and attitudes could become more a part of your life at work. Write these down. If you are doing this as part of a workshop, discuss what you have come up with your fellow group members.

Exercise Three: Design a program of training that would help others in your organization/community develop and strengthen their resilience skills and attitudes. If you are doing this as part of a workshop, you may have the opportunity to design this program with others. Try to answer specific questions such as:

- What would the training look like? Be specific:

- How would it be presented, who would present it and when and in what format?

- How long would it be?

- How often would it be done?

- How would you get people to attend and participate in the program?

- Would it be mandatory or voluntary?

- What resources would you need to deliver the training? Think about such things as training materials, videos, PowerPoint slides, etc. In the next section we will be talking specifically about resources that are available to assist you in developing workshops and classes in your organization and community.

If you decide to make an active effort to develop these skills in others in your community or at work, your plan needs to also focus on how you will maintain your resilience while you are doing this. To help you keep this in mind, review the eleven skills and attitudes that we have been discussing and answer the following questions:

- What support network will you utilize both in and outside of your home/organization/institution?

- How flexible will you be?

- Are your plans realistic?

- Will you take action?

- With whom do you need to open or increase communication to ensure the success of your efforts? How will you do this?

- What feelings will you have about what you are doing and how will you deal with them?

- How self-confident are you about the success you will have with your "project"? Will doing this activity build your self-confidence?

- Will doing this activity be meaningful to you? Will it add meaning and purpose to your life? In what ways?

- How will your level of optimism or pessimism impact what you are doing and the success of your project?

- How will you take care of yourself while doing the project?

- How will you keep a sense of humor while doing the project, especially when things go wrong?

Module VI

Materials And Training Resources

Self-Study: *Duct Tape Isn't Enough* and the DVD *Daily Heroes* were designed as a self-study program and guide. They are excellent selection for reading groups and clubs. There are other books (we've included a list of suggested titles in Appendix V) that can be used with the resilience materials. We would suggest that you make a checklist of the eleven resilience skills and attitudes and as you read a novel or biography or watch a movie, notice whether the characters are making use of these skills and attitudes. If you and some friends are reading the same book or watching the same movie, the checklist can spark a lively discussion. This activity is one way of reviewing these skills and attitudes. You will get better at applying them as you practice them.

I would also encourage you to visit the American Psychological Association Help Center at APAhelpcenter.org for additional information on resilience and other related topics such as the Mind/Body connection. The American Psychological Association also has an excellent bookstore online where you can find one of the resources that was used in writing *Reaching Home, In the Wake of 911,* which explores, in some detail, terror management theory. A complete reference for this work is in the reference list.

Organizing A Workshop Or Class

These suggestions come from our experience delivering this program to a number of different groups through a number of different formats. *Reaching Home* was released in late October 2006. The Maine Resilience Program, making use of *Duct Tape Isn't Enough* as a workbook and trainer's guide, was introduced in January of 2007. As of the publication of this edition of *Duct Tape Isn't Enough*, we have delivered workshops to a diverse audience ranging from Resident Assistants at a local university to residents of an elderly housing program and their staff members. We have provided this program to first responders, including fire fighters, police, emergency medical service personnel, health care providers, Red Cross volunteers and the general public. The length of these workshops has ranged from an hour and one half for the Northeast Chapter of the National Association of Professional Journalists to a six-hour Train the Trainer program for the Maine Education Association. Most of the workshops have been six-hour workshops and have focused on training individuals to serve as trainers to their organizations and their communities. Maine Resilience, since its inception, believes that these skills and attitudes are relevant for every member of society and has set as its goal reaching every citizen of the State of Maine. We are currently in the second year of a three-year grant from the Emergency Management Agency of Cumberland County to offer these workshops to the residents of Portland and surrounding communities.

We have obtained sponsorship from a number of community organizations, specifically **Alpha One**, which is the Independent Living Center for the State of Maine. We initially trained persons with a disability to serve as co-trainers in the program since we believe that persons with a disability have some real expertise in resilience, having been able to survive in our society. As the program has developed, we have added other co-trainers to our ranks of individuals who have demonstrated resilience through their lives, their work or their profession. The program is continuing to grow and evolve and we are hopeful that similar programs will be developed in other states.

Timeframes

The program has been designed to provide a minimum of three to four hours of classroom time. The bulk of the program is to be completed through self-study. As with anything, if the participant is going to learn the skills and the attitudes they have to practice them. The program and its activities are organized in such a way as to allow for this practice and repetition. Adding discussion groups and other exercises that allow people to observe and use the skills and attitudes can reinforce the learning process. As indicated previously, the format is important. I prefer conducting the training over time rather than in one sitting but much has to do with the motivation of participants. A six-hour, one-day workshop can be very effective with motivated participants.

For participants to learn the material, they need to be willing to read the materials, which will take 12-14 hours and to complete the exercises and the discussion questions that will take an additional 7-10 hours. Repetition, practice and the reading and discussion of materials are the keys to integrating these skills and attitudes into your life at home, work and in the community.

Formats

To teach the basic skills and attitudes of resilience, we would suggest a four-to-six hour program (see Appendix I). Participants will do most of their work outside of "class" reading and working with the material. Each participant should be provided with a copy of *Duct Tape Isn't Enough* a few weeks before the training so they can begin reading *Reaching Home.* The four-hour "classroom" program can be offered in one sitting or can be divided into two, two-hour programs. The program consists of four modules. The first is a two-hour presentation, Module I and Module II, with a break in between so that people can work with the materials. Participants return in two-to-four weeks for a presentation of Module III and Module IV. This is the format that we have found a number of organizations prefer such as first responders, e.g., police, fire and rescue. This has also been a format for delivering the program in elder living facilities for both residents and staff. These organizations have limited time available to train staff which may mean that training modules have to be compressed into an hour and a half or two hour format and presented by one of their staff whom you trained to deliver the program.

Other groups, such as educators, have preferred the six-hour Train the Trainer program, in part, because when it is offered, Modules V and VI allow the educators to do program design and to create "take aways" from the trainings. Once trained, these educators can offer it to their peers in 1 ½ - 2-hour professional development seminars and integrate it into the classes they are currently teaching, whether it be history or math. This does not have to be an "add-on" program or a separate class.

Using The Time Between Classroom Presentations

I prefer dividing the workshop into segments and allowing two to eight weeks between the presentation of Module I and II and the presentation of Module III and IV. This is primarily a time for reading and self-study but it is also an excellent opportunity to conduct small discussion groups, either face-to-face, online or by bridgeline/conference call. A "meeting" could be held after participants have completed each section of the book, e.g., four sections/four meetings. Meetings could be for 30 – 45 minutes in length.

CEUs. It is important to some of these groups, such as social service providers and educators, that you offer Continuing Education Credits. We have provided six hours of **CEUs** for the six-hour program and four for the four hour program through the University of Maine Conference Center we provide a certificate (Appendix III). In order to obtain CEUs, participants must complete a quiz and an evaluation (Appendix II and IV).

Videotapes, DVDs and PowerPoint Slides. In addition to the written material, we have found that using short videos can be another way of teaching the skills and attitudes. A popular one is *Where's Herbie* — a ten-minute documentary of an elderly (early nineties) Maine fisherman. To learn more about this video and for purchasing information please go to www.reachinghome.com.

We would be happy to also provide you with the PowerPoint slides and a DVD of the presentation of the six modules. We have videotaped my presentation of Module I and Introductions to Module II through VI.

We have also created a DVD, *Daily Heroes*, which is based on my interviews with eight individuals who have demonstrated resilience in their personal and professional lives. I would like to thank them and John Nunan and his staff at Alpha One who skillfully edited the interviews and created this extraordinary DVD. The individuals are referenced by profession and the challenges they have confronted. They have all the blemishes and the vices of ordinary people as well as the courage and strength that we all possess.

To order additional PowerPoint slides, Videos/DVDs please visit our website, http://www.reachinghome.com or e-mail us at rhcf@gwi.net.

Another excellent video, *Aftermath*, was created by the American Psychological Association as part of their public education resilience program that was developed after 911 and was presented by APA public education coordinators and their colleagues in 2004 and 2005. The videotape still has as much relevance today as it did then. It looks at one block of State Street, in New York City and how the lives of these individuals were impacted by 911 and by other events. It can be obtained by contacting Public Relations at the American Psychological Association at 202-336-5899. You may need to work with your state Psychological Association Public Education Coordinator in using the tape.

Learning From The Videotape/DVD Presentations

Listen carefully to the videos that are presented in the workshop. For each video, answer the following questions:
1. What skills and attitudes did the person make use of in dealing with the challenges that they were facing? Be specific.
2. How would you have dealt with the situation they confronted?
3. If you are participating in a Resilience Workshop, discuss your answers with your fellow participants.

Donations and Sponsors

Don't hesitate to ask. Explain what you are doing and who you are training. We have gotten free space, donations of coffee and donuts and sandwiches. In some cases, if you pay half, they will donate the other half, especially if you are doing this with a non-profit or for first responders.

Magnets

We have found that creating refrigerator magnets with some of the Resilience Skills is another way of reinforcing the learning process with workshop participants as well as advertising the program. The cost per magnet is low and they can be ordered in lots of 1,000 through our web site, www.reaachinghome.com. Sponsors like having their name paired with resilience. We recommend that the magnet include the following:

8 Factors To Build Your Resilience:
1. Connect with others.
2. Practice flexibility.

3. Make realistic plans, then take action.
4. Open lines of communication with others to solve problems.
5. Manage strong feelings. Don't deny them.
6. Build self-confidence through action.
7. Create purpose and meaning in your life.
8. Keep a positive outlook — negativity will not help you or anyone else.

Bridgeline Calls

We believe that an excellent way of staying in touch with each other is to schedule a regular conference/bridgeline call each month with individuals interested and involved in the program and to offer this as a free follow-up for individuals who participate in the training. We have made use of FreeConferenceCall.com as a resource in doing this and, as the name implies, the conference call is free. Participants, however, must pay the cost of the long distance call to dial into the conference call. We notify participants of the call a few days ahead of time giving them the call in number and the access code which they must punch in when the conference call operator answers.

Tips on Facilitating a Workshop or Discussion Group

1. Make sure that your equipment works, specifically your computer. Play the DVDs and PowerPoint slides. Know the equipment so that you are comfortable using it during the workshop.
2. Check the room that you are using before you schedule the training. See where the outlets are and what is the real capacity of the room. Remember that you are going to be doing break out groups and that you need space for this, either in the room or in adjoining breakout rooms.
3. Learn some relaxation exercises. These will be especially helpful for you on the day of the training or the discussion group when the equipment that you checked the night before doesn't work. Instead of opening a vein, take a slow, deep breath. (See *Maine Guide To Relaxation And Stress Management* at www.abilitycoach.com.)
4. If leading a discussion group or standing up in front of people is really difficult for you, refer to some of the tips on conquering fear on our web site www.reachinghome.com. You may want to spend some time with a counselor or psychologist, learning ways to deal with your stage fright. Doing this program may be a way of finally conquering this fear.
5. Don't assume other people will always do what they are supposed to do. Check or have someone else check to make sure that workshop notices have been mailed or e-mailed out, materials copied, etc.
6. Rehearse the first few lines of your introduction to the program. Say them out loud so that you can make changes in your tone or cadence. This may also help you deal with your anxiety before the program. Anticipatory anxiety is usually the most difficult. Once things get going, the anxiety often decreases or subsides.
7. Show up early for the training. This allows you to make sure that things are in order and working and to arrange an alternative plan if they are not.
8. Have a glass of water nearby when you're doing your presentation or discussion. Room temperature works better than ice cold.
9. Thank all the people who helped you, your co-trainers, or facilitators, people who provided the space, donated the coffee and donuts, etc. Recognize and reinforce these people for their efforts. After you introduce yourself, allow the participants in the program to introduce themselves. Depending on the size of

your audience, this may or may not be possible. Listen! The better you know the audience, the better trainer you will be.

10. Look at the individuals in your audience or discussion group as you do your presentation. Talk to specific people. This may help you relax.

11. Ask questions. Get your audience engaged. Again, the more you know about them, the better for you and the program.

12. Take a break every hour to hour and one half. The six modules of this program and the breakout groups allow you to do this easily.

13. Answer questions, or at least try to. If you don't know the answer, admit your ignorance. If possible, find the answer and get back to the person asking the question.

14. Encourage participants to stay involved with the program. Use the workshop and the discussion group as an opportunity to recruit supporters and co-trainers. Ask for feedback (Worksheet Evaluation Form – Appendix VI).

15. If you say you will follow up with someone on an idea or a workshop opportunity, make sure you do.

16. Don't take yourself too seriously. You will make mistakes. I certainly do when I do a workshop, such as forgetting names, or that really important point that I really wanted to make but forgot. Relax. You're human, too.

Tips For Specific Groups

If you are doing the program for fire and rescue, offer (if possible) a different program for volunteers versus career fire fighters. Use or record stories of fire fighters or police and, of course, obtain their written permission to use the stories as part of your training. Do this in a very simple interview format. Your local community television station may be willing to record the stories for you. Having senior police, fire or rescue personnel talk about their lives and how they have made use of these resilience skills can be quite convincing to young fire fighters and police who may still see themselves as ten feet tall and bullet proof. That's why we created the *Daily Heroes* DVD.

If you're doing a workshop for first responders, try to get representatives from each group to attend a six-hour Train the Trainer workshop initially. This is a good idea since they could develop workshops and programs that will be for all of the fire, police and rescue personnel in their township or county. This may improve communication and the ability of these groups to work together in an emergency. This is certainly one way to reinforce that process.

It may be difficult to get police involved since many see themselves as having problems unique to their profession and are often unwilling or uncomfortable talking about their lives or their jobs in front of people who are not involved in law enforcement. You may need to develop a special workshop just for police.

In working with educators, using, the six-hour format, form a committee of educators to design "take away" activities prior to the workshop. This may include lesson plans and may also allow the educators participating in the program to develop professional development workshops in their schools.

Working with Businesses

We have just begun working with business owners to help them see the relevance of this program for them and their employees. We plan on working with Chambers of Commerce and have talked with the Emergency Management folks in our State about developing a program specifically for businesses that would focus on both the nuts and bolts of restarting a business after a disaster and on preparing employees through resilience training to be able to connect the nuts and bolts and operate a business during and following a natural disaster or terrorist attack. This training, especially given the economic mess we are in, has relevance to employees and their families in helping them to deal with the everyday stresses and crises that they face, not just the "big one".

We would encourage you to pursue conversations with businesses in your area and to be creative in finding ways to encourage them to integrate this program into their operations and their planning. The best emergency plan requires people, with the resilience skills and attitudes that this program teaches, to carry out the plan.

Technology

Take as much advantage of technology as you can. The resilience skills and attitudes could be put on the website of the different organizations and groups with which you're working. Create your own website or blog or both. Produce an e-mail newsletter. Write an article for your local paper about your project. Use television and radio. We introduced Maine Resilience on "207" a news/talk program of WCSH, the NBC affiliate in Portland in late January 2007. Most stations are looking for program ideas *after* the holidays.

Webinar

View the "Building Resilience: Expecting the Best, Surviving the Worst" webinar by Ron Breazeale on the KidsTerrain web site http://kidsterrain.com/products/product.php?productid=12&cat=2&page=1. Use the webinar to promote your program and educate others about resilience.

Internet Interview

Hear my interview on "Talk To Me . . .Conversations With Creative, Unconventional People With Host Rita Schiano" on Blog Talk Radio, where we discuss the politics of fear versus the politics of hope and building resilience. http://www.blogtalkradio.com/rita/va/2008/04/08/talk-to-meconversations-with-creative-unconventional-people-with-host-rita-schiano.

Keep in mind that "one size does not fit all" and that the beauty of this program is that it can be adapted to the different groups with which you are working. Be creative!

Contact us if you need our help:
      E-mail: rhcf@gwi.net
      Phone: Dr. Ron Breazeale, 207-773-7993 ext. 25

References

Goleman, D. *Working with Emotional Intelligence.* New York: Bantam Books, 1998.

Pennybaker, J.S. *Opening Up: the Healing Power of Confiding in Others.* New York: Avon Books, 1990.

Prochaska, J.L., Norcross, J.C. and DiClemente, C.C. *Changing for Good.* New York: Avon Books, 1994.

Pyszczynskiki, T., Solomon, S. and Greenburg, J. *In the Wake of 911.* Washington D.C.: American Psychological Association, 2002.

Seligman, M. *Learned Optimism.* New York: Free Press, 1998.

Whitworth, L., Kimsey-House, H. and Sandahi, P. *Co-Active Coaching.* Palo Alto, California: Davies/Black, 1998.

Appendix I
Maine Resilience
www.maineresilience.org

Program Outline

Modules 1 – 4 - Basic Resilience Training

9:00 A.M. **1 hour** **Module 1** – Introduction to Resilience: This module defines the skills and attitudes that make up resilience and the need for training and coaching. *Lecture, discussion, PowerPoint, and video (Aftermath).*

Break

10:00 A.M. **I hour** **Module 2** – Learning from the Past/Learning from Role Models: This module encourages participants to examine the skills and attitudes that they have utilized in a crisis in the past and what they have learned, both good and bad, from role models and themselves. *Small group discussions facilitated by coach/co-trainers and video (Where's Herbie?).*

11:00 A.M. **1 hour** **Module 3** – Learning and Teaching Resilience Skills and Attitudes through Story Telling: This module utilizes *Reaching Home* and the *Duct Tape Isn't Enough* guide as a tool for learning and teaching these skills. Participants have an opportunity to tell their own story. *Small group discussions facilitated by co-trainers after an individual writing exercise, and video (Daily Heroes).*

Lunch

1:00 P.M. **1 hour** **Module 4** – Developing your Plan for Building Your Resilience: Participants develop their own plan utilizing materials from *Duct Tape*. *Small group activities and discussions facilitated by co-trainers.*

Module 5 – 6 – Teaching and Coaching Others In These Skills And Attitudes

2:00 P.M. **1 hour** **Module 5** – Application of Resilience Skills to the individuals, groups, classes you are working with, in the setting in which you are working, e.g., public schools, fire and rescue. The module focuses on how to integrate these skills into the activities you are presently doing with these individuals, groups/classes, e.g.. "Wrapping" the program around a developmental reading or math skills program. Integrating the program into firefighting training. Participants are asked to look at the challenges that they will face and how they will deal with them. Who they will need to sell and how they will do this. *Individual writing exercise and small group discussion facilitated by co-trainers*

3:00 P.M. **1 hour** **Module 6** – What's your individual plan for maintaining resilience while working on this project? Participants will review the eight factors/skills/attitudes that make for resilience and answer the following questions:

1. What network of support will I utilize both in and outside of the organization while developing and conducting this project?

DUCT TAPE ISN'T ENOUGH: Survival Skills For The 21st Century

2. How flexible will I be?
3. Are my plans realistic? Will I take action?
4. With whom do I need to open or increase communication?
5. How invested, feelings-wise, will I be in this project? Why?
6. How confident am I about the success I will have? Will doing this activity build my self-confidence?
7. Will this project be meaningful for me and others involved in it?
8. How will my level of optimism or pessimism impact what I do?

Individual writing exercise with small group discussion facilitated by co-trainers. Wrap Up, Quiz, and Evaluation.

4:00 P.M. Adjourn

   Follow-up – Monthly, one-hour bridgeline (conference) calls facilitated by a trainer to support implementation and follow through by participants with their plans for building and maintaining resilience.

Appendix II

Resilience Quiz

*Best Answer

Please answer the following ten questions by circling the correct answer.

1. **Self-confidence is one of the best buffers against feeling anxious:**
   A. * True   B. False

2. **A SMART Plan is:**
   A. Specific
   B. Measurable
   C. Time Specific
   D. *All of the above

3. **Optimists are more likely to see both good things and bad things as being temporary rather than permanent:**
   A. * True   B. False

4. **Talking about how one feels is:**
   A. More likely to occur with men than women
   B. *May be directly related to what we learned in our families about how to deal with feelings
   C. Not something that we can change
   D. Both A and B

5. **"Correctly" assigning personal blame is often difficult to do and is:**
   A. Frequently a waste of our time and energy
   B. Is something that our society is obsessed with
   C. Is accountability with a heavy loading of blame
   D. *All of the above

6. **Being optimistic in these difficult times is:**
   A. An indication of one's naiveté.
   B. Can have major health benefits
   C. Involves frequently saying, "This too will pass"
   D. *Both B and C

7. **Resilience is:**
   A. **More common than we thought**
   B. **Can be learned**
   C. **A combination of skills and attitudes that help us deal with and bounce back from difficult times**
   D. ***All of the above**

8. **Being flexible is:**
   A. **A sign of weakness**
   B. **Makes you into a "flip flopper" who never sticks with anything**
   C. ***Is one of the best indications that an individual is emotionally healthy**

9. **Which of these is not a Resilience Skill or attitude:**
   A. **Assertiveness**
   B. **Problem solving**
   C. ***Keeping your feelings to yourself**
   D. **Taking care of yourself physically and emotionally**

10. **Management of anger is a resilience skill:**
    A. *** True   B. False**

Appendix III

DOCUMENTATION OF ATTENDANCE

This is to Certify

that:_____

has attended, in its entirety, the Following Continuing Education Activity Sponsored by Alpha One

**Program Title: Maine Resilience:
Teaching 21st Century Survival Skills**

**Program Location:
Date of Program Presentation:
Number of Contact Hours and CEU Credits:**

**Approval has been granted for xx CEUs
by the (fill in information)**

Signature:_____
**Debra Porter
Continuing Education Conference Coordinator**

Alpha One of South Portland maintains responsibility for this program.

Appendix IV

Suggested Titles On Resilience

Adults

Braestrup, Kate. *Here If You Need Me: A True Story.* New York: Little Brown & Company, 2008.

Giovanni, Nikki. *Rosa.* New York: Henry Holt, 2005.

McCullough, David. *1776.* New York: Simon and Schuster, 2005.

Mitchell, Elvis and Timothy Greenfield- Sanders. *The Black List.* New York: Atrium Books, 2008.

Pausch, Rand & Jeffery Zaslow. *The Last Lecture.* New York: Hyperion, 2008.

Pelzer, David J. *Moving Forward: Taking The Lead In Your Life.* New York: Center Street, 2008.

Salak, Kira. *The Cruelest Journey: Six Hundred Miles To Timbuktu.* Washington D.C.: National Geographic Society, 2004.

Salisbury, Gay and George I. Hicks. *The Cruelest Mile: The Heroic Story Of Dogs And Men In A Race Against An Epidemic.* New York: Norton, W.W., 2003.

Schiano, Rita. *Painting The Invisible Man.* Wilbraham, MA: The Reed Edwards Co., 2007.

Walls, Jeannette. *The Glass Castle: A Memoir.* New York: Scribner, 2005.

Young, William P. *The Shack.* California: Windblown Media, 2008.

Children

Conner, Leslie. *Miss Bridie Chose A Shovel.* Boston: Houghton Mifflin, 2004.

Dalgliesh, Alice. *The Courage Of Sarah Noble.* New York: Scribner, 1991.

Jones, Brenn. *Learning About Resilience From The Life Of Lance Armstrong.* New York: Rosen Publishing Group, Inc., 2003.

Kimmel, Elizabeth Cody. *Balto And The Great Race.* New York: Random House, Inc., 1999.

Lowry, Lois. *Number The Stars.* New York: Random House Children's Books, 1990.

MacLachlan, Patricia. *Caleb's Story.* New York: Harper Collins Publisher, 2002.

MacLachlan, Patricia. *Sarah, Plain And Tall.* New York: Harper Collins Publishers, 1987.

MacLachlan, Patricia. *Skylark.* New York: Harper Collins Publishers, 1997.

Appendix V

<u>Workshop Evaluation</u>

Workshop Name: _____

Presenter(s): _____

Date(s): _____

Presenter Information	Poor	Fair	Good	Excellent	N/A
Presenter was knowledgeable and well-informed					
Presenter was responsive to questions					
Presenter was engaging and held your interest					

Comments:_____

_____

_____

Course Information	Poor	Fair	Good	Excellent	N/A
Information presented was useful and applicable					
I gained insight and knowledge that I didn't have before					
Presentation was clear and well organized					
Handouts were effective and relevant					

Comments:_____

_____

_____

What did you find most beneficial about this workshop?

What changes would you suggest?

What future topics would be of interest to you?

To obtain additional workbooks and training materials or learn more about upcoming trainings and workshops:

My Address: _____

E-mail: _____

About the Author

Dr. Ron Breazeale is a clinical psychologist with over thirty years experience in the fields of mental health and drug and alcohol treatment.

Reaching Home is about the world he grew up in as a child with a birth defect in the "Atomic City," Oak Ridge, Tennessee, where his parents lived and worked. He has worn a prosthetic hook most of his life.

He is married and has one child, a daughter, and now lives and works in southern Maine.

Training Products Available

The book *Duct Tape Isn't Enough* — $29.95

Train-the-Trainer package* includes:

- The book *Duct Tape Isn't Enough.*
- *Daily Heroes*, volumes 1 and 2. This two-part DVD set shows the compelling stories of 16 people who have demonstrated resilience in their personal and professional lives.
- Modules 1 through 6. This 1.5-hour-long DVD shows Dr. Ron Breazeale presenting these modules.
- The DVD *Where's Herbie?* This award-winning, timeless documentary has a heart-warming message no one will forget.

Train-the-Trainer Course
This online course is offered through the University of Maine, Augusta, and offers 6 continuing education units (CEUs)

A 50 percent (50%) discount on future orders of two or more copies of the book *Duct Tape Isn't Enough.*

Inclusion of an additional staff member in the online course will be offered at a discounted rate.

Products also available separately:
Daily Heroes, volume 1— $49.99
Daily Heroes, volume 2 — $49.99
The DVD *Where's Herbie?*— $12.95
Modules 1 through 6, presented by Dr. Ron Breazeale — $149.00

*Course to be offered starting in the fall of 2009. Price to be determined.

All prices referenced above are subject to change. For current information on programs contact Dr. Ron Breazeale at 207-773-7993, extension 25.

About Maine Resilience

Maine Resilience teaches participants to manage adversity to bounce back more quickly. Benefits include improved morale, decreased medical and mental health problems, increased team spirit and cooperation, and better relationships among co-workers and community members.

How Maine Resilience Got Started

Maine Resilience began in January of 2007. A major focus of the program has been to obtain sponsorships and continuing support. In December of 2007, the program received a grant from the Cumberland County Emergency Management Agency which will allow the program to offer five workshops each year in Cumberland County for the next three years. In addition a number of organizations have funded training programs for their employees and members. The program has been coordinated with the effort, materials and information offered by the American Psychological Association and the Maine Psychological Associatoins through their Public Education Programs. Clark Associates has also provided funding for seminar training and promotional materials.

Maine Resilience will continue to seek support from business who pride themselves on the resilience of their company employees and products with the goal of making Maine Resilience self-supporting and self-sustaining.

Maine Resilience Goals

- Assist citizens of Maine in building resilience, readiness and response techniques needed to bounce back from tragedy - whether a national disaster, or a personal one.

- Train people with disabilities to utilize their untapped resilience skills to become trainers/coaches for Maine Resilience and conduct workshops to teach others the techniques needed to adapt in the face of disaster, and in the ups and downs of daily living.

- Recruit first responder professionals - fire fighters, police, EMT's, Red Cross personnel and other community leaders having resiliency skills, to be trained by Maine Resilience as trainers/coaches who will then conduct resiliency workshops for Maine businesses and the public.

- Invest in the citizenry of Maine to create a more effective and resilient response to crises. Both disabled people, and society as a whole, will benefit together by increasing resilience in communities.

- Participants to overcome adversity more quickly. Benefits include improved morale, decreased medical problems, better mental health, less sick time used, fewer accidents, better team spirit and cooperation, more rapport and relationships among co-workers and community members.

- Use story-telling to bring across the techniques of resiliency - permission has been gained, and use donated, for locally authored books, *Reaching Home*, and *Duct Tape Isn't Enough*, the readers and coaches guide to *Reaching Home*, to aide individuals and groups as they learn and teach the concepts and skills involved in resilience.

- Organize and conduct Train-the-Trainer workshops in the Portland and Bangor areas. Resilience Trainers/Coaches recruited will be disabled persons, emergency first responder personnel, and other community leaders. They will be compensated for their coaching time and expertise.

- Schedule conferences and mini-workshops with Maine businesses and community groups to provide resilience training workshops with continuing access to follow-up support sessions. A strong focus will be on partnering with local businesses and other Maine organizations for employee and citizen resilience training.

- Coordinate the program with existing efforts, materials and information offered and sanctioned by the American Psychological Association on resilience.

- Obtain sponsorships, partnerships and continuing project support from corporations, organizations, and foundations created on ideals in-line with the mission of Alpha One.

- Offer future components of Maine Resilience training tailored for: 1) schools, focusing on all grade levels; 2) pinpointing specific resiliency issues in time of war for Maine citizens; and 3) supporting Maine's war veterans and their families upon returning home.

- Offer Continuing Education credits for attendees participating in future Maine Resilience training sessions.